Kenneth McKay

THE MASTER
AND THE MESSENGER

A CIP catalogue record for this title is available from the British Library

Hardback ISBN 9780956237101
Trade Paperback ISBN 095623710X

Typeset in Baskerville MT by Hewer Text UK Ltd, Edinburgh

Printed and bound in England by CPI Antony Rowe

Kappamak Books
Rowellan House
Bellevue Road
Ayr KA7 2SA
Scotland

www.kappamakbooks.com

For Paola
and all her Italian virtues
and
for Harriet, my daughter

Reaching Out
At time
A friend
At straw . . .

I

There is a sweep of light that is like gold in the American fields of Idaho in the early morning. It is a sight that can lift the heart and yet bring it pain. Swooping like a bird on this landscape one would find a stillness many Americans never find in a lifetime. Over the range of colours bathing this land sat an off-white clapboard farmhouse inside which Greg Keech Jr contemplated his death. Nothing moved outside in the fresh breeze as he felt all the weight of his young years. In the semi-darkness of the tiny bathroom, while the light spread everywhere outside, he took himself away from his reflection in the mirror to a red-stained towel on the floor. A few steps from him, motionless on a poor bed, lay the woman who had allowed him to love her until the realities of their lives made for their decision. Greg and his girl, Carla, had brought another life about, a small soul she would call it smilingly, and with a mixture of joy and terror they cut away from those who could but would not help them. With a while before dawn, nestled in the fields of America, Greg's girl had some violence done to her, a violence that used to call on many girls when this land was a darker place, which cut off the life connection between mother and child.

There would be no rush to any emergency service, no run from the house onto a track for assistance because young Greg could not leave. Carla had begged him to stay. And Greg stayed and shook as he sat with Carla who had decided that to be alone with her child would be another act of violence to bear. So with Greg she smiled as she gently loosened her grip on life and let her blood flow. She died before the stars in the sky disappeared, before the morning bird had yet to call and before Greg had fully realised that loss could be found everywhere in his young American life. He had his history, and now it was tinged with brutality.

Brutal experiences never soften people; they only lead to a life of getting back. 'All people who are hard have never wanted to be,' a man said, a military one, who had come to his house to bring news about his father, General Gregory Keech, when a younger Greg still had his eyes half shut to the world. The man wanted to talk well of him when no one else in America did, he wanted to say things for Keech's son to grow up with, to keep him strong, because too many of the country's young men were growing up abandoned and too many could not bear the strain. Now Greg was to take a step like his father and walk away – so it would appear to those who were to begin the hunt for him.

While the day settled over the clapboard house, Greg wept all his tears for Carla, who had given herself to him almost a year to the day when she left this earth and followed her baby's spirit.

The day did not pass, not even when the stars appeared again and Carla's body had lain still throughout. The day would not pass. The day baby was wrapped and held and walked and talked to, which gave Greg's heart a moment of lightness, his body and limbs, too. The day did not pass as he sat close to Carla while the house creaked. All the tension in her young life was gone, and while his heart ached for her and the baby he held the night returned to him all his fears. As the decision he was to make rushed to him, he could hear Carla's voice saying, *thank you Greg, you've killed me, over and over.* He stopped the rocking motion with his baby, placed it in Carla's arms and walked out into the darkness. Greg did not walk very long and he did not walk very far before the rough physical approach of police officers made his perceived wickedness seem a much kinder act.

Greg was twenty-three when the court and its jurors decided that young Keech, son of the traitor general as the media implied, had indeed been responsible for the deaths of his girlfriend and her baby. His unsettled state, which had taken hold in High School where he displayed the arrogance of a young man going wrong, was highlighted to the court. No one came to the courtroom as his friend, and those who had predicted his downfall when he was barely a teenager were mighty pleased on hearing again of his actions as those of a cold emotionless youth who had matured to adult violence and gross neglect. How could he sit and watch the mother of his child have life drain from her as she bled to death; he could have saved her, them both, the court heard, but instead he sat back and saved himself from the burden of mother and child around his neck. He let them die. It was that simple, the court was sure it was right, as do courts in every state where there is a shunning of insight and tolerance for those Gregs who make up what is human life. All those involved in this lawful decision felt relief that they had triumphed again. Any doubt that could have penetrated an uncertain soul that day would have been buried away with a verdict that made everyone stronger and closer to God as Greg began his time away from freedom that was Idaho and its sweeping fields where, somewhere, Carla and child lay.

Young Greg Keech was travelling south and east to his destination. Behind the bars of a prison vehicle as it passed by his neighbourhood he could not see the high state mountains he had grown up with, the majestic view that had during his childhood made him majestic, too. He sat shackled in the semi-armoured wagon and that refused him the sight of the sky before he entered the brutal architecture that was to become his home. It was difficult to think of the last months; he had always thought that America's enemies, his enemies, were over there somewhere, over oceans and unfamiliar mountain ranges, out of sight from his world. It was a shock to come face to face with them and their power in the court and in his own land. Carla and child were gone and no one in the Justice Department could tell where. Impotent to the real matters of life they dressed with serious faces without serious thought, men and the occasional woman who saw a world, their world, as a model for all the Gregs to follow. Cleaning up Greg with prison time, away from nature, was simply a strategy to wipe him bare, shake his bones and reduce his heart even further. So Greg never had a chance. His life would have been preferred but in a *civilised* society there were rules about lynching, so they took his freedom and added enormously to his insecurity instead of offering their hand. Carla and child were not lost because of Greg and he could feel no guilt about that and that alone might have given him a modicum of comfort, but now a prisoner of the penal system he felt he could not survive, it would break his head his inner voice kept repeating. The voice would sometimes clash with any good memory he could find before his head would fall and close down. There was no one to call on, all he found love in his heart for was gone; the moon and the stars above him would be all that was on offer. He had lost a small, small family: life had just swallowed them up. He ran it over and over in his mind what he might have done, could have done, re-visiting that night as dawn was creeping into the corners of the room. He had been back every time he was left to himself and like a spirit he would return floating in the space where Carla, his soulmate, lay on the bed, her words as a whisper. And just as he sat with his hand in hers and believed she might sleep, Carla died when Greg had momentarily dropped his eyes to the floor. Her last request was that he stay, just stay. He could not have left before then when she was becoming weaker and the baby had become still. Carla went quietly away with Greg as her last touch with the world. He could not forget how an initial surge of fear took hold of him while Carla lay gripped by the spread of cold in her body, how her colour had faded and her heartbeat, which had raced to deliver the little blood she had around her body, slowly ceased. He would remember how her head rolled from side to side as she was gradually losing consciousness and how his own heart responded and trembled. That was the last impression of that early morning when nothing moved and life passed by. Carla! Carla! He had called out ever since.

As Greg survived what he was dealt with for the love of Carla, the story that was his father's was mostly unknown to him. But you do what you can, thought Greg, and live it best you can. The day his father was to take him along an uncertain road had lasted a long time, but his hopes to get back on track, as he was all those years ago, began in a small way when he received a letter from a woman in England who had, with difficulty, made herself known to him some two years after the verdict. Jilly Dorian knew what Greg Keech did not, that her letter was not some casual contact some prisoners are lucky to get while they live their days locked away from the world; hers was because she believed she shared something with Greg Keech. It had taken her a long time to reach the age of twenty-four, she felt, and it had taken her more time to write to Keech. A young woman sending her airmail out of the blue like that, there had to be a reason. Jilly Dorian lied about that and created a picture of herself that anyone would have accepted, as Greg did.

Letters usually came once every two months to the State Penitentiary, and up until Greg's release Jilly had become a story-teller of how things they had experienced they could share. She knew Greg's story, everybody knew, the general was a man who could be remembered easily for he had wounded his country by his actions and paid for that. Jilly, too, had her own war that she somehow kept at bay when she wrote to Greg. She, too, was wounded. It was many years ago but if one felt the pain as great, it was no time at all. After the general had made his move on that fateful New Year's Day, the wheels of concern had turned and turned the young lives of Greg and Jilly astray.

2

West Germany, 1 January 1983

'John, I can't sleep. I feel dizzy.'

'I don't want to sleep. Christ, Shirley, it's New Year.'

He made a movement that brought her laughter. 'Shirley, do you know what's so funny . . .'

'What?'

'Your old man is out somewhere, straight out on his back somewhere in this camp.' He tried to hold his laughter. 'He's so stoned he won't see daylight for hours.'

'I can't sleep', she said, 'not like this . . . here.'

He moved to her. 'This is not the best bed for a body like yours, but I'll try to compensate.'

'John, stop it, go away', she giggled.

'Sssh, the walls have ears, I could lose a stripe for this.'

She playfully knocked twice on the wall but no one returned it. The celebrations had left most in drunken positions but for one, who lay listening in the dark, waiting for his hour of departure.

'This is Radio Free Europe broadcasting to all friends in Eastern Europe on this New Year's Day. Today will be cloudy, but it will clear in parts with some sunshine getting through. Temperatures in most places in Bavaria will be minus 4 centigrade. Road conditions are good on autobahns out of the city. Now, while the temperatures drop we'll climb the American charts with a little country and western . . .'

The US base, Camp Braddock, was completely still; the morning frost held tightly to the roofs and car tops and painted over the greenery of the neat sectioned off areas that were lawns. Anyone on duty did it with no movement. The huge Christmas tree outside the gates with its message of peace and happiness fluttered quite silently in the light morning breeze. At the far end of Camp Braddock, where the higher military ranks had their quarters, general Gregory Keech moved about quietly. The New Year's Eve party which had ended just a few hours before still hung in the air. General Keech dressed, in uniform, in front of a full length mirror, his golden spiky hair patted down slightly with his hands, his face steady as he watched. He placed his hat carefully on his head, brought his hands down slowly and stood erect. He then opened the wardrobe on his right and brought a blue woollen coat and put it on. He checked his watch before switching on the radio. The broadcast was in German, which did not interest him, so he twiddled with the wave band for some seconds and stopped at the sound of an American voice introducing something from *way back*: it was an old McCartney song, something about a long and winding road. Then the voice returned: 'It is 9 am on this first day of January and Radio Free Europe will be on the air throughout the day giving you the news of what's new in the American charts. But now, what's been happening around the world . . .' General Keech listened in a half stoop, his fingers on the volume control as if the sound might increase without warning, then the music returned with a thump of drums. He switched off. He picked up a black briefcase that lay on the bed and opened the door.

The air had a sting to it that made him pause before he headed towards a dark Chevrolet saloon and got in. On duty at the gate that morning was a young soldier of twenty from Rochester, Minnesota.

When General Keech arrived at the gate the young guard paid particular attention – the general had wound down his window and wished him a good year. 'Thank you, sir,' the soldier beamed, 'for you too, sir.' The general smiled and nodded as if it was his intention. The guard held his salute as he followed the car past the Christmas tree, which was returning slowly to its natural colour as the frost slipped away, then past the fir and pine trees towards the road.

Keech listened to the car radio babbling on about road conditions while telling how quiet all the major roads in the country were. The music came on, the beating sound that was neither good nor bad: it wasn't anything. He searched for something he could understand. There were many American stations all over Bavaria, all pumping out the same music to the youth of each country they penetrated, all emphasizing how great it was to be on this side of the fence. With a fast twirl of the radio knob he rushed through all the voices and then silence. The empty road made it an easy drive for the big Chevrolet; he had passed through three farming villages some kilometres back but no one was about, at a window, or doorway, there were no children, none on their bikes on the pavements, none anywhere. If ever the Red Army decided to do it, to pick up their guns and come across, the first day of any year would not be a bad time. Whatever their priorities were that made their lives worthwhile Christmas time seemed to be the West's, thought Keech. He had been around a long time, had spent Christmas at home for the first twenty-five years, then had gone overseas and tried to equal the number in foreign parts but still had a way to go. Christmas didn't make people good, he had learned, but it was the job of Western governments to create the belief that people in favour of Christmas were good people and others not. Good and evil were as clear as the stretch of brick and fence that ran through Deutschland. And if the other side were so bad why had they not come, made their move, when their military

9

was at its strongest while NATO forces were struggling just to keep up? Why had they not crossed over the dividing line on a day like that when the West was too drunk to give a damn? 'If they fear us,' the general was now talking aloud, his voice quite raised, 'if they want to dominate us, why have they not come across?' He slapped his hand hard on the wheel and said no more.

As he drove on he saw himself in a park on a sunny day – with his family and his mother and father. There was a lot of laughter, mainly created by their dog who had gulped his ice cream while he scolded his young son. He remembered how the whoops of laughter almost laid him out. His mother was filled with concern as he lay unable to control the constant image in his head of the dog and the ice cream. The horn from a car ahead disturbed his memory for a moment as the road filled up a little. His parents had given him so much, love and kindness and all their support throughout his life; he could never forget nor would he ever want to. But they were gone now, one quickly after the other. Once in a moment of desperation he had thought that if you let your emotions go, brought out all the sadness, all the pain, stretched it out as far as it would go, you would be alright, you could return drained and tired and ready to build yourself up again. Gregory Keech tried this the night after his mother died; he let go his control, let the sobbing and moaning run free, alone with the door locked, until he was rescued twelve hours later. They found him on the floor, his left arm moving from side to side, his hand almost intact with four fingers – the fifth lay stained and pale beside him, cut clean to distract the other pain that had raged within him.

The white metal notice board with its red lettering was clearly visible as Keech slowed, it was there for him and any other American soldier to read carefully and turn back. He pulled the car off the road some yards before, sat for a moment and read: "US Forces Personnel. HALT 1 km to Czechoslovakia. Do not proceed without authorization." The border crossing with Czechoslovakia was some hundred metres round the curve in the road.

Keech turned on the radio, found an American station, wound down the far side window, slid over and got out. The American radio voice sounded happy and excited, and it followed him while he walked purposefully away, round the curve and down the slight slope in the road towards the crossing point. First he had to pass the West German side of the border and then make his way to the Czech side, which was a further three hundred metres beyond, three hundred metres of no man's land between the two sides, a stretch of empty road lined with magnificent pine trees soaring skywards and giving the road a dark and sinister look. As Keech approached, a heavy articulated truck pulled in off no man's land to have its papers checked by the German Custom officers. Behind the large plate glass office window two officers were idly chatting as Keech passed and walked a further twenty metres. 'Hey you. Halt!' This Keech did while the German bodyguard let loose a mouthful. Keech half-turned to him. 'Where the fuck are you going?' the German demanded, then looked at Keech's hat, he had not realised. 'American?' Keech walked away. 'Halt! Halt!' He began to run. The German ran after him for a short distance. 'Halt! Christ's sake! American! Stop!' He couldn't very well drag him back, he had no power to, even if he could turn the six-foot-two general. He stood watching the American get farther along the road, farther away. He ran back to the office, grabbed a pair of binoculars and focused in on Keech. Three Czech guards had stopped him and he was seen to unbutton his coat and reveal his uniform. General Gregory Keech had gone over, had crossed to the Eastern bloc.

Paris, January 1983

The snow had fallen evenly on Paris and it looked a pretty picture, something not many tourists see. Paris under a heavy snowfall in January was missed, very few came to photograph the effect, the stunning way winter could be, as if this white cover captured all the elegance that had all but slipped away from the city. Everything was enhanced; even the pigeons seemed to fly with more grace.

There was a snowy sludge lying in the forecourt of the Gare de Lyon; an attempt had been made to clear it but despondency had set in and it was left, discoloured and watery. Edward Fisher stepped out of his taxi and immediately negotiated the crumbling snow, then made to board his waiting train. At ten minutes past noon the Trans-Europe-Express would depart for its journey south to Switzerland and Italy. That day, 3 January, Edward Fisher boarded the TEE train and chose from the many unreserved seats a window one in an open carriage; with him was a business colleague, Pierre Halin. There were a few other passengers, rich and warm with expensive furs, returning from the capital now that the celebrations had died away. Their coats were removed and folded with great care and neatly placed on the rack above, their cases had been left in the luggage space further down the carriage.

Lunch was being served until two, but no one seemed willing to wait and most left for the restaurant car before the Paris suburbs had been cleared. After their meal Fisher and Halin returned to sit opposite each other and discuss business until, with Dijon twenty minutes away, Fisher gathered his papers and locked them in his slim black business case. Through the large carriage window he watched the snow, which was falling heavier with each kilometre, thick and high all along the sides of the track. Settling back in his seat he produced a pack of Christmas cigars and lit up. Both men were in good spirits. Halin leaned forward to explain a French joke, which brought a burst of laughter.

Further up the train two men got up from their seats and walked down, carefully studying the passengers as they went. When they entered Fisher's carriage they paused, then continued and stopped. 'Monsieur Fisher?'

The Englishman looked up. '*Oui.*'

'Could we have a moment with you alone, please?'

'With me? Why?'

The man, large and heavy, smiled. 'A moment, Monsieur Fisher, just a moment.'

Fisher looked at his companion and replied to him, 'I don't think I will.'

'There's nothing to alarm you,' said the man. 'If your friend would leave us . . .'

Halin jumped up to leave but Fisher asked him to stay.

'It is no disturbance to me', said Halin.

'Stay here', insisted Fisher, 'I'll see what they want', and he left.

The train pulled into Dijon ten minutes late and remained there for another ten. Fisher had not returned, and Halin's concern brought him out of his seat and to walk up the train. The top carriages were deserted, there was no one as Halin searched and felt a strong desire to turn back. Then he spotted a patch of hair some distance up over the top of a seat, black hair like Fisher's. He rushed up the aisle. Fisher sat still and stiff. The train came to a halt shortly after in the white wilderness of Dijon.

'My name is Campbell, I'm from the Embassy.'

The lady who had opened the door looked puzzled. 'The Embassy?'

'Yes, may I come in?'

She stood aside and the man entered.

'Mrs Fisher, I have very bad news.'

Her mouth opened as if to speak and she raised her hand to it. 'My husband?'

'Your husband is dead, Mrs Fisher. On the train yesterday. I'm very sorry.'

'Yesterday?' she repeated.

'His body will be brought back to Paris. The French notified us late yesterday evening. I could have telephoned, but it's not an appropriate way to communicate such news.' He watched her, she was lost elsewhere. 'Please sit down, Mrs Fisher.'

A tear eased fom her eye as she sat. 'How?'

He knew she would ask, he hoped she wouldn't, not there, not him. He sat down at the edge of the sofa and looked at her. 'Your husband was murdered, Mrs Fisher. That is what the French authorities have told us.'

Her hand was still half shielding her mouth and now she placed a finger between her teeth and gripped hard.

'Who? Why?'

'I have no details.'

'How? How was he killed? Tell me!'

'I don't know.'

'Shot? Was he shot?' – He could give no answer – 'Was he knifed? Why are you not telling me?' She took a moment and used her handkerchief. 'You can't come to a person's door and tell her that her husband's been murdered and expect to walk away just like that. In the minutes you've been in my home . . .' She stopped and used her handkerchief again.

'I'm terribly sorry, Mrs Fisher. We are told not to linger, to convey the news as delicately as possible but not to linger.'

Mrs Fisher nodded. 'Why have the police not called?'

'They thought we should do that. The French police are not noted for their command of a second language; I should expect them later in the morning.'

Her tears were running and she pushed her face into her handkirchief, locking herself away, for the seconds she was allowed, in her self-created darkness where everything was fractionally more bearable. 'I'm sorry, but my husband is dead and I don't know what to do.'

'I understand.'

'Is it Edward, you're sure?'

'Yes', he said.

She squeezed her eyes tightly and tried to push back the reality of it.

Campbell rose and walked to the door. 'If I can be of any help . . .'

"Yes, you can. I want to take my husband back . . . home to England.'

'I see. It's an expensive business.'

He waited; she stood in the small lobby, her dark hair swept behind her ears. She didn't care about expenses, her clothes, her furniture, her walls with their elegantly framed watercolours made that quite clear.

'We'll see to the necessary documentation for you, Mrs Fisher.'

She tried to smile. 'Thank you.'

3

Jilly had pretended not only to Greg but to herself that his plight had captured her; as she boarded the plane on her journey to meet him, her pretence was strong. Young Keech had been given early parole, much earlier than he could have hoped for, and set to put out distance between himself and the land of Idaho. His appearance was lean in a way that told anyone that his look had been forced upon him. His features were held well by his youthfulness, and his smile, while he waited for Jilly at Los Angeles airport, was ready to show itself bright enough, he hoped, to make her feel her long journey would not begin in disappointment.

It was a strange meeting with much apprehension, standing on the airport floor, waiting for their connection to each other. While he stood he saw an image of Carla with child nearby and then a distance away. Carla kept fading in and out like that as Jilly brought herself through the arrivals door. Greg did not spot her quickly enough as she walked up to him extending her arm. 'Hello', she said. He took her hand and stared at her. 'I don't know what to say now', said Jilly looking back at him. She took her hand away. 'Good flight?' She nodded. 'Good.' She wanted everything to be good.

The arrival hall had filled with some excitement with raised voices and squeals of nervous laughter. The tannoy system put out information but few, if any, heard it. 'Got everything?' Greg looked at what she had. 'Let's go.' They both walked to an exit but before going through it, he stopped her. 'You came', he said. 'Yes.' At that point he had forgotten her luggage. 'You came', he said again and gripped her heaviest piece as they walked to the airport parking.

Jilly had come to America where there were new sights and new pictures of another kind of life, but she did not feel she had come alone, with all the signs of human relations at her first stop in LA, she was happy to be reminded of who she was and what she had come looking for.

With the airport behind them and the wind from the ocean slipping into her hair, Jilly spoke to Greg as she would have done had she been writing to him.

'I'll be your guest in America and hope it'll be alright.'

At first it was difficult to say who the American was and who was not. Greg had much to say but was unable to say it, so much gratitude to show and so much affection to give his passenger who had given him her support while he was living in the darkness.

'What are you doing?' Jilly enquired. 'You never said exactly,' she said with a smile as the road appeared so long before them.

'Not being myself, that's what,' he replied. 'I bounce all over this land,' he sang in and out of tune. 'If I had a hammer . . .'

'Yes, I know the song,' said Jilly. 'So this is America.' She viewed the passing scenery.

'Yep,' confirmed Greg. 'There are many Americas and there are some you don't want to know about.'

'I've come to know.'

'Have you?'

'I want to know America as you do, the good and the bad,' Jilly revealed her intentions.

Greg changed to a higher gear, his foot pushing on the throttle, squeezing all the energy out of his old Ford to overtake the slow traffic ahead. They rode for another half hour while their hearts beat to a contented rhythm that neither could say was familiar.

4

London, January 1983

'I know you know the story but I'm going to go over it again.'

Sinclair was all you would expect an Intelligence boss to be: a distinguished man with alert searching eyes, confident without the arrogance, a suspicious man who concealed it with a sincere display of friendliness, who listened intently when told what he wanted.

'There is a small town in East Germany by the name of Hansbach, a quiet sort of place, farming and that.' He wanted Alex Dorian to follow him as he went, every word of the way, so he kept hold of him, eye to eye, word by word. 'The sort of place you'd find muddy roads and dung heaps and strapping farm girls. Well, the town of Hansbach has all that and more, and this is why I'm having this confidential little chat with you.' – Dorian rested his right leg over his left knee and listened – 'As you know, on the first day of this month the Americans lost a general from one of their bases in Germany; two days later he turns up on East German television declaring himself free from the West and happy to live the rest of his life on the *right* side of the fence. I must say he did look rather happy . . . drugs I suppose. Anyway, the Americans were shocked, stunned; dear old America had taken a knock and it was all a bit worrying to see a superpower looking so fragile.'

There was a pause and Sinclair got up from behind his desk. 'They want the general back, of course. They don't believe a word of it. And they want our help.' He returned to his desk and sat down. 'They want our help,' he repeated and bit his bottom lip.

Alex Dorian watched the delight creep into the expression on Sinclair's face. He could understand that. British Intelligence had been out of favour with them for a long time, *a slack bunch of Oxbridge boys who weren't living in this world – the real one.* They didn't need the British, they said so. They had their spy satellites and their aircraft and worldwide operations and all the British had was their spies and the disclosures in their funny little papers. But now all seemed forgotten, they had asked for assistance.

'Do they? Why?'

'Yes, I wondered at first, then they sent one of their top boys over to explain nicely for us. It appears the Russians don't want their general, they want to hand him back for one of their own. He hasn't been taken to Moscow, or, if he has, they've returned him mighty quick to Hansbach. That's where he is now.'

'Was he taken or did he walk?'

'That's another thing, Alex. The Americans say he was taken, well they would. We simply don't know.'

'No one's talking?'

'No one.' A pause. 'The Russians want one of their own, Grigov. They want Morrison, too. Oh yes, they don't want to be seen abandoning the American. The master and the messenger, as the Supreme Court judge labelled them before he passed sentence for twenty years each. Well, this nice young fellow from Langley told us there's not a chance in hell. What they didn't do was tell the Russians.'

'What exactly do they want?'

'Oh simple, Alex, they want their general back for nothing.'

'To go over and get him?'

'That's it. Look, they know how we run things, and how we operate. They admire us, Alex, and now they're telling us. We have been asked to get their man back, they want him pretty bad.'

Sinclair wiped the corners of his mouth with a stiffly ironed white handkerchief taken from his jacket pocket, then folded it back as it was.

'The Americans don't feel they can do it,' said Alex. 'But somehow they think we can?'

'No, no, their intelligence people are quietly seething about the whole thing. No, the reason we've been approached has nothing to do with intelligence, it's political. Washington has little faith these days in its intelligence service, not enough anyway to risk a cock-up. They shudder at the thought of fouling up. They'd much rather we took the risk.' He stopped and looked around his desktop. 'Cigarette?' His fingers had eased the lid open of the shiny cigarette box.

Alex reached across. 'I don't know where Hansbach is and I don't think we should find out. Why should we? Risk one of ours for their soldier boy?'

'Could we do it, Alex?'

'Probably not. A small town in East Germany. How far in?'

'About thirty miles. He's being held in a country villa just outside town.' Sinclair watched with a well-what-do-you-think look. 'This American fellow impressed the DG, he's for it – through our German people, of course. The DG understands the American position and feels it's our chance to get on an even keel with them.'

'Just suppose', said Alex, 'this general walked across, it's not likely he'll walk back.'

'It's a matter of trust here, Alex. The Americans say he didn't, we would have to go along with that, accept it that he didn't.'

Alex widened his eyes. 'Trust?! Nobody uses that word here, you know that. We're a suspicious bunch of . . . ., well, you know, trust can never come into it.'

'Well, whether you like it or not, the DG does, he doesn't see it your way, Alex, and we need to keep our friends in this business.'

'In this business,' replied Alex, 'it really is quite difficult distinguishing who one's friends are. We would have to check out everything they tell us, and that takes time and I suppose they wouldn't like it – not in a matter of urgency. So we'd be pressed from the start.'

'Very well, Alex, I've got it', Sinclair said abruptly, 'I'll pass your comments along,' and closed the subject like the slam of a door. 'Are you busy?'

Alex gave a little unsure nod. 'I might be.'

Sinclair smiled at his reply. 'Give my regards to Susan.'

While the Paris snow turned dirty on the streets, Edward Fisher's body was flown back to England. There was a respectable service in the small church with its patches of lawn at the front and sides and the grey sandstone that was put together quite a long time ago and now protected a corner of the town. The same church Fisher had rejected for his marriage. Nice words had been chosen for him although the vicar had little recall of the man. But unremembered dead men – just to be safe – were good men and he spoke well of him.

His murder was an open case in France, and in England it had aroused interest. The British Embassy in the rue du Faubourg St Honoré in Paris had, as all Her Majesty's Embassies, the presence of the intelligence service. Someone working in a clerical position was the usual thing and in Paris this was the case. When the police contacted the embassy on the day of Fisher's death, their interest lay with his family; a man murdered on foreign soil can be more difficult for his family to bear, and the foreigners he has lived among can become as guilty as the murderer. They thought an embassy official would be a better choice to visit and inform his family. It was also thought by a member of the embassy staff that someone should go along and view Fisher's body: a murdered British passport holder deserved their attention.

The day Fisher left his seat on that Swiss-bound train, he was carrying all the things one would find on any businessman: an American Express card, a wad of notes in a simple leather wallet, a Rolex watch, a couple of Parker pens and a paper thin calculator. There was also an address book with friends' names and business ones, all neatly written. With them, alone, was a Paris telephone number; there was no name or address, it was just by itself on the page. This number was noted but no one called it: the Soviet Embassy does not invite callers; at least not those with questions.

It was a rainy, miserable day when they called. The little bungalows behind their wrought iron fences and squeaky gates spread the gloom down the treeless street, where a couple of cars were parked, one on each side – retired people's cars: an Allegro and a Marina. A caravan stuck out in a driveway with a red canister of gas beside it – holiday time seemed far off. As they walked up the path, the garden hedge and shrubs blew ferociously.

The ding-dong of the bell brought a figure behind the lace curtain on the glass door.

'Mrs Fisher?'

'Yes.'

'We have called to ask you one or two questions about your late husband.'

'Police?' – the men slightly nodded – 'Come in, please.' Mrs Fisher closed the door on the weather and led them through into the sitting room.

'It's always been a depressing place in wintertime,' she said 'but when the weather brightens and the sun comes out we forget how it can be – like today.' She smiled and the men responded.

'Mrs Fisher . . .'

'News about Edward?" Her voice lifted as she straightened herself. 'Any news?'

'We've heard nothing from the French authorities. Nothing new, Mrs Fisher.'

Her eyes emptied then. Before they held surprise, hope, a look of waiting but now all that was gone and she sat looking across at the men: both young, perhaps at the last stages of their youth. They were dressed expensively for policemen, she thought, and the one with a moustache and large hands, the one who had yet to speak, said much more than he intended.

'You're not from the local force, are you?'

The smaller of the two men, who had for some reason been elected to do the talking, answered no.

'From the city then?'

'That's right. Mrs Fisher, there are a couple of things we want to clear up, things that are, most likely, simply explained. Now, if you could bear with us and allow me to go over the same questions I'm sure the French have already asked . . .'

'Alright,' she said softly.

'Your husband worked for a company called Paristec. He was travelling to Lausanne for a conference on computer data systems. Is that right?'

'Yes.'

'Was it usual for him to attend conferences?'

'There were many scattered throughout the year but he was not enthusiastic about them, if that's what you mean. He was rather successful in attending as few as possible.'

'When did he start with Paristec?'

'In '78.'

'He moved to Paris then?'

'No, he was already in Paris at that time.'

'With another company?'

She paused. 'Yes, you could say that.'

The policeman looked at her. 'Another company, Mrs Fisher?'

'He was a teacher before . . .'

She buttoned up the sleeves of her blouse then pulled the two sides of the collar together. Her eyes had a sunken look, dark and withdrawn, she looked tired and a little afraid. Was it because of the two men who had come in out of the rain or was it being so suddenly alone in the world?

'My husband was a teacher for fifteen years, at a big comprehensive in one of those areas you wouldn't want to live in. He was a good teacher, one of the few who didn't need the teacher-training year.' She sat back in her chair. 'In 1970 a new head came to the school. He introduced himself to all the staff, he had brought bottles of wine, which had a very positive effect, they couldn't believe it, being so lucky. First impressions could not have been better. The next day he had a chat, as he called it, with each of them, privately in his office.' The story brought a little laughter from her. 'He told them in words anyone would understand that the *ride* was over, not only was discipline coming back for the children but they too must expect it. He went on and on about how he saw his school and how teachers could no longer teach irresponsibility in the classroom. They were all politically motivated in his eyes, and if he could have taught all the subjects running from class to class he would have done it, he would have been sure then that his way was being followed.'

'So your husband left?'

'Yes, but not immediately. You don't give up your career immediately; he waited as anyone would for things to improve, but they never did.'

For the first time the other man with the moustache spoke and her surprise brought her forward in her chair. The man's silence had made her forget about him, her attention being with the other.

25

'Why did he go to Paris? Why not find another school?'

'He left in '75. He was completely disillusioned; he loved teaching, it was all he wanted to do but the state system in this country wouldn't let him. Or that's what he thought. He got a teaching job in Paris and we stayed.' She paused. 'I'm sorry, I haven't offered you anything.'

'Thank you, but no,' the moustached man said with polite firmness. 'Do you know how he got the job with Paristec, Mrs Fisher?'

'Not really. He made contact with many people, giving English adult courses, travelled all over Paris where the work was. Those were lean times in a very expensive town.'

'He certainly seemed to have made up for that.'

Just when she had sized up the smaller man and his questions he now appeared to have nothing to say. It was the other, who ran his finger over his hairy lip, that was showing interest.

'Flat in Paris. Bungalow here. Expensive furnishings etc. Your husband became a wealthy man in a very short time, and if you tell us how he managed this we might be that bit closer to identifying his murderer.'

She looked at him, at his eyes then the rest of his face. He wore the look of a person who knows more than he says, who has caught on to something and now waits to be told it.

'My husband, Mr Policeman, had no secrets, had nothing to hide, if I got your meaning correctly. He did not own the flat in Paris; it was rented, we had to live somewhere. We bought this place at a very good price and why shouldn't we, most people own their home – we're no different. My husband is dead, he was still a young man who was lucky to find a good job in a foreign country, something he couldn't do here.' She gave a sigh of tiredness. 'I believe the investigation into his death is a French one, so what exactly is your interest?'

The smaller man spoke again; having got angry with the other, they switched over for her. He then produced Fisher's address book which had brought them a good distance on that wet winter day.

'This book contains the names and addresses of your husband's friends and business acquaintances – it's what one would expect to find in an address book.' He flipped through the pages.

'Well?'

'Well, Mrs Fisher, there is a telephone number here,' he held the book up at her. 'Would you look at it.' He got up from his chair and took two steps towards her. 'It's a Paris number. There are many Paris numbers, but here . . .' he opened the book wide, 'here . . . Do you recognise that number, Mrs Fisher?' – She shook her head – 'Could it be a friend?' Perhaps, she said. His voice had raised noticeably then quietened. 'Do you have a telephone, Mrs Fisher?'

'Yes.'

'Could you bring it through, please.'

She got up and carried it through from the hallway.

'Just rest it there.'

She placed it on a small coffee table with a glass top.

'Fine.' He sat down beside it and picked up the receiver. 'Would you come over here, please?' He dialled the number from the book then gave her the receiver. She had not expected this; her eyes dropped to the mouthpiece and she waited until she handed it back.

'What does it mean?'

'You cannot tell us, Mrs Fisher?'

'I cannot tell you anything,' she replied.

5

When life was young and the days began with the sun and ended at dusk, there was a rhythm, it seemed simple that one step forward would be followed by another. Then the world inside Greg's head was easy and that's how he thought it would always be: straight and uncomplicated like an ancient Roman road, where young hearts strode ahead and minds never fell behind. Somehow all that had stopped and the road had changed; the world Greg was born into had become another place, and he thought in a different way where his mind worked and lived in reverse. Things that were yesterday, were also today and he knew would also be tomorrow. And after his time in prison he had learned how twisted and dangerous this new road was for many. Picking up life's ways like this was no preparation at all and maybe, he thought, all those guys behind the walls and wire were there as children on a beautiful stretch of road that still existed in their heads. Out of his cell and released to the open road that was deserted at that early hour, Greg had looked at where he had been, the walls and the towers appeared enormous, and as he gazed at the parking lot, he wondered if his father had parked properly before abandoning the car and walking away. He never knew much, no one wanted to say, he had to imagine almost everything by himself. The road outside the prison was straight, Greg had noted, a bus was coming along and sunlight was striking its silver frame – it was a child's road with a magical bus and Greg was going to board it and head into tomorrow.

Tomorrow had arrived. When the car stopped on gravel outside a white two-storey building, Greg remained at the wheel. 'I worried about you comin' . . . When you first wrote I didn't think it could go on, letter after letter. But it did,' he said half-turning to her. 'I would lose you over and over and then a letter came. I can't explain what they were for me . . .'

'I can't imagine,' Jilly said quietly. 'We've all got things no one else can imagine and that's a lonely time. But I'm happy you're free again. I'm happy we wrote and that I'm here.' She turned to him. 'Have we arrived?' She stepped out. 'No matter how far you go,' she said over the roof of the car, 'you never seem to have travelled at all.'

Greg looked at her. 'Just what I was thinkin'.'

'Really?'

'Nah.' He laughed as he pulled out her case. His struggle with it brought out more laughter.

'Greg!'

For five months after arriving in California with another shaky car that had all but expired some hundred miles short, Greg had felt the sun like the first time. A new road out of the past and into a job on a university campus as a patch gardener. The Idaho Correctional Board had considered that young Greg deserved a chance to start again, to get away from the Keech name in his home state, to move on. He was given an area here and there in the grounds to tend, to plant some seeds, to care and help them prosper; maybe something in that would help the garden and the gardener; no one knew what Greg could do, least of all Greg himself.

'When you said you were comin' I went a bit frantic. I was

runnin' around this place, you know, I don't have a house here, don't have much, but people have been friendly, and there's Ugo, a nice guy as long as you don't try to slam an aitch on to his name. I told him about you, he knows a bit about me, and he's pulled whatever to make a nice room available for you.' Did this please her, he wondered. 'You'll be a student like everyone else.'

She smiled, 'I can't imagine you frantic.'

'You don't know me. I can get high on frantic.' He laughed and so did she.

Home in America was going to be alright, she was fine, Jilly was sure. The sun was like having someone smile on you, the trees in the grounds were waving and the people she had yet to meet would be like family. Little rooms she had known were very different in different places, but, here, Ugo had been so kind and given her a room to keep her fears away. She had now taken the final step along her lonely and private road, and maybe before the decade was out her destination would be reached.

Jilly Dorian seemed to have no ties to anyone, she could write a letter about someone one day and they would be gone the next, her world seemed to be ever changing and no one's name was solid with her. If Greg had been somewhere else when he received her letters he would have felt her happiness in her nostalgia, but being cooped up like that he couldn't read properly, couldn't breathe, couldn't, couldn't. Jilly had a chance to look in a new mirror and see a new self, all that promise that used to be in England and was no more, had returned in America, she was sure. Away from home for so long, home had begun to gnaw at her, and she could now see herself like never before she arrived in California.

6

London, January 1983

Alex Dorian's wife was a romantic woman, a person who would not think it odd to have a kitchen lunch with candlelight. It was something Alex could not understand, why she worked so hard to get the feel of things right. There was always an atmosphere for the moment, she believed, and it was important. Anything could create a mood, a piece of furniture or something hanging on the wall. All props to make people feel better. Susan found it hard at times living with a practical man; sometimes he was another person to her, someone who cruelly destroyed what she had created. They had been married ten years – he was quite late but he had never considered marriage a commitment he should urgently seek – and they had a daughter, Jilly.

It was a quiet dinner with a couple of good friends that brought the American general back into Alex's life. Jack Kirkland, head of Bonn Station, sat beside his wife Kathleen, a fuzzy brown-haired woman who had put on some weight since Alex had last seen her, whereas Jack was just the same, more or less, looking good and keeping in trim. Most of Alex's friends, he realised, were older than he was and only a few years before he wouldn't have noticed, but now, he did. He remembered when he reached forty he stood naked in front of the full-length bedroom mirror and took his chest, waist and hip measurements and proceeded to struggle with press-ups. This show of concern was quite out of character for a man who had shown little interest in fitness. But the leap from thirty-nine to forty shook him and he had not forgotten, he walked more now, did his carpet exercises and listened to his wife about his dress. Now at forty-three, he noticed his friends ahead of him, the angle of a face, the hands, the attitude. He had not seen Jack Kirkland for two years and then it was in Germany, a business visit and home again. Friendships apart like that could go on for ever, nothing sour ever had the chance to get in the way. It was not the best, and if he had thought about it he would have realised he knew little of him. The years had deceived them both; what they thought was a deep and firm friendship had hardly ever dipped below the surface.

Kathleen enjoyed telling stories, usually funny horror ones about other people. The Germans had been libelled numerous times and her contagious laughter stirred her listeners. There were some who refused to find her humour catching but most failed. With Alex and Susan she found no resistance, they enjoyed her stories and her German impersonations, although Jack could only manage a polite chuckle most of the time. Kathleen insisted she help Susan prepare the coffee. For guests Susan used an octagonal-shaped Moka coffee-pot and brewed a strong Colombian blend. Alone, the Dorians used the instant stuff because Alex said he couldn't tell the difference.

'It's good you could make it,' said Alex. 'We don't see much of you and Kathleen.'

'I know, Alex. Sometimes I feel I don't see much of anyone – anyone, that is, I really want to see. There seems always to be an ulterior motive for meeting people, you know what I mean? It's not enough to be with them but there are other reasons.'

'There are?'

Kathleen and Susan were talking as they waited for the coffee to bubble up.

'It's about the Keech business,' said Jack after a pause.

'Ah, the GI.'

'Well, he's a bit more than that. You've had a word with Sinclair?'

'That's about it. He asked me what I thought of our people staging some kind of rescue operation and I was against it.'

'We've been asked to consider the feasability,' said Jack. 'The DG wants a positive response, I hear.'

'It's mad,' Alex said. 'There's too much we cannot verify. We're being asked to believe what we're told, what we don't know. And in my experience that is something we shouldn't do.'

'It's a political decision; you know that, it's got very little to do with Intelligence. Sure, they want a report from my Section but they want it to make good reading. We've been given a chance to tell them all the reasons why we should go over and bring Keech back.'

Alex sat quiet. Kathleen called through that the coffee had eventually appeared in liquid form.

'Alex,' said Jack with his head slightly forward across the table,'it's too much for the people in power to ignore. The DG is thinking of his own, he doesn't want Six downgraded any more than it is. To refuse the politicians the opportunity to assist the American President they've all come to love means just that; friends in Whitehall would become less so and without them . . . Well Alex . . .'

'Espresso or cappuccino?' asked Susan.

'Cappuccino for me,' replied Jack.

'And for me. Lots of cappuccino,' added Kathleen.

'Nothing for me,' said Alex.

'How can you resist that beautiful smell?' asked Kathleen.

'Oh, he does quite easily,' said Susan, 'lots of self-discipline.'

'I hope not too much,' said Kathleen seriously.

Everyone laughed.

When the women returned to the kitchen with the cups, Jack cleared his throat a bit and asked Alex for help.

'I do think the Russians want us to make a snatch for Keech, they're sort of dangling him in front of us. Keeping him as close to the border as that suggests to me Keech walked over, and to return him the Russians think will do them no harm. A high-ranking soldier walks out on the freedom-loving US, it's not the kind of copy Washington needs. To have a military traitor on the other side of the world is bad, but to have him returned is infinitely worse. Of course, the Russians being Russian will try to get the most out of it; they've asked for Grigov but they're not going to get him and they know it.'

'Jack, if all that you say is true, why don't the Americans just leave Keech where he is, just forget him?'

'Because they want the Russians to appear as evil as they really think they are. The story of Keech being bundled away to the other side is a good one for them, so if he can be seen to be rescued it will in part remove the impotence which they displayed in Iran.'

'Can be seen?' questioned Alex.

'Yes. They won't allow Keech to make it alive, a dead Keech looks even better.'

'They'll kill him?'

'They'll have to. What else can they do?'

Alex got up from his chair with more than a little surprise.

'It's not very nice, is it?' said Jack. 'But the plan has been drawn up and our people are enthusiastic.'

'You asked for help.'

'I don't want to go along, but what else is there? I would like to bring Keech out – alive. And you I can trust. I can speak to Sinclair.'

Alex stood silent at the far end of the room. He thought for some time before finally raising his head and giving a nod in agreement.

"No one knows when the moment will strike, today or tomorrow or a few years in the future, but everybody thinks about it. When Bennett opened his eyes, he did not swing his legs out of the bed and begin the day, he lay still looking around the room. There was no sound, no distant voice; only a dreadful silence that sank on him, pressing deep into his body. Bennett had tried to find a reliable source of distraction, something that could coax his thoughts elsewhere, but . . ."

Alex stopped reading. 'I never used to read this kind of thing,' he said. He sat with his pillow wedged behind him. 'You've had considerable influence on me, not all good, let it be known.'

Susan lay listening to him, her deep brown hair looking deeper on the white pillow-case. 'I enjoyed the book,' she said, 'but I'm not surprised, I didn't really expect you to.'

'It's not my kind of entertainment. I get angry when I'm halfway through a book and I'm still waiting for a reason to be at this stage.' He closed the book then opened it again, slowly turning the pages. 'It's annoying, depressing. Depression is like a cold, it comes when you never want it and you can never be ready, but you're stuck with it and you try to cope. I don't want to settle into bed with this bloody thing.'

'It will be banned from the room forever more . . . Alright?'

He lay silent.

'How did you find Jack?' she asked.

'More or less the same, I suppose. His voice was a little different – older, I think. And you?'

'Yes, there was something but I can't say what it was. Kathleen seems content in middle age, settled quite happily into it.'

'Kathleen was in middle age ten years before she arrived there,' said Alex.

Susan found that unfair but funny. 'What did Jack want?' she asked.

'Oh, just a chat. He trusts me, you know.'

'Why shouldn't he?'

'Oh, I don't know. It's just when I'm told that someone trusts me I find it unsettling. I like to know, but not to hear it. If you know what I mean.'

Susan turned to him. 'Jack and you are close friends; you work in a secret business where trust is defined to its last letter.' – Alex slipped down a little – 'Whatever he told you required him to say that nothing in the friendship had changed, everything was as it was.'

'I got that much, but I never use the word in this business and it makes me wonder when I hear it.'

'About what?'

'Everything . . . To survive in this business you have to on the look-out.'

'For what?'

'For someone who's out fishing for you.' – Susan gave a puzzled look – 'Of course, you have to be a fish before the line is dropped.'

'You're talking in the dark again, Alex. I don't believe you're talking to me at all.' She looked at him. 'You're playing safe, that's what they call it, isn't it? You can't talk to them and you can't talk to me. Am I right?'

'It's all paranoia, nothing to worry about, it keeps us alert.'

'What else did Jack say?'

Alex had slipped down more and ready for sleep. 'Mmm . . . You read in the papers about this American general.'

'The one who jumped over the Wall?'

'Well in a manner of speech, yes. The Americans say he was taken.'

'And was he?' Susan's interest took away the sleep that had been gathering in her eyes.

'Good question. Jack thinks not and so do I. But it seems our masters have another mind and they want to bring the poor fellow back into the arms of mother. Jack wants my help.'

'How can you?' Susan looked serious.

'Well, it seems I'm one of the few he trusts . . .'

'I see. Then what would you be a fish for?'

7

It was some days after Jilly had arrived and seemed settled
that Greg spoke to her, far from his patch and in something
like a whisper. He began to say that he had tried to make
the job work but he couldn't. He had no rest, he said, in fact,
he couldn't see her as he'd like to. He couldn't see anything in
a good light. He sat on a bench, his legs spreadeagled with the
sound of a gentle ocean some hundred feet below. There was a
worn look on him, the excitement of meeting Jilly seemed over.

'Is it Carla you think about?'

'No, it's not.' A pause. 'I've got her here.' He pointed to his
heart. 'Quietly. She's no disturbance. And she shouldn't be, she
wouldn't want that.'

He came forward on the seat, his arms resting on his thighs.
'It's my father, he's become so large in my life when I've tried
hard to make him small. Now maybe that ain't a bad thing, but
it's killin' me.' Listening to what he was saying Jilly found her
pictures. 'My father, Christ, was a general, and everywhere I've
been told to forget him. He's dead, they say, let the dead lie.'

But it was a long time ago, Jilly wanted to say, such a long time
and yet the pain she found in Greg's voice allowed time nothing.

'For a long time I hated him. I knew friends who had bastards
for fathers; they cursed them, belittled them, got their laughs that

way. I thought my father was the same, you know . . . It took courage for me to call him a bastard, I'd no idea what I'd feel or how it would sound, but once I said it I believed it.' He sat up erect. 'So many people wanted to pity me, the family. We got American Stars and Stripes in the post to help us retain our patriotism.' He almost laughed. 'I wanted to tell you more in my letters but I had to focus on where I was. Had to survive, I suppose.'

Jilly listened.

'You came out of nowhere for me. Some guys I met in there would've considered a turn to religion for that. When you've got nothin' goin' for you, you can become like a dog; a touch, some consideration from another human being can make you utterly grateful, overwhelming it is, grateful.'

'Did I overwhelm you?' asked Jilly as softly as she could.

Greg did not reply. He chuckled. 'My father, General Gregory Keech, sounds good, don't it?'

'That's my friend there.' Greg's old Ford sat some feet away. 'I love it. The engine can falter now and again, but it ain't ever died on me. It's strong in its own way.'

Jilly felt strong too and said, 'I've got something to tell you, Greg, something I've never told you. Can we go back to the car?'

'Sure.'

There was no wind noise, only a squeak or two from the car as Jilly looked out at the sea. 'If I didn't know that was the Pacific Ocean, I could believe anything.'

Greg sat and waited.

'The story of your father wasn't new to me. What you told me about things in your letters, I already knew. I wrote to you not just to keep you afloat but to keep me afloat, too.'

Greg looked at her but she didn't look back.

'Your father and what he did had a huge effect on me as a young girl, I just didn't know about it till later.' She wound the window down and took in some air. 'You've got your pain and so have I.'

The sky was beautiful, the sun dipping slowly while Greg was stirring to speak without finding a word. He opened his door and let it hang wide on its hinges.

'Because of your father's decision,' Jilly went on, 'your country set out to get him back. The world was a different place. Your father caused a huge stir. Of course, you know that.' She paused. 'Everything was more threatening; if you weren't West, then you must be East. The politics were that crude. We should have been young enough to avoid all that . . . So here I am in the U S of A, on this lovely road telling you my story which began at the time your father made his move.'

Jilly stopped and waited, there would be something from Greg, a burst of anger, an explosion of rage. What was she telling him? Did he know?

'I don't want to hear,' said Greg, 'I really don't need it. I've got my own baggage and up until now it's been bloody heavy.' He sighed as some birds crossed his vision.

'I need to tell you,' replied Jilly. 'You need to know.'

8

Hansbach, January 1983

General Gregory Keech was being looked after well; he had his own room with a single bed, two wooden chairs, a wash-hand basin and white walls all around him. He could not walk in the large gardens without having someone close by. He was not being treated, he felt, as a VIP. The food he complained about continually, and the hours he was locked alone in his room brought his head to fall into his hands as he sat on the bed. His plan of changing over and abandoning the people back in Idaho and starting up a life again had overpowered him. Everything was clear, new life, new people, new Keech; he expected that. They would be friendly and set him up – home, job . . . They would consider his move honourable; a man alone for so many years in his country had put down his gun to begin again. But it hadn't turned out that way – not yet. And as he was beginning to sink, unable to grasp anything, a clear shaven-head soldier came suddenly into his mind, a Vietnam Veteran and prisoner of the Viet Cong. He remembered the boy, his thin white face and black eyes before a room of fellow soldiers, all hoping that one day they would have their story, their pain, their pride. He told of his four years in captivity before the room stood and the applause loosened his tight young face.

The applause went on and on inside Keech, bringing his own pain to the surface. The pain of shedding his skin in the hope of receiving a Soviet one, and the pain of his memories, his marriage, his children. The applause went on; the boy's story of so far away had reached home and all Keech's pain was there – back home and far from Germany.

A sudden change in the weather had brought freezing conditions sweeping across West Germany and the chill sneaked in through the cracks in the window frame. Keech wore a roll-up sweater and a pair of shapeless trousers. He got a blanket from the bed, tightly wrapped it around him and sat on the floor with his back pushed against the radiator. He remembered things there; saw many faces, mostly cheerful and laughing. The sad side to his life did not surface there, no old wound had appeared to cut him again, just silent laughter from some good day.

A key was pushed into the lock of the door and a man entered with a small tray.

'Coffee?'

The man had a pleasant face, in his thirties and rapidly going bald. His hair was short at the sides, which did nothing to conceal his large ears.

The tray was laid on the bed.

'How long does this go on for? When does my life begin here? Why am I not in Moscow?'

'Questions, questions,' said the man while he poured milk into the coffee.

'You're damn right,' said Keech getting to his feet, 'I have been here for weeks, in this room, in this closet of a room. I can't open the door. I'm trapped.'

The man continued to attend the coffee.

'Do you hear me?' Keech's hand held to the man's shoulder. 'I've taken this step,' Keech quietened his tone, 'to leave my home country and come here. I did expect more of a welcome.'

The man's eyes never left him. Keech's hair had lost its spiky look, it was now longer and he looked younger.

'You are a military man, General, based at Camp Braddock and Camp Braddock did celebrate Christmas and the New Year. That is so?'

'Of course, it's a worldwide celebration.'

The man smiled. 'It's a time to get drunk and lay your women, nothing more.'

'For Christ's sake, it's a time for children. Christmas is for children,' Keech explained.

'We in the Soviet Union don't think so. Your country is an imperialistic one that has claim to a god. Am I right?'

Keech nodded, 'Yes, we believe in God, if that's what you mean.'

'What I mean, General, is the Christmas you in your country profess to celebrate for your god: you get drunk and lay your women. You're supposed to be celebrating the birth of Jesus Christ and the beginning of the Christian faith, but you in the West get drunk and take your share of women.'

Keech shook his head. 'It's not like that.'

'General Keech, we think you got drunk at Camp Braddock on New Year's Eve, maybe drugs were available. No?' – Keech had turned away to look out the window – 'When you crossed through to our side you were still recovering from a dizzy night.'

'Not t all. I had planned it months before; I did not get drunk, my actions on the first of January had in no way been due to an impulsive thought brought on by celebration alcohol.'

The Russian looked unconvinced.

'For Christ's sake! I'm a defector. I'm a high-ranking military officer in the US army and I expect to be treated as such.'

'What if I were to say to you that you might be a CIA plant.'

Keech laughed loudly for some minutes. 'You guys are crazy; your suspicion's tying you in knots and these knots will tighten . . .'

'And what will they do, General?'

'What?'

'The knots. What will they do?'

The men looked at each other, the Russian and the American. Keech had his back to the window and his face appeared darker, more shielded from the gloomy day.

'They will end your suspicions.'

The Russian stretched his mouth. 'Your coffee is getting cold.'

He walked out and turned the key noisely to lock.

9

Jilly Dorian had the body of a happy woman and the eyes of a sad one especially when she had no words piling up inside her, words to convey her thoughts to someone who would listen. It was a mood thing, a deep lingering mood that could retreat for a time to allow the other Jilly to be seen and then it would return. Her body and limbs were in happy unison but her psyche had taken too many beatings too long. She could also appear to slump, a weary slump, a tiredness brought on by a heavy load. She had a face that could be misread, a smile that could hold back what was going on inside and in times when she felt small. Jilly thought she had a destiny and it was being with her father, that was all she carried in her head, all her energy was there. While Greg listened to what she was telling him in silence, she sat still and talked more about who she was.

It was a wonderful feeling to be free again to speak of where she had been and how it had come about, while the sky and the sea shone together out over the large expanse. To come out in the open with Greg and tell him how by accident she had read the story of the Keeches after Greg had been convicted. How she had learned that the family had been strongly advised to bury their father as deeply as they could in their minds, to throw off the stain of treachery, which they were now smeared with, by denouncing openly the name of Keech. Jilly had no such advise, not publicly anyway. But there were times, as a teenager, when she had weakened and turned away, gripped by anger for a second, a moment, while hatred rushed around her young head, and in that time it was like her own heart stopped. Now, where she sat on the coastal road, she felt strong, like the sun in the sky things would come back to her the way they were.

'I don't know what to say to you.' Greg had made a fist of his right hand and he was tapping the steering column harder and harder. 'Christ, Jilly.'

'I never told you anything that wasn't true, I just didn't tell you . . .'

'No you fuckin' didn't. Fuck! Fuck!' He got out and struck the bonnet hard with his hand. 'Here I'm thinkin' that I'm in the shit because I have an old man like nobody else, I'm just so unlucky that my dad thought it was time to screw his country and his family.' He thumped the bonnet again and walked erratically around the vehicle as Jilly remained inside. 'That I've got an old man from hell and wherever this dream called Jilly came from, it was not like mine. It was never going to be like mine. You, Jilly, were supposed to pull me out of where I'd been, don't you see, out, now I'm back in.' He put both his hands on the bonnet and seemed to wish he could fly out over the ocean.

'I was attracted to what you were going through. I thought I could understand. Greg. It was good having you in my life, writing to you, Greg, I'd been alone for so long . . .'

'Everyone's alone, don't you know that? We're all fuckin' alone.' He moaned a little, 'Oh Jilly, Jilly.'

'I'm sorry.'

'It's all screwed up,' said Greg. 'I needed you to be normal, normal with normal history.'

'I will be. Once I know in my heart that what I'm looking for can't be found . . . Once I know.'

Greg leaned on the open door and looked at her.

'Come back in.'

Greg sat in, his tension easing. 'Wow!' The key was turned, and the engine caught, the tyres rolled off the gravel and slipped onto the smoother surface that would take them down to the sea.

Greg and Jilly had their own ideas of the way things that had invaded their lives had come about, and maybe that is how it can only be with memories and other people's reports, they rarely match any other, they are just snapshots.

IO

London, February 1983

Alex Dorian had worked in the German Section in the early '70s, and he had met Jack Kirkland about the same time. Germany was far from a peaceful place then with the savage acts of terrorism that had struck the country. Jack was five years senior to Alex, he knew because they had birthdays together. It was Kathleen who discovered it; Jack's was on the fifth and Alex's the eighth. When Jilly was born Jack was godfather. The recent years had made it impossible for the dinners and weekends, Jack being in Germany and Alex in London. But now a job was on involving the Americans, and how much their involvement would be no one was quite sure.

'Sometimes talking in the park is the only way, if you can get free from your desk. But sometimes I get the feeling they don't understand why a warm comfortable office is not preferred.'

Both men had the collars of their coats up, and Jack had a scarf round it tied at the front. It was February and the park almost empty; a jogger in the distance, a woman with a high pram and a dog running from tree to tree. The trees were much darker after a two-day lashing of rain, everything was wet and pools of water lay waiting on the footpath.

'This is a hush-hush operation. The Americans insisted on that and we have agreed. You heard it; we're the chosen few.' Jack inhaled noisily.

'I thought you could have put across your points a bit more forcefully,' Alex said. 'You don't believe in this operation, so why . . . ?'

'Because they believe in it, damn it, everybody believes in it. I wasn't going to storm out. No, Alex, I listened to them and I listened to you. You surely know they wouldn't abandon the Americans, as you suggested.' They walked quite slowly. The sun could have been out and the birds could have been singing a summer song.

'I'm just surprised that this meeting took place at all; there was a face or two I did expect to see there, where were they?' asked Alex.

Jack looked away. 'I want you to come over with me, back to Bonn. The weather is much the same as here but it'll be a change for you. What about it?'

Alex had a pair of leather gloves on but they did not prevent the cold getting through as he would bring his hands hard together to generate some heat.

'What's the situation?'

'Oh, nothing has changed. You've just heard the official story; the Russians have got Keech and they want to exchange but the Americans won't.' Jack stopped and turned slightly to him. 'You've heard what the DG thinks; he believes the Yanks, stupid bugger. He said that if the exercise was feasible a plan should be prepared to bring the general chap back.'

There were two small boys playing with a black and white football: they were keeping it up with their heads and counting aloud each time it passed from one to the other. They were good and Jack and Alex stopped to watch in silence.

'Why is it,' asked Jack, 'when I know it's a long time ago when I did that, it seems hardly any time at all?'

'I don't know,' answered Alex. 'Maybe life's like Halley's Comet; it appears every so often then vanishes, but keeps, if only for a moment, returning.'

Jack frowned. 'I don't get you.'

Alex's attention was on the boys. 'No, maybe not.'

The boys had had enough and let the ball run on the wet grass while they picked up their school bags and chased it.

'Well, can it be done? This American?' asked Alex.

'At the look of things I would say no, but that's because I would prefer to have nothing to do with it.' Alex waited for an answer and Jack went on, 'As I said to you before, I feel they're dangling Keech, asking us to take him. If I'm right we have a problem. We don't know their game. To ask for an exchange and seriously expect it, we can understand that. But what they're doing is difficult to fathom. I mean, Alex, a general in the American army is someone worth having, they don't get many of them.' A pause. 'But they're treating him like a farmer's boy.'

'Can he be got out?' asked Alex. 'I don't suppose,' he went on, 'we would be walking here if the answer was negative, would we?'

'Right, Alex. Against all my better instincts there is a possibility. It hasn't been evaluated yet but for our political masters evaluation is something that comes after action.'

Alex smiled; he hadn't heard Jack complain like this for years, his part of the sufferer, the one no one listens to. His suffering was beautiful to Alex, because there was no pain in it, no torment, it was just a way of being for Jack, a way that worked for him.

'What about it then?' Jack returned to his question, as Alex stopped and fastened up his top button. 'I'm being polite, Alex, you know that.'

Alex nodded, 'If you think I can be of help.'

Paris, February 1983

It was a good day in Paris, it was cold, very cold but there was a feeling of promise about, something that made all of life's problems that bit smaller. Some streaks of sunlight had shot through breaks in an otherwise even mass of cloud and for a few moments they gave colour to the Champs Élysées which seconds before had been black and white.

Nikolai Levchenko was stretching his legs. He had taken the Metro from central Paris and got out at Concorde; from there he walked up the Champs Élysées, crossed over and headed back down. He wore dark clothes: dark grey trousers, black coat and grey scarf tucked inside, grey hat with a black band round the middle. He occasionally stopped at a shop window, one where the pane shone giving a perfect reflection of the traffic behind him. He then stopped at a newspaper kiosk to buy a French daily, doubled back up and smartly stepped into a cafe.

The cafe was a tourist's delight: it stretched out onto the pavement and was boxed off with large glass window frames; the small round tables with their basket chairs were situated in lines from one side to the other; visitors that day seemed to prefer the first rows and sat just as the chairs were positioned. Levchenko stepped deeper inside to sit with a younger man who had been waiting. A couple of coffees were ordered and delivered before the men spoke, then two envelopes, one large and one small were exchanged across the table. Something else was said before Levchenko rose and quickly left.

Pierre Halin checked his inside pocket where he had slipped the Russian's envelope, then pulled up the collar of his coat and walked out.

Nikolai Levchenko worked at the Soviet Embassy, he was the KGB's number two in France. His movements had been of great interest to the French security service since the day he arrived in the capital, three years before. Levchenko was known for his walks in and around central Paris, in the Montmartre district and the Latin Quarter where any surveillance could be easily lost in the dark narrow streets. To have a watch on someone like Levchenko would have brought a charge of harassment from the Russians and caused French-Soviet relations to dip further, which no one wanted. So the French watched as closely as they could without a cry from his embassy.

When Nikolai Levchenko stepped from the Metro station onto the Champs Élysées that afternoon he did so knowing he had been successful, his French watcher had been left – underground, three stations back. But he was not to know that the British had decided also to keep an eye on the KGB staff in Paris and their movements. The murder of Edward Fisher had got them; his brutal death was for no apparent reason, there was nothing whatsoever it could be linked to, no robbery or revenge. Fisher's colleague on that train told the French investigators that he had seen no one: Fisher had got up to visit the toilet and had not returned. On the Champs Élysées, while Levchenko walked briskly between stops at various shop windows his British watcher kept reasonably close.

The French police had almost let go on the Fisher case, in truth there was nothing to hold on to. They had made their enquiries, of course, and discovered a girl, young and innocent. It was a quiet little affair not worth disturbing. They had the names and addresses of Fisher's fellow passengers but they had called on no one. They had not been informed of the British interest and they suspected none.

London, February 1983

'Sometimes I can't contain myself at how devious the human species can be,' said Nick White. 'When it surfaces and you can see what has been going on, you can be so captured that you lose sight of the wickedness that has been revealed; disturbed like that you can only attack it, human nature insists on that immediate response. Of course, we enjoy the darker side of humans – men; that's why we do this work.'

Nick White was a man no one liked too much. He gave the impression that everyone was a tiresome fool, it wasn't new with him, not a sudden change, no, it was a long established pain which came into his eyes that made anyone talking want to conclude quickly and rush away. But there could have been a reason for Nick White's pain, something that lay elsewhere, a reason that had turned him sour on the human race. He had an unsteady voice and a troublesome nose he would blow with a crumpled handkerchief with such ferocity one half expected a locomotive with carriage to rush from either passage. Before him on his desk were photogaphs of his wife, a slim soft-looking woman, and their two children.

'I've heard it said,' White continued, 'that it's sickening to watch liars lie, the excuses given, the breakdowns with their explanations, but I don't believe a word of that and I would suggest you don't either.' A pause. 'You didn't get a photograph of this Halin chap?'

'No, I didn't, sir,' answered Gull.

Frank Gull had returned to London as requested, to lay down the facts as he saw them. Gull was young, with fairish hair and bluish eyes. He was an SIS officer based at the British Embassy under cover of First Secretary. There was a look of formality about him and he was proud, always proud. He was also ambitious and very impatient to find out, to know. Treachery could be found anywhere for Gull, it was everywhere and not an isolated crime, not something rare; it was much more ingrained into society and everybody was capable of it and he hoped to prove it.

'Well, now that you're here tell me what you know,' said White.

'On 3 January,' Gull began, 'Edward Fisher . . .'

White waved a hand at him and said he knew those details

and to move along. Gull inhaled strongly and continued, 'On the TEE train at Dijon, Fisher was found dead in his seat, the discovery was made by his business colleague who found Fisher strangled. A cheese wire had been used; it had been pulled tightly around his neck cutting deeply into it.'

'Cheese wire?' asked White. 'Yes sir, it was deeply embedded and left dangling on each side.' There was a pause as both men looked at their own images. 'We were notified and I viewed Fisher's body at the morgue. I went through his personal effects and found a telephone number in his address book.'

'Stop there,' said White. 'Let's move on to more recent stuff, shall we?'

There was a hint of annoyance on Gull's face at being interrupted again before he returned to his thoughts. 'As the number was that of the Soviet Embassy I decided to assume that it was not an above-board business contact.'

'Why did you assume that?'

'Fisher was an English language teacher, he was not a businessman, he was not selling anything for his living and yet he had this number. If Fisher was involved in some way with the Russians, if he was an agent, then, I thought for a while, whoever was running him would be someone of the lower ranks of the KGB.' He paused. 'Fisher worked for a city-based company called Paristec, a computer data systems outfit; their technology is good but no better than a number of others and competition is fierce. Fisher was a teacher there, he organised courses for key company staff, he also translated for English versions of their manuals. But he had no knowledge of computers, even if he translated documents of the most secret kind it is unlikely he would have realised their value.'

Nick White listened joylessly. He had been sitting in that chair for a long time listening to various faces in front of him; he would sometimes take his eyes away and look at each family member. But he did not drift too much with young Gull.

'So I thought,' went on Gull, ' if he was not passing company secrets to the Russians what was he doing? Whatever, I guessed it was more, and if so, at a higher level, and this would merit higher rank.'

White put his forearms on the desk. 'And?'

'Well, the security employed for the KGB's number one is all that one would expect, so I looked at their number two, Nikolai Levchenko. The French keep a close eye on him except for the day the Russian lost them. It was neatly done in the Metro. Levchenko boarded at St Germain then appeared to try and get off, then again at Opéra. He had waited until the outgoing passengers were clear and the incoming ones were boarding and then he made it for the exit. He struggled his way through then changed his mind and stepped back in. The train ran along another two stations when he made his dash at Concorde. The French watcher dared not take his eyes off him as Levchenko made for the door. He was wearing a hat and as the train stopped he took a step foward and removed it, so on the platform he was just another head, nothing to distinguish him from any other. In a cafe in the Champs Élysées he did his business with Halin and left; no time was wasted.'

'So,' said White, 'whatever Fisher's business was with the Russians you think it was with Levchenko?'

'Yes, I do. And now Fisher's dead, they've got a replacement.'

'But it takes months to replace an agent,' said White. 'How could they do it so quickly?'

'There's a contradiction here, sir,' replied Gull. 'If Fisher could be replaced with unusual haste, it would suggest two things: Fisher was not a big fish, shall we say, in the operation and yet the very presence of Levchenko would suggest that he was.'

'Now that is something, Gull. A minor doing an important job.'

'Like a Securicor driver going round the banks,' said Gull.

'Yes. A postman delivering a Littlewoods cheque. What could

Fisher have been delivering?' A pause. 'I want you to go quietly on this, it's your territory and nothing is sure. We don't want to upset the French – not yet anyway.'

'I thought I might call to see Fisher's wife, find out what she knows.'

'She hasn't given anything away to anyone. Be careful, Gull. When we're feeling our way like this, we could be babes . . . you know. You get my meaning, don't you?'

Paris, February 1983

Rosalind Fisher had returned to Paris. After a wild wet time in England she had decided that she wanted to come back, to try and keep what pieces that were left of her life in France.

She cleared some untidiness around the room while explaining how she had been away, then asked the gentleman to sit down.

'Gull? Is that an English name?'

'Where its origins lie I'm not sure, but I can trace it back to the sixteenth century.'

'Really, that's interesting.'

'Yes. I don't want to intrude on your time, Mrs Fisher, but I need to ask a few questions.'

She nodded. She had expected another call from someone and understood.

'Murder is never nice but sometimes it can be easy. Someone's dead but the reason is known and the murderer is caught. But with your husband it's quite the opposite and I'm sure you'll agree with me. A senseless murder without provocation.'

'Yes, I do agree with you, Mr Gull. But although it's heartbreak for me, it's surely not for you. How many English people die abroad every year and die violently?'

'British citizens abroad who die violently and suspiciously do receive our utmost attention, and fortunately they are very few. Your husband's death is receiving our attention and it will continue until we are satisfied why someone decided to kill him.'

'You're quite different from that other man, Campbell, wasn't it? He didn't have the same policeman approach as yourself, and that's what you are.'

'Mrs Fisher, your husband was an English consultant with Paristec but his salary hardly suggests he could afford this place. Where did he get the money from?'

'I know my husband is dead. I know he's not coming back. Don't you know that too? You're chasing my husband for nothing. All the good and the bad he has done in his life is over. Why are you here, why? I need to be by myself, to remember him, to have a clear picture.'

Gull waited till she had eased back in her chair, the colour slowly returning to her face.

'Your husband's life is over and his death is a mystery. He was not robbed on the train, he was not beaten, nothing like that. He simply left his seat as one usually does on a long journey, and found someone waiting for him.'

She played a bit with her hands, fingers, nails.

'Did he have enemies here in Paris? Any debts?'

She said nothing.

'He certainly had something that someone took offence to.'

'A crime of passion maybe, Mr Gull.'

'You knew of his affair with the French woman?'

'I did, but it never caused angry scenes or anything like that. He needed her, he said. He needed both of us, he said that too. I believed him – a man, a woman, might have a need for two people. I don't think that makes that person wrong or inadequate.'

'So it didn't bother you?'

'We're supposed to respond negatively to such a situation, aren't we? Separate, divorce, shout at trust being betrayed and cry a lot. I knew that was not the way.'

'Where did he meet her?'

'If you know of her existence, Mr Gull, you'll also know that she is an employee of Paristec but he met her before that: he gave her private classes two or three times a week.'

'Had he many classes?'

'Oh yes, plenty. His nights were booked Monday to Friday. Some came here for classes.'

'To the house?'

'Yes. It was because they lived too far out for Edward to make it worth his while.' She remembered something which made her smile.

'I never thought the French were that enthusiastic about learning English,' remarked Gull.

'But they were not only French, there were also Spanish, Turkish, Greek, African. There was even a Russian.'

'It's amazing,' said Gull showing a little amazement, 'that so many people from around the world come to Paris and learn English. Even a Russian you say.'

'Yes. A nice man who spoke the language very well but had little opportunity for conversation. And that's what he wanted from Edward, just conversation.'

'Do you remember his name?'

'Name . . . Yes, I remember. When he called the first time it was me who answered the door. He had a heavy briefcase and he had noticed that it had caught my eye and he said that they were English books. He introduced himself then as Monsieur Levchenko. He came some more times after that, but I never saw him again.'

'When was this, Mrs Fisher?'

'Oh I don't know . . . some Christmas time. I don't know.'

'When did the classes stop?'

'I don't know if they did. A few months ago he phoned; I think he was cancelling a class. I remember after the call Edward was a bit restless. It was what happened if one had private classes, they were unreliable sometimes, they would phone with thirty minutes notice and cancel, there was nothing one could do. This uncertainty about classes and income made life difficult. Nothing was sure.'

She put a king-size cigarette to her lips and held it tight to the lighter flame. She was wearing a beige dress with a belt that tied at her side allowing the shape of her thighs to come through it, and Gull realised for the first time that Mrs Fisher was an extremely attractive woman.

'Can I get you something, Mr Gull?'

'It's the money question, Mrs Fisher. Suppose your husband was a busy man, could his income from Paristec, which was not high by Paris standards, and from private classes, bring all this?'

'I don't know how much my husband earned; I only know he could afford what you see.'

Gull looked around then got to his feet.

'Are you going home now, Mrs Fisher – to England?'

She moved with him to the hallway. 'I always thought if things should turn bad here there would always be home. But England has changed, we both have.'

I I

There are many changes that can take place without one knowing, and although Jilly and Greg had found themselves lost in the world, cut off from any guiding force, someone had noticed when Jilly had arrived and where she had come from.

Jilly had come to believe that there were people who had a slant on life that could not be satisfactorily explained, she had met them, one way or another, on different streets of life. Their slant was a preference to be in the presence of heartbreak and pain, not as a medical person would volunteer to this arena to ease it, no, those people's way was to keep it alive, to increase it. Jilly had been alarmed by those people: the sick individual, the brutal institution. But as she had her fries and coke and laughter and music and was lulled away from her hard times, she was being considered as a problem which had not yet reached its full potential. Her letters to Greg had come only recently to light and there was some unease around that any long-time stay in the US would bring further anxiety. It was best to pull the plug on her.

The room Jilly was sleeping in had been given generously by Greg's employers, which was a surprise to him. It made him happy to feel at long last he was being helped, so much so, that with the news he spoke excitedly on the phone with Ugo.

'Your girl's comin' over, that's great,' Ugo said.

'Yeah, the world's not a shithole of a place after all, is it?' Greg felt his happiness running all over his body. 'I feel great.'

'I can feel your energy, man,' said Ugo.

Greg laughed and laughed. 'I've got so much fuckin' energy,' he spluttered down the line.

Ugo listened as Greg raced on. He was older, ten years could have been in it, and it was what Greg was looking for when he arrived; someone, he thought, like him, a casual guy who spoke in that way, and who saw the world with the eyes of the people he could have been but was not. Ugo was more a student than some of the deadbeats on campus, Greg told him more than once. Ugo would thank him and say the fact was he was not and they were. 'They've got three of a kind and I've only got a jack. It's the way it is.' But they'd been cheating, Greg would explain. And Ugo would study Greg's face and say, 'I know, I know.'

The air was still as the hour reached half past a black two a.m. A few hours before Greg had realised that something was up, something Ugo had said about how lucky Jilly had been with immigration, an easy ride through, he said. These people held a hell of a lot of power, he went on. Greg was not sure then what he was saying, not until the campus was asleep did he spring to life, jump up in a startle and in the darkness he rang Ugo's number and let it ring and ring. In minutes he was running over damp grass with anger and fear to Ugo's room.

'Ugo!' He rapped on the door. 'Ugo!'

The door finally opened and Ugo showed his face. 'Yeah!'

'Let me in. Come on,' Greg insisted.

'Come in, come in.' Ugo looked strange. He was dressed as he was hours before.

'Don't you sleep?'

'I am fuckin' sleepin'.'

'Well I can't fuckin' sleep.'

'Life's a bunch of trouble.'

'I wanna know about Jilly.'

'Greg, I don't know. We all try our best but sometimes it ain't good enough. We've all got troubles; one day they're yours and one day they're mine.'

'What the fuck are you saying? Tell me?'

'I can't tell you. When you're screwed as much as we are, you can't tell anything. That's a fact.' He stretched himself out on the bed. 'That's the world. That's dear old America.'

There was some sound from a radio which could not be heard when their voices were in the air, but now as Ugo lay still, his worldly cares manageable and Greg silent in a chair, the night music sounded meloncholy and uplifting at the same time.

Ugo had once been a bright star, he had it all then, he was to become part of the elite, that small percentage that keeps America moving forward. The journey was to be smooth because it was all there for him: background from upstate California, high school whizz kid, money and influence. But it didn't turn out for him. He lost his bearings or so he was told. He lost his respect almost overnight for all that was waiting for him, he began to die and the very thought frightened him that he was being asked to be the proud young man he had every right to be. But he wasn't proud and while he lost his image he began to lose his friends. He couldn't understand because, then, he couldn't articulate what was happening to him. Self-questioning is something some people try never to do and Ugo was urged to do the same, but it was no good, and the more he questioned the money, the influence, the smugness, the moral highground folks on the hill, the more they wanted to isolate him. He couldn't be allowed to run through his twenties discovering himself if he was going to discover others on his way. It had been hard for him but he didn't feel isolated too much, there were communities everywhere of people just like him, he told Greg, capable and incapable of so much. 'We're not bad, we've just been too honest. Be careful, Greg, don't become too honest, the world doesn't want to know.'

'But you came from somethin',' Greg sounded bewildered.

'If I came from nothin' where would I be now? I sometimes wonder. I screwed up somehow, gave my folks a hard time and that's bad.' Ugo sank on the bed. 'Gee,' he smiled with his half-closed eyes at the ceiling. 'Listen, man, I like who I am, some days I don't, but I'm okay. I'm a black man who can't be sure if the ground below his feet is his.'

'Neither can I,' said Greg.

'Yeah. How many blacks were sharing things in that High Security government residence?'

'Didn't count.'

'No, Greg. Couldn't count.'

Ugo could shine into Greg's gloomy night, as welcome now as when he first arrived those months ago. Greg's gloom was more worry and it could only be his own, Ugo had his, which he kept in his room with just the lightest of a smoky haze to comfort him.

'Will Jilly have to leave?' Greg asked.

'Mmm. She'll have to go.'

'Why?'

'She's trouble. That's what they say.'

'Who says?'

'It don't matter. I'm sorry, man. This ain't a good time.' He rubbed at his eyes and asked Greg to switch off the light when he left.

Greg walked back thinking of the men he had lived with in prison, how they all needed someone, sometimes anyone. Back on the damp grass he knew they all needed a buddy, so lonely were they; now alone in the small hours with his brain at war he felt the stabbing jabs of his own loneliness. In the quiet night he wanted to live the best way he could, to be what he had every right to be; so to silence the voices of those men back in Idaho he took some comfort in the memory of his old Ford that had brought him down through the desert where the nights were still and nothing seemed to live on the earth.

The desert was a drive away, the job a bit further, and he had never had a car that he could be sure about, not anytime; his cars were someone else's first and second, then maybe his after, but he would forget that as soon as the key dropped into his hand and he sat in. The air then was drier than what the best of the Napa Valley could produce, and most of all there was a sense of freedom and being free that would make him happy about himself. On the road in an old dog of a car that could not promise anything from watering hole to watering hole, his gratitude grew immense as the miles passed and his disappointment equally so until it all came to an end, and he had to let it go or pay a repair bill that would have been out of his reach.

Before man and machine parted he stayed awhile in the desert as dusk fell on the sand. There was some time to wonder at the stars, which he thought he had done before, as a boy with his father maybe, he did not know for sure. He sat wondering where he had been and where, in the newness of the desert, he would go. Life had been so heavy just making his way, and he could not try any harder, there was no room left for that extra spurt; he was whacked. In the warm darkness he considered his fight with everything, thought of his mother and his sisters, saw them prettier, heard them, too. Sometimes with tender family pictures there would be an ugly shot, a face, trying to intrude – this ugliness his father seemed to know, he seemed to have little love for his mother and so it became for him. She was another kind of woman and she had made her daughters the same, and because of that he lost all three. He didn't know it then that his anger was not all for his father who had walked off to the end of the earth, from them . . . and from him. Perhaps it was there in that still place under the stars where you could feel how you functioned, what kept you upright on the planet and how it revealed the thread that everyone lived by the grace of, that a route could open up for young Greg, a pathway to real significance, a direction he never had before. The stars could do that, they could take you to a crossroads and although you might struggle with confusion, you could feel any road offered would make you happy, you might even be told which was the road for good and which for evil. There were choices that awaited Greg, and as he stretched away from what he was in Idaho, he was slowly evolving into another kind of man far from the one who had been wandering the state all his life. He, in his Ford, could not just see the stretch of road ahead, he could see demons he had thought then were friends. There were Gregs all around the world with their just causes and they spread themselves touching and breaking lives on their way, from Idaho to Paris.

Greg had a focus that was some days clearer than others. He had wounds he sometimes felt deeper and had thoughts that might have been his father's: a man at war, betrayed, abandoned and punished. But Greg had no war to remember and no buddies to mourn; still his rage, which could dip and rise, was picking up momentum.

12

London, February 1983

Pierre Halin had risen early, when Paris was still half asleep, when the morning air was still fresh and the smell of baked bread sucked up his nostrils as he made his way to Charles de Gaulle airport and his London flight. He knew the early morning from his youth, which was not very long ago. Returning home from the many parties and discotheques, from some hours shared in a strange bed and being rushed out as the hands of the clock approached dawn. Halin didn't know it then, but he enjoyed the panic, the run down the stairs and the quiet morning street. He had not wanted anything else; love in the middle of the night was enough, he didn't need any other time, but somehow he got it. He got married, he became a father, he never saw the early morning quite the same and the smell of bread now meant little to him.

The Air France Airbus came into Heathrow and Pierre Halin slipped through Passport Control with unusual ease. He made directly for the Inn on the Park and had breakfast. For most breakfast was over, the table tops with their crockery lay disarranged, some orange juice had been abandoned with a crust of toast. Halin sat with a paper stretched out as his continental breakfast was served. The clearing up of the tables had started at the far end of the room and became decidedly noisier before he escaped it. He then called at the desk and asked if a package had been left for him. His name was Adam. From the office the clerk retrieved a brown envelope, well sealed with the name clearly on it. With no difficulty Halin walked away with it safely zipped up in his briefcase. Outside he took a taxi and directed it back to the airport. The taxi was allowed to journey a few hundred metres before being stopped. Pierre Halin was requested to step out by a large man in a grey suit, his briefcase was taken by another equally grey-suited man and they drove away with no protest or surprise from the Frenchman.

The room was small and windowless, the walls creamy and the faces of the two men blank. Halin had spoken a few words, forced into it to break the silence, but the silence was allowed to return. No one seemed worried; Halin didn't, and the men didn't try to change this, not at first.

One of them flicked through his passport. 'Halin,' he said loudly.

'A'lin,' corrected the Frenchman.

The man raised his eyes to him. 'Pierre A'lin,' he said. 'I forgot, it's all accents in your language, isn't it?' The passport was closed but he didn't let it go, his long fingers had a good grip. 'Been to England before, Mr Halin?'

'Many years ago.'

The man nodded, 'I like France.' He paused, thinking of something he remembered and liked. 'The people I've always found friendly. Paris is a beautiful city, the attitude to life there is something not many people see, I think. They go at peak times to grab all the sights, they hardly pause. You're from Paris, aren't you? I don't suppose you see it quite the same way. What do you think of London?'

'I don't know London very well.'

'Ah, you haven't been here long.'

'I arrived this morning. I don't know why I'm here in this police station.'

'You eat much better in France,' said the man, 'you consider food. You're interested in what you put inside your body. I understand that. Here, nobody cares. They talk about it being fuel for the body, the ones who don't care. Different attitude. I don't know why you're here, Mr Halin, I'm just passing some time with you till someone arrives.'

Halin looked at the other man farther back from them – his arms were folded and his face had changed to serious. 'But I have to be back in Paris today.'

'There's plenty time, Mr Halin, plenty time.'

Halin sighed, 'Is it my passport, is there something wrong with it?'

The man looked at it. 'It's fine, just fine.'

Halin sighed again.

'I have a friend,' said the man, 'who lives abroad; he's English but he'd rather live away. There are many like that who just cannot take their own country. I think it's sad but not wrong. No, no, you should live where you're happy, and here, England, can only be happy for some.' A pause. 'I suppose it's the same in France?'

Halin didn't know what he was listening to and the longer it went on the more he worried. 'Yes, some are, some are not.' He glanced at his watch, then stretched his arms out and picked up the envelope which had lain on the table from the beginning.

'Just put it down, Mr Halin.'

'It's A'lin, A'lin, you keep forgetting the accent.' The envelope lay on the table as he stood and then walked round his chair. 'What am I doing in this place? What do you want?'

'Well, shall we talk about you, Mr Halin? Then a picture will emerge for both of us. I'll start off by telling you a little, then you tell us a little, shall we?'

Halin blew out his cheeks and sat down. The other man seemed pleased that the Frenchman's excitement appeared over.

'You work for a company called Paristec; you sell data systems, you earn a low basic salary with promise of much more on sales and you're not as successful as you'd like. Four years ago you married and became a father and your eighty-square-metre flat began to close in on you. Like so many, Mr Halin, you didn't think it was fair. In such an elegant city as Paris you struggled, not forgetting your wife and child. When Edward Fisher arrived at Paristec you saw your chance to improve yourself and decided to study English. The world of data systems was an English one and you acquired a second language.' – Halin sat hard in the wooden chair – 'Then your bonuses started to increase, small at first but it was a step in the right direction. That should have been the end of that little story but then something happened, didn't it? Something quite out of the blue.' – Halin frowned – 'Something unexpected, Mr Halin. On the train to Lausanne, the man who taught you English got himself killed.'

'But I had nothing to do with that. Is that why I'm here?' Halin stared at him with appealing eyes. 'Nothing.'

The room fell into silence.

'Tell us about Levchenko.'

'Levchenko?'

'That's the name, Mr Halin, or did he use another with you?'

There was a long pause. Halin made two attempts to say something, a denial, an explanation, perhaps, but little came, only the sounds of a man caught between his thoughts.

'If you're working for the Russians that's too bad, Mr Halin. Many have done, been lured in because of weakness – an incomplete life, uncertainty, usefulness. There are many reasons. I think yours would be fear, Mr Halin. Was that it? Fear of France? Fear of living there? Was that it? Was that it? Are you afraid, Mr Halin?'

'Can I have some water?'

There was a jug on a small tray on the table with three glasses. Halin's questioner filled up a glass and passed it across.

'You are young,' said the man, 'and you are lucky. You're in a foreign country and you've committed no crime here that we know about, but back home . . . well, I'm sure you know better than I do.'

'I'm not a spy if that's what you think. I've been passing no secrets, no rolled microfilm. You know that?' He took some more water. 'I've done nothing. I'm not anything.'

'Oh, you are something, Mr Halin. You're in with the Russian, he tells you what to do and you do it. Now, that is correct, isn't it? You're rubbing shoulders with this Levchenko for some meagre pittance that keeps your life together. Isn't that it? You're his bloody messenger.' He rose and placed both hands on the table and stared at Halin.

'You're trying to provoke me,' said Halin. 'You think I'm English. I'm not, I'm French. You don't know how to provoke the French. By raising your anger you hope to to raise mine, but you can't.'

Alex Dorian got up from his chair and Halin's questioner sat down. He held a pad of paper and a pencil which he rested on the table. The pencil rolled a little, then more and more until it rolled off and crashed to the floor.

'Open your envelope, Mr Halin.'

Halin slowly picked it up but Alex took it from him and stripped off the tape holding the envelope flap down. As his hand eased the contents out further and further a small spring, which had been held to the inside with a black adhesive, sprung up and detatched itself from the black gum-like substance. Startled, he let the envelope drop.

'Christ!' he said in a loud voice. 'There's nothing, just pages from a paper, just bloody newsprint.' He slid a foot over a loose sheet, 'They'll all have to be checked,' and turned and went out.

Halin looked across at the other who pulled at his tie and slackened it.

'How long will you be away?' asked Susan.

'I don't know, shouldn't be bloody going at all,' Alex replied.

'What is it, you're pacing. Please sit down and tell me. Do you want a drink?'

'No, I don't want a bloody drink.'

'Are you ill?'

He stopped and thought to himself, 'Yes, I suppose I am.'

'Tell me.'

'I'm going to Germany, you know Jack asked.' – she nodded slightly – 'To bring back some damn crazy American who somehow – and this is unclear – got himself to the other side. Anyway, that's where I'm going.'

'And you don't want to go.'

He looked up at the ceiling. 'Jilly?'

'Yes, fast asleep,' she replied.

He took quick steps to the door. 'I must see her.'

The light from the hall entered Jilly's room as the door was gently pushed open. He stepped in and pushed almost all the light back out, leaving only a corner of her pillow top visible. He had little time to observe her during the day, just to watch. There was always something that took his thoughts elsewhere, something to distract him. His daughter now could do all the things he had wished she could when she was so much younger and he never quite focused on her then. He wished he could go back, and sit and watch and watch.

He kneeled at the side of her bed and looked at her little face, in the quiet. He felt like wakening her up, giving her a mighty squeeze then telling her to go back to sleep. But he let her sleep with a thumb in her mouth, a habit she had promised to stop but could not. Hanging by her bed was a large picture frame filled with photographs of various sizes, taken at different times during her eight years – different stages of growing up. Alex looked at them with some surprise and remembered them all. But he didn't use the camera much these days, didn't look in at the camera shops in the High Street or think about buying a film. The thought never came anymore.

'How is she?'

'Fine. I love to see her sleep, it's then I can fully realise what she means to me. We're very lucky to have her.'

Susan was perplexed, 'Is there anything wrong?'

'No, nothing. People are mysterious, you can't expect to understand them all the time. There are moments that pass between us that we cannot hope to begin to tell each other.' – Susan looked suspicious – 'You're right, I don't want to go. I'm not supposed to tell you anything about the office but I trust you and that makes a big difference.'

'Let's both have a drink, Alex.'

He brought a bottle of whisky to the table.

'Now will you tell me?' asked Susan.

He unscrewed the cap and poured. 'I had a Frenchman in the office today. He flew in from Paris to pick up an envelope and to fly out again.' A pause.

'That's bad?'

'I think so, but as the envelope contained nothing secret, nothing that would worry anyone, it was decided I could be released and head out to Bonn.'

'And the Frenchman?'

'He's all patched up and gone home.'

'But he will be investigated and you'll not be there, is that it?' Susan smiled, her worry had been for nothing, there was no real news, Alex was going away for a little while and that was all.

'Inside the envelope . . .'

'Well?'

'Inside there was nothing, scrap paper. But to be sure no one looked in, a small spring was fitted inside and when it was opened and the paper pulled out, the spring jumped and detatched itself.' He looked at her. 'What do you make of that?'

'So when the envelope reached its destination it would be seen to be tampered with. Did you stick the spring on again?'

'Yes, we did, but the adhesive used was a primitive type gum, thick, black, like those liquorice rolls you could get at the school shop all those years ago. We couldn't locate anyone in the city who supplied it at first. It was a close thing.'

'What are going to do now?'

'Nothing, remember I'm off to Germany. It's for the bloody politicians too. But this Frenchman can surprise us, he may not know it but the man running him sent him on a dummy run.'

Susan sipped her drink. Alex was not talking to her anymore but thinking out loud. He needed to go over it in his mind, just let his thoughts come out and spill over Susan. Once when he went upstairs to kiss a sleeping Jilly goodnight he didn't come back for over an hour. He said the darkness of her room cleared his head. Susan understood.

'Dummy run?'

'Yes. You see someone in this country leaves an envelope to be picked up and someone comes over from Paris, collects and goes home. But this time the messenger has changed, there's a new face, so his master in Paris arranges for his own envelope to be picked up by him just to check out the replacement, to be sure everything's well.' Alex cursed to himself and poured more.

'And whoever's leaving the envelope,' said Susan, 'it's worth travelling all the way from Paris for.' She paused. 'What exactly are we talking about, Alex?'

He looked over the rim of his glass at her. She knew but she couldn't say.

'Someone is passing something,' said Alex, 'and you know what they call that.'

13

The month of May in this southern end of California is a more restful time if the visitor arrives with no preconceived ideas, no great expectations to be met, no household baggage from wherever he has come from. There are many battles going on here, battles for everything that take away the beauty of the place and of anyone who lives to battle. Jilly was into love and love had taken her into battle, and there were times, before she was a woman, when she feared to lose and that had stuck with her since. All the years when she had still to reach her full self, she always had the strength to go that extra mile, for Dad, she would say to herself, but many times it was for her calm. Now in America where the sound of her presence on the road had awakened her more and begun to stir others into their actions, unaware and still alone, she lay in bed more like a teenager than the tired woman she many times felt, quiet like the night. There was a belief, or at least a hope, that in favourable places answers could be found, the dressing of anywhere could determine success.

In this silent hour with a touch of light in her room Jilly lay soft and still, while Greg was far from sleep; in a rushing moment he jumped from the chair he had rested on to think of Jilly and scrambled with his footwear before the sound of soft tones of the telephone ringing brought his movements to a halt.

'Hey man, what you doin'?' Ugo asked down the line.

'Can't sleep. You?'

'I'm alright. Just thinkin' about you.'

'Have you ever thought what you're doin'? I mean, ever thought of goin' home?'

'I'm at home.'

'You're in a couple of hundred square feet. That ain't home.'

'It's all space and time, man. And nobody knows what that is.'

'Ugo.'

'I know. Can't sleep, can't talk, can't do fuckin' nothin.' Then don't, Greg, don't do anythin'. This is a good place. Don't lose it.'

'You gotta lose some things to keep others, didn't you say that?' Pause. 'I wish I had what you've got. I wish, I wish.'

The call had slowed Greg; Ugo, he knew, was still on the line but he had no more to say, so he allowed the receiver to slip into its cradle without another word. There was nothing to lose. Nothing. He made that walk over to Jilly, brought on with a worry to unload, worry and fear which he was going to dump on her doorway. She didn't deserve that. He still could be amazed at how she had helped him from an ocean away, how she wrote and wrote. As he approached, he cursed his situation and Jilly's.

There had been a letter, written when Jilly had found a period of peace during their correspondence which Greg didn't know what to do with. It was a different kind of letter that touched more deeply all the sores he had, it was a moving letter and Greg fought with himself not to be moved. Jilly had no right to be so bloody caring, so warm and civilised, while he was holed up in darkest America. Where did she think he was? If ever he was uncertain whether to love or hate the land of his birth, Jilly's letter was showing him how life could be, how human beings could make a difference to each other. With his fingers slipping over Jilly's pages, he lost his pain for a while as he imagined more and more of her. It was a certain kind of agony for him to receive the daily abuse and Jilly's care together, and he cursed both camps. Jilly had made a mistake, her softness had come at the wrong time just as he was sliding to the bottom of his life.

Now, in the night, Greg tapped Jilly's door while his heart thumped heavily. She cautiously opened to find his head resting on the door frame. He put a foot in and leaned toward her ear; speaking softly he brought her out of her room. She stood obediently, stiff against the corridor wall, the pulse in her neck revealing her anxiety. 'What?' she whispered. She was beautiful there, stripped of what adulthood had made of her, and as the seconds passed she returned to an earlier time when her happiness had yet to flee; in that Californian morning, before the first bird song, a younger face that was all Jilly was seen.

Greg had driven to a little place waiting to be found, somewhere on a ridge, where the bends in the road seemed to go on forever and where gravity was seen as a friend by those who leapt towards it. California is a lovely place, but it can be as tough and hard as Idaho. It is not a place for the needy and the desperate, it is not a place where wounds are treated, not a reaching-out place, not in the valleys and not on the ridges above them.

'Greg, what's going on?' Jilly looked closely at him while she sat uncomfortably. 'Greg. What?'

'I don't know,' he replied.

They sat in a cabin sort of place, and outside there were peaks of rock shooting up to an impressive height all around. Jilly had her hands wrapped round a coffee cup of enormous size, and the liquid inside was doing its job, heating her from the outside – there was no need to drink it.

'You'll soon be leaving,' said Greg.

'Will I?'

'You're going to be asked to leave.'

'The country?' There was a childish look of surprise on her face. 'Greg.'

'I'm sorry. You must worry them. They know something. Everything.' Greg could not keep looking at her and searched for some distraction.

'Greg.'

'You'll be back in England and you'll forget all this.'

'This isn't a break for me. I can't go back like this, I'm alone there. Do you understand? I need to stay. I must stay.' Jilly found a slight tremor in her throat as she spoke. Outside there were some gusts of wind that rattled something of that out-of-the-way diner. Greg felt her nervousness as she went on, 'I'm strong. I'm not going anywhere but I'll stop being your guest. I'll get out.'

'Jilly, they want you back home.'

'Who does? Who wants me to leave?' she asked with a shout.

'They don't want us together,' answered Greg. 'It's my father, it's all about him.' He sat moving an unlit cigarette from finger to finger. 'Your father and mine, Christ, Jilly, they've fucked us up. It's been goin' on for years.'

Jilly was fighting the shivers that had crept into her body. 'We can do something. If we let things just lie . . .' she wondered about things just lying, like a cupful of coffee left on the table no one returns to.

'We've got little money,' said Greg.

Jilly wondered more, some pictures of the past appeared, some talking, too. Little money. She knew about little money when she and her mother were together, and Jack, her father's best friend, decided not to be theirs. They had been left to themselves when they needed money and people so much. So they turned on each other: instead of holding closer, they pushed apart. Two small units adrift. That was what Alex was afraid of; when he was a part of their lives, every time he was called away, a day, a week, they would become less, not in importance but in physical size inside his head. When he returned the house was less, too, and love there, with welcome home signs in pink crayon, could still be felt, but all love sounds had been turned down.

'We've got money. How much do we need?' she announced and questioned in the same breath. 'We'll go and find your father and mine. That's what we want, isn't it?' She pushed her cup away and it fell on its side. 'Everything will be easier, Greg. It will.'

'Will it?' asked Greg.

'Did you see your father's body, Greg? Did your mother? My mother had nothing like that. I had nothing to go to. There's no burial place for me to know where my father is.' She paused. 'They told my mother something and she told me. But it was nothing, nothing, and that's how it's been all through the years and now, here I am, in my twenties. I've asked questions in London and they've said nothing in reply. I think they thought I'd remain a girl all my life with my girlish questions. Or I'd become distracted and go away. They don't want to know me because they don't want to answer or explain.' She looked around where they were sitting – the overhead tube lighting clashing with a glimpse of dawn. 'I hate them,' she said with little hate in her tone.

'Hate?' enquired Greg. 'Everyone I've met encourages me to have it.' He looked out. 'I haven't disappointed them. Now it's a quiet hate, it isn't so obvious, but it's me now.'

They sat for a time in their own worlds and from a distance they looked as a starry sky would appear, peaceful and still, no indication at all of the turbulence going on out there.

14

West German-Czech Border, February 1983

Beyond the open field was a forest but you couldn't see it, not at that time, just the mist, wet and cloudy, hung before you. There was also a wire fence some metres away and another beyond that with automatic shrapnel guns between them. It was strange to see the guns pointing inwards, towards themselves, towards the very people who had placed them there. The fencing and the guns ran along and followed the contour of the land, mile after mile. And when the mist lifted the farmland of Czechoslovakia would look as good and normal as it did anywhere in the West. The road that ran by, parallel to the fence, was narrow and deserted; there was a village half a kilometre away but this road made one feel much farther. And as the mist cleared slowly, a gun tower could be seen beside the trees just as they were in POW camps during World War II.

Jack and Alex were sitting in the car looking across. 'Keech crossed some kilometres farther south,' Jack said, pointing the direction.

'And then they took him north?'

'That's what we think. They took him to Hansbach, a farming community outside Zwickau, and from there to Moscow, we believe. But Christ, Alex, a top US military man falls somehow into their hands, they must have taken him to Moscow.'

'And then they brought him back?'

'And quickly, after just a few days. Now you know how they do things, they don't do anything quickly. But with Keech they moved bloody fast.' Jack paused, and turned to face the window. The mist was moving back, the engine of a tractor could be heard in a far off field. 'Along this stretch there are many hamlets, a scattering of houses and farms. Some villagers have been reported suffering from nightmares, it's the mist that disturbs their sleep: just before they jump up breathing heavily they say they saw the mist lift away and there the Red Army was, facing them,' Jack smiled.

'Just how the Germans on the Normandy beaches must have felt when the ships appeared,' said Alex.

'You know, Alex, in this business one needs to be always awake, to be always questioning, wondering how things match up. You know, you know what I'm talking about. It's a mental exercise, you've got to watch it with everybody.'

'Yes Jack, I know.'

'Recently I've been thinking . . . Why does Control want me here, out here. Why have I been thought so suitable for this. And don't give me my location bit. It makes me wonder . . .' He looked out ahead. 'Do you know anything? What are they thinking, Alex?'

'I don't know.'

'There isn't anything.... Christ, Alex, they're consulting with the FO every bloody day.'

'Things are not that bad, Jack. Sure, there have been one or two unwise, shall we say, appointments. And the FO did ask to be kept up-to-date and someone goes along, usually Simpson, and he tells them what they want to hear. But Control is Control. It's a bloody nuisance, they all say so, but it costs little.'

'Is that right, Alex. You're sure about that? There's nothing worrying going on?'

'Worrying?'

'Yes Alex, when people lose their command and have dialogues with the government it has always been a sure sign in the past that all was not well. If a problem has risen in Control, they'll sit on it until they figure out a way. And if during this time the government requests SIS to assist another country in an operation which I think is madness and they go along with it, what does that suggest to you?'

Alex thought.

The sun had come out and Jack had turned the car heater off. Nothing had passed on the road.

'One would have to ask what is worrying them so much . . .'

'And what could that be?'

Alex felt prodded by Jack and he didn't like it.

'We have to tell each other, Alex . . . what we're thinking.'

'If you know, then speak, Jack.'

'Only a mole could worry Control the way I think they're worried. It would explain their decision and why we're here talking on this country road.'

'No, I don't believe that,' said Alex. 'I agree it's a political decision but it's not a suicide one, is it?'

Jack sighed. 'We've put our necks out for the Yanks because the government thinks it's a good political move, and Control feel they have no option because they will need their friends if and when the news gets out that there's someone in Curzon House trading with the Russians . . .'

Alex interrupted, 'Jack, you've got no proof about any of this. You can't fix your mind like that, there's nothing to go on. It's just a feeling and you should know. Feelings have no place anywhere. Isn't that how it's supposed to be?'

Jack didn't answer.

'We're here to do something.'

'You're right.' Jack turned himself round in his seat and started up the car and with some difficulty reversed before turning back towards the village.

'Have you told anyone this? . . . I mean, what you've told me.'

He shook his head. 'Just you, Alex my boy. You can only tell something like that to someone you trust.'

The car climbed a slight rise and headed on, leaving the fields and the wire behind it. The men were silent as they bumped their way along the road. A thick mud had formed after a heavy rainfall and seemed to cover all of the village. They could have been in the East, the picture looked as if it belonged there except for the parked Audis and Volkswagens. Alex stared out, clearly preoccupied. Jack drove on in low gear.

'Do you fancy a coffee, Alex?'

They both scraped the mud from their feet before entering through a dark heavy door into a large bar which had yet to waken to the morning. Jack stood for a moment listening for a sound before knocking hard on the counter, while Alex settled at a table with his arms resting on the bare top. A thin man appeared with an apron down to his knees and a black waistcoat over a shirt with its sleeves rolled up to his elbows. His arms were ugly with the veins bulging down to his hands, which he wrapped in his apron like in a towel as Jack enquired about the area.

'I've ordered coffee but I can't promise that's what we'll get. There are many Germans today who like to advertise how miserable they are, and I'm afraid I've just been speaking to one of them.'

Jack took off his coat, folded it twice and placed it at his side. Alex waited for the coffee with his coat still buttoned up.

'Your trouble is, you've been away from the Northern Line too long,' said Alex.

Jack laughed loudly. 'The Germans are over there too?' He laughed again.

'You've settled well here, you miss nothing. Maybe moving, a new place . . .'

'Alex, if you want to get on in this business don't look to get away from it. It suits us quite well here, most of the time, but there are others who know exactly what they want out of it. I'm not that dipped into this work; I can breathe easier out here, and for that I shouldn't expect anything grand.'

The coffee came in thick rounded white cups with a bowl of sugar and teaspoon; Alex ignored the spoon and used the one in his saucer, Jack didn't seem to notice.

'Maybe I'm getting older, Alex, but people mean more to me now, their presence is much more important.' He sipped at his coffee while Alex added a spot more sugar. 'But there are very few, do you know that, bloody few.'

'I haven't reached that point yet,' said Alex, 'I understand it but I've still to arrive. I' don't expect to get myself behind one of those big desks back at Control, I've thought about it but I can't see it. But we've got to go on, haven't we? Right to the end.'

'What else is there?' asked Jack. 'We have all our places here, our rules and our orders and we have to follow. Do you want another?' Jack pointed at Alex's cup. Alex placed his hand over the top of it. 'Think of it, Alex, just some hundred yards across there,' he stretched his arm out in the direction, ' there's another world. After the wire and guns, there's another world. What do you suppose Keech was thinking when he walked over, presuming, of course, he did just that?'

'I've no idea, Jack. Many have gone; disillusionment seems to be their confession. They say they don't recognise their country anymore.' Alex thought a bit. 'It can't all be one-sided, the country has to take some of the blame.'

'You think so?'

'I think if Keech was sick of America, of capitalism, where else could he go? If you're sick of the female body it doesn't necessarily mean you prefer the male one, but that is the way of our thinking.'

Jack looked at Alex not quite sure what to make of that. 'You could be right.' He dug his hands deep in his pockets and brought out some loose change. 'Could you sort that lot out while I have a pee.'

Gruff German was being spoken as Jack disappeared through the bar room and the waiter came round from the counter with a fistful of cutlery to set the lunch tables. Alex put aside the pfennigs, half marks and marks and made neat little columns before Jack hurried back, lifted his coat and they both walked to the door.

As they trod with care through the mud Jack said, 'While you're here in Germany with me we'll stay in Bayreuth, it's fifty kilometres from the border. If Keech is meant to come out, that's where he'll come to before his fellow countrymen call to collect him. What do you think?'

They stopped at the car while Jack waited for a reply. The promise that was in the sky an hour or so before had gone, there was nothing up there but a mass of cloud, dense, heavy cloud.

'Who'll be bringing him out?' asked Alex as he studied the mud on his shoes.

Jack hesitated, 'You see, Alex, we have to be careful, we have to watch our step. If Keech gets out it'll be a young German chap we'll all need to thank.'

'What am I here for?'

'I told you, Alex, I trust you.'

'But you don't need to, not here.'

Jack turned, opened the door and nodded to Alex to walk round and get in.

'If I didn't have you here, I'd have another. This . . . For me, this is a job I'd like to run away from. Now, I can't do that. So considering that, I didn't want someone coming over. Who the hell could it be? Carlton? You've met Carlton?'

Alex nodded, 'Our hands have actually touched in greeting.'

'Have they. Now there's a chap who can be very quick, sharp – that I can admire – but he has no need of people, he's quite ruthless. Now that's fine, I can listen to that from a distance, but he has no business anywhere near me. No, Alex, I did think you might have something on yourself, something secret. You didn't, did you? I mean, you didn't leave anything, to help, for friendship?'

Alex couldn't understand what was going on in Jack's head, he seemed worried, unsure, perhaps afraid, afraid that this operation would fail. Or was he sufffering from more than that, was there panic about him? Alex sat back and watched the country-side pass. Susan seemed far away; it had been sometime since he had been away from her and it had given him time to think how easily even the strongest tie could be undone. Nothing could be sure, he thought, not Susan and not Jack.

15

The drive back was when the white moon had become less distinct, and when Jilly's weariness had caught up with her as she opened her mouth in such a yawn that Greg remarked, 'Jeez!' Jilly spluttered at that and laughed. 'The size of a canyon,' said Greg. 'I have been told,' said Jilly defensively, 'perfect in all proportion.' He laughed and she joined him, and the ride for the next few miles, turning and twisting, down and down as those rocky peaks disappeared, was happy and excited.

Jilly was dropped off to gather her things, their spirits higher than before, their minds lifted from gloom to that place where happiness can be found fleetingly, and where the colours of the world are seen everywhere. It was the place to be. Before they met up again Greg called on Ugo; a tap on his door brought no response, a muffled call of his name was the same. He wanted to have a few minutes with him, a casual friendly word of thanks. To ask him to care for his patches, patches as big as the potato fields of Idaho, Ugo had teased. He wanted Ugo's good wishes, to have his hand, to embrace him. But behind Ugo's door was a man lost to the night.

With the car in low gear Greg slipped along to Jilly's building. It was an anxious decision, for sure, but one that would bring its reward. Something they had to do: like donating blood or a kidney, like opening your heart. But nothing was guaranteed, Jilly more than Greg knew that in the end no one might be rescued or found and the heart might not be enough. With the air still fresh and Jilly feeling cold, Greg drove past the boundaries he was supposed to stay behind and took them both away.

'They won't find us?' Jilly asked and answered in one.

'They know me. They know you. And they know this old car.'

'But will they be looking? Really looking?'

'It's what they live for. It's what makes them tick. They don't want a good ol' America, they live for the bad one. They're all-over-the-top pieces of shit, all out of control. Must be the same in your country.'

'We're on the run then?' Jilly slapped her hands together. 'Wow!'

For a few miles they sat quietly as they climbed higher.

'Is it out of love?' Jilly asked out of the blue. 'All this?'

'Love?'

'Job gone. No money,' Jilly explained. 'You had a deal, you told me. Early release with restrictions. Wasn't that it?'

'Let it go.'

'With the road up ahead . . . who knows!'

'Let it go, I said.'

'Why let it go?'

'I want to know more, just like you. We're the same, we're looking for a nice comfortable explanation that we can sleep with.' They had entered a road of tall trees which guarded them while they drove through. 'I don't know if we'll get it.' Greg pulled the car into a rest area and brought silence to it. 'We might never get it. If I thought I could shake my troubles off, I'd rest with that. But I'm a hateful guy. If you could get to know where my hate takes me, you wouldn't be here.'

'And you think I don't have the same hate?' Jilly jumped in. 'You think I'm a tourist in the dear old U S of A?' Her anger had raised her in her seat. 'My father went away to help an American soldier . . .'

'General,' corrected Greg.

'I don't bloody care what his rank was.'

'He was a general.'

'So what?'

'It matters.'

'What matters is that my father was taken fom me and I want him back. I don't believe he can't come back.' She sat fully and exhaled loudly. A little traffic was heard on the road while they uncovered their emotions behind a bushy screen.

'Maybe it's good we'll be looked for,' Greg said. 'As long as we can stay a few days this way, we might get good coverage, our stories will come out.'

'So they won't hunt us down and shoot us?' Jilly asked half seriuosly.

'It really depends who they want us to be. If they want us dangerous then they'll have us that way.' Greg had realised what he had said. 'Yeah, they want us dead. They'll want rid of father and son.'

'Why would they?'

'We need help, Jilly. All our yearning, for what? Alive or dead . . . .'

'Alive. Alive. You've got to believe that. It's a lifetime to you and me, but to others it's nothing.' She wrapped her arms around her and Greg asked when someone last did that for her. She heard the question but she could not say. 'Everyone imagines America in their own way and everyone makes a mistake. It's what a person brings to wherever he's going, taking a piece of history that makes a new place okay, a place to stop in.'

'Not here,' said Greg. 'You can't bring things like that here, you're here to start fresh, that's what people think, strip them cold. That's how they want you. That's the way it goes. America's got it all for you, the states of plenty dreams.' He thought of dreams. 'And plenty nightmares. We cater for all.'

'America,' responded Jilly, 'isn't here on this planet to break me. I can't be broken. Tell America I can't be broken,' she tried to say strongly, but in the car, which gave her little confidence, she barely got it out at all. 'Tell America. Tell.'

Jilly and Greg sat in the car staring out at the trees while a soft radio sound played music for the desperate and the broken. It was surprising how gentle and caring notes could be as they questioned whether the listener should live or die. It was an intimate moment for thoughts and memories rushing around their heads, pulling them this way and that. Suddenly Jilly felt she had found her way and said, 'I need to roam with the few dollars I've got. Just go out there,' she extended her arm to the screen, 'and find things for myself.' She turned to him. 'We're too sad to be together, Greg.'

'And too sad to be apart,' offered Greg.

'Maybe.' The trees were handsome and protective as Jilly looked admiringly. 'I can't return as I came,' she gave a little laugh. 'Hope to die before I get old.' She beat her thighs like drums and repeated the line of the song that amused her. 'Before I get old and before my father's story dies.' She pushed open the door and felt the cool air.

'Jilly,' Greg jumped out, 'it's all my fault, I always thought your letters were only for me. I was lookin' at it that way. I thought you were comin' for me. I thought that.' Greg walked round the car and touched her for the first time.

'I'm sorry. I'm a desperate woman,' she smiled, 'I really am.'

Greg thought of Carla as he came close and placed his hands on Jilly's shoulders and took the distance away from them.

He contemplated the thought of Jilly not being there, gone, like she had never been. Yet it was more than likely now that the news had got around campus. She was leaving and again he just waited. Waited as he had back in Idaho where no one knew how he was with Carla as she lay with all her strength ebbing away. The trial was unfair, a tabloid affair out for revenge, and as he stood waiting for their judgment, he saw America looking the other way. They had walked him into court with shackles from ankle to ankle and wrist to wrist, and anything he might have had that could have given him the smallest measure of strength was hoped by one and all to have fled him. He stood waiting weakly. If he could have run, like his father had, out of the court and out of America, he would have. He and his father together on that road with the tall trees and all the promise. In court, surrounded by a sea of unknown faces, he stood a forlorn figure who could not break out of his silence and had no words of sadness and none of grief for his girl and his baby. But he was sad, he had grief and love, he could have a lot of love . . . then he could not. With a lawyer selected for him, a professional aide who failed as such, Greg was allowed to drown in the courtroom, in front of the judge, the chosen jury and members of the community. He simply waited.

'Gregory Albert Keech, the jury has found you . . .'

He started up the engine and sat burning fuel. The smell of gasoline entered the car and then entered him. It was a strange moment of déjà vu, a time when a smell of impending failure could be sensed. It was worn on one's shoulders and seen settled in the eyes. Such a moment could be seen in Greg who instinctively reached for the little cross and chain he always wore. This small memento could maybe make an impression, safeguard him from an angry world, even become a friend.

The crucifix, which looked more golden in the sun, could not be fully possessed nor could it be disregarded, it was all that was left behind after his father had gone. It had been brought by a military man with rain dripping from his peaked hat and cape and had been put out of sight since, until Greg found it in his hands one sad day. When Keech walked out of Camp Braddock, he left the crucifix, like a calling card, on a piece of furniture. Now in his palm, Greg tried to imagine his father with it, around his neck, in his pocket, pressed against his lips as he had seen others do. It was brought by the visitor with much dignity, as if conveying a death notice on the family. It looked beautiful in his hand and in later years when Greg found himself in the darkest of hours, when all its protection was called upon, the beauty of it surpassed all the pain he was in. Life was a mystery he would say in his stronger moments, the reason he wanted to believe was in his hand, and if it gave comfort to his father, he wanted to be a part of it. Idaho boys had been lost in Viet Nam like boys every-where, and there were those who were never found, still and tragic, never recognised and never brought back home. When Greg heard the stories of young men and their one-way tickets, dressed for hunting and swearing to die, he knew he had missed his time. Viet Nam was his place to be, to show the world himself, who he was. Face to face with another, a moment between two strangers. Although Greg did not enter any zone of combat, the ones his father struggled in, he knew his father's story, had been with him, had died in front of him and had been cradled by him. In the darkness as sleep was pulling him in, young Greg created his moments with his father who would talk tenderly and tell him what it meant to have him in his life, and, until another time when all would be revealed, Greg was happy in his bed where horrors could visit; he was lighter than at any time, being cradled by his general father in some zone where restless departures were all around.

How could Jilly know him, Greg wondered as she said, 'Go back. I'll go and be that tourist for a while.'

'You want me to leave?'

'Yes.' She took some steps and looked out at the horizon. 'The stars are always there. Imagine, Greg . . .'

'What?'

'There's more to us than we know.' She turned, 'Do you know?' She swept all the sky before her. 'I've read amazing things about parallel worlds. Do you know about that?' The sound of the wind was the only reply. 'Nothing is what it appears. Nothing. Your pain and mine are really not necessary. Can you imagine? Greg!' She looked for something from him. 'If you believe. If you believe.' She paused. 'If I could only know more.' She kept her eyes to the sky. 'Go back, Greg, I'll find my way.'

Greg found no struggle within himself. 'If that's what you want.'

He started up the car and pulled away. He dropped Jilly close to a couple of tourist buses parked facing out over Lake Tahoe. He left with her promises that she would not disappear, promises he made her repeat before he headed back to his boundary. He had let her go and he had said nothing. When she asked him if there was anything he wanted to say, he said nothing. He agonised. He could slow and turn, he could, or he could speed up. The seconds ticked away before he thumped hard on the dash and sped away.

16

Paris, February 1983

The envelope rustled in his hands as he turned it over, then with finger and thumb he pulled at an edge at the top and tore it open. He widened the sides and peered in.

'Everything is fine, just fine.' Nikolai Levchenko folded the envelope and placed it on the table with both hands on top. 'You understand, you now have a new position. Because of Fisher's untimely death we've had to rush for his replacement and you seemed most suitable. I know you, Monsieur Halin, let me be clear about that, and you know who I am, let there be no mistake there. Fisher's job was that of a messenger; he would deliver and collect small and not so small packages between the two capitals. He was very good at it and he prospered as you will, Monsieur Halin. We understand your needs, your system is such that it is natural for you to have them, but we could never accept them as an excuse, should your loyalty ever stray. This is a commitment, Monsieur Halin. You must understand that. Do you understand that?'

'It's a job for me, that's all.'

'I want you to realise that it is more than that. When you work for us it has to be taken seriously. Your work before has never been as important as it is now. This time you will have no further contact with the others; it will be with me from now on, always.'

'And money?' Halin asked. There was a lingering pause. 'I know what you are and what you can do, but I need money. Here everybody needs money.'

'There will be money,' said Levchenko. And Halin's smile was full of relief as if he had had a thought, for a desperate moment, that something had changed and now there was going to be none.

'How can I contact you?' asked Halin.

'You don't. We're being serious, Monsieur Halin, contact will be left to me. But there is always the possibility that you may need to get through to me – a life or death situation, nothing less – and you will ask for King's Knight and then hang up. We will use a series of meeting places all coded. If you should make this emergency call we will meet two hours later. If I'm not there return the next day at the same time.'

'This will cause me difficulties,' said Halin, 'it is not easy to have this free time.'

'*Monsieur*, you will invent for time, invent an illness, a sadness, but you will invent.' Levchenko was calm as he spoke.

There was a pause while Halin considered his new involvement – his second job, the one that would raise his standards; but he had a worry, one he couldn't chase away, and there, he brought himself together and asked, 'Why did Fisher have to die? Where was the need in that?'

Levchenko pushed his cup to one side; the envelope remained exactly where he had placed it in front of him. 'We don't know who killed Fisher, you were on the train with him, you were there. We were not.'

Halin couldn't believe it, there was no one else who could have done it. 'Fisher was killed by you, your people.'

'No, he was not.'

'Impossible, it had to be. Fisher made a mistake, no? He was followed onto the train and . . .'

Levchenko sat with one hand resting on the other across the envelope.

'Fisher made no mistake, he was doing very well, he was reliable and safe. We did not kill him, that would have been our mistake.' He stopped to show a hint of a smile. 'You will be intrigued, Monsieur Halin, we are too, but be assured, we did not bring Edward Fisher's life to a close because of anger or anything. Someone else is responsible for that.' He waited a second then rose.

Halin watched him as he slipped a glove on.

'Money, *Monsieur*?' He pulled the glove back off and dropped a small envelope, taken from his inside pocket, on the table. His large pale face watched Halin pick it up. 'I hope that will satisfy your needs. *Aurevoir.*'

When Levchenko was safely gone Halin counted the French notes.

Charles Gull was back in the French capital where he had some watching to do.

Halin had been accepted by Levchenko; the need to replace Fisher had been hurried by Russian standards and this had heightened Control's interest. But they were not ready to act, they were still finding their way. Someone in London was passing information, that much was known. Before Halin, Edward Fisher came over once or twice a month to collect a *package* from various points, then returning to Paris and Levchenko. It was the source, completely unknown, that worried Control. It could be anyone from anywhere. Fisher had never met him and Halin would surely do no better, only Levchenko knew and his immediate superior. The source was well protected, there would be no contact, he would know what was desired, he would be autonomous. But with a switch of the collecting point, Fisher had to know. Did it come from Levchenko or was Fisher contacted direct? Soviet gratitude was most certainly what paid for Fisher's lifestyle and kept his head well above the Paris waters. But at that point everything dimmed for Control; nothing could be certain until the bad blood amongst them finally got sick and called for help. They could only wait for Halin to receive orders. Gull walked the streets a lot where Pierre Halin had returned to the bright lights and his youth.

17

Toby Cullen was somewhere at thirty-three thousand feet when a powerful beam of sunlight burst in through his window. It was a welcome surprise. Much of the east coast and mid-America had been swept with unseasonal weather – storms, flooding, nature beating up on nature, and it had been long days since sunshine was seen. Everyone on the flight seemed to respond positively as the craft filled with more and more light. Cullen felt now he was leaving old weather and old days behind. But he knew that however high he climbed, it was only to be temporary, he would soon return to the man he was on the ground. He was still youthful looking and maybe by not seeing the cruel decay of time on his reflection he could lose track of where he was. Maybe he had remained the young Cullen too long, and this did no favours for anyone, least himself.

Cullen had his history which made up an interesting résumé, he was an agency man who had had some input with that mission General Keech had brought about. He had taken the years in-between to become the man he wanted to be, like many who pass the years fleetingly, caught up by their own status. While he sat he found himself thinking backwards in time, where he had been and what he had done; it was strange because history was dead to Cullen and the dead made him angry, but as he would not cast an eye at it, his history was surfacing more with each day. When he boarded his flight at dawn he had a good journey ahead of him, a time to look backwards, back in Germany, back on the road to Camp Braddock when anxiety had gripped everyone as the snow lay tight on the land. Young and short-cut smooth then, he was told that what he did not know he was to fill with cock-sure confidence and some invention. *Tell them stories that will release information. We live in a world where little is real, we make it what it is, that is our control and that is all we ask for.*

There was a man who Cullen looked up to back in time, back in Langley, Virginia, a kind of father figure but so different from his own and yet he seemed to bond more with him. He thought that he was the man he wanted to be while his own father was not. This man was strong, decisive, someone Cullen believed in completely. He could see no signs of weakness in him as he stood before him day after day, and no sign of his own while he was in his company. Men like him gave Cullen hope that they weren't all on the same road, there were some, had to be, who didn't decline and disappear, thank God, they simply changed their location, became someone else. He had great difficulty believing otherwise. Then the day came when the man was visited by ill health, which shook him and shook Cullen, too. He was at a loss as to what was going on as he watched the man diminish in front of him over days and weeks.

The man in Langley had fought as well as he could and Cullen maybe saw it more than the man did, he even brought the news home with him and spoke of the man's struggle and how he hadn't bowed to it – words like, no compromise, no change of direction, no selling out for some deal, *it was Custer-like, Mum, Dad.* He made him feel strong, he said. *Do you know, Dad, he told me to be my own hero. That's what he said – this man.* His father replied how nice it was to be spoken to in that way, but he should remember that they weren't at war there. The man at Langley had much control over his life and to do that he had to be constantly alert, on a war footing with life, yet this power couldn't help him now. *But Dad, it's war, every day of our lives is a war day, don't you understand? Why is it? His* father would ask. *To say it's war is our attempt to elevate ourselves to a higher plain, to dignify our murderous side. We are simple human beings with simple urges: to love a little and to kill a lot. War, don't use that term here, it's a lie. Look around the world and show me courage, show me on the ground where we confront an equal, show me in the air. We are just the dominant force. It is not a decree from God. War is not killing each other, that's just barbarism and a whole lot of fear which can be a stumble over a figment of someone's imagination. Surely we can agree on that? To my mind that is not war. War is going beyond ourselves, it is a life-lasting conflict to pull ourselves out of the shadows, an honourable desire to leave our primitive side, a state we all inhabit. That is war and should be your war, too. You're not Mr Good Guy, son, you're just brainwashed into thinking you and your crew are. Be your own hero, sure, step away, be greater than the CIA, the army, the missiles, war is what we don't know, what we don't comprehend, don't waste your time, cross that bridge, son, and get out of the human battle zone.* Cullen wasn't ready for his father's wisdom when strength was already on offer and, although it was a shock to see the man lowered into the ground, he would be as strong as Custer, in the desert, overwhelmed when the battle came; if he couldn't win the war, every battle had to be his.

At thirty-three thousand feet one could feel like the person one would like to be on the ground, in fact, touching down again could be the most underrated disappointment in life. Because of history Cullen had to return there and read the whole American story along with the British one. When the stewardesses began a final clear-up, the captain announced that the flight was on time, but with less than an hour out from LA there had been a warning of weather fronts clashing over the city. The smoothest ride from east to west was over. And while swirling air engulfed the craft buffeting its passengers, Cullen sat tightly strapped uncertain of what awaited him on a slippy runway.

America had looked out from its stations worldwide since the momentous fall in Berlin, and the Cullens of its secret service network were to stand at ease. A new era had been established. East and West and the Iron Curtain were history and the world was full of hope with a warmer political climate. The icy chill had ended except for a small matter that had been born in Idaho and continued to be felt. Below the cold air of its mountains and in rooms in Washington D.C. certain people became ill at ease, and with it returned a decision of the old mentality. A hunt was ordered.

*   *   *

Sixteen years earlier in certain offices in Thatcher's England, there was an icy chill of betrayal about and a hunt was quietly started. No one knew who he was nor were his personal targets known, but there was a feel of him, and everyone in London had their private moments with him and yet he remained unknown. It was a time when Jilly had begun to notice things more: a world that flowed and made her happy and secure. She could remember it like yesterday, and the more she remembered her happiness the more she felt the pain of today. Had her life just been unfortunate or had a crime been perpetrated against her? Sometimes she could be back in primary school where all her movements were run and jump and her dad was always in her pocket, like her candy money or a lucky something. But then that changed, the money was lost and luck was gone. Jilly was extremely articulate but when her emotions were aroused her words would run away. *I can't, I can't, I can't,* she would scream when her mother tried to encourage her to say what it was that kept her mourning, and it was true that she could not. So Susan worried that Jilly's health would suffer and tried to call in someone her daughter could talk to but, to her dismay, no one came alone, they brought their questionable training, their attitudes, their prejudices, and left the human being aside.

Jilly had asked Susan to go to Germany and find Dad, he needed their help, she would say, but Susan had become exhausted, too much so to be urged or coaxed and too afraid to tell her what she believed. *We'll go when you're older, when school isn't having all those exams.* But that, Susan realised later, was her big mistake, school should have waited, not Germany. It would not have been a wasted journey because Jilly carried her father about with her, and taking the physical journey into Germany could have saved her from the troubled girl she had become. So Germany stayed far and now so did Susan. Jilly slipped away and, maybe in her mind then, she thought that if this news reached her father he would somehow come to end her pining, maybe he just wouldn't stay away any longer. With every day she struggled – it had become her life – and Alex, whom she had looked out for so long, was not expected anymore, he was on her horizon and there was where he stayed.

18

Hansbach, East Germany, February 1983

The air had changed, the biting chill of the day before was not there, the crunch of frost beneath the feet was gone. Now only pockets of snow were left in the sheltered parts where the sun could not penetrate. Gregory Keech walked in the grounds of the big house, whose fading yellow colour had almost evenly spread over the three storeys. The influence of the Italian Renaissance was clearly there, on the roof and the windows – the first and second floors had large shutters two metres high, the ground floor thick iron bars. The dying yellow sank into, more than blended with, its surroundings. Everything looked broken, brought down and dirtied, cracked lines of plaster ran down the walls, cutting into what was once a handsome house.

Keech waited for his hosts to decide that there was a place for him, that he was exactly who he claimed to be for so long: a bona fide defector. But although his briefcase was filled with classified information of considerable value, Keech was not believed. They played games with him, stupid games and afterwards they spoke to him as a man of great importance. And it went on like that day after day.

The effect on Keech was predictable: he cursed them loudly,

kicked the furniture around his room shouting bastards, stupid red bastards, then there would be silence and an eye fom outside would watch him through the door as he lay, both arms covering his face, on the bed. But he was allowed to walk and enjoy the trees that stood bare on the sloping ground. There was no locked gate or high fence with prowling dogs that guarded the house, there was nothing like that. Keech could have walked away at any time, and maybe he would have if he had known. But he stayed fairly close to the house, using the many paths that criss-crossed the grounds.

It was now warm so he took off his jacket and laid it on the faded grass and began running fifty-yard sprints then walked back swinging his arms before him getting set for another. Having done this a few times, he began swinging his arms around him pushing his chest out as he did so, then took a few minutes rest.

'You military men like to keep in shape, is that not so?'

A tall man had come down from the house; he had walked over the grass ignoring the paths. He smiled in a friendly way at Keech and approached him extending his arm. 'My name is Andrei.'

Keech stopped his arm swinging and took the Russian's hand.

'You are right to come and exercise, it's good, it purifies the body and takes pure oxygen to the brain. I too like to be fit, it heightens the senses and stimulates what we are.'

'KGB, Andrei?'

'Yes, of course,' he said softly. 'Shall we sit?'

Keech fetched his jacket and the two made for a paint-peeling garden seat.

'It's very still here, just the fields and the trees. I was brought up on a farm and it was the same there, except for the damn cockerels at five o'clock,' he laughed – Keech smiled – 'I think Russian cockerels make the loudest noise in the world.' He looked at Keech. 'No, I'm not just saying that, it was a maga-zine of yours. Yes, I read it some years ago . . . What was it . . . National, National . . .'

'The National Geographic,' assisted Keech.

'That's it. The National Geographic. A very good magazine which taught me many things.' There was a pause. 'It's been a long time since I've been back. Ambition takes you away from what you love, is that not so, General Keech?'

'Yes, I suppose it does.'

'And ambition is our greed for self-achievement . . .'

'It's progress, individual progress.'

'Yes, there is progress, but before the progress there is the greed to do better because if we do better we are rewarded better.' Andrei looked at Keech and laughed a little. 'General Keech, our thoughts are different, some of them anyway. Do you smoke?'

The Russian produced a packet from his pocket. Keech shook his head and the packet was returned.

'What do you have to say to me?' asked Keech.

'There is no particular target, General Keech, I've read all that you have said . . .'

'And? And? What am I doing here?' Keech stood and looked out towards the fields. The sun was low in the sky mixing pink and orange with the clouds. 'I have not been made welcome here, why is that?'

'Because we're not sure.' Andrei stood beside him. 'I understand your feelings but we're not sure of you.'

Keech turned his gaze from the sky to Andrei; their faces were close but neither retreated.

'It took a long time to make my decision, you must understand that no matter how much I believed in your system it took time before I could say without doubt that your country was where I wanted to be. To do that I had to consider my family; I knew they would never follow me.' He paused. 'Men follow men, that's the army way; you can go through fifty miles of jungle and they'll still be there with you . . . Families . . . Families are just convenience, they lack the natural emotions that all people need. And they're everywhere, they run this world, they make us what we are . . . Christ, you should walk down my street in the States and see what families are doing for each other.' He looked hard at Andrei. 'Look,' he stood proudly, 'I'm no misfit or wino in my country and yet I'm talking about real experiences, real family experiences.' He stopped and took a step back. 'You must understand, my family were hooked to the capitalist system, the banal television programs, the trashy journalism in our papers. It was all that . . . crap, there was no substance in all that, no real worth. So, alone, I made my decision to leave.' He stopped and turned to the ever changing colour in the sky. 'I brought what I could and it's quality stuff . . .'

'What you brought,' interrupted Andrei, 'was quite little and we had known about most of it. So, General, what were we to think?'

'I don't believe that. How could you know? I had the sites of the Pershings in Germany, I had their flight paths and eighty per cent of their targets. How could you know that?'

'The Pershing missile has its flight path changed periodically, General Keech. It would be wrong for us to assume that its onboard computer would not instruct it on a new path perilous to our defence.'

'What do you know. That's all crap. Who do you think your enemy is?' He began to laugh. 'Flight paths changed periodically, is that what Moscow believes?' He turned away. 'If you only knew how weak and stupid we are . . . Our onboard computers you talk about are no pieces of magic, they're downright dangerous,' he turned back, 'they could easily turn the bloody missile round. We're not safe.'

Andrei listened.

'Alright,' said Keech, 'you don't want to hear that, you only want to feel the threat. Alright. What about the rest? Don't forget that.'

'The rest, General, is old, out of date.' Andrei said that the

104

way a doctor might tell his patient bad news, there was some sympathy Keech could feel. 'We were happy to receive you,' he went on. 'We understand that your decision was a courageous one. While you served with the American military you were our enemy, were a threat to us and the world. Then you decided to leave . . . very courageous.'

'Well,' said Keech, 'what the hell am I doing here?'

A film of water appeared over Keech's eyes; the air had turned sharper, and the rims of his ears looked stiff and red. The colours in the sky were soon to disappear and Andrei suggested they return to the house.

'We don't know why a high-ranking military official such as yourself would throw away his life and his military career and walk over to enemy territory with a briefcase filled with yesterday's secrets.' – Keech stopped – 'Yes, General, everything you gave us belongs to yesterday, there is nothing there to convince us of your sincerity, to prove who you are. You could be anybody.' Andrei was being stirred in the semi-darkness. 'A part of your government's dirty tricks. Is that what you are? CIA, General Keech? Are you there?'

Keech turned on Andrei and held him tightly by his coat lapels. His coat and jacket beneath slid up to his chin and Keech squeezed the material in his hands.

'You've been clear, Andrei, the fog has lifted. Now I'm going to be equally clear.' He could feel his knuckles push into Andrei's chin. 'I'm no part of no plot with no agency. I'm quite alone in this. Do you understand? I'm a man who got tired of military life, got tired of all the crap one has to listen to there. I got tired of watching American faces on the TV screen, of American voices. All that crap I've listened to; I got tired of it.'

Andrei was in an uncomfortable position, he had been raised onto his toes and Keech was not ready to release him. 'The political system doesn't work; it has broken more people than made them. But you'll know that, Andrei, because you know everything.

You stupid bastard, don't you understand, I left all that, driven out by what my countrymen had become.' He loosened slightly at Andrei's coat. 'I simply lost my hope. You'll understand hope, Andrei?' Keech loosened more and more as he slipped to the ground unconscious.

19

There was a glow in the damp night sky stirring people in a hamlet some distance from the main road leading out of state. A fireball, they thought, a disaster a bit out of reach to be of too much interest. The absence of a bright moon left all unsure, so the doors of their homes were closed behind them, as Greg's old Ford was consumed by fire.

Greg had returned on the route he had come along with Jilly, and as the car filled up with his silence Jilly was seen at the airport, seen taking the breeze from the sea, seen standing in her night clothes; these moments had taken away so much of his concentration that he had not realised how the car had picked up speed. Only when it was showered by a downfall did he feel its movement. He jumped in his seat and inadvertently pressed the radio button on while he struggled to make a gear change. The brake pedal felt soft and the road ahead looked promising with the radio voice encouraging everyone to have a good time. The car was squealing round the bends and, to his surprise, Greg had time to see where he was heading – cold and still on a slab. His mind slowed down – maybe it was time to go with the car, just go with it. The offside front wheel suddenly sank in a pit on the road, which caused the door to burst open, and Greg and car headed off into the trees. He was to remember his thoughts then, how he should stay, just to take the ride. Be courageous, be his father. He was out there, wasn't he? When the car dipped again, jolting its frame as it went, before resting heavily at the foot of a tree which was almost lost in the darkness, he jumped out. A distance away on higher ground Greg looked on, saved by his quick decision to throw himself out early before impact, to see the first flames taking hold. There was a boom which seemed to take all the life from the vehicle to the top of the tree. Greg watched in the thick brush while flame was all around, his opportunity to be free now gone. He sat shivering as he imagined himself there, trapped in the car, burning, yet he was so cold, and he could see Carla the same, cold and asking him not to go. As the car burned, he could hear her say she couldn't lie alone with herself. 'Don't go,' she pleaded, 'I'm lost here. Greg. Greg.' He was on that line everyone straddles on throughout their lives with little drama until it becomes a precarious ledge. 'I've felt tenderness. I've felt the stroke of fingers,' he had said to Carla when he didn't want her to think there was little warmth to him. He had feelings, he wanted her to know, even when he didn't feel anything. 'I know about that. Don't think I don't know.' Carla knew. He had told her things from his life and things from his dreams. She was sure it was his troubled self that made him the way she saw him. She smiled.

Some distance from the car Greg waited, surrounded by the outline of the nearby hills against the sky. It was a memory of a picture he had seen before where attack helicopters would suddenly appear over the hilltop, approach and deliver their venom. 'The rotor blades from Nam can always be heard.' An army officer was being interviewed by TV journalists, and everyone in the Keech household was watching around the set, faces locked to the screen. 'When you've heard that sound in a conflict situation, it's with you forever.' Could that sound have driven General Keech to do what he did? Could that explain his actions? The officer wouldn't say. Could the sounds of machines and conflict not be silenced? Another asked. 'What for?' the officer snapped back, 'it's that very sound that keeps all our men standing tall today. When Keech walked away, if he did, he would have had the sound of those blades coming up from behind. He would have thought then that he was far from being alone.' The officer stood tall and stiff. 'He was wrong. Very wrong. But he has not become my enemy.' He paused. 'No, not my enemy.'

Greg gathered himself and let his mind rest as he walked away from the burnt-out shell his car was soon to become. By the break of dawn the car was still smouldering with a swarm of police around it. They had come in the blackness with their trunchen-like lights only to wait the hours till first light. It was not going to be routine procedure of car careering out of control with its occupants trapped in the inferno, it was going to be more. The driver and any passenger there had been on the road and then off it, they had been in the car and they were not there now. They could be in need of medical attention and they had to be found. Toby Cullen was inclined to think they had run, out to make a bloody nuisance of themselves or to become dangerous runaways.

20

Hansbach, East Germany, February 1983

'Good morning. The hours pass quickly with sleep. How are you?'

Keech lay fully dressed on the bed. He brought a hand up and spread it over the back of his head.

'It's still early but you must be hungry.'

Keech was silent.

'No?' Andrei sighed. 'Lonely?' Andrei waited. 'It is natural. The body needs food and it also needs comfort. That is something the world is agreed upon.' He smiled and opened the door. He snapped his fingers to someone in the corridor then returned to Keech. 'I believe you. I know a man can get tired and just walk away, like you did. But we have to be sure. There are people who believe nothing at all and these people you have to convince. But that is for later.'

Footsteps could be heard outside the room – two people. Andrei stepped out and allowed a young woman to enter.

'This is Hanna.'

Keech looked at her, she looked back.

'Take the comfort she can give you, General, it's therapeutic.' Andrei closed the door.

Hanna stood quiet like a virgin and Keech looked at all of

her. She was slim with a small face; her hair was tied up loosely allowing strands to fall down past her ears. She had nothing on her face, no touch of false colour, no reddened lips. Her eyebrows had been left unclipped and eyelashes undarkened. She had been wakened for him, her shirt had been rushed on and pushed with little care inside her skirt. The skirt, Keech followed past her knees. He swung his feet off the bed and held out his hand to her. For some minutes he held to her.

'Hanna.'

She looked.

'Speak to me.'

'What should I say?'

He sighed, 'Nothing.'

She took the buttons of her shirt from their buttonholes with one hand. 'What would you like?' she asked.

'Just you. All of you.'

She spread herself on the bed, her legs apart as they wrestled. With every movement the bed squeaked, with every thrust and pull it acknowledged until Keech held her buttocks still. It had been a moment of forgetting for him, lost in the flesh of a woman, in her breasts and below. She sat quiet on the bed, straight and proud looking. He was half turned to her.

'Put off the light,' she said.

'I can't,' he replied, 'I need to see you, your body.'

She smiled and stood. The sky was dark and the window reflected all their movements. The room, although small, had not filled up with their presence, it felt empty, unwanted. The woman threw a pillow to the floor and lay on it. Keech responded coming down and putting himself everywhere until she groaned. They lay until their bodies turned cold but she did not complain; her orders were to please until he was satisfied. The morning light finally came, a break in the darkness revealed the outline of the trees, a distant dog barked at something – or nothing – and Keech and the woman, Hanna, lay tight together.

111

'Are you allowed to speak to me?'

'I have no secrets so I am allowed,' she answered.

'I love your eyebrows,' he said – she laughed – 'I've never seen a girl with full eyebrows, just left alone.'

'No?'

'No.'

'I'm sorry.'

'No, I really love them. You're beautiful and you have thick eyebrows.'

'Can you not find a woman in America with thick eyebrows?'

'No chance,' he said, then gave the question some thought. 'Your name is Hanna,' he paused. 'I'm Greg. You know who I am?' – she nodded – 'Who are you? You're no pro?'

'Pro?' she looked puzzled.

'Prostitute. You're not?'

She smiled, 'I'm just Hanna.' She pulled the blanket from the bed and covered them both.

'I've been here a long time, or so it seems, just me and my thoughts in this room or in the garden.' He paused. 'I never knew how I would react to being left to myself, no politeness nor friendliness. You see I can't go back, that can never be looked at as an option. Do you understand?'

'Yes,' she said.

'If your people decide they cannot welcome me . . .'

She listened, her large clear eyes watching him.

'You were beautiful.'

She smiled at him in a tender way, a way that conveyed a sincerity about her part in their meeting. 'You needed a little help,' she said, 'a little human touch.'

'Do you work for Andrei?'

'I'm not allowed to answer that question.'

'Just keep all matters to the flesh. Right?' He closed his eyes. 'Hanna, Hanna. When you stepped in I saw you beautiful. I can't tell you how, but after all that time I've been here and all the things I've wanted, prayed for, to get out of this . . . this room, you stopped me. I was happy just to look at you. You could have come to bring me coffee.'

'It is this place, your feelings are misled by this place. Our meeting was not natural; I had been ordered and you had been deprived. It would be wrong to place any importance on feelings now.'

She got up and put on her shirt and buttoned it while he looked at the new day.

'The sky looks promising and for me that makes everything promising. Will you promise to come back?'

'Personal promises are meaningless here, they have no value.'

'But you can promise,' said Keech.

She turned to him, 'I can be ordered but I cannot promise.' She dressed and left.

Gregory Keech waited for a decision, for someone to decide what to do with him.

21

Greg had bruises on his leg, pain in his ribs, a general feeling of being beaten up, and his heart crying out. The car had gone and so should he – gone, gone. If there had been a gun, now, he would have taken it and placed it well, yes he would have, damn it. Placed it well, now, right now. The new day seemed indifferent to his being alive, and nothing would have changed if he were dead. *Oh Greg. Oh Greg.* Jilly had called as he distanced himself from the car and his desire to have a gun.

His desire came from a place, a memory, which could not slip easily into the recesses of the mind, no matter what age a person is, a gun has a way of getting attention. Just the sight of it, metallic and heavy, a sinister instrument with the power to change a life, something Keech wanted his son to know. But young Greg became excited when he sat down beside his father to learn about guns. 'Don't touch. Don't talk. Listen,' his father said more than once. 'Don't talk, listen. When you see a gun, that's what you do.' He learned what guns were and what they could do while his hands longed to touch and hold.

It was the day after his father had spent time with him, thanks to dad's gun, in the early evening when the house had become dark after some rainfall and after some turmoil had been witnessed in the earlier hours with voices raised and emotions released, Greg saw his dad's gun again, and again it overwhelmed him. It was in his father's hands, some feet from him through a doorway. Still as a statue, small boy Greg watched with his lips apart as his father, a little drunk and playful, aimed at targets in the room. The gun would be caressed with the palm of his hand, then it would be held by both; this display of affection surprised Greg because he had never seen his father in such a caring way; he watched him and became a little frightened. His mother had broken the thread of love that they surely had or thought they did when Greg was younger or just simply before he existed. He did not know. His mother had become a woman of the Mall, she had also become big and confrontational as she stepped about and lost any art and care for herself and her family. He thought he had begun to hate her before his father did, and that was in his mind as he kept looking through the small opening in the doorway where he hoped to share in the happiness his father seemed to have. He felt himself light inside, father and son like that, he could have hugged him for being his dad and for bringing this moment about. As he waited, with eyes bright and clear, his father had turned his gun around and was pressing it hard against the underside of his chin. All Greg's hopes which had lifted him to a new height then plummeted and his body filled with tremble. How strange to see the man he loved take a gun this way and threaten himself. To end his life, his friendship with him, to get away from him. He had watched his father's mood change through his actions, saw him become unhappy and angry and felt his boyish heart race. He heard his father's words: *Don't talk.* The turmoil of earlier that day filled his young head. *Don't talk.* And if he could have known he might have heard all the noise in his father's head, all the disturbance trapped inside: the rotor blades, the screams, the agony of anticipation, noise, noise. *Don't talk.* The gun had begun to shake creating a frightening moment before it was released and slowly placed away.

Don't talk. An anxious time had passed, man and boy rested, one in ignorance, the other in silence.

*   *   *

Toby Cullen did not know when his compassion had been reduced to what it was today, it was hardly a question he asked himself and no one else had. It would have been a long time when self-interest took its hold of him, it could have been eighth grade, he would have supposed, when nothing was given and everything was taken. That was the education then. He knew, had he allowed himself the thought, that much had been lost in his lifetime, all to gain hold somewhere in America. You can pay a price easily if you don't feel you're paying it at the time, it's like the car, the house, so that many mortgage their life for: Cullen was fully mortgaged. This way of living had his grip on him before he reached thirty when the Cold War was still cold and the thought of losing it unthinkable, like losing wife and family, your mother . . . your dad. Cullen had become nervous along with those at Langley, and he had become cruel, too, but maybe that part of him had always been there, lying at an unknown depth for years and then . . . Cullen could do that, disguise his dark side while still using his youthful intellect until his youth passed and he lost track of why he was on the planet. It was a sadness his fifteen-year-old self would have felt if there had been some way to see the future. But Toby Cullen was not thinking too much of where he had been – an open door for tomorrow was a door tightly closed on yesterday. But he had to return a little, back to the Keech affair, back to what was known and what was lost. It was a failure, Keech could not return, not for Cullen and not for patriotism. It was a disappointment, he recalled, on an early morning country road in a divided Germany. It was in the past, he thought, but now the story sprang to life again when a call directed him to Greg's blackened Ford.

'Do we have a firm identity of who was in the car?' Cullen asked the first officer he came to.

'It appears to be driver and passenger,' was the reply. 'A man and a woman.'

'How do you know that?'

'From the plates. The owner of the vehicle is a Gregory Keech, whose address is at the university in Santa Barbara. We understand that he left there recently with an English woman. They were travelling together.'

Cullen stood wondering if a miracle had occurred, was it just Keech's boy or had the general returned home? Sixteen years was a long time to play dead. But… If you waited long enough things came round, a belief that had become stronger as he made his way along the corridors of Langley.

Toby Cullen did not believe in death and he could say that this belief sustained him in the most difficult circumstances. After his sister's death – which had been accepted by everyone – Cullen alone decided that it was only a disappearance and that she was somewhere else, one day she would show up. It was something he had to believe, there was no option, it was a deliberate thought, more like a mechanism inside him had been switched on or perhaps off. Mother's tears, father's sadness were too much, *she'll be back*, he wanted to reassure them but he never did. He thought there was a trick about, emotionally and scientifically, that all around was not as firm as sometimes he needed it to be. But other times it was good to know, and he knew, he could feel it in his bones that nothing was lost to him or to America. He could be cocksure when it was strong and shaky when it was not. It probably all began years before when he didn't even know it, when he was fighting with himself and thought it was the world. The cycle of life had become unacceptable to him, and he became more convinced of it in a mid-west town one day, a day of celebration when there was happiness in the streets and everyone wore a smile, when he saw his long lost sister who had been taken in a drowning accident.

From twenty yards she sat on some grass and looked as he had always remembered her. She was lovely, a little older, more adult, her complexion as it had always been, in full bloom, and she was smiling at the world going by. She sat, it seemed, for as long as he wanted her to, because he sat a long while being sure and unsure as he trained his eyes on all of her. Her happy face captivated him. 'Margaret,' he said under his breath as he edged closer till he met her eyes. 'Margaret.' She was now looking at him. 'Margaret.' She softly shook her head and said sorry. Cullen was absorbed by the moment; his sister, who had been out of his life for so many years, was there before him, nicer than he, better than he, and he found himself filling up with pride for her. All that he was before he made the trip was somewhere else because all he felt was emotion, and he had taken it for granted she would rush to him as he had always imagined her doing when the day came. But Margaret sat not confirming that she was that person, how could she, while Cullen had moved along the years, his Margaret had remained the same. As she turned from him, Cullen watched her walk away, her hair lifting on her shoulders as she went. He did not know why he let her go, he had let her go in the water, he wanted to believe; it was never told that way, but he knew he could have done more. He confessed one day soon after seeing her appear before him and let his secret out. But instead of it lightening him, it enraged him that he could have walked off the street and into that position. 'I let my sister go.' 'Go where?' he was asked. He hesitated and his posture fell as he prepared to be the Toby Cullen he had always denied himself. He had let Margaret be taken by the water, he said. 'Why did you?' he was asked. 'I'd never lost anything I loved. I wanted to lose.' Again the priest asked why. Cullen answered that he wanted to know how strong love was. 'And now?' the priest gently enquired. 'Her name was Margaret.' Cullen's sadness brought no more. Cullen could think but he couldn't communicate; *one-gear Toby,* he had heard someone say. It was a lonely world which he thought was for everyone.

The Greg Keech he was to begin hunting for was perhaps the general to him, and with patriotic authority he had promised Keech a thorough job. But perhaps in young Greg he recognised himself in days far off when Margaret had been allowed to slip away and her going had brought a terrible silence from him that reduced her value to nil. While Margaret lay somewhere waiting to be acknowledged, Cullen lived behind a facade, secure and insecure for too long. In young Greg he saw more of himself than what was there and if he thought that, if he thought that Keech's son was suffering, too, where could he find his anger and damnation for him?

22

Bayreuth, West Germany, February 1983

Alex and Jack were in Bayreuth, the festival town of Richard Wagner. The town itself is an unremarkable place, there is nothing that would steal one away from the nearby autobahn and bring one through its streets, except Wagner and the Festival Hall. Like an industrial piece of factory building, the Hall, where Wagner's music is celebrated throughout the summer months, stands tall in red brick for the many visitors who flock there. Nearby, in the gardens, a bust of this German son is held high on top of a marble column; but Alex and Jack had little interest in famous men, they would have left the next day if it meant the Keech affair was decided – failure or success, either way their job would be over.

'You may remember this, it was some time ago. I was visiting Germany, it was my second time here but my first in Berlin. It was '65 and I wanted to see all the sights. I didn't take Kathleen. Were we married then,' he asked himself. 'Anyway, I was introduced to some people there by the Station Chief, Adamson. I don't think you met him, Alex; nice chap. He died some months later.' Jack's face held the surprise he had felt at the time. 'I don't know what it was.' A pause. 'I met a family there; mother, son

120

and daughter, a very nice threesome. I spoke with them. The husband had known Donald.'

'Donald?' questioned Alex.

'Adamson. Donald Adamson,' replied Jack. 'The husband worked for us, he was on the payroll. Then he died. What happened was, their apartment was broken into in the middle of the night. The family were of course asleep; no one heard anything. It was clearly robbery, much was taken. But the strange thing was, as his wife slept next to him and the children in their rooms, one of the thieves woke Matthofer – that was his name – and with a knife at his throat brought him out of bed, disturbing no one, sat him on a kitchen chair and drove the knife through him. Then they left with their booty and disappeared. Now, Matthofer didn't die, not there and then. His moaning finally stirred his son to get out of bed and find what must have been an awful sight that was his father. Just hours from death when emergency surgery could do no more, he told the police. It was murder, Alex, pre-meditated murder. You see, they had to take him from his bed; he couldn't very well disturb anyone lying there, so the intruders thought, and so they arranged it to look that way, that they were disturbed and in their panic they lashed out at him and ran. And if Matthofer had died immediately there is no doubt that is what would have been accepted.'

The men were high up in a hotel room overlooking the town. It was a modern building in a modern complex. Below the street was wide with the trees still deep in winter.

'Matthofer's boy couldn't get over how someone had deliberately destroyed his father. I mean, Alex, I think the poor lad had that clear mental image of his father on that kitchen chair every minute of every waking hour and more than likely in the darkness, too.'

Alex lifted the coffee-pot from the trolley and poured a refill into his cup.

'Whatever ambitions the young man held at that time changed

then. Or maybe they died. He wanted to do his father's work, to work for us, even if it meant being an errand boy, just to get in. We turned him down, of course. We couldn't have an emotionally disturbed lad looking for vengeance, looking for a way to get back. So he went away and that, we thought, was that.'

Jack studied the traffic below, silent movements in a thick drizzle. 'About a year later Matthofer's wife wrote to us asking for help to find her son. He had gone, left home, like many do everywhere, and although we had more reason to help Frau Matthofer than anyone, we couldn't. She wrote and wrote, angry, pleading, but nothing gets through to us, you know that, Alex. When we have a choice we play safe, we hardly ever do the decent thing.' He pointed at the cup in Alex's hand, 'Is that coffee still warm?'

Alex wrapped his hand round it and Jack walked across with cup and saucer in hand. He sat down opposite Alex, sipped the cold coffee and lowered his voice, 'Then the boy surfaced. He sent us a letter, it was addressed to Adamson who was by that time long dead. He had obviously heard his father mention the name and he had picked it up as a person his father trusted. He introduced himself should we have forgotten the name; told us what he could do and what he wanted and went about proving it. He gave us four names all working for the West German Jungster company in Frankfurt, all East German agents who had been with the company for years, had security clearance on practically everything; he held them up to us and we were impressed. So we thought about young Willy Matthofer. We did feel, or some of us did, that we owed the Matthofers a bit, we thought we'd try him out, get to know his feelings. There was no address on the letter, just a meeting place in Leipzig.'

'How did he get the letter out?' Alex wanted to know.

'We presume he got someone to take it out – it had a West German postmark. He never did say. Willy Matthofer had become an East German. You know, with the routine movements of West German citizens and divided families, a simple swop could be done . . . well something of that kind produced Matthofer in the East and his papers were immaculate. Of course he used another name but his position there was not at all precarious. This young man had made up his mind to get back at those who had murdered his father, and that's where they were – over there. It would have been better for him, perhaps, if it had just been a robbery gone wrong, maybe he would have accepted that, maybe justice would have helped him there, but no. Now, over there, he didn't just want a quick bite at revenge, he wanted to be biting all the time. It's a dedication, Alex, to have something like that burning inside you. I marvel at him.'

'It's misdirected hate, Jack. Even hate can become honourable in the right eyes.'

'Strange to hear you talk like that. Willy Matthofer deserves admiration. How can you deny him that?'

For a moment Alex was silent, then he said, 'Should we admire sorrow, grief, when they're allowed to rot and rot? Don't get me wrong, Jack, I know which side of the fence I'm on, but is it right for a person to be devoured by hate, to sacrifice his life to it and for us to use that hate. This Willy Matthofer might be doing great things and risking his life, but it's all driven by hate and I wonder if we should talk about the Willys of our world. Just let them get on with it.'

Jack studied Alex. 'Maybe you're right, maybe Willy's a fool who can't let go. Some people who are struck by tragedy commit suicide, and some call that taking the easy way out, others have great sympathy for them. Some lose a chunk of themselves and want revenge. It all depends on what's important to you in life. I don't believe, for example, if a busload of kids crash because of a drunken driver that the parents should receive a meagre sum of compensation and end it at that. What else can they do, you might ask. And I would say I don't know. But that doesn't mean, Alex, that people can or even should slip back into the mainstream of everyday living – they have to burn themselves out;

maybe Willy will do that but he can't – not yet. Willy's burning away over there; you might not admire him but I bloody well do.'

He pushed himself back in the chair then picked up the phone and asked for room service and more coffee. He was flushed with only the areas beneath his eyes looking pale and anaemic. His anger had raised his pulse level and he now sat and waited for it to return to its regular rate.

Alex didn't say anything, he had upset his friend but he couldn't apologise, apologies never came easily to him. He had noticed how people did it and he didn't like it, it was embarrassing. The facial expression used, the stretch of an arm, all the built-up sincerity. He remembered how on a rare occasion Susan called him a bastard, a cruel one, and how surprised he was. Susan stared into his face and found what she needed, then blurted out sorry, sorry, while she held to him. Their faces were pointing in the opposite directions and he was thankful for that, he didn't want to see her, so he held to her and let the moment distance itself from them.

Alex cleared his throat. 'So it's through your Willy Matthofer you hope to free Keech?' he said.

Jack lowered his head fractionally.

'How can he do that? If he has positioned himself where he has become valuable to us, if he is an East German citizen with papers, with work, can he walk away and do his liberation bit for the Americans without someone noticing?'

There was a knock on the door and Jack got up quickly to open. A second trolley of coffee was wheeled in, with a large plate of thick cake slices. Jack pushed something into the waiter's hand as he removed the empty coffee-pots and cups.

'Alex, I have to go back to Bonn – overlapping business, I'm afraid.'

'Can you get back that easily?'

'Oh yes, from the airport here you can fly to most major centres in the country. Sorry to leave like this. It'll give you time to try the local beer, bloody good, too, brown, called Schinner.' Jack poured in the cream to his coffee and watched it swirl around the surface then sink.

'You will say hallo to Kathleen for me?' said Alex.

'Will do.'

Sometimes, when there's a moment to spare and there are no obligations to fill it, no wife or children to pull at you, things can appear in a way they otherwise might never be seen. Jack had literally flown away; he announced his intention at the last possible moment, had a quick shower and left. He had got angry, had a burst for this Willy Matthofer. Alex was puzzled. He had never heard the story of Matthofer, it was completely new to him. He looked at his watch, said *Schinner* aloud and took the elevator to the bar below.

There was a young girl serving a couple of dark-suited men on stools while having light talk with them. Alex waited. He scanned the show of bottles and stopped at the girl. Her eyes never moved from the men as they told her something funny. 'Maybe she wants them, he thought, the two of them, together, at once.' He smiled at his thoughts, he hadn't had such erotic ones for god knows how long.

'*Ja?*'

'Beer.'

She turned to the bottles.

'Brown.'

'*Braun*,' she repeated and picked up a bottle.

'No. Schinner,' said Alex.

'*Ah, ja.*' She poured and asked, '*Englisch?*'

'Yes. Do you speak?'

'A little,' she replied in a modest way.

There was something about her that was very appealing to him; there were many appealing things, but if Alex had been pushed to be exact it would have been sex and bed and all her nakedness against his.

'Do you like Bayreuth?'

'It seems nice. I had expected lots of snow.'

'Oh, it has been and gone and it will come back. It never misses a year, twenty-thirty centimetres. More than England, yes?'

Alex had never known a time, except when he was a virgin, when his desire to rush a woman to bed was so urgent as it was now.

'I've never been to England. It is very nice?'

He thought about England. 'Yes, I suppose it is. I never seem to get around very much when I'm there.'

She left to attend another customer and Alex discovered a new beer. As the beer slipped down he remembered making love to Susan the night before he left. It was natural, he didn't know when exactly he would be back, so they met a little earlier that evening. It was not unexpected but arranged some hours before in the kitchen when Susan had her hands dipped into some-thing far from bodies and bed. This part of their life was never unexpected; neither ever surprised the other. And now as he sat surprised and excited by this young foreign girl and all her flesh, Susan's body on that last night stretched across his mind in positions that he knew were hardly real.

'Would you like another?' the girl continued with her English.

'Yes. It's very good.'

She poured and smiled at him. 'You are my first *Englisch* customer,' she said, 'but I've been here only a short time.'

'Your English is very good.'

She beamed but didn't believe it.

'We are talking, we understand each other, no?' – she smiled again – 'Are you working here all night?'

'Most of it,' she replied.

They both waited for each other, she to present an opening somehow, he to suggest a meeting. He found it difficult to go on and his pause took the girl away again.

When she returned he asked, 'Will you have a drink with me later?'

'It will be late,' she said.

'Sometimes the English language is at its best late.'

She opened her mouth to laugh but there was no sound. Alex now had an appointment and the local brown beer was put aside. He had an unappetising meal in the restaurant and returned to his room. The local American radio station had brightened his surroundings and the delicious young German girl was almost certain to brighten him, but Jack took his mind away.

It was nine when he dialled Jack's number in Bonn and got through to Kathleen. 'Hallo. I'm a colleague of Mr Kirkland's, could I speak to him, please?' The voice was far removed from Alex, a little Sussex, a little Wessex.

'I'm sorry, my husband is not here and I don't expect him back for some days.'

Alex was shaken. He politely thanked her and placed the receiver.

Jack had lied. Now why would a man in his position do that – to someone he trusted?

23

While activity was mounting for two young people on the slopes of their own mountains which had taken them all their lives to reach, there was to be a determined effort to discourage them from climbing higher. The meaning of life had changed in the world, but it was seen that Jilly and Greg had not changed with it, they were still with the past and no one wanted that. General Keech was gone, a fact, said many. Alex Dorian was seen to die on a cold road in West Germany. Neither man had been seen again. When she was told that Alex was lost, Jilly's mother could not produce a sound. The man who sat opposite her had tried to find a response, something that he thought would be familiar for him to offer himself in the best way he could, but Susan gave nothing. Jilly, who had not been with her when the man spoke, had quietly entered the room; sensing a tragedy, her young face, conveyed a beautiful sadness. The man had become almost silent as Susan beckoned Jilly with outstretched arms. Jilly remained still. 'Jilly.' The man stood up, feeling uncomfortable, he had to leave. 'Jilly.' He had said what he had come to say, Susan asked Jilly to fetch something she could not possibly find, to give herself a moment to ask her visitor what she could do, she was alone with her daughter and . . . and . . .

He gave her a number to call should she be pestered by the press. As he stepped off her doormat he warned her that her husband's pension would, of course, be affected.

Susan closed the door on the man and the mean day, and dimmed the lights before taking her place in front of a dying fire. Death and suicide can lurk within families when life has climbed high upon them, and it was then when Susan thought she had travelled too far from any relief that Jilly's young voice was heard. 'Daddy, don't leave,' she cried, more to the room than to her mother. A child, their child, had realised everything, but instead of calling to stop him, she wanted to travel with him. She called again, 'Daddy, don't leave me alone.' Susan dropped her head into her hands and held as much of her pain as she could in her created darkness. Jilly's sobbing began and never really stopped, it was there for all those difficult years when love and hate were so easily interchangeable and harsh decisions were made which destroyed all that Susan and Jilly hoped to be or become.

As she grew and the years became more turbulent, Jilly left for destination after destination; in that time Susan's mother died and with her death there came full realisation to Susan that Alex was gone. On the day Jilly's grandmother was buried Susan stopped believing that it was still possible Alex could somehow return; it was a moment when she could have found despair, just buckle under the weight of more loss, with her living a normal life on hold for so long, she instead held to the memories that were Jilly. In the semi-darkness of the night before, Susan held her mother's hand for a time while softly speaking to her. She then took a typed letter from her handbag, written for Alex to say how she loved him more and more, and before her lips fell on her mother's cheek, she slipped the letter into a pocket of the garment she was leaving this world in.

*   *   *

Jilly allowed another birthday to pass without a word to anyone as she walked into a small town after, in a nervous moment, getting off her bus early. The walk was not a burden as she let slip aloud how so many birthdays had come and passed. There was a visible gasp of shock from her when the thought of how near her quarter century was, entered her mind. But today she looked younger than she was – her hair, her dress, very un-English, her possessions carried in her bags – and alone with herself her strength seemed to weaken as she thought her good thoughts and then the other ones. She was tired, her power felt gone. She remembered telling her mother on a rare occasion how she had always lived without power. 'Do you know what that's like?' she questioned, her emotions straining her. 'Like having no use of your limbs. Can you imagine?' She all but screamed: 'How can I put things right, Mum? How? I need a little power. I need a little support.' Susan replied Dad would want mother and daughter to support each other. 'Dad! Dad! Where is he? That's why I rage. My life is rage.'

Jilly passed herself off as an Australian tourist for the second day, and surprisingly she felt happy with that. She thought about it, imagined a map of the country she had never considered visiting and yet felt for a little while a part of it. She let out her birthday news in a communal room, a place of timber and open grill smells with happy strangers who brought a relaxed buzz to everyone. All the recent tension was now lighter as she became what everyone thought she was. As the night darkened and Jilly slipped out of her day, her thoughts of past present and future were sleeping. Her head hit the pillow easily and it was some hours before she saw her father again, in a city street, a short distance from home: she was walking with him as a little girl when a car pulled up alongside and two men rushed out. They ran to them, voices raised but she understood little. Jilly's hand was taken from her father's as they jostled with him. Whatever was said was to frighten, because she could not remember him looking that way before. The men's bodies engulfed Alex, so that from her position she could not find him although she knew he was there, and, as her heart beat in a flurry, another car rushed to them, braking hard. Two other men, eager and excited, put on a show of making a difficult arrest. They wanted conflict. Alex gave them none. He was pushed into one of the cars and Jilly, who had almost been ignored, took her seat beside him. Before they drove off the front passenger turned in his seat to face them with anger and agitation, looked violently at Jilly and said that the Social Services would have to be called in. Alex's words, the only ones Jilly had heard throughout, asked with some force not to do that, to let his daughter go home. She could do that, he said. *Please.* Jilly remembered his voice in a heartbreaking way. He looked at Jilly who sat so very still, her lovely little hands clasped together. He took from his pocket the house keys, placed them firmly into her hands and left her standing on the pavement as he was driven off. Alex kept his eyes on her as she followed him until the car turned away.

That evening Jilly heard him tell Susan that he had abandoned her; had let her down. But it was the police, Susan said. 'On the pavement,' he went on, 'what was she thinking then? Walking alone like that after seeing me being taken away. I could have killed then. Susan, I would have killed. To put me in a position . . . To endanger my daughter for their own bogus priorities. That will trouble me that I lost power to them.' He paused. 'Think . . .' Jilly walked along that street while cars sped past, her head so young and her situation so unexpected. On and on to her door, to an empty house. Alex thought.

Jilly dreamt on and let the memory of that time slip as she stored up her energy for the coming day.

In Jilly's new lakeside accommodation with the night almost spent, there were some early stirrings around the house and outside the sound of car tyres on wet surfaces. Her room had heavy drapes which had kept the darkness tightly around her as slivers of sunlight tried to penetrate the thick low-lying cloud. There was some tinny clatter from the kitchen – breakfast preparations, she guessed, were in motion. The other sound she heard was of someone breathing, she was sure. She lay listening with her resting pulse beginning to race. Oh, she cried silently, as fear gripped her muscles and her imagination produced many pictures. With her eyes tightly shut she tried to wish her situation away, with her parents suddenly swimming everywhere in her head. By the time they left, her heart raced on as if it were on her body's surface, and only with her eyes opening to find Greg kneeling at her side did her fear disappear and her fury became known.

'I couldn't move a limb,' she raged at Greg, 'I could have died! I could have died there,' she pointed to the bed. Her movements wild, she would be facing him, then not, ready to weep, then . . .'Greg!' she shouted. 'I'm sorry. You shouldn't leave windows open.' 'You're an idiot.' 'I've been out there in the rain all night.' 'How did you know where I was?' 'I made a call to a few places you could have been. It's a small town, especially for an Australian.' 'Why have you come?' 'I lost the car. It's a burnt-out wreck.' 'You okay?' 'Yeah.' 'You?' 'Suppose so.'

The house had wakened up, morning activities could be heard. 'Just in time for breakfast,' he said. 'And after?' she asked. He raised a hand northwards. 'With me?' He nodded. She smiled. 'You might want to shower first, comb your hair, get a fresh shirt . . .' 'Yeah, yeah, yeah.'

Greg's entry to her room gave Jilly the chance to fear for herself, it was terrible and wonderful. When the moment came she had the pictures she wanted, and when the moment passed she felt a surge of hope, her dad was there, and before she had opened her eyes she had invited her mother, too. She knew that hope was the strongest emotion on the plus side, but love had soared to another place and it couldn't be defeated.

'Jilly, this is our chance . . . to make a break.' Greg urged her. 'We're all screwed up.' – Jilly knew – 'I lost the fuckin' car. I should have stayed with it. You should have seen it explode like that.'

'Did you think of staying with it?'

'Yeah, I did.'

'But?'

'On another day I probably would have.' He brought a fist hard into his open hand and the crack of knuckles on palm startled Jilly. 'Think!'

'You think,' she called back to him, 'I'm here, at rest with the world. Do you know that? Rest.'

'It'll be a short one,' replied Greg, 'because . . . because.' He saw her at rest, still running but without the jaggedness, without the strain. Who would she be, he wondered, if she could rest forever? 'With them at your back you'll soon be home. And your dad, where is he?'

'I don't know. I don't know.' It was exactly what her mother had said when the two were face to face and Jilly's hands were smaller and her mother used to hold them.

But mother and daughter somehow could not be together, Jilly was sure, even though Susan was not, and all the pain and torment each had seen in the other for all the difficult years came to a stop. Susan and Jilly cried alone in different places and life turned them colder.

As she sat on the bed in this new America Jilly heard all of what she had become – her words, her actions, and her mother pleading with her not to go, not to go. She did feel strong then, right and justified to choose her path and break her mother's heart. Carrying memories like that could disturb her, could bring her close to make some kind of contact, a sweet *hello, I'm okay*. It could also allow the idea that Alex had done exactly what she was doing: staying away. Dad didn't die, he just couldn't come back. Maybe he thought no one wanted him back, not really. She hadn't asked him to come back, not properly. DAD! She would scream to herself.

There had been some movement in another part of the house and a bird or two had a long time begun their song.

'Jilly,' Greg reached for her hand, 'let's go.'

'How will we go?'

'We'll put our names up in lights. We'll be everywhere. We'll be famous.'

Jilly became a little excited. 'We'll tell the world. We'll make a splash.' She had found hope again.

'Right. We'll make waves, huge fuckin' waves,' Greg announced. 'Or . . . .'

'Or what?' Jilly was caught up with how she saw the days ahead. 'What?'

'They could shoot us.'

Jilly let out a gasp of disbelief, 'Greg, don't.'

'I'm serious, if they really don't want attention. My father attracted a whole lot of that. Sure did. Christ, I'd love to meet him, talk a little. Christ, is that too much to fuckin' ask for?' He coaxed her from bed, 'Come on, we're on the hunt. You want to hunt? We want to hunt, don't we? We want.' The energy in his face stretched the skin and a little madness could be found in his eyes.

Jilly began to dress. She thought that the road ahead might be the final stretch; the horizon where all her dreams lived seemed that bit closer. If she considered all that lay there at the wrong time of day her emotion would overcome her, but now away from England, where all her problems were born, now in America she hoped they would die. In the tiny bathroom into which Jilly had squeezed all her hopes, there alone with herself she studied her features, while the light from the small wall lamp sneaked out through a finger breadth's gap between door and frame. There she looked back at her eyes and remembered herself. She needed a dose of normal healthy life with trivial thoughts and laughter, to be around and in that kind of life. She was lucky that she had been given beauty, so short in supply that those who possessed it could never share it – it was either to have or not. Hers was an unstable beauty, she believed, when it sometimes could not travel the short distance from the subject to the eye of the beholder. Jilly was mistaken, what she was everyone could see.

*   *   *

When Alex was still around and there was a buzz going on, at home and out in the cold world, and others were being pulled into it, Jilly was happy then, laughing and being silly. She thought so, young in England, in America. When Jilly last felt on solid ground, Toby Cullen was almost thirty and he, too, had his own excitement, the surefire certainty from way back that came from saluting the flag at summer camp, being stirred by pride with every clash of brass symbols, being American. Even heading out of high school as a teenager when the pictures of his country were shown around the world, he did not feel a sense of shame, he stood strong and lost many friends because of it. When the pictures of American panic on the embassy roof in Saigon were seen in everyone's home, and when the helicopters made speed with the few to the open sea, he did not feel bad, as many around insisted he should, he just felt sad for his country and inadequate as an American. But with time young men's ideals can and do change, and the American flag which could bring a tear to the eye could also dry it up completely. What was it, he asked himself, that dried up General Keech on the day he turned his back, and walked away from America?

'Have you ever lost something dear to you and couldn't accept it? What would you call that?' Cullen had stopped for a blueberry something, which he didn't get, and a coffee. The man he had put his question to was a temporary driver, someone who had brought him quickly to Greg's burnt-out old Ford. 'A kind of denial,' the driver answered. 'Yes, denial,' agreed Cullen, 'but for years?' 'I don't know, sir.' 'Got to find this man Keech.' He looked at the driver and almost saw himself, the way he was years before. Same look, same tailoring, same lack of joy about them, as if unhappy being around this part of the world where nature seemed to take a gentle pause.

'Do you know this man Keech we're looking for?' asked Cullen.

'No sir. I know of his father. The army general who walked away, over to the Russians.'

'Right. What do you think of that?' Cullen wanted to know from anyone who might have an opinion after all this time.

'It was a long time ago. America's changed, I think. Keech was an unwell man, sir. I read. The sick should have our understanding, people would say, sir.'

'Do you say that?'

'I'd like to think so, sir. That's my America, to go the extra mile for the individual.'

'Really.' Cullen was surprised. 'The extra mile. Is that our country today?'

'Yes sir.'

24

Paris, late February 1983

Nikolai Levchenko had got into a routine: he had made himself available, to anyone watching, three mornings a week at eleven. At that time he would walk from the embassy building and through the large embassy gate into the street; for the next hour or so he would walk around Paris centre, stopping and moving where he pleased. But he had arranged no meeting with Halin and there had been no further trips across the Channel. Control waited for a movement that would tell them that, before Halin, Fisher had made pick-ups regularly in the capital and taken them out to a foreign port. And to receive Levchenko's personal attention would suggest their man was a valuable source of highly classified information. But they waited before engaging themselves in a high-level hunt; Control had gone along this road before when they had housed a damaging leak, and, since, they had never been so fearful that another would be turned and it would start again. Anything was possible.

It was a wet night, there was only a handful of days left of February and the rain, although falling fast and hard, had less bite to it. It was a welcome sign that winter was going, slipping away. The night in Paris under a dark rainy sky glittered with life. The cafes and restaurants offered hope for anyone who needed it, for anyone lost in the world. And for Frank Gull it made London a sour and sad place, a sleazy mass of decay that he was glad to get away from. Paris he loved, another kind of civilization with a language that made him feel someone else. Pierre Halin that night looked what he had always hoped to be: rich and loose. He had made his way from cafe to cafe and never a stranger in any. There was always a greeting waiting, a firm shake of hands, a touch of cheeks. Gull noticed him different, his hair was darker, almost black, and short when before it was brown and longer. Everyone seemed happy that he had called and the initial laughter never quite died away. But Gull was sure Halin had a destination that evening. Somewhere at the end of the night's road Halin would drop the social chat and mirth and meet someone. It was unlikely to be Levchenko; he too had his social activities and it was important that the right people saw him, his working Paris street clothes replaced for a dinner jacket. But somewhere further into the night Halin would receive his master's orders – it was all Gull waited for and he had waited long.

Since Halin had been released in London, Gull had kept a watch on him night after night until Halin went home. Now, that night, as Gull waited and the river slapped at everything that sat on her and the wind had gathered to curl round every corner, Pierre Halin decided to make his last call of the evening. Gull followed him, first by taxi, then on foot for a short distance to rue de Castellane. Before entering the building at number twelve, Halin used a call box on the other side of the street, then replaced the receiver, crossed back over and entered. Gull stood annoyed with himself that a possible connection with the two had not occurred to him. It was right that Mrs Fisher could now find Paris a lonely place, that she could open the door to Halin and replace a part of her husband at the most silent and empty time of her day. She must have known Halin well; perhaps Fisher had invited him home to dinner. Expatriates are never too fussy, they try immediately on arrival to start up like before, and invite, invite. Fisher would have certainly invited Halin, and when Fisher was murdered, Halin would have called round. But Gull hadn't calculated this tie, at a time when Mrs Fisher would need someone he forgot about Halin.

As Gull waited and the night deepened, a dark car pulled up a hundred metres or so behind him, almost silently. It sat at the kerb quiet and still like a jungle cat watching. Gull decided to move and crossed over to the call box. The off-side door of the car opened and a figure got out. Gull walked past the box and quickened his step. He would walk on a little more, he thought, then cross back over. But the car had crawled up on him, and as he made to the road it had arrived.

'Get inside, *Monsieur*,' said a voice behind Gull.

The two men got in and the car moved away. They returned to the centre, to the buzz of the traffic, turning left and right before briefly stopping. The car door opened and Gull was pushed over, while the other returned to the front.

'This will be pleasant,' said the new arrival. 'No heroics or anything like that. You are Gull, are you not?'

There was no reply.

'No response?' The man looked away. 'Don't be tiresome. You are a minor in this professional business and unfortunately minors can be very brave, stupid people.'

'Who are you?' asked Gull.

He could not see the man's face clearly; although the city street lights flashed through the car, there was always a part of the face permanently in darkness. The squelching sound of flattened water as the car headed away from the centre gave Gull a feeling that chilled him, as if the water noise heightened his senses and he knew where the pools of dark would lead him.

'You are Gull. What do you think you are on to? You do think you are on to something, don't you?'

'Was it you who killed Fisher?' asked Gull.

'Oh, you are not interested in Fisher. That is not it at all.'

'That's exactly it. Fisher was a British citizen and his death is our concern.'

'No, no, Mr Gull, I will not take this from you. You know very well what it is I want, but you will try, as you feel you must, to keep your interests in another quarter, keep me away from what you know.' The man's voice hushed and he pushed his face nearer to Gull. 'Our game is a dangerous one, you know that. We are taught to defend, defend, protect, protect, all our actions lie there. Now, we are in this car together for these reasons; you have something to protect and I . . . well, I have, let us say, something to defend. And what is more, Mr Gull, it is not necessary that you return back on this road, not really absolutely necessary. Take a moment, Mr Gull, look out of the window, touch your hands and consider life and death.'

With every kilometre the night became darker. The surrounding suburbs of Paris were quiet, the traffic reduced to a handful of Peugeot and Renault cars.

'What can I tell you?' asked Gull.

'Just tell me what you think you are investigating. What has Fisher's death sparked off?'

'Fisher worked for you as a messenger. He collected, we believe, classified information in London on a regular basis from some we have yet to discover.'

'So you think you have a spy on your hands?'

'It would appear that way.'

'And how far along are you with your investigation?'

'As I said, we don't know who the leak is or what exactly is being leaked.'

'Yes, but to whom is the information going?'

'To you.'

'And who am I, Mr Gull?'

Gull turned more to him, 'You are Levchenko . . . KGB.'

The man did not reply. The men in front were silent while the engine noise filled the car.

'Your people have no idea who they are after?' asked the man.

'None at all.'

'They don't know what is being passed?'

'No.'

The man thought. 'Mr Gull,' he sighed, 'I believe you are still protecting. I can understand and I'm not without some sympathy. It must be difficult in your position. But it is what we have been taught and what we have accepted that we must follow. Is that not so?'

'I have told you all.'

'Any action that strengthens defence is admirable; is that not what we have been taught? That reduces the danger and weakens conflict.'

'You mean the end justifies the means?'

'Yes. To prevent a dangerous situation everything must be done to rescue it. It is its rescue that is our only concern.'

'But I've told you all. You've learned everything.'

'Yes, you have failed to protect, Mr Gull, but your position was not a favourable one. You judged it accurately. I can understand.'

In the blackness of the countryside the car drove steadily on. Gull shivered a little.

'Are you not turning? Going back?'

'Not yet. Not yet.'

'This man, whoever he is, will be found,' said an increasingly nervous Gull, 'his existence is known now. He will be found. It's not up to me. You know that.' Gull's hands held together, squeezing on each other, holding his fear in.

'We must defend, it is what we have been taught. The British, too, teach it. You, yourself, have been taught it. You understand, our positions are clear to each other.'

'Please,' said Gull, his voice just short of pleading.

The man tapped the driver on the shoulder and the car slowly pulled in close to the side of the narrow road and stopped. The rear passenger door opened and one of the men stood waiting. The interior light lit the face of the Russian and Gull stared into it.

'It's no use,' said Gull in a burst, 'it's all for nothing.'

'No, it's not. I have told you, it is for defence. We understand each other, that is important.'

Gull was encouraged out of the car and with the driver the three men walked away. Gull was going to die and he could hardly believe it. While he was walking through the wet Paris streets only a short time before with the neon signs flashing their happiness, he never considered how close death was. The people, the laughing, the music had made death seem impossible. Ridiculous. There was only life in the streets, the best of it, just life, life, life. But in a short time he had moved a world away to a field somewhere on the outskirts. He could see a light from a house in the distance across the field and he searched through the darkness for another.

'Stop,' said one. And Gull stopped.

He had been taught many things in London; his work required him to learn a lot. But how to stand in a field and wait for the moment when everything would end for him had been forgotten. He could not plead or search for their compassion; they were allowed none. And just when the sky began to clear and a few specks of light could be seen flickering up there faraway, there was a shot like a cracker at a festive time. Then there was another and the light at the other end of the field abruptly went out.

Two days later, where the open countryside lay still and upturned and no one travelled along the pot-holed roads, some crows were sighted and Frank Gull's body was rescued.

London, February 1983

Nick White squeezed at the skin around his eyes then across his forehead, completely affected by the news. He had lost Gull, he knew that, the danger Gull had put himself in had not been recognised by him, and he suffered. Sinclair did not feel it was time for laying any blame if there was any at all. But he was worried, Gull had died for something, for someone.

'I've read what Gull had been doing and I can hardly believe it,' said Sinclair. 'The KGB? Their number two? Are you sure of all this?'

'If I wasn't before, I am now. I told Gull to be cautious, to watch his step but I admit I couldn't see this Levchenko involved in the leg work he described to me. But I let him go, mainly because I had faith in him, I thought he should go as far as he could with this and then come back and explain how things really were. But he can't do that now, Christ, I gave him no support, nothing.'

Sinclair let White's regret rest with him for a moment, then asked, 'What do you think now?'

'I think we have someone here or, if not here, damn close who's found a new master. Someone who's been turned.'

'You know what you're saying?'

'Yes, I bloody know. Gull bloody knew. I could do with a drink.'

Sinclair got up from his chair and poured a generous measure for him and an equal one for himself. 'Gull was no fool, Nick. I know we feel there are the odd one or two who could get lost in the tube but never Gull. He was young but sharp, sharper than maybe we were at that time.'

'He wasn't sharp enough, I'm afraid. I know, I appreciate what you're saying, but I have lost Frank Gull and I don't think I should have. If I could see a way where he was stupid, something where I had no control I could, perhaps, accept what you're

143

saying, but I see nothing.' White drank some more and helped himself to the bottle on the desk.

'This Frenchman,' said Sinclair, 'Halin . . . he's been interviewed and released?'

'Yes. Alex saw him. A bit strange that was. Halin flies over here, picks up an envelope at a west end hotel and about turns back to Heathrow.'

'Strange?'

'Yes. The envelope is of course sealed, which Alex opened only to find sheets of newsprint with a further but more subtle seal.' White explained Alex's discovery in detail.

'And you let him go?'

'We had to, there was no other way. But we frightened the French boy. He has agreed to switch.' White stretched over and laid his glass on the desk. 'Levchenko is running him, which indicates his source is high; what Halin collects is good stuff but I believe also it's the KGB's way of assuring their source of their best protection. No one kows his identity but Levchenko and the top brass in Moscow. I suggest we tighten security around here to strangle point.'

'You think it's here?'

'Could be. I hope not,' said White, 'but I cannot say I'm optimistic.'

'We can't give this to Alex, he's away. And Gull has to be replaced.'

'I would take it myself if I could. But after saying that, I would say Fraser should be considered. He was with Alex, he spoke with Halin. He's good.'

'Good,' said Sinclair.

'If we can't find anything here, nothing tampered with etc, I'm afraid this can't be any guide that the leak is elsewhere. Whoever he is will know about Gull, he'll know he's been stopped and he'll probably know who replaces him. Our position is out in the open while this bastard looks out from the forest.'

'What are you suggesting?'

'I'm not suggesting anything. But in a perfect world we would pick up Levchenko and extract every bloody detail. Simplicity in itself.'

Sinclair frowned. '*Senior Russian Diplomat Tortured*. That's a headline for you, Nick.'

'It would be all for Gull. This world's not fair, is it?'

Paris, February 1983

Everything seemed to be happening at once; Gull's murder had shaken Control and stirred feelings of retaliation, but it was no use, there could be only one way of getting back, of really getting back. Tom Fraser moved out of London to Paris and waited for Halin to pick up his ticket and cross the Channel.

Eating out in France could be a pleasure. Eating out in Paris a delight. Fraser didn't know food very well, the result of an accident of birth and bad education. But happily he was not in denial about those shortcomings of his life, he welcomed a new experience.

'The food's bloody good,' he acknowledged. 'I suppose you don't have a spare minute in this town?'

'At first, sir, there was a lot of getting to know, but eventually you calm down and take things a bit easier,' said Lee, an embassy boy getting to know his station.

'Gull liked it here, didn't he?'

'Yes he did. There's something good about being a foreigner in a place like Paris. An outside feeling, perhaps.'

'No commitment, Lee, that's what it is. You enjoy the good things but feel not to blame for the bad. Must be wonderful.'

Fraser drew his napkin across his mouth and filled his glass with the red table wine. He was a tall man with a gravel voice that deepened his accent which after many years in London had for some reason become even stronger. Paris was his favourite city.

His discovery had come a long time ago: as a rugby enthusiast he had travelled with a coach of followers in Scottish national dress to witness a sorry defeat. He had not got back home for four days; the coach had left and Fraser had walked miles round and round discovering another Paris as a defeated but unbowed rugby supporter. He grew up in those days and now had an affection that one might have for one's birthplace.

'I didn't know Gull. Never really had the chance. I'm sorry he didn't quite recognise the danger.'

'I knew him,' said Lee. 'He was left alone too long. He became obsessed with the Fisher murder.'

'Did he tell you?'

'No. But after Fisher's murder he suddenly was not available – for anything. Socially he closed himself off.'

'That's exactly what I'll be doing,' said Fraser, 'I'll be living quietly in one of those romantic pensions, but I'll be alone. There'll be no callers. Gull died for something; you've heard the stories, haven't you?'

'Yes. London has a leak.'

'That's it. London has a leak. Now listen, lad. There'll never be a time when London doesn't have a leak, we can't expect that. Do you get me?'

Lee wasn't sure.

'Never mind, it'll come to you.'

'I would like to know what you think, sir.'

'It's a matter of two and two, Lee. You can see that, can't you?' Fraser watched Lee's young face. 'It's this. It used to be that a London leak would go through a London handler. Right? If you were running someone you couldn't appear to be an absent mother, you had to be there with your presence. And you could also gauge the water temperature. Most of the time this is the way of it.'

A waiter interrupted, '*Café, messieurs?*'

'*Deux, s'il vous plaît,*' said Fraser. 'You do want coffee?' – Lee nodded – 'Getting back,' continued Fraser, 'Gull discovered something else. The KGB here was running someone in London, in another country, using a messenger for pick-ups. All the leak had to do was choose his location each time, put his choice in any one of the classifieds that the papers and mags offered, as much as a couple of weeks before and leave it.'

'But why does the KGB here run him and not London?'

'Because there's saturation coverage of the KGB strength in London, and in many cases the local Rezidentura are forced to run their agents via a continental case officer . . . but that's not the whole story. In this particular case this situation is preferred because it's safer that way. Safer for the man in London and for them. We don't watch the KGB here, not really the way we'd like to, we leave it to the French. And when Gull began showing interest they killed him. They wouldn't scare him off first, it's too unreliable for the Russians. Death they understand much better.'

The coffee came. The small restaurant was quite full, loud laughter had cut Fraser's train of thought so he finished the remains of his wine.

'Where could the leak be?' asked Lee.

'Well, work it out, lad. I've given you something you can work on. Obviously he's a self-assured bastard, he can work alone without any contact. He goes quietly slipping things away, sealing them up in an envelope and then he goes back for more.'

'Government papers?'

'No, no.' Fraser shook his head. 'Politicians don't become that sick of their country as to lead to its downfall. They sincerely believe that as long as they're about things can be saved. Don't you know any politicians?' Fraser watched Lee, he wasn't catching on, he wasn't trying, he was just listening. 'No, it would be someone who could see the country from his personal view-point, someone who knows how we are, hidden from public view. Someone whose affection for the land of his birth has soured over a long period. Someone who's had enough and instead of quitting, taking early retirement and buggering off, stays and allows his hate to grow and then strikes, feeding the other side.'

'And nothing is discovered.'

'Nothing. Remember we're talking of someone at the highest level. This person is completely trusted. They've killed for him and have no doubts, Lee, that they'll do it again. Have you got me now?'

'Recent history would point to . . .'

'Exactly, just read through recent history, all the answers are there.' He took a thick-battered wallet from his jacket and brought out what he considered was the likely cost of the meal.

'Just go about your business at the embassy meantime and leave me your number and pray we get more of a chance than Gull got.'

25

While Greg left Jilly's room the way he entered, Jilly paid what was due and said goodbye. From the moment she took herself away a new world waited. She was going to splash herself around, get attention for that long-time coming reunion. After boarding a bus for another road and town, she and Greg sat together like strangers; in the silence the countryside seemed to expand before them. There was a man of uncertain age with a guitar who had chosen the back row of seats.

'I hope he doesn't play,' said Jilly. 'No music, please,' she whispered.

Greg leaned over and told her what he had heard his father once say. 'When I hear a piece of music that moves me . . . moves me, that's when I decide about it. I hate it from then on. Can't have a string of cheap notes embarrass me, can I?' Greg smiled. 'That's how he was then.'

'Are you like that?'

'No,' he said in a sure way.

Jilly asked no more as the bus rolled on and sat comfortable with herself and only a light strumming of strings in the background. A relationship had begun with the general's son, the idea had been swimming about in her mind, an idea, one that might take shape. Her ideas were many, always had been, like bursts of energy and then gone. But there was one idea, or more, it was a promise, made at the heaviest of times, a promise she swore by, on the bus to the airport to her flight to LA, that by the year two thousand her life, as it was, would be over. The second after the midnight hour and the leap taken, her old life would stop, cease, end, be over. Two thousand was the time and on the bus then and now she counted the months with her fingers. She had not known of a relationship, not as she understood it to be; she had seen others, when she was a girl, place their efforts on appearing interested and to what heights they would fall from to be wanted, to be part of the circuit. She saw them more and more as she grew, and more and more she walked away from them. She could see no beauty then. Maybe she saw everything that way, life all around was seen ugly and false, and the people everywhere had been caught up in a pool of dirty water. But it would soon be over, she felt with certainty. On the bus, her fingers counted again, she smiled for Alex and in the same instant for Susan.

The strumming guitarist, moved by his own sounds, was singing something in the lowest of breaths and Jilly and now Greg were taken to different places on the bus, on the road – there was a highway for everyone.

*   *   *

There is a road in Idaho that weaves its way a good while, and in that time one might not know where one is. Buses with soft upholstery and passengers on a tourist trail never know of it. It is a strange haunting road designed, it seems, to tear at the young hearts of those who travel on it. Young Greg was part of that road, it took him up and down while he was biting at his journey through his youth. That road had a name, a route number, an interstate status but it did not matter, it was a killer, a road that somehow invited those with horrors in their head to come and scream at the world.

One late summer Greg was travelling on it when the year was closing in and his self-perception was raging, after a dewy dawn had revealed two young bodies one mile apart on a loopy section of it. The discoveries highlighted in the media frightened Greg since, it was claimed, the killings were so similar that the police were looking for a killer in the singular. A man out of his head on drugs was not discounted because of the brutal treatment the women received; the killer might not be quite aware of where he was at the time of the killings or of what he had done. Greg thought of his own whereabouts. Maybe he was high on something, maybe, he would think, maybe he was there. He could not remember. Greg was too alone: that and his rage helped him to turn to any chemical that could lighten him. He did not know how sad he was then.

When his father never came back, he heard someone say that he was now the man of the house, he had to be strong and look after the women. He found pride in himself that he could be considered by anyone for that role, but it never happened, the women in his house never wanted him and scorned him mercilessly until he withdrew from the idea. From then on Greg harboured anger and fear, and it was the fear that troubled him most. In his sleep he would dream about his father being taken away by strangers in the night, and he thought that one night, when America was asleep, strangers would come for him sometime after he had climbed into bed – he just knew they would call – and when they didn't, his fear was suspended until another night. And so it went on until it wasn't only the night but a call could come at any time. While he was waiting, his world would climb over him and he would explode, the house would shake and he would appear ready for violence, but violence never came. It was too much for him, drifting in and out of school, too much without a friend, someone who loved him. His introduction to some drugs was not a wicked acceptance to turn criminal, it was a normal response to what could have been a prescription for a chronic pain given by any doctor. It offered relief, a new world, a better one, but in fact it was just a cap smothering the real Greg; some days it would be good, great, and others it would bring him to his knees. He began to think about the times he couldn't remember, the times he felt so happy but he couldn't remember when. There were blanks in his head and at first he didn't care too much, it didn't matter because there was so much he wanted to forget. Then the bodies were found, one after the other, and the nights started again, sounds of strangers coming for him. He began to believe more and more that his terror was real, and if he had not made his decision to escape it would have been unlikely he would have made it till Christmas. He had a plan that before he could wake in the dead of night, listening to the heavy thump of his heart in his ears and before the night sounds returned, he would be somewhere else, somewhere south and far in Mexico. He would sell some things he used to treasure, get some money, and in the night he would take his mother's car, the family car, he always thought, and steal away.

Mexico was more than what Greg could have imagined, it was not the picturesque country with lovely *señoritas* in colourful dresses, with guitar music and song playing through the night; US travel guidelines to those who planned to visit were cautionary ones, anywhere on the other side of the Rio Grande was potentially a dangerous place to be, advice was to stay on safe tourist routes. But it was not widely known that the border town of Ciudad Juarez was wild and dangerous, yet for some the place to be. A town high in drugs and violence and low in humanity, where the women did not matter too much as a life force, as they disappeared on a regular basis only for their bodies to be found at a later time. Death and killing were in the air, and people who were ordinary in their life and in their beauty lay amongst the desert nature, still and lovely. All had been abused and defiled and almost all were strangled before they were discovered in the desert sands north and east of Juarez. Young flowers of the town all now melting in the sun, and with every discovery a police officer would kneel closely to examine the wound, the blow that took them away, and a frame-by-frame picture of their lives could be seen and known.

Death was a different experience in this part of the world; it was rarely a something, most times a nothing. And nothing had changed for decades when Greg journeyed towards and reached the crossing at El Paso. Juarez city shared its sun and blue sky with the southern edges of the US but its ugly face was all its own. Ciudad Juarez had its name, its reputation which all of Mexico knew of, but Greg, who thought only of newness and escape, had little idea of it. He had travelled south with an excited heart to a town from hell. He dreamed he was heading to a Hollywood depiction of Mexico, a kind of Brig o' Doon Latino style. So for a while he sought opportunities in Juarez, local deals in local ways, then roamed Highway 45 which was a direct link to Villa Ahumada, a one hundred mile stretch south. A small town where even the local police had been known to abandon it so much were they in fear of their lives. It seemed young Greg had chosen a land of destruction to ease his pain and he may have been right because any bullet or any wire ripping through a *señorita*'s neck would finally remove all one's pain. He had thought he had a plan to move on from his life in Idaho, steer away from his old self and let his baggage just drop to the side, but on arrival and ever since things never turned out that way. He stayed in Mexico until the winter grip in the northern US states slipped away but until then he could find no big bucks and very few small bucks, instead he was met with US style pain that the Mexican nights could induce. He took comfort from the women who entered his life the way a kiss is given to the deceased.

Juarez opened his eyes; there, where only the dead had the beauty, Greg sometimes longed for it, too. So far had he travelled and still he carried his full weight until one day in his spartan accommodation, where the smell of food was always around, he saw a news report on his small television screen of another body found out there on the desert plain. The camera work scanned the blue sky, the mountains in the distance, the vegetation, and then the lovely face of a woman. Beside her was a black shoe with a light brown trouser leg filmed to the knee. It could have belonged to a military man who was there to watch over her, to give her the protection she now no longer needed. The voice-over on the report was an unusually sad one and the cameraman was allowed to linger as his camera toured the woman's body. Greg sat motionless as the sun cast deep shadows over her face.

The next day Greg rose at dawn and took himself out of his one-room-and-a-bit apartment and out of town. The sun was light golden and it had a voice to him: it could sound like his father never did, like his mother never could and like his sisters never would. There was an occasional squeal from a bird as it soared while Greg stood and imagined how the woman had lain. A light haze had suddenly appeared to reduce his horizon as he searched for the woman's resting place. He covered some distance until he found a stretch he could lie in, like the woman in her stillness; he crouched himself to touch the sand which had yet to feel a warm sun then lowered himself to rest. With his eyes closed as she had, he thought about her, could he have known her, her name, her business in the world, her voice. People were passing him by and he was not holding on to anyone, never to know, not their names, nothing. In the morning, in the desert, he was invisible; maybe it was just like being dead, he wondered aloud, and again quietly, until he heard the engine drone of a small aircraft. There on his back he spotted the shiny silver glitter of a plane. It swung round a couple of times before tipping out its cargo. On impact with the sand a plume of dust rose from the site and Greg's worry rose with it. The propeller craft then flew off allowing the dust to settle.

Greg was a good distance away, a good twenty seconds to reach whatever it was that stirred the desert sand. In a crazy thought he imagined his father there on the ground, dead. This idea stayed with him too long because he froze for a time believing that his father had been thrown to him. After all his years of torment, that was it – your father, have him. The *dirtbag* that he had been told he was and heard him called was ringing in his ears. In a stooped position he ran between bush and shrub to the landing site to confirm that living down Mexico way could be responsible for your heart breaking. The smell from the black plastic bag, the size of himself, did not disgust him, it brought him sadness because inside were the last remains of a once life. Greg did not feel sick only his tears welling up for this stranger. The smell had now become the scent of honeysuckle from an Idaho spring and was filling up in his memory. The trauma of life under a southern sky had become too much and the squeals from the air too loud.

With only a handful of silver Mexican coins and a few dollar bills there was no getting away, Juarez was to remain home until a better time when a deal could be made. Greg waited till he got too scared to stay. He returned to what was home thinking how death was on his shoulder but its smell had yet to be sensed. He sighed with – it was only a matter of time and death would call, sure it would call, sure it would – on his mind.

26

Bayreuth, late February 1983

The barmaid was right, snow would come and did. Ten centimetres had fallen on the town, mainly in the darkness. By morning
the clouds still hung heavy but there was no more.

Alex had been on the phone to Susan; Jilly was ill, nothing
too serious, something that only children were prone to, it would
pass. He was full of concern for her; an only child ill becomes
that bit more precious, that bit more worrying. It was not what
Susan wanted – one child – but Alex argued that they shouldn't
have more because his time was taken, he couldn't be there and
he would feel guilty and Susan would be much more their parent
and that would be wrong. And although she argued back that he
could change his job, it only changed the atmosphere, which did
not allow for the making of love or babies. Susan held him to the
phone longer than he wanted; she was happy to talk, she liked
talking to him on the phone, she liked his voice alone. Just his
sound with no criticism in his eyes of her weather reports, school
reports and eating reports. She was free with him on the phone,
much more, she felt, than when they were together.

Before, when she was younger, she had a clear picture of how
she would marry, of how married people, like the fingers of two

open hands, interlocked with each other. It was not a dreamy idea thought about in a dreamy way, it was how love would naturally bring the union together. She was convinced. When Alex came into her life she couldn't understand why she was attracted to him, how she could love someone she didn't like. She tried hard to deepen her dislike but it only deepened her love and that ended her self-questioning. She was deeply his, two different people like two tightly closed fists. She had always thought a marriage could never be like that, like hers with Alex – separate, no agreed path, no aim, almost a casual way with no shared dreams or hopes. After they married she found herself studying the marriages of friends, she was sure she had got it wrong, theirs was the odd marriage out. Her mother told her that on paper it would certainly indicate that the horse had gotten the wrong rider or vice versa, but the Grand National had been won many times by such misplacements, she said optimistically. Then Jilly arrived and she stopped wondering and searching. Alex changed about then, too, the effect of a quietened wife, she thought. His job was pushed more into the background as if it had lost its importance. He made it sound dull with dull people in dark offices chain smoking and whispering top secret sentences to one another. He would laugh at that, which encouraged her, and the subject would go with the laughter. It was only recently that he had begun to talk more, complain and get angry, like it used to be, and she had missed all that in-between, listening to him. Now she wasn't sure what was best. You had to have a need for each other in marriage, that was something she still believed; and recently and now on the phone Alex, in his way, was telling her that.

An alarm sounded outside the room as Jack unscrewed the cap from a whisky bottle. It began as a cold shrill then continued as a moan. It lasted some seconds and stopped all Jack's movements.

'I felt I'd been caught there,' said Jack.

'Caught?' replied Alex.

'Yes, you know, doing something wicked and then the alarm goes off.' He held the bottle cap between his fingers.

'Nobody likes to get caught,' said Alex.

'You haven't been wicked, have you?'

'I thought you had.'

'No, the real wickedness lies on the other side, we're no match for them.' He handed Alex his glass. Another noise intruded on them, this time from the street – a patch of road was being dug up and the drill was ferocious.

'Do you know where the centre of Europe is, Alex?'

'Well, I couldn't put my finger exactly on it but at a guess I'd say it's somewhere east, quite a bit probably.'

'Actually it's just a little bit,' said Jack. 'It's here, less than an hour's drive away.'

'Should we know about it?'

'Listen Alex. If you were over there preparing to bring Keech out, you would like to have some options – a couple anyway. To bring him out through Czechoslovakia could be considered, you know that. Different people the Czechs. They remember the Red Army stomping in over them, Christ, they're not likely to forget. It could be easier that way. The centre of Europe is marked with a wooden tower and sits on our side of their fence. It's in the middle of the countryside with beautiful views of the rolling Czech landscape.'

'I see,' said Alex. 'Your Willy Matthofer needs a marker.'

'Exactly. The tower is fifteen metres high, it's on a slight rise on fairly open ground. There's an outdoor cafe which I don't suppose has seen many visitors . . . too out of the way to attract. And for a small charge one can climb the narrow winding stairs to the top and imagine how the other half live beyond what your own eyes can see.'

'And there'll be no stretch of wire, no automatic firing system, only some guards in their towers keeping watch. Right?'

'It's attractive, but there are problems. At this moment Keech is not in Czechoslovakia, as we know, he's in East Germany, and that's the major problem. If we could be sure of getting Keech from there into Czechoslovakia, then things would be a lot easier. I've thought a lot about this, but it is fact that the border points between East Germany and Czechoslovakia are bloody tight; it would be a double hurdle for them and their chances . . .' He gave a hopeless look.

'The double hurdle you talk about is there any way you look at it; every patch of soil at the East German border with ourselves is covered. There's little choice there,' said Alex.

'There's a time factor, Alex. To move Keech through into Czechoslovakia and then out would take time, and this has to be a quick operation from the word go. The other way is certainly dangerous but it's faster. If Keech is going to make it he'll find out about it sooner. He'll find everything out sooner. And you're right, the hazards at the East German border are considerable, but thankfully, there are blind spots.' Jack paused. 'Look here, Alex,' he spread a map of the border area over the small table between them, then ironed it out with his hand, 'look, there is a scattering of farms all over this area and Willy will know that.'

'I hope he's got a better plan than that,' said Alex. 'A few open fields may look attractive but I can see nothing easy in crossing them to the wire and then cutting through.' He walked to the other side of the room. 'If that's what your Willy chooses then they won't make it . . . Christ, Jack.' He turned his eyes from him to the window and Jack looked again at the map. 'Look at the weather out there,' said Alex. 'How long has it been wet like this? Weeks? Months?' Jack didn't answer. Alex sighed. 'The rolling Czech fields you talk about presumably extend to East Germany; they would be a nightmare to cross on foot, and it would have to be on foot, any kind of engine noise at night would alert the guards. Christ, Jack, their lives would end there, in the mud.' He turned and looked at him. 'And your Willy boy would be dead.'

159

Jack pulled his tie up tighter and straightened it. He ran a hand up and down one side of his face feeling the bristles of hair pushing themselves out into the open. Some men shave two or three times a day in an effort to hold back this constant advance. Jack was like that, he would caress his face which had become lined, in parts deeply, with his obsessive use of the razor. A clean face was for him a youthful face, and he needed that; at the wrong side of forty he needed something to compensate, so he shaved and he felt the result and it helped.

'A few months ago a young East German brought his mother and girlfriend out,' Jack said after a pause. 'It didn't make the headlines, it doesn't anymore, but he did and well too. Somehow a tractor was left in the open and the three of them climbed onto it and drove through a hail of fire before tearing down the fence. They had not a scratch on them, a little shocked, mark you, but physically untouched.'

'They had the luck at least to have a tractor,' said Alex. 'They had help. Your friend Willy will not.'

'Oh Alex, you're wrong there, why do you think we're here, we'll have to help him.'

Alex was more puzzled but concealed it from Jack and even found himself nodding. But Jack had prompted many questions and they all lay on Alex's tongue, all waiting to be thrown out.

'We'll have to assist in some constructive way. We couldn't expect Willy to do it all by himself. No, no, he'll need us at the right time.'

'Jack,' Alex stood resting his bottom on the sill of the window, 'I think you know a damn sight more than you're giving away and I don't like it. I'm not just here so you can have someone to talk to, and anyway, when did Jack Kirkland ever get lonely?'

'Alex, I don't mean to upset you.' Jack was filled with concern, his voice soft and warm. 'You know how it is, surely Alex. This is something that cannot fail and to be bloody truthful our control is not what we'd like it to be.'

Alex had noticed over the recent chats he had had with Jack that his language had changed; he felt there was a man with a lot of sincerity to convey, it was the last *bloody* that began a little worry in Alex.

'It's the Americans, Alex. Christ, you know how this government is, they don't want to let them down.'

'Yes, I know all that, you've told me.'

Jack got up and stood for a moment looking at a picture on the wall. 'What is worrying you, Alex?' He turned and looked at him. 'We're friends. If I thought you should be worried I would tell you.'

Alex remained at the window and Jack sat down. The telephone rang and Jack answered.

'It's for you.'

Alex frowned, 'Yes.'

Jack had walked into the bathroom. Alex was brief.

'Giving out your number?' asked Jack standing in the doorway. Alex could say nothing. 'A girl – here in Bayreuth?' Jack widened his eyes and his forehead creased deeply.

'From the bar,' explained Alex. 'She poured the beer. Schinner – right?'

'Did you like it?' asked Jack as he turned to close the bathroom door. 'Good,' he muttered himself.

Alex felt he should offer no explanation, his newly acquired German friend would make Jack curious but nothing more. There was an uncomfortable silence between them. Jack had picked up some papers and was studying them or so it seemed. Alex had nothing in his hands just a heavy feel of silence waiting to be broken. He dug his hands in his pockets. 'I know you're in charge of this. I know that. You've chatted with the top and it's been made clear to you what is expected. I know how they can be . . . but you can't keep me in the closet opening it little by little, telling me bits and pieces then closing it again until another time. Should I expect that from you?'

'I don't know what you should expect. We've got our parts in this affair; it was explained, you did accept . . .'

'What the hell are you talking about? Jack, what are you talking about?' Alex's anger rushed out from nowhere and Jack rushed out his.

'Don't jump at me. Alex, there's nothing you don't know. You see, there's more to this than just you and me waiting in this hotel room, but the bastards didn't tell me. You're right of course, I did chat with the top and sipped their hospitality and was told, told mind you, that from all the intelligence reports this was no mission impossible.' He brought a hand over his shaven cheek. 'Sometimes Alex, I think there's more than Five and Six, there's more than SIS, there's another, a super secretive agency operating from a bed-sit in darkest London.'

'It's what I've suspected all along,' said Alex seriously.

'The last person I spoke to before leaving was Sinclair and he gave me no more than what I already had. In fact he said, I'll see you when you get back then. There was nothing in his words or tone that would suggest the Keech rescue was going to be complicated.'

'You mean it is?'

'Not from our side of the fence. No, but my Willy boy, as you like to call him, is getting help. Now exactly where this help comes in I cannot say, not yet. You see, I'm being fed bits and pieces and by it one can only just measure the rate of progress on the other side. So if the secrecy of our world is at its tightest now, we can't help but feel it.'

'I thought it had been left to you.'

Alex paced across the carpet, furious that Control had decided to play their way in the name of security.

'It's bloody annoying, Jack. You know there are times when the little men back there in London are nice, just nice. They can extract feelings of friendliness from you. You talk with them and you leave feeling you've spoken to very nice men.'

'It's important that if we don't love them we, at least, like them.'

'So we have an invisible master in this affair. Who the hell could that be?'

'When I realised there was someone I gave it five minutes thought. We can't give it anymore, not now.'

'When we get away . . .' said Alex.

'Away? Don't you like Wagner?'

'Some find his music stirring; it shakes me.'

Alex walked into the bathroom and closed the door.

'Oh Alex, you couldn't have heard about Gull.' After a few seconds the door opened. 'Gull,' said Jack quietly, 'he's dead.' – Alex had slipped his head between the door and its frame – 'The Russians murdered him.'

Alex thought about what he had heard, then withdrew and closed the door.

27

The bus was cruising along roads that looked perfect, smooth and rich, which kept Jilly's eyes closed, her heartbeat steady with the ride. The swoosh of things passing was soothing and no voices could be heard from others as everyone approached, mile by mile, their destination. To travel in this way in America brings different views of what it means to live there. Jilly had seen sadness in the happiest of faces since her arrival, and it was hard to understand. What was this sadness? Why was it there? Maybe, to the American, life was harder because of its foregone conclusion that it couldn't be won, and that was so unacceptable, to find happiness without victory. Maybe hearts there could not be full and content and families could not hold on to each other as they should. But Jilly was new there and yet . . . she and her mother used to be as one a time ago. Susan lived her life in the shadows now, and Jilly never called. The link between them was so much less. Jilly had been into punishment, it had grown with her, for her mother and herself. Loneliness was her big thing, her character was gregarious but she lived the opposite, she would insist on the opposite, every occasion she indulged in the opposite. Loneliness can be such a deep sorrow for the young, a deep blow to their heart, and for Jilly it affected her eyes and only illusions appeared for what was now her sight. Each bend of the road Jilly sat dreamily, her pain gone, and her thoughts for Susan nowhere.

Susan loved her more and more, and she would call on Alex, as she had always done when she struggled with her hope, to love her, too, wherever he might be. But there was no Alex, no physical place where he rested, he had just disappeared. After a time it was expected she would get over Alex, and Jilly's phase of anger and rage would calm, someone said, another person who had studied and qualified, someone who knew the workings of the human mind but did not understand Jilly's. The better tomorrow Susan prayed for never came and with the absence of Alex she feared her love may not be enough to save Jilly yet she called on Alex when her heart was down, called and called to him. And this was Susan's life for a long time; always thinking of Jilly and of Alex, every occasion brought one or both to her thoughts and so it was when she took the short walk along her leafy street into the buzz of traffic. That day it was the flower shop she went to, then found herself alone on the pavement with a small bouquet in her hands. She felt some purpose about her, on a buoyant kind of day when your size, your person, your worth meant something more. She strolled behind two women and found herself walking away from town. It was not a long walk and with something in her hand it could appear she had a destination. She had walked from the tarred pavement onto a gravel pathway where she stopped. As she looked over the small stone wall and passed her eyes through the open gate, she shivered. Alex came flooding back, then Jilly. Where was Jilly? Where? She placed her flowers carefully on the wall, took some steps back and under her breath called on Jilly, her name bringing a lump to her throat; then angry and feeling afraid she returned, empty handed, home. It was terrible, the walk, the flowers, her heart pounding with fear and thinking this way and that, terrible, thinking maybe there wouldn't be a way home for Jilly, there just wouldn't be a way.

Jilly, at that time, was not thinking of a way back and if she did she would not know how. She was going forward and on her way superstition had entered her life, things that should have meant nothing, acquired a significance that, perhaps, was not normal. Her search for Alex was not normal, many had told her so, she was too obsessional and sometimes bizarre. The more she heard the more she stayed away and maybe that was the answer: there was only one gateway to her father, as long as she remained by herself, no mother no lover, there would be no threat that her pathway could be blocked and lost. She always felt closer to where she wanted to be when there was activity in her body and in her preparations. 'Suppose,' someone said when she had stopped and when another human being had got closer to her, brought the person closer to her, 'suppose you never find him, he's just not there – you'd be like millions of the rest of us who have no father to call on. You'd be like me. I'm surviving.' Jilly listened and told her friend that she did not want to survive. She also said that when her father spoke with her for the last time, her mother said that dad was being forced to say these things, that he was stressed and that was why he was gone. She knew there were people who could tell her where he was now. Today. She was sure. On that last call something happened to her. She was young, but she changed and that was for good. She would tell those whom she liked that she couldn't follow their dreams.

They would ask how she could leave others, family and friends without a thought. They questioned her motives for magnifying herself and her pain while reducing everyone else; sometimes they got through with their questions and could trouble her. It was true, she would distance herself from everyone who criticised her and it was also true that her young life was moving speedily along and much of it had been wasted. It was not what her father would have wanted, she heard that many times and mostly from strangers. So from friend to friend she moved, each hearing her story, which was good because Jilly could hear it too. A belief was something that was not negotiable and should not need to be explained, it was a belief and it helped her through the day and through the night, she would strain at explaining. Sometimes she would find herself full of shame, she had said openly and privately, ashamed at her needs but she hoped her father understood. She hoped. She sometimes spoke as if he were in the room. And sometimes as she spoke she would repeat a story that made her warm inside, a story of when she was younger, much younger and when night-time was earlier. Her head would rest on her pillow with a furry friend or two beside her. Her father would come in for the last time and sit at the edge of the bed, talk a little until it was time to leave, and there he would lean down to kiss her cheek and say, 'Daddy loves you.' Jilly, her head resting and her eyes almost closed, would respond with, 'And I love me, too.' At this he would drop his head like a stone onto her pillow, which brought tremendous laughter from Jilly. His weight sort of flattened her to the spot, and he played dead. Mortally wounded by her reply. 'Daddy, Daddy,' she would call, but Daddy was dead. She laughed and laughed, when she was younger.

There are many places in the mind where someone could take shelter, but normally these places are rarely sought because without the desperate need no one ventures deeply enough. Jilly's life was not normal, she had become quietly desperate and she did visit those places for calm and joy. And then in the blink of an eye that world could be lost to a noise of today, any noise could do it . . . like a knock on the door. It was not too early, a little sunlight was striking a piece of furniture while Jilly lay in bed. The mornings can be sad for some; all the rushing about, all together like that can take the individual out of the person, but Jilly's individuality was not under threat in that way. Then there was another loud rap on the door. She took the trouble to pull herself from her warm position to approach and open. Her body as a young woman could still be seen as a girl's, a teenage girl, the girl Susan thought of every day. There was an envelope waiting for her signature and it had arrived in a roundabout way from her mother. After five years away Jilly still did not want contact with her, so she kept her address secret to avoid more of the letters Susan had written to her when she first said goodbye. The pain Susan put into them seemed to push Jilly further away. They were received and read at first, but then they were simply received, opened and peaked at without leaving their envelopes. But what Jilly held now was the first letter for as long as a year. Her mother's pain had not gone away, it had just changed direction and never found the page the same as before, all the tension she lived with had somehow exhausted itself and she was now left limp. The man who had knocked and brought Jilly out of sleep had also brought news for her to consider. Susan had called Jack Kirkland, whom she used to know before Alex went and before Jilly went away, too. He was a family friend in those days, like anyone could be, a man who had surprised himself by being Jilly's godfather, he and Kathleen were valuable and Susan used to see them. Then it stopped, and Susan started believing that nothing was sure and nothing real – Jack had just been a face in their lives, it was painfully realised, his soul, wherever that was, never visited, not Alex, not Jilly and she had not seen or heard from him for a time she could not measure. And Jilly? Jilly had gone. Selfish reasons, selfish. And love? Love was a let down, just that.

It was not easy, Susan hated it, to make contact with him, but Jilly, her daughter, demanded all her thoughts, her care and efforts to do the best even if that meant calling on Jack. He was surprised to hear from her, his tone said all, but happy to hear that she was fine. He and Kathleen were in good health and maybe it was down to the sunny escapes they took when they could. How long had it been? He asked, and then, without a pause said that it was too long to think about. Susan was hesitant on the call while Jack flowed a little too much, wary, perhaps, of her and what was on her mind. He could tell Kathleen that he had been speaking with her and maybe something could be arranged. He tried to wave away Susan's attempts to talk about Jilly. She'll be fine, was all he wanted to say. It was a difficult time for young people but fortunately his work was still going on, spoken with the tone of complaint. Susan could feel his desire to replace the receiver and her heart sank then before she called, 'Jack, I haven't been getting any help. You know that.' Jack knew but could not say. He heard the timber in her voice quiver when she said that she had been treated cruelly and unfairly and no one cared. She had Jilly, remember? He was supposed to be something in her life, wasn't he?

Jack listened but had the ability to see nothing disagreeable about himself, it was remarkable how this mould of a human being could take shape, and it was deeply regrettable that Jilly had ever met him. 'You do know it hasn't been easy, Jack, it's been very hard.' 'Yes, I know, but considering the circumstances . . .' 'How long do I have to do that? Tell me?' 'Susan, speak to Kathleen . . .' 'I'm speaking to you. Jilly needs help. You can help.' 'I'll see. I'll let Kathleen know.' He placed the receiver and sat in his office thinking of times when Susan had called in vain and Alex …. silent, but on his mind.

The letter was one Jilly had not received before, written to her with so much hope that she might reach out, not with a hand, but maybe a finger. The pages held her still while the door had yet to be pushed fully closed; there she discovered who she had been and what she had become. Some steps along a worn shabby floor where she paused from the world, the spring of her bed creaked and steps to a closet bathroom could be heard. It was how Jilly passed her quiet days away, in someone's arms but nowhere else. There would be touches of tenderness and threats of violence to be found after she had walked away from those who criticised but cared for her. She had gone backwards in her journey and the letter she held was offering her in the softest of ways to stop the decline. It was a letter showing her the way out and it was written with Dad nearby, Susan said. 'All those years without Dad,' Susan went on, 'and today, today he's here. Jilly take yourself away from wherever you are and learn some things, go to college and remember where I am. I'm your mother and I miss you very much.'

A door banged, a voice was raised and Jilly pushed the pages under her white top against her skin, out of sight.

'What are you doin'?' her friend asked. He stood looking at her trying to convey his interest. 'Who was at the door?'

'It was a priest,' Jilly replied.

Her friend stood untidy, his body, hair, look, nothing was well, least of all the grin that appeared in the silence. 'You kiddin' me?' He never knew when or how to smile, his face was just there, ready to scoff or to fight.

'I think I want to become a Catholic,' Jilly said with some relief in her heart.

'Like hell!'

She moved about the room, her letter sticking to her increasingly sticky body as her heart picked up pace. Nothing was said while her friend watched her gather her bits and pieces around the room and when he could wait no longer to argue, he used a limb to beat any object across the floor and the silence was over. This was Jilly's world. What had happened, she would ask herself, when the night was still and her wet tears told her that everything was real, what had she done? But on a morning when she decided to bring the church to her aid and later found herself in their halls and sensed their beliefs, she knew a new step had been taken. Susan had asked her to see Jack, to make a call, please. He was her daddy's friend, he could be of help. She left out the spiritual guidance he had committed himself to, because it was clearly something he regretted now. 'Call today, Jilly. The world can be a better place. I'm here for you, as always. I'm here and yes, I'm turning into a lonely old woman. Some days I think

I see you in the street and one day I will reach out to a stranger and think I'm hugging you. Do you ever see me? A few years ago I decided to have a photograph taken on my birthday, a snapshot that you could see later. Little photos of me for you. Do something with your life, for yourself, for Dad, for me.'

28

London, early March 1983

Nick White was making his way through a glassy wet night where the beads of rain clung to the screen allowing a distorted image of the neon lights of London life. He had taken a taxi from a restaurant in Little Howard Street and now sat back patiently waiting as his driver, with equal patience, crawled through the traffic. Nick White was getting old, faster than many others his age; he was flabby and the grip of decay had firmly taken hold, it was a decay he had expected . . . sooner or later. His attitude was a realistic and clever one, he thought; the anguish of aging would be less, it was all a matter of attitude.

He shivered a bit and buttoned up his coat and pulled up his collar. Only an hour before he was sitting at a neat table covered with white stiff linen falling half-way to the floor. His wife sat opposite, her hands a little nervous as she played with her fork while the waiters hurried from table to table. Marian White was not any younger than her husband but she looked very good, a woman one could observe for a long time. She had a kind of Lilli Palmer beauty that could catch one's eyes quickly although she did not look like her. She was someone who did not have to be interesting or anything, it was just enough to have her there. And if her eyes appeared a little sunken, a little darker around the corners, it took none of her beauty away.

The Whites had been married twenty-nine years and Nick White had somehow forgotten that, forgotten who he shared his life with and who lay beside him at night. He had forgotten and it wasn't yesterday, it could easily go back half their life together. For Marian White it wasn't something she missed, not with her husband anyway. She had decided that she would take a risk and fill her physical needs with others, not with one and only one, but two, three . . . That way would avoid a possible attachment, a possible shift of her love. She could do that, lie in rooms around London corners and keep loving Nick. It was her explanation, one that she needed before she set off all those years ago.

She couldn't remember when they last dined alone like this, but on the phone he had said to come in something nice and she did, and to distract from the nakedness her low-cut dress revealed she wore a necklace, thin with a bead of a dark stone that he had bought a long time before she had set off. He did not see it or did not seem to as he spoke short sentences to her and she replied with the same. The waiter arrived to serve and Marian White finally let her fork rest.

'So everything's fine at home?' said White.

'No tragedies if that's what you mean,' she replied.

'No, I didn't mean that. We've never had any tragedies so why should we start now.'

'We've been here before, haven't we?'

'Have we?'

'A long time ago.'

'And you remember?'

Marian let the spoon rest in her soup. 'Yes.'

'Well I don't remember.'

'Then why did you choose this place?'

Nick thought. 'I think I saw it advertised . . . in the tube. I was going up or down those stairs and the walls, you know how they're filled with posters as you glide by . . .'

'It's to catch you while you're not thinking for those seconds,' said Marian.

'Yes, I know it is, but I'd prefer something more eye-catching.'

'A naked lady or two?'

He took the last spoonful of soup to his lips. 'In the tube?'

'Why do you try so hard to be old Nicky?' asked Marian. 'Why, why?' Her voice wanted to shout. She had come a little forward in her chair when the waiter arrived and smiled at her as he took her plate.

'Maybe it's the work I do,' he said, 'it suppresses the libido or something like that.' He brought out a slim silver lighter that could slip into any pocket without anyone's notice, and then a cigarette case, as silvery as the lighter. 'I know it's been difficult, that's why I've said nothing.'

'You're losing me a bit,' she said.

'No, I don't think so. You've wandered away from me for many years, I know that and I thought what else could she do?'

She played with the white napkin which had a postage stamp of embroidery at one corner – she always had to find something for her hands to do when her pulse quickened.

'I think our dinner is coming now,' he said.

The waiter served again what was a fairly conservative meal brightened only with a massive green display of broccoli, seasoned with olive oil. The bottle of French red popped and they were left.

'I hope we can enjoy this, Nicky.'

She was the only one who called him Nicky; before he had always been called that by friends at school and university, but those times were faraway and those people almost lost. He hated being called Nicholas, it was artificial to him, it belonged to a statue or saint. Up to her death his mother refused to call him anything less; she thought any name that ended with a 'y' was trivial and carried no respect. But he longed for a little less respect and perhaps a little more familiarity; then someone called him Nick one day at the office and he let it go, which was to his later regret, even today after so many years.

'It's nice to be like this,' Marian said, 'just the two of us in a roomful of strangers.' She drank a little and watched him cut neatly at his meat and followed the fork to his mouth. 'What is it?' she asked. 'Are you angry?'

His chewing stopped momentarily as he stared across at her. His eyes had become smaller, she noticed, they were less blue than they used to be, more bluey white, like a trace of a cloud over them.

'Angry? I don't know who has the right to be angry here: you for being untouched by me for so long a time or me for being cuckolded by you so many times.' He pushed his plate a little away from him.

'Is that why we're having this meal together, to talk about our weaknesses,' said Marian. 'We'll soon be old, we should be talking about our strengths. Can't we do that?'

'You see, Marian, I understand your needs, I'm sorry that I can't fulfil them, but I understand you had to go looking, shall we say. But I don't believe under those circumstances you were happy because there must have been many times, maybe in the early days, when I could enter your head and flood it completely. Your moment then couldn't have been happy. And now we're in our fifties and things don't come easier, in fact, our fears increase.' He paused. 'What I'm trying to say is, when I called you today I listened to you tell me something and I wondered then, at that moment, if I still loved you.'

Marian listened intently.

'Because,' said Nick, 'because . . .'

The waiter had stopped at the table and noticed that their meal lay unfinished.

'Lovely meal,' said Nick quickly – the waiter smiled – he looked at Marian.

'Lovely,' she agreed.

The waiter gave a little bow and walked away.

'Foreign chap,' said Nick.

'Because . . . ?' Marian urged.

'Because we have to know what we want.' He could see he was not being clear. 'Have you ever thought of living without me?'

'You mean parting?' she asked alertly.

'Yes, parting.'

'No, I haven't.'

'Why not? What do I possibly give you?'

'Stop,' she snapped. 'If you want a divorce then say it, just say.' She made to get up. 'I hadn't expected this, Nicky.'

'Give me a few more moments.' He stretched an arm out to her. 'Marian.'

She turned and reconsidered.

'On the phone today I asked that question, and I do. And I arranged this to hear it from you. I don't want to embarrass you but it's been a long time and the years pass. It's important, I need to know.'

'You want to know if I love you? It's very strange to hear you ask, Nicky, and I wonder what's started it all off.' She looked down into her open hand, then turned it and looked at the rings on her finger. 'You are a part of me, Nicky, and I would never want to say goodbye to you, never want to turn away.' She looked up. 'Is that love?'

'How would you like to get away from London?'

'A holiday?'

'More than that, a new environment, a new outlook.'

She was puzzled. 'A new environment? Why would you want to do that?' Unconsciously her hand reached forward across the table between the spaces. 'Here is our home.'

'I want to get away, not for a month or six, but away. You can understand that, Marian. Twenty years and more ago we used to dream of being wonderfully isolated in a foreign country. Well

176

we didn't . . . Marian, I feel old here, frightfully old – here in swinging London,' his voice raised a bit as she dropped her eyes. 'Are you listening?'

'Yes, I am,' she said. 'Where do you want to go?'

'Oh, I don't know. Tell me your feelings about the idea.'

'I don't know what to think, Nicky. What can I say? My conservative husband wants to change his life.' She gave a little laugh of surprise. 'It's so un-you, so rebellious, to turn your back on the establishment a few years before pension time. And for what?'

He listened to her with his hand around a glass of wine, rich and red and dazzling with reflections.

'Why? I have to ask why?'

'I have great difficulty, shall we say, in communicating with you – with anyone. It's terrible,' he said. 'Where is the coffee?' He looked for the waiter and Marian looked at him, not sure what he was going to say. 'You know what I do and how I cannot open my mouth. Well, now I want to open it to you but I cannot be sure . . .'

'You cannot be sure – about me?' she asked.

'How can I be sure?'

'You mean . . .' she paused. 'It's about trust and loyalty,' she gave a dry smile. 'And I haven't been that kind of wife, have I?'

The coffee came very brown and the milk Marian added had little effect. Both tended their coffees in silence, their eyes away from each other.

'There have been many times,' she said, 'and I've wondered why I let you down. Was it loneliness? My need to be wanted?' She sounded regretful, unhappy and disappointed with herself. The coffee had stained her lips and the red beneath was very dark. 'I don't know, Nicky. Men have girls when they can, it builds them up, perhaps it makes up for their failures in life. I think I took men to stay young, to create situations where I could remove the heavy cloud in one's life. Maybe to pretend that life was full of fun and to be always someone's girlfriend.' She stopped.

'There's a problem at the office,' he said, letting her confession go right past him. 'There's a bloody big leak there and an investigation has started up and I'm afraid they're looking for someone quickly before the search escalates and others start sniffing around.'

'My God, Nicky,' Marian looked amazed. 'They don't suspect you?'

'Yes, I think they do.'

'My God!' she said again.

'Before you ask the answer is no. But I don't want to go through it all.'

'You must,' she jumped in.

'I can't.'

'Why not? You're nearing the end of your career and you allow yourself to be stained like this. My God, you'll go to prison.' The more she thought the more she shook.

'It's better . . .'

'What's better,' she interrupted, 'why should you be the solution to their problem? How do you fit in? There has to be something. Oh Nicky, you've frightened me.' She put her hand to her mouth. 'The children – we cannot run from them.'

'Let's go home,' he suggested.

'No. Please, I'd rather stay. I want these people,' – she looked at the other diners – 'around me. Please.'

'It's a strange world,' he said. 'Do you know we haven't spent this length of time talking face to face like this for years. We have made each other sad, terribly sad. Do you ever feel that if only, if only . . .' He smiled at her. 'The office needs to show it can be effective in its own house. They've got a cleaning job to do and they've done some calculations. Believe me, they've calculated wrong but I don't want to stay and fight. I'm not strong enough for them.'

'Have you spoken with Sinclair?' she asked.

'No, I haven't. He would say it was a touch of paranoia anyway, and would suggest a medical visit.'

'He's your friend.'

'Marian, there's no such thing in my business. Christ, don't you know that?' He got angry. 'Where do you think I've been spending my time all those years – at a refined civilised club in St James's? Sinclair means something to me, of course he does, but he won't put himself out for me. There's no nursing the sick; if you get sick you die.'

'But you're not sick.'

'I'm as sick as they want me to be.' He saw her anguish in her lovely eyes and knew she wanted to know more: she couldn't understand. 'Recently we lost a man in France,' he began to explain a little, 'I can't give you the abc's but before he was killed he had come to me. He told me a story – well I thought it was a story – and I let him go back to gather more evidence. Shortly afterwards the Russians killed him. Now look at it this way: if I were the leak I might have panicked, might have wanted only to stop him. It makes sense, doesn't it? I might have arranged his murder, don't you think so?'

'Maybe,' she said. 'To avoid discovery,' she whispered almost to herself. 'But it's not true.'

'Don't be naive. They can't have a hole in security and take no action. Don't you realise they'd rather pick someone from the street than leave it exposed.'

Marian could see he had made his mind up and she could feel herself pulling away from him; just when he needed her close she sat opposite getting further away. She was frightened and wished she hadn't met him and now she wanted to get up and leave. 'I can't go, Nicky. Our home is here. I'm not leaving.'

'Marian, they'll put me in prison, you said so yourself.'

'No they won't. They'll retire you quietly, they've done it before.'

'Maybe they would but not in this case. There's a murder involved and they'll want me for that. They might even kill me for that.'

'I'm going, Nicky.' She pushed her chair quickly back and stood. 'Stay, please. Let me go alone.'

'Marian, sit down, don't walk away from me, you're my wife.'

'STOP IT. STOP IT.' She clutched at her purse and left.

Nick White sat helpless. His wife's raised voice had turned everyone's head but he didn't see them, he only saw flashing images of Marian's face. He could see her clear and beautiful, someone he wanted to embrace, someone he loved. Then like the sun hidden by a cloud he lost this picture and his anger rose and he hated her, hated her.

Now in the taxi he wrapped his arms around each other shivering more. He was surprised that the temperatures had obviously fallen so much in just a few hours. The blood was draining from his hands and he squeezed them closed letting his nails sink into them. But they remained cold. He could not understand what was wrong with him; he could remember being so cold before, in London, days before Christmas, eight or so years earlier. The frost which had covered everything that morning had brought with it a chill that took his breath away. His feet and legs ached and he had palpitations as the cold affected his heart rhythm. Only when he stepped into the car and put the heating on at full blast had the terrible cold slipped away.

As he sat huddled in the back he thought where Marian might have fled to, whose bed was she squirming in. He allowed his eyes to fill up at his thoughts. He was getting colder; finally he wrapped his knuckles on the glass partition. The driver slid it open.

'Could you allow me a little heat here in the back?'

'I've got it on,' said the driver. 'It's been on all night.'

White sat back, and as he gazed out past the driver his chest heaved like a mighty sigh which opened his mouth. The blow had sort of pinned him to the spot. He groaned at the damage he felt then slumped over onto the floor.

'It appears nature can be more vicious than the Russians,' said Sinclair sitting at his desk. 'It was a heart attack and it killed him in minutes.' He pulled out his handkerchief and sniffed into it. 'It must have felt like a hammer blow, the doctor said.'

Alex listened, he had just hurried out of Germany to be there, to hear from Sinclair the surprising demise of Nick White. Jack was far from happy that their little operation had been disturbed, he could see no sense in it, why should White's death need Alex's presence in London? Alex had not complained, he had packed and left rather business-like.

'You don't know what's going on, Alex, but not many people do.'

Alex waited for Sinclair to get it all out, to tell him what he had been brought back to hear. But with Sinclair one never got a stream of sentences, one right after the other, no, there would be lots of stops and starts, a bit here and there, so Alex made himself as comfortable as he could and wore the expression of an interested listener.

'When Frank Gull was murdered, Nick was filled with guilt; he was here, I listened to him. He was undoubtedly in great distress.' Sinclair raised his eyebrows as if to ask, 'What do you think of that?'

'Natural, I suppose,' responded Alex.

'Very natural, Alex, but have you ever heard of Nick White coming out like that, being so openly in distress?'

'No, I haven't. And I haven't heard of him losing anyone before.' He paused. 'If he thought he was responsible for Gull's murder, shouldn't he feel that way? I know I would.'

'Yes, yes, Alex, in normal cicumstances we wouldn't question his behaviour, but when do we ever have normal circumstances?

I liked Nick, known him for years, of course, and if I could I'd just like to say goodbye to him, you know, some flowers, a quiet moment of thought and then back to the living. But we can't do that here, not with our own.' He searched for something on his desktop. 'Drink, Alex?'

'Thanks.'

'The usual?'

Alex sort of nodded. He never had a usual and he wondered why Sinclair thought he had. The usual was a small flat bottle from an obscure distillery where the Gaelic was still the dominant language.

'You'd better add a spot of water,' said Sinclair. 'Here.' –Alex held out his glass– 'You know we have a problem.'

'Yes, I know,' said Alex.

'Well, tell me how you see this. Our boy in Paris gets a sniff of something and he brings it back and tells White. Gull's story is hardly considered because no one else hears it, just Nick. Gull then returns and within days he is murdered. Nick plays the part of the grieving father and soon afterwards he, too, is dead.' He stopped and waited for Alex.

'There could be something, a connection but . . .' Alex's voice trailed off.

'Do you think it was murder or suicide?' asked Sinclair.

'Didn't you say he died of a heart attack?' – Sinclair nodded – 'His was a natural death.'

'Alex, the threat of murder can induce a heart attack, you know that.'

'And suicide?'

'Suicide is a bit more complex. Anyone with a wish to kill himself usually prefers the quickest and the most painless way. But, for example, if you had the desire to hang yourself it's possible that the preparation – it would take a bit of preparation – would heighten you, get the adrenalin flowing, the heart pounding. So it's possible that in your final hour, say, you would be in an excited state.' He unfolded his handkerchief and blew long and hard.

'If White did plan suicide,' said Alex, 'but his own heart failed him before he could go through with it, there would have to be a reason. Why should he? Nothing I presume has been found out about him, nothing to say White is the leak, and even if there was he could have made a run for it. Suicide is a desperate act to escape. Was Nick White at that point?'

'We don't know. But we want this leak plugged ... and quickly.' He gathered some papers together and slid them into a drawer. 'How's your business in Germany?' Sinclair asked the way he might have asked about Jilly's progress at school.

'Progressing,' replied Alex.

'Alex, we're hoping in a way that Nick was the leak. It would take care of not knowing. I spoke to Marian, lovely woman.' He thought about her for some seconds. 'She's shocked of course.' He gave a heavy sigh. 'Nick could never be, but here I am searching for the shadows in his life that could tell me that indeed he was.'

'What do you want me for?' asked Alex.

'We want you back here as soon as possible. We can't lift you out of Germany just like that, you're needed there, but we can't give you much time. This American is important; we don't want a failure there. Success would bring the powers that be to smile upon us, and that would be most welcome.'

The little bottle sat on the desk quite forgotten. Alex had his empty glass in his hand and would have liked a drop more.

'I expect to see you back here when all is over,' said Sinclair.

'Who's taken over from Gull?'

Sinclair bit lightly at the corner of his lip. 'We've got Fraser there; he's very active, just keeping a watchful eye.' He got up. 'How's the weather in Bavaria?'

'Like here,' Alex said.

'The weather people have informed us that spring's likely to be late.' He sniffed and looked serious. 'So April won't be the cruellest month this year, more likely to be May.'

The crowds in Piccadilly were heavy for a March day. Alex didn't like Piccadilly, too many people pushing and shoving, it was a strain just to make one's way. He didn't like crowds anywhere, they made him uncomfortable and there were times he didn't like London, not a part of it. A few steps from Oxford Street he found the relative quietness of a pub all brassy with dark red walls, and there he decided to call Susan. An unexpected flight back had left him no time to meet her, he would have liked that, she would have brought Jilly and would have loved to see her, them both. Once, when Jilly was still struggling her way out of babyhood, he returned home after three weeks in foreign parts and she could not recognise him. He spoke to her in various voices to turn her small serious face into a smiling one but failed. Susan laughed at his concern and he realised then how he could disappear and little Jilly would go on, grow, and anything she knew of him would fade until that, too, disappeared.

'I've been in the city all day and I'm flying out again in a couple of hours. How's Jilly?' Alex listened. 'I don't know exactly when I'll be back.'

Susan wanted to call Jilly but he said no, he didn't want to hear her, not on the phone. He said he would ring the next day or the day after then replaced the receiver.

He sat down to his beer. Maybe Susan should have had another child; he didn't know why he should think that, maybe without him his family seemed awfully small, mother and daughter like that on the phone. He drank his beer. Alone like that he couldn't see their strength and wondered if it was there at all. Nick White was dead. This thought sprang into his mind with some force although it had never been far away. He then remembered the book Susan had given him and how he discarded it. Alex didn't want to read about how fragile life was, no one needed to read about that. Susan was not frightened, she could be entertained by it, nothing terribly disturbing ever entered her head, she was somewhere else, on another level. But when it came for Nick White he couldn't have known too much about it, and now they want to investigate, to check up on a dead man. He smiled into his beer and the bar erupted in laughter.

29

Jack had not been sleeping well, his career, his life, was winding down. He had begun fearing that Kathleen might leave him, just one day not be there. It was a thought many must have in their lives, he was sure, but when the thought came to him in the night, the many were not considered. In the darkness he could find no place to go. He was yet to be old, but one day in the centre of London he caught a glance of his reflection and that decided for him that he was. Then there was Alex, out there, who could not be touched in the day or in the night. Jilly was a beautiful girl when he last saw her and since he had deliberately avoided contact by avoiding Susan. How would those two lovely people look upon him after Alex? In his nights he had his remorse only for it to disappear in the sunlight.

Jack was sitting alone when Jilly arrived. She had not found it easy to find his choice of meeting place, and, as she searched, her attention to what she wanted to say to him had been taken. Before slipping into her chair she stretched her hand out to him. Jack stood and greeted her with a, 'Jilly, how are you?'

She smiled and said she didn't know that place, wasn't her part of town. She sat in front of him offering a full view of what Alex's daughter had become.

'Are you well?' Jack asked.

'I'm okay,' she said with her eyes leafing through a menu.

'Oh,' said Jack, 'please, what would you like?'

'Green tea.'

'Green?'

'Antioxidant and that,' Jilly explained.

'Ah!' He looked for service and finally found it. 'You sat down without really knowing who you were looking for.'

'I knew,' she replied.

Every time she would look away momentarily, Jack could be caught observing her. He did not want to see Alex but if he could in Jilly he would. 'I haven't seen your mother for a while.'

'Don't you want to?' Jilly asked quickly.

He sat quietly. 'It's difficult. Things to be done and things that are never done.' He looked into her face.

'What things?' Jilly wanted to know.

Jack sipped his coffee and gave a shrug of his shoulders that said, *you know.*

'You want to go to university but you don't have the entry qualifications and time's passing,' Jack said, moving on to the reason for their meeting.

'I don't know,' replied Jilly.

'It might be something I can help you with. Maybe not university, but some kind of college.'

'A college?'

'Yes. Something that would say you were there. That's what you need.'

'Did you go to university, Mr Kirkland?'

'Jack, please call me Jack. Yes, I did.'

'Then I couldn't go to anything less. I'm my father's daughter, and he's an extremely intelligent man with beliefs and principles which you may not hold, but he does.'

'We're not talking about your father, we're talking about you. This is about you. I told your mother I'd do what I could. I can't push your name as a prospective candidate when you've got no results to show.'

'If my father wanted me to go to college, he would have ensured that I got what I was capable of, he wouldn't have pretended that his least efforts were his best.' She looked boldly at Jack and he said he was not her father.

With that remark Jilly sank a little in her seat. No, he was not her father and her father's friend would not have said that. Who was Jack? 'I'm sorry for taking up your time.'

'I don't agree that your father wouldn't encourage you to go where the opportunities are.'

As she stood over him, Jilly said, 'You don't know my father.'

'Jilly, your father's dead.'

'I don't believe that. You were with him that day and here you are sitting here. I don't believe any of it. You can't put your hand on your heart and tell me my father's dead.'

'It's official. There's no mystery. I was a witness.'

'Then where is he?'

'Sit down, please.'

'Where is he? Why can't I visit him?' Her voice was loud then quiet. 'You were with him and you came back without a scratch. That was lucky. I can't believe that. I won't. Don't expect me to believe that my father died out there and somehow he stayed out there.'

'There was a full report.'

'Written by whom?'

'By me. And another by an American.'

'Who?'

'I don't remember. We couldn't get to your father, it was beyond us. He had to be left.'

'That's what you say.'

'Yes, it is.'

Jack thought of that time when it was cold and when he was sure he was on the right side of the fence, the moral and the political one, where rights and wrongs were clear. It was a good time for Jack, good against evil. There was an enormous buzz from being that self-righteous English patriot, which enhanced his appetite for all the good things in life. He had lost a friend in Alex, but, he reasoned, before he was that friend, all the good in him must have been already drained. He was wrong though, and the years since had all but told him that he was never Alex's friend – Jack did not have friends, they were just people to him, no real exchange of love and trust between them. As he sat with Jilly he could remember how he was as a younger man who had allowed to short change himself somehow, and he did wonder in the night what kind of person he was. A wrong turning on a busy road taken years ago might explain the deceit and deception, not for any ideals, but simply for the job of exposing honest, if misguided, directions of others. The smug satisfaction of watching Alex drown in his ideals, watching and dreaming of where he was taking him, was something that even today, face to face with his daughter, he would never surrender. What explanation could there be for that? Another kind of Jack would have felt for Jilly instead of trying to patronise her.

He watched Jilly go when he had planned to leave first. It had not been a long meeting and he was sure he would never see her again. A young woman in his life but there would be, always, Alex. Many days and weeks after that cold night in Germany, when he had settled back in London and after the report, a report that, he was told, had to be watertight, he let Alex go from his mind without triumph and without grief. He heard how hard it must have been for him, being side by side with Alex, knowing and not knowing his mind. He did not know what to make of it. Alex was Alex and they did not know each other well, not really. Alex had been a troubled man for a long time.

'Alex,' he now wanted to say, 'Alex, I'm troubled, too.'

*   *   *

On the bus when the light outside had changed in darker skies, Jilly felt some danger. Who knew why pimples would appear on the skin when there was no obvious sign of a threat. It sometimes would be followed by a tingling sensation that brought some panic to her. But this time she was not alone, Greg sat next to her and he wanted to talk, to tell her how he had begun to miss things. Outside some rain had lightly hit the window, little beads all seemingly eager to be on the other side. They might have had a voice as Jilly watched them run.

'I miss things, too,' Jilly said. 'Sometimes I think I miss things I never had, when all I want are the things I had.' The way she looked at him made her appear vulnerable. 'This is a long road, I suppose.'

'It's as long or as short as you want it to be,' Greg replied.

Visibility had become less in all directions.

30

Northern Bavaria, West Germany, March 1983

The autobahn was choking up: construction work ahead had slowed the traffic to a crawl but it was orderly, no one tried to gain a few metres here or there. A grey cloud hung persistently, a blue sky could not be remembered for days or weeks and yet springtime was not far away. And it looked as if a gradual approach was not for that year, more a sudden burst of arrival.

Toby Cullen had just flown in and the car that met him was now far from the city and had missed the jam on the autobahn by slipping off an exit road a kilometre or two before. With its green military colour and markings the large American car slowly weaved its way round the bends on the tight secondary roads heading towards Camp Braddock. Cullen sat clean in the back of the car, boyish features, short hair but not quite military style, suit dark but not too much, fitting neatly. His coat and briefcase lay at his side and he viewed the road ahead by sitting on the right. The American flag flapped in the wind as the car came out of the trees. The final turn-off had brought them close in to the wood where the dullness of the day was hidden. The car proceeded then through the gate.

Toby Cullen had come on no political orders, his arrival in Germany from his own base camp at Langley was an intelligence one. As American Intelligence found their British counterparts impossibly secretive, it had been decided that American interests were too great to be left to a foreign camp. The British were unlikely to volunteer anything and so Cullen left by domestic carrier under an assumed name. It was never thought that the British could pull Keech out, rescue him from his captives, but the British did and the Americans worried. Although the reports on Keech firmly resting on the desks of the CIA's high command since the early days of January were glowing to the point of making him the US army's finest military man, no one believed it. And no one wished to point it out, certainly not when the politicians pulled their own intelligence people out. General Gregory Keech was allowed to grow in the American people's mind, he was allowed to become bigger than life as the television networks poured over him. They had interviewed a *strong and courageous* Mrs Keech who spoke with a tremble in her voice at how she hoped and prayed he would be released. But no one believed it, not at Langley and they could not believe the British did, and yet with political nudging MI6 had agreed to help and stage a rescue for their general.

Cullen settled into a room that had been set aside. His presence at the camp was not wholly welcome by some; although it was stressed that he be received with the utmost discretion, he could not easily be passed over as someone from IBM. Word got out among the officers and Cullen made the most of it by interviewing them and discovering Keech for himself, the general who was liked and disliked, and another picture emerged from the one the written reports had created.

'Mr Cullen, we know what's goin' on, sure we do. A US Army general was snatched and taken across by the Soviets and they want to do a deal but we don't seem to want to play.'

'I don't know about that, General.'

'Yes you do. You know about it. I've got friends in Washington and you've got yours. Isn't that the way things are?'

'Just a moment, General, let me ask if it is not possible that general Keech was not snatched?'

'You mean you'd believe that drunk at the border post who claims that he tried to stop Keech. That's just a cock and bull story. The guard was drunk, he had been celebrating. It was New Year's Day.'

'All I ask is if it's possible.'

'No, it's not,' the general was upset at Cullen's suggestion. 'General Keech may be many things but he is no traitor. Do you know, Mr Cullen, if a story like that got out here, morale would drop. Do you understand me? We're a very short distance from the East German-Czechoslovakian border, it is of immense importance that the men have good spirits.'

'I understand,' said Cullen. 'It's true that there are some people back home who have doubts about the general. The government, of course, has much praise for him and we understand their motives . . .'

'Mr Cullen, General Keech was taken and I'm ashamed at the efforts your people have put in to get him back.'

'Was Keech unwell?'

'What?'

'Was he unwell?' There was a slight pause. 'General, when you last saw him did he appear unwell?'

'No.'

'Had he been unwell?' A pause. Cullen leaned forward. 'I'm asking, did you, at any time over the past few months, notice a change in him?'

'What are we talking about?' The general stared across at Cullen. 'You've read everything including medical reports.'

'I want your opinion. You're trained to notice men, their morale, their fitness. Was Keech a healthy man in all senses?'

'He was the same as any of us. We're all flawed, Mr Cullen,

even CIA operatives. Gregory Keech was – and I'm not here talking to you to paint a pretty picture, to protect the army – he was a man who had his ups and downs, one day close, the next distant. You should be talking to the medical officer.'

'General Keech never called on him; no stomach ache, no fever.'

'You think that odd?'

'No,' said Cullen, 'I suppose not. But it doesn't prove much.'

'It proves everything to me. Keech was a fine army man and a healthy one. So whatever you're looking for, Cullen, I suggest you try elsewhere.' The general rose from his chair.

'The country wants to believe the Soviets took him; it's understandable, how else would he have made it across?'

'Precisely, Cullen, there is no other way.'

The general walked over to a wall where there were some photographs, large and framed. Two were of a small group of men in uniform. Another was in black and white, of a man looking half serious, half smiling, with a white background suggesting that it had been taken in a studio. Perhaps it was the general many years younger; if it was, Cullen could see no resemblance.

'We're not at war with anyone, not militarily, that is, and that makes a difference,' said Cullen. 'I understand that this affair has had an unsettling effect that reaches all the way back to Washington because, to be honest, no one can be sure if Keech walked or was taken. And that is a fact, General. In war you might close up and get right behind Keech, support your man in other words and handle it yourself. But that's not what we have here. There's no war and no secret, everyone's looking in – the politicians, the networks and ourselves. The story on Keech has got to be the right one; the American public, already gripped by a wave of patriotism, are waiting to welcome him home. If Keech isn't the hero they insist he is, if he's not the father who longs to see his children, then Gregory Keech is a lie, and you know as well as I do that some people suffer more than others in such a situation.'

'Mr Cullen . . .'

'Please, General. As it is, our reports to date haven't been enough to satisfy Washington. We're out of favour these days and they think the army can handle it. They trust what you tell them, they don't expect a backlash, my God they don't. But we wouldn't be surprised, we're uneasy about certain aspects of this affair. Some of your men don't believe the official explanation, they're more open now. In January they wouldn't open their mouths to us. Obeying orders. But now they've been talking and their picture of Keech is that of a man who was hot and cold, soft and harsh, a man you could have sympathy for. General Gregory Keech. Am I describing him fairly? I want to know, General, if he's over there on the other side because that's where he wants to be for whatever reasons. I know the army will suffer; traitors have their effect and we cannot pretend that he's not exactly that. No one would believe he suffered from mental problems, the name of Keech has gone beyond that for anyone to accept mental illness as an explanation.'

'Just a minute. Just a minute.' The general lifted his forearm from the desk and extended a finger. Engine noise from a nearby heavy vehicle climbed to a roar and this was allowed to die away before the general lowered the palm of his hand to the desk top. 'Let me tell you something: Gregory Keech was not a brave man, not, in my opinion, that bit more than his fellow men. He was hot and cold; he would flare up in a wave of anger at something, verbally burst out and exhaust himself, then either forget it happened or praise his victim the next minute for something slight. When one saw him then, in full blow, it was easy to forget who he was and what he was. But no one thought he was unwell; it may have brought me to think for a moment but no longer. This camp is active, there are other things. You'd have to do something quite mad to get much attention here.'

'But you have hundreds of men, doctors, nurses . . .'

'Yes,' the general nodded, 'we have more than you think

and there are times when a soldier blows up. We expect that, it happens in every army. But we're talking about a general, high rank, and at this level you can do and get away with a damn sight more. You can be as mad as hell, I'm sorry to say, and as long as it's not too noticeable, meaning you're not going round slapping your men or worse, things go on as normal. You should know that, Cullen, I can think of a name or two behind big desks in Langley who should be in Rest Homes for the disturbed.' – Cullen gave the expected smile – 'But I wouldn't say they're at risk of setting up home elsewhere, would you?'

'Where does his bravery come in?'

'His lack of it, you mean. Well, you have his file. It says he was honoured in Nam, in a place . . . Jesus, I can't remember.' He gave a little disappointed laugh to himself. 'I thought when I left Nam I would never forget the strategic landmarks I had learned and seen. I thought their names would be clear forever.' He slid open a few drawers of his desk and brought out a pack of cigarettes and holder, fitted a cigarette carefully into it and went on, 'Anyway, Keech was there, where the jungle is a hell-hole and where much hand-to-hand combat took place.' He leaned forward, his voice dropped, 'Do you know hand-to-hand combat, Mr Cullen?' He stared at him, his eyes doubting whether the young man in front could.

'No, I don't,' replied Cullen.

'Well, it's all that you think the Coliseum must have been like all those years ago, when gladiators fought for their survival. It's all that but more. In Viet Nam you struggled for your life in another kind of darkness; the jungle is a dark place and the animal sounds there make it so strange that the dark becomes intense. There can be a sudden silence – the reason only the animals know – and this silence increases the fear and that invisible line between living and dying is crossed over and over again. It's hard to convey to you what it is there, in the steamy air as you desperately try to kill. But you find out more about life and death, and it's damnable because you can't say what. Keech was never equipped for that.'

'But he got his medal there.'

'And that medal lifted him up the ladder. It's an opinion, but if Keech was there he would have stayed there, I don't believe he could have got himself out.'

Cullen frowned.

'Those who returned, and there weren't that many who had to enter that dark zone, are remarkable men. As I said it's difficult, our language is not equipped for things like Nam; feelings and experiences have to remain on the whole untold.'

'Are you saying Keech is not a remarkable man?'

'That's about it.'

'Then how was he awarded his medal?'

'I don't know how he did that and I'm not going to try and find out. The war is over. I don't believe his award abuses anyone. It's not right, but many things were not right there.'

'So Keech is not a brave man, he's a fraud.'

'You see, to do what some would like to believe Keech did on New Year's Day, for me, requires a certain amount of courage. To pack up and go like that . . . I don't think it would be easy.' The cigarette holder was stuck between his lips, the cigarette remained unlit. 'Keech didn't do that.' A low-flying jet screamed overhead and the windows rattled for some seconds. 'Where do you go from here, Mr Cullen?'

Some wind had sneaked in through an open window and fluttered the small flag of America on the general's desk. Cullen looked at it silently.

Hansbach, East Germany, March 1983

Some distance away north by east where the tall forest trees stood so close together, Gregory Keech was again alone. He had been given some books, replacements for the ones he had surprised himself by getting through, writing paper and pen to encourage him to put it all down – all that they thought he still had, his reasons for changing sides. For Keech it was April, perhaps later, he had no idea what the day or month was; a sunny morning was a spring one, he never looked for the tell-tale signs, an early flower or the shift of winter air as he walked in the grounds. If he had looked for something outside, the way the sun would drop behind some hills in the distance perhaps, he would have noticed the icy glow that seemed to surround it, it was bright and colourful but it was cold. If he had recognised the signs he would have known which month he was in.

He was alone with his books and they left him that way for a long time. And when the silence did eventually break, it was he who broke it. It started with his reading a sentence then repeating it, then he would read loudly a word or two from a passage. It started like that, sitting on the bed, his legs crossed and a book open and held firmly before him. Then he began babbling. He would look at the pages of the book and babble about things that could not be found in the text. But before the babbling he would play-act, talk like a lawyer in court would to a defendant, accusing and doubting his credibility. His voice was strong and righteous and each sentence would begin with, 'This man . . .' He would play this role for an hour or so and then be silent for a little while. He was allowed to go on, to let his mind run and then the coffee would arrive or a beer and later he would sleep. When he woke he would ask for Hanna and he would be asked why he wanted her and he would say that he needed her, all of her. But Hanna never came.

Keech's strength was gone – his mental strength – and physically he had stopped exercising in the grounds, doing his sprints, keeping up his body. One day when he returned from his walk he found the yellow walls of his room smeared with cow dung. For the many weeks he had been there his room had become a refuge, a shelter from everything and everyone, and although he had no control over who entered, it was his, a private place where he could rest and where he could go over and over that ultimate decision he had made on that first day of January. The cow dung was to destroy all that, to remove the emotional corner in his now new life, to strip him. With a blanket he scraped and rubbed at the walls, but his nostrils were filled and he could only curse and curse. Through the spy hole in the door Andrei watched him, silent and still. Andrei unlocked the door and entered. Keech did not bother to raise his head; Andrei sat on a wooden chair a little distance from him.

'Do you think we are treating you badly? Do you think we do not care about you?' Andrei paused. 'Do you think we are so filled with hatred that we don't care about your agony? If the positions were reversed, General, and I were you in America, would I not suffer?' He pulled slightly forward. 'What would they do to me, can you tell me that, General?'

Keech had pushed his bed against the wall and there he sat with the stained blanket across him. 'They'd give you a big house and a hundred thousand dollars.'

'Yes, I know that. If I were good. But if they thought I was neither night nor day, if they couldn't be sure, what would they do?'

Keech lifted his head. 'They would shoot you fucker and bury you.'

Andrei smiled and nodded, 'American humour. It's not quite unlike Russian. We take it a stage further and lay flowers on the grave. The punch line lies there.'

Andrei actually laughed, a real laugh which didn't affect Keech that way. The Russian stretched his face with his hand wearily, in a way that said, 'I like you General Keech and I do want to help, so let us try and get it right this time, let us get out of here.'

'I have nothing new to say, General. I only wish I had.' He paused, his eyes waiting for a reaction. 'I have a wife waiting in Moscow. I would like to see her. A leg, a thigh, they are important to a man. Of course it varies with men. What do you miss, General?'

Keech thought of a leg, Hanna's legs, her thighs, her hands.

'Would you like a woman tonight? I can do that for you.'

'Hanna?'

'Yes, Hanna, if you want. I can give you Hanna every night. A very enjoyable woman.'

'She's been with you?'

Andrei laughed in a controlled way. 'Hanna was not born the day you arrived, she had not been kept pure for a runaway American general. You're not in love with her?' He waited. 'No, I don't think so. You have other things on your mind and I would imagine feelings of love are very far away.' He paused. 'No, things of the heart and of the flesh are for later, it is with now we concern ourselves. We can reach no agreement about you and this to a Russian mind is unbearable. Do you understand what I'm saying?'

Keech sighed, 'Yes. Yes.'

'But we have the capacity to think about you for years, to work you out like a game. Where there is doubt, General, there is a flaw, and where there is a flaw there is danger. You, at this moment, represent a danger.'

Keech was quiet, he had heard it before in many ways, there was nothing to say, no denials, no words. He had got used to the blanket and he had lifted his feet from the floor and crossed them on the bed. He wasn't sure what Andrei meant; although he had heard him, he hadn't thought of what he might be saying, his mind was taken up with images elsewhere: of a young boy in short trousers running away from something, a rainy night where the beating rain was like a whiplash a thousand times at once, and the many voices of Radio America building up their own images they so excitedly talked about.

'Are you thinking of home, General?'

In a dull voice Keech asked, 'What are they saying about me?'

'Nothing now. At first, of course, there was a flurry of interest, they made you the victim of KGB abduction. We were supposed to have taken you as you celebrated goodwill to all men. But then the voices on the *murky affair*, as your newspaper people called it, fell silent.' He paused. 'Your death was announced only a few days ago.'

'I'm dead?'

'They've killed you. They don't want to know.' Andrei watched Keech with the blanket across him, his hands out of sight underneath it.

'How did I die?'

'Oh, suspected heart seizure. Something quick and without warning.'

'That is a lie.' He woke up and became alert, tossed the blanket to the side and stood. 'It's a lie.' He gave a short laugh, 'Holy Mother.' He laughed again. 'Do you know something: I'm living in this world and there's not one bastard I can trust. Not here with you and not where I've come from.'

'Trust, General? We barely know each other, we're from different camps. Trust belongs to friends and we can hardly be called that, not in this atmosphere, not here.' – Keech had sat back down – 'All your life has been in America, it was there you discovered trust and distrust, over there we had no influence. You should not rage at us, General, we are not your mother.'

Keech sat at the edge of the bed, his eyes closed, holding a pincer grip with finger and thumb high up on his nose. 'Don't tell me it's not the same, your Russia's not the same, don't tell me that.' He rubbed at his face. 'When I was young, very young, I got to know about lies and how people used them, and how they laughed them off when they were found out. I used to look into their faces to see the lie and it was always the faces of men. I thought it was something like swear words, only a man would say them. And that is what I thought for a long time, that men lied and women did not. When I discovered I was wrong, totally wrong, that everybody lies, West and East, trust doesn't exist . . .'

'You were shaken,' said Andrei, 'down to your army boots.'

Keech ran his fingers through his hair which had never been allowed to grow so long for over twenty years. 'Get out!' he shouted.

'Not yet, General, I'm not finished.'

Keech sprang at him and pulled Andrei from his chair, half dragging him across the floor before releasing him with a thud. He stood over him and in a sudden burst of anger kicked hard at his body. Andrei squirmed on the floor to get away but Keech kept at him with a foot. The blows directed at Andrei's body had brought no sound from him, he just kept moving away, crawling over the wooden floor. When he reached the wall Keech pulled him up to a sitting position and slapped him twice; the sting from the second one brought a red patch from cheek to chin.

'Am I dead? AM I DEAD?' Keech had lowered his face to only a few inches of Andrei's. He was breathing hard and ready to go again, to lash out and break the Russian on the floor.

'Your body was flown to an air base,' said Andrei, 'the American flag was draped over the coffin.' – this gripped Keech – 'Your family were waiting.'

'Family?' Keech said quietly.

'It took up many minutes on the national news.' Andrei stopped, his eyes firmly on Keech. The skin around his mouth had broken at one side and the blood was running, following a course before gathering and dripping onto his jacket. 'Let me go, General. Let me get up.'

Keech stood back and Andrei picked himself up.

'You think you have physical power over me because you are a military man and I am not. You are supreme, that is what you think, no?' he smiled. 'Well, General, there are many ways of bringing agony to a man. I will not have you beaten, I don't want that. For your mind I know what pain is required.'

Keech made for him, jabbing his finger in front of his face.

'You are a man without country,' said Andrei, 'you have nowhere to go. I was the only one here who could have helped you.'

Keech turned from him not interested. The door of his room closed loudly and Andrei walked down the corridor with its hard floor.

Keech switched off the light and crossed to the window. The darkness was not total, there was a half moon and the light picked out the forms of trees and bushes, the shape of a house and its television aerial. There was a light about two or three kilometres away moving through the night – car headlights. He followed it until it disappeared.

There was a road that led to Hansbach but Keech had not known of it. Keech was not there to escape and so he never looked for anything, he just waited for Moscow to eventually welcome him. But now in the darkness of his room he stood looking out into the night, trying to work out where the road was. He waited some time before another vehicle came along and in the moonlight he could make out it was a truck. The lights from it excited him as if they had shone through his loneliness and ended it there on the spot. He pushed his face to the window and held on to the truck before it too disappeared. It was a main road, he thought, carrying freight from town to town, city to city, but that was all he knew.

He then tried to find star patterns in the sky, but the Great Bear and the Seven Sisters could not reveal his position. He had always been amazed by the stars; it was something that, although it completely mystified him, also gave him hope. When hardly anything is known, he thought, there has to be hope. It was not a hobby with him, he had no telescope back home, bought none of the science magazines, he had no interest in that. Where his interest lay was looking up anytime he found a clear sky, there he would stop and be caught at what he could see and what it did to him. What it did to Gregory Keech was to make him think of his mother: as he lifted his eyes the loss of his mother would creep into him, and the more he looked the stronger her presence would be. He never knew why the stars in the black sky should bring his mother to him, they just did, every time.

It was two hours later and Keech was asleep when the door opened. A man walked in and laid a mattress on the floor. Another man entered and gently lifted Keech's wrist and handcuffed it to the bed. A woman stood in the doorway then the light was switched on. Keech wakened and saw Hanna's face. 'Hanna!' he called. But she just stood. The two men removed her gown and dropped her hair which had been tied. She opened her mouth to receive one as the other removed his clothes.

Keech watched silently, unable at that moment to do or say anything. Her body was being caressed by both as they fell on their knees on the mattress. He began to bawl: 'Hanna! Hanna! Don't Hanna! Please!' But the lovemaking continued. He sat tied two metres away, he didn't want to see but he had to, had to listen to their bodies become sticky. And while Hanna brought each to his peak, Keech wept. But the agony was to go on and the men found new positions for Hanna who complied with all their wishes. His sobbing could be heard along the corridor. 'Hanna, Hanna,' he called more to himself than to her.

The door then opened and Andrei stood. Keech had his head buried in his hand. The two men left, Hanna stayed naked on the mattress.

'As I said, General, there are many ways to bring a man agony. But you will recover. Hanna had two men before your eyes, but what does it matter, tell me, why does it hurt?'

He looked down at Hanna. 'Put your clothes on and stay with the general.'

'Get her out of here,' shouted Keech.

'Do you hate her now, General? Oh come, military men have

different attitudes to women and love, they have no hold on either nor do they want any.'

He took two steps forward and removed the handcuff from Keech's wrist and left him still on the bed, while Hanna, dressed as she was, waited. 'Can I sit?' she asked. 'I would like to sit.'

Keech did not reply and Hanna edged herself onto a chair which had been pushed into a corner. Between them was an unease, an anger that a quarrel usually creates in a home, when silent sentences tumble out and every word is thought of before it is released aloud.

Keech kept his face hidden. 'Did you . . .' He stopped.

She looked. 'Did I what?' She paused. 'What was your question?'

'I've got no question, there's nothing to ask.'

'I heard you,' she said, 'I did hear you . . . *Hanna, Hanna.*' She wrapped her arms around her. 'Andrei has his job to do, to get what he wants from you. I'm a tool to him. Women are tools to men, no? It is so here – here in the East and in your West.'

Keech gave her no response and she got up.

'You sit like a wounded man, General. Like a wronged man.' A tear gathered in her eye and began its slow descent, quickening all the time. 'But you cannot be wounded, there is no reason. I have all the reasons.' She wiped away another tear just as it fell. 'I have all the reasons.' Her voice had lost its strength as she leaned on the wall beside the door. 'I'm leaving.'

'It's better that you don't,' said Keech. He raised his head. 'Andrei doesn't want to see you now. Stay, it will be better for you.'

Hanna covered her mouth with her hand and stared at him.

'Stay away from him.'

She shook her head while keeping her hand over her mouth.

'What is it?' Keech asked. She then placed a finger over his lips. 'Microphone? Is that what you mean? I found it a long time ago, and they've never replaced it.'

'Are you sure?' Her relief brought her question quickly.

'Sure,' he said confidently.

'It is dangerous,' she said, 'they put sometimes two in a room and let one be found.'

'There is nothing. The room's almost empty as it is.'

Hanna began looking, at the ceiling, at the walls. 'I'm frightened.'

'Just stay and you'll be alright.' Keech's anger had gone, his voice was comforting.

She sat on the mattress with her knees up and her arms around them. 'Andrei wants to show you his power.'

'He has a sick mind.'

'Has he?' she asked with a little surprise.

'Well, wouldn't you consider being forced to have sex with two men in front of me sick?'

Hanna dropped her head. 'No, it is not sick, General. Would you not like two women?' – Keech didn't reply – 'Women have such fantasies – to have more than one man.'

'Okay, okay. But in front of me?'

'Andrei wanted you to see me with them, he knew your mind – puritanical American. He knew your response and he was right. In another situation men like to watch their women with others.'

'For Christ sake, Hanna, are you saying . . .'

She placed a hand over her mouth, footsteps were approaching. The door opened and Andrei stood looking at them both.

'Gather your things up, General, you're being moved.'

'Where?'

'Downstairs. Another room. Larger.' He turned to Hanna. 'You too, get your things and come downstairs.'

Keech took only moments to bundle his belongings into his arms while Andrei waited, stiff and aloof like a top class hotel manager. Hanna had begun to shiver slightly as she walked along the corridor in her partial dress. Midway down the cold staircase Andrei stopped and turned to them.

'This move is not for the view you will see of the garden, it is not to allow you more space, which you will have,' he smirked, 'it is not for humanitarian reasons. Nothing like that. This will be a short stay, and if at the end of it we are still unsatisfied that you, General Keech, are indeed a defector . . . if that is the decision we finally come to, then it will be unfortunate. I'm sure you understand me, General, but I will be very clear. You will then be charged with espionage and if found guilty you will be executed.'

Keech stood motionless, and as Andrei looked up at him, he was somewhere else, far from the big house, far from everything.

'Let us hope that will not be the case,' the Russian said, as he continued down bringing out some keys from his pocket, choosing a large one from the bunch with his fingers while letting the others drop on the ring.

As he unlocked the door Keech noticed there was no spy-hole, no obvious sign of a watcher being employed to visually guard him. On entry the room was warm and pleasantly bright, with a large bed with a heavy wooden bed-head against the wall. There were two rugs on the floor and a mirror hung on a white painted wall. The two windows were naked.

'Through that door,' Andrei pointed, 'there are toilet facilities.'

'Why?' asked Keech.

'You mean the change?' said Andrei. 'We want to welcome you, General. We want you to get settled in your new home in Moscow, but we cannot have any doubts. Here we hope to dispel the doubts we have, in an atmosphere of friendliness.'

'And Hanna?'

'Hanna is your companion. Settle in, General, we'll talk tomorrow.' He closed the door behind him and Keech dumped his belongings on the bed.

31

Tom Fraser had died a little since reaching the age to take on a new life; it had always been a worry that all would come to an end, one way or another. There were many lives a person could lead, and then one day there would be none. He would envy those people who never looked back, things back there were never remembered as they really were, he had heard so many times. But the harder he tried not to live in the past, the more he was there. Places to think of and faces to mourn. Some days it was too much and instead of embracing more the unknown years ahead, he argued and fought with them, wanted to destroy them.

With all those overhead clouds in his life, the call he received one morning came when his blood pressure was climbing and Helen, his wife, crying. The caller was enquiring, was he enjoying his retirement? Was he getting out, foreign travel and that? Such friendliness was theraputic and Fraser could feel his tension ease when he was asked to come over and help put fresh colour onto a fading picture. He was to recall all over again where he was when death was intruding in his life and he was to remember the American that Jack had put in his report after the Keech mission was over. To Fraser, Cullen never had a face, he was, as Jack described him, the typically brash Yank who was an unnecessary

208

witness to a sad evening. But Fraser wanted to know more and through a name in Washington, another he had never met but had spoken with on occasions, a link to the American mind, he thought, could be had. The picture he got through this contact was that Cullen knew it all, just when Jack would have denied being there, if he could, this Cullen man was clearly painting it as he saw it. But Cullen wasn't that man anymore, he had reached higher ground in his career, had shed his boyhood determination and, it would seem, settled back for the ride through middle age.

Fraser was to know little more except that he and Cullen had little to show for all their early eagerness to fight off the enemy; every perceived victory was nothing more than a blip in their existence, every perceived danger was an excuse for any action that gave them some worth. Fraser had lived this way too long – too late now to turn his life around. Cullen, too, knew this road and he was destined for nothing more. Loneliness was part of him and he did not know it, he felt it but could not recognise it until Margaret moved more and more into his thoughts, so much so, he knew it was time to make a turn. Tom Fraser did not believe in men making turns, you were what you were, and that was that. He was too unaware of things, too content to live in his self-created fog and make his judgements as he saw fit. Being in America with his history an ocean away would be like money in the bank, he would be free to meet Cullen, to shake his hand and know his number. He would be back and life would be purposeful again, it was all he ever wanted. But the Americans knew about Fraser's losses, they thought they knew his number, too; no one was impressed and in their way they loved it, they loved to see the smugness wiped away from their counterparts on the other side of the water. Fraser felt a hard bump as his flight touched down, gathered his hand luggage then waited in line in the aisle before stepping off the aircraft and placing a foot on American soil.

*   *   *

Placing a foot on American soil could be a dream for many, just breathing in the country that was seen as the most hopeful and positive place on earth. Those people on distant shores had their hearts filled with the Stars and Stripes and tales of freedom and security. No one really knew or wanted to know of any other picture, so strong was the feel-good image of the US. But for some Americans, this America seemed to pass them by; that foreign view was simply that – foreign. Brought up and living on the edges, adrift from the mainstream in all but every state, they knew as firmly as anyone who they were and where they stood; but it did not matter, their lives somehow were less recognized and all that good which was seen to be their country passed them by. Still they dreamt their dreams, and the years passed by and a new generation picked up the thread of hope that once was as thick as rope, and life moved on.

Young Greg Keech had dreams – he had dreamt of criss-crossing his America time and again, it was a sort of exercise; others may dream of hiking for days and do it, scale a mountain peak and do it, but Greg dreamt of pacing the land, back and forth, because America was all he had and was ever likely to have and he still had to do it. In his mother's house in a low-income neighbourhood of town, the family status gone, he too often sat at home. Low-income areas had dimmer street lights as if those in charge of street lighting thought that the less money people had, the less vision was another price to pay. Greg sat in one room while his mother moved about the kitchen. Over the years he had watched her more, every day, her movements, her features. She had become fat and he did not know why she had. There used to be a photograph of her, Mum and Dad on their wedding day; they did look happy: he was fit and strong looking, and she almost as tall as he with a figure to admire. What had happened? She never spoke to him about growing up, about being a man. The thought never seemed to enter her head. She shouted a lot and her language deteriorated after the time the family shot to fame, when the cameras were all recording their lives. His mother was excited then. She did think – he was sure because he had heard her say, once on the front pages, always there – that all the attention was the beginning of a wonderful new life. Until the day came when everything died and she realised her life was over. The lights in her life were fading day by day and he, her son, gave her nothing. She was not thankful that he was in her life. He wondered if she saw him at all. Her daughters had no voice simply because they had nothing to say. Girls can be like that, sucked into a life shaped by those who are nothing themselves; within a home, a school, a community. Like diamonds considered as stone. Greg, too, could have gone that way, been sucked into oblivion, but he was saved: he had his anger and his hormones which fed it. While his sisters were quiet, Greg had his dreams.

At home in this way with the dimness of life like the street, his mother took a call at the door, and called Greg. Before he had taken a step, two police officers entered his room. He was told to sit down, which he did reluctantly.

As one kept an eye on him, the other moved around. 'We're not here to ask you anything, we're here to tell you what we know.'

Greg did not like sitting while they stood talking down, so he got up.

'Sit down,' shouted one.

Greg moved away to another part of the room.

'You little shit!' he was called as some steps and an arm reached out at him. 'You're goin' to jail, son of Keech.'

His mother was back in the kitchen, and she remained there when the officers left with Greg. He could be held for as long as they wanted to; when the street lights were dim, he had now learned, abuse could be found anywhere in America. Their charges were bogus, he had committed no crime. He was at home that very night, that very hour when a thief made his mark.

His mother knew it and, if she had shown any interest in her son's plight, she could have said so. Greg sat in the station room. The men on view there, officers, their hands on the telephone, holding a night-stick, pulling at their fat faces, lifting their crotch, whoever these people were Greg wanted to spit at them. They spoke about his life to date, where he had been and what he had done.

'Mmm, you're a desperate man,' an officer said, while putting the weight of his hand on the telephone receiver, as if he expected a call he didn't want, a call he could prevent from getting through. 'I'm not just saying that, it's here.' Greg looked at the file he was holding where his life's history was supposed to be all recorded. 'It says you're a cold, unemotional young guy,' the officer seemed pleased to read that. 'Is that true?' – Greg said nothing – 'It says you've got potential to go way off track, to become another of the good ol' US of A's shit class. Wow! I'm honoured. A man of potential.' He was inflicting wounds on young Greg who disguised every blow. 'You can get out of here. Go!'

Greg raised himself from his chair and made for the door where he turned and shouted that if they were serious about the shits of America all they had to do was look in any mirror. 'I'm Gregory Keech and my father's a great man.' He was surprised he had been given time to speak before he was grabbed. As his body was squeezed, his legs gave way, and he was bundled out to a nearby cell. After a dull night he returned home with his nerves jangling. A step inside, no one wanted to know, not his mother and not his sisters. The care he was looking for was absent, love had flown and his silence was all he had. Whatever had happened to his family he decided he would never know. He would never look for an explanation and although their blood was his blood, they were not the same. Maybe he could live with this cool approach in the years ahead but as a young man, who was sometimes a boy, he had come to know strong feelings of hate and rage as they coursed their way through him.

'False, false!' he wanted to shout. 'It's all false, Mom. I should have a lawyer. Why can't I?'

'If you've got the money,' a sister said.

'Will you come with me?' he asked his mother but looked at all three.

'Where?'

'To a lawyer.'

'I'm not goin' anywhere near those people,' his mother said determinedly. 'Even if they'd killed you, I wouldn't go near them.'

Greg turned away and found an empty place where, as a boy sometimes and more recently, he would break down, then muffle his sounds even though he wanted someone to hear.

When Greg called on a man, his legal representative he thought, someone who said he would see what he could do, it was *magic*, *just magic* he said aloud. But there was no magic because Greg was too weak, too small, too vulnerable to make any headway. 'Forget it, for God's sake. You won't hear from him again,' his mother said with some anger, and a sister with a laugh inside her agreed.

Greg walked out into the street to the roar of a bike. The rumble of noise came closer and closer, before it passed him and disappeared into the distance. He had a friend who owned a bike, a big masculine one painted red and black. It was awesomely aggressive, and it was this aggressiveness that was the killer, his friend had enthused, that was why he loved it. He could not wear this raw attitude the way the bike did. It was magic. He had thought of painting himself red and black and being at one with the bike. What did he think? Greg was asked. Greg hoped he would hear that roar again as he walked on remembering his friend. The bike was gone, lost somehow, and so was he. He had last seen him standing on a street, with the same old jeans, the same cool suede jacket and his smile which had attracted Greg to him at a time when he and his family were sinking, in their new home, their new town.

It was a time when his mother had become insecure and all her new pills were somehow to combat that. Greg didn't know what they were or how they could do that, but his mother always had a smile when she was close to them. He believed for awhile that those pills were just for his mother, he never imagined that others, in their hundreds, thousands, also had a similar relationship with them. He did not know then that his friend had started on pills long before. It was sweet honky booze, Greg had it explained to him, except there was no sensation on the tongue, it was all up here, his friend had said slapping the side of his head. It was just booze, nothin' special. *Like the song, man, years of booze helps you choose – your destination. It's okay with beer, with coke, milk, and sometimes a double dose; it depends what you want.*

There was a cloud of terrible sadness over the area where Greg now lived; the area had a name but he had refused to recognise it, what was the point, he couldn't see a point to anything. This sadness, Greg thought at first, was only over him, but when he understood the pills and their purpose, he knew it was over everywhere like condensation on everyone's window. But somehow the roar of the bike could make life seem carefree; sitting astride Greg would tour the town and the countryside, just moving was a pleasure, and about five miles out of town there was a clearing where everyone would meet on Fridays. It was always at night and sometimes there would be a brilliant black sky with stars sparkling like crystal. The hum of happiness was in the small crowd, maybe because, from there, their lives could fall to dangerous depths. It was a family to Greg: love could be felt in that clearing and it was so good. There were many times like that, he would meet and be happy, and sometimes on the bike when his feelings would be overwhelming, he would have wanted to wrap his arms tightly around his friend, a moment when his love urged him, but he did not; resisting, he held to the seat bar behind him while the bike travelled on.

Then there was the call to say that his friend was dead. It seemed a simple call that required a simple acknowledgement. The caller did not know much and didn't try to imagine. Neither had much to say and Greg was left holding the phone with a, *see you*. In small town America there are not too many places to run to when a person is struggling every day, any bump or collision life can serve up can be felt as a wave of momentous despair, and Greg, who had reached sixteen that summer, wanted only the clearing. In the drizzle that had been falling all day, he walked out of his neighbourhood and arrived through the rain and his tears at the place where everyone came to talk and touch and be as one. But the clearing was empty and darker with the sky covered over, there was no laughter and his friend, his friend was dead. He was walking round and round smiling at memories and crying at reality, sniffing back his feelings then letting them fall. It must have been an hour or so when a roar was heard maybe a mile away – a bike with its light bobbing over the uneven road was heading his way. The sight the rider got of Greg standing so forlorn might have been heartbreaking if Greg had not welcomed him with a huge smile and whoops of joy. 'Man, you're bizarre.'

The engine of the bike ticked over as the rider remained astride.

'Who else is comin'?' Greg asked. 'How many?' He looked into his face and waited to be told that everyone was coming, that he was the first but soon everyone would be there and laughing. The bike engine was shut down and its light shone like a torch with rain drops darting through its beam. 'Have you seen . . .' Greg wanted to say his friend's name but it never came.

'We've all heard,' said the rider.

Greg shivered and said, 'Didn't know where to go.' He held himself tightly.

'Let's go,' the rider suggested.

'Was he killed?'

'You mean, Danny?'

'Danny,' Greg repeated.

'He killed himself,' the rider replied.

Greg thought about that and gave a smile. 'What a guy,' he said with admiration.

'Let's go.' The rider started up the bike. Touching the machine and mounting it, Greg whispered, *Danny, Danny*, and as the bike raced back toward town, he put his arms around the rider and squeezed out all his heartbreak.

*　　*　　*

Toby Cullen had found a bed in something between a motel and a hotel, in a room loudly decorated. All that was needed was there: big bed, big TV, big breakfast, big big big was all that was on offer. A few days earlier, on the east coast, before he was called to re-fresh his memory of the Keech affair, he had received some junk mail, one of which contained a question from an organisation that wished to put no hands on its reader but simply to ask that whatever he or she had done yesterday, whether out of love or with hate, passiveness or violence, was it not time to come out and show themselves? Wherever you are going, it read, we are all going too. There was more but Cullen let it go as his life urged another tempo. Sitting on the big bed he had time to think of how he would be if and when he came face to face with the children of that affair, when one of their fathers had lost his bearings while he pretended not to see. When he had paced up and down on that road that was almost frozen, but he never felt it because the coming success of his mission was warming him. On that road before anyone else showed up, and afterwards when a wintry sun appeared, he was gone. He liked that then, a professional work done well. All the shades of truth and lie wonderfully interwoven, a tapestry of deceit, that was the beauty of it. Oh, it was fun. He was young and America could be bad.

There were enemies around to become involved with. Ah, those were good days. But Cullen, a few days on the west coast, could see where he had been; the story unfolded again and not too far a distance from his room, some miles west, in a Californian coastal town, living in a typical timber-framed house was a man he was to call on.

Nikolai Levchenko had his life there, a pensioner now. He had arrived after the Keech affair with his wife Tania and a strange looking little dog. It was a kind of reward for his cooperation and he began his new life eagerly. But before a year had passed his wife stopped living and died. His dog disappeared, returned home, he preferred to think. Levchenko had now many things, but what to do with his loneliness was a puzzle he had never prepared for. He was not as free as he imagined he would be in America. All his deception to help the West had not turned out at all well. He would still drive the short journey to Tania when the world was felt farther away and there he took some rest on the grass and brought her to life. He enjoyed dusk there when the sea and light seemed to dance together, he could be tranquil and maybe Tania was, too. His son and daughter on the other side of the world never wrote to him and never would, he knew. Too many shadows in their father's life, too many secrets from them, and, with their mother lying in America, they could not forgive him. Levchenko had made a mistake, and it was in America that he was paying for it. On the grassy slopes standing with his hand on Tania's stone, he could see all his mistakes.

32

Paris, March 1983

Pierre Halin smoked furiously as he waited. The little art shop behind him had just turned on its lights and the paintings displayed in its only window caught his eye. Nervous as he was, the originality he faced calmed him noticeably. Paris was full of art and everybody liked to think that what they took away with them was the work of a yet undiscovered genius in a bed-sit high above the city with flower boxes on the window sill. Halin had tried his hand at forming art more than once, he thought he might be good and he enjoyed the image it created. But his pictures were just pictures, pleasant but empty and few sold. This was when he was ten years younger and everything was still possible, before dressing up in suits and plain shirts, before stepping out to sell the data systems of Paristec. There was a painting of a clown in all its colours, looking out with a hesitant smile. Its legs were slightly bent and its arms were in a juggling position, but there was nothing in the air. For a moment Halin forgot his troubles.

'Monsieur Halin?'

He spun round, his thick black eyebrows shielded the jump in his eyes.

'You will remember,' said Fraser, 'that's all you need to do for now. Just identify who you are talking to.' He looked in at the window. 'Not my kind of thing that. I've been watching you for twenty minutes and you appear to be quite alone.'

A large car came up on the narrow street, squeezing them onto the narrowest of pavements until it passed.

'Let's go, Mr Halin.'

They walked round the first corner and then another some distance farther up until they reached a little smoky bar. The small tables were being wiped as they entered. A girl was stretching herself between two customers to reach a difficult part with her cloth; she exposed herself like that to the men, which gave them serious thoughts about how she must be under her tight jeans. Fraser and Halin brushed past and decided on a table.

'It's not the best part of Paris,' said Fraser, 'but it should do.' He took out a packet of cigarettes and offered one to Halin, who accepted. 'Well, Mr Halin, how's business these days?'

'I'm going over tomorrow,' replied Halin.

'Are you now. We're on the move at last.' Fraser looked at the thick cigarette he held. 'The early morning plane?'

'Yes. The same as last time.' Halin drew deeply on the cigarette then released the smoke quickly.

Fraser sat opposite flicking what little ash he had collected into a large glass tray. 'I'll get a couple of beers,' he said, getting up.

If sincerity could be placed as a physical mark on a person, this mark was totally absent in Pierre Halin. He was a person Tom Fraser had decided upon back in London when the Frenchman shook but did not fall and a deal was made after the white walls began to rattle him and Alex spelt out that he either changed his loyalties or returned to a welcome in Paris with the French police. If Fraser was not buying a beer for a sincere man he certainly was for a frightened one.

'Am I getting any money?' asked Halin.

'Do you need money?' replied Fraser.

'This is dangerous, you know it is, but you don't care about me.'

'Mr Halin, do you want to run away? Is that what you want?'

'I'm doing something here for nothing. Giving you information for nothing.' He raised his glass and took a mouthful. 'You'll get me killed.' He became agitated and turned frequently in his seat, his body never resting. 'I'm going to stop,' he said.

'How much money do you need?' asked Fraser. 'Tell me?'

'A lot,' said Halin. 'A lot, a lot.'

Fraser leaned toward him. 'Look, Pierre, let's see if we can have a good view of this picture together. You work for the number two KGB in France. He wants you to go over to London and pick something up. What does that tell you?' A pause. 'Never mind. Then you return with it, collect your money and wait till the next time. Right?' – Halin listened – 'Now there's been a change. Before you return this time we have a look at what you've collected, that's all.' Fraser finished his beer and went on, 'Dangerous? It would be if our little secret got out, but there's no reason why it should.' – Halin shook his head in disagreement. – 'We will pay you, but there could never be the kind of money you're thinking of. Your position doesn't merit that. Do you want another beer?' He turned, '*Deux bières, s'il vous plaît.*'

'It won't always be like this,' said Halin, 'sitting here drinking beer. It'll get worse. When you find out what it is I'm collecting and who's giving it away then you'll stop and I'll be left.'

'Oh, come on, Halin, you're as quick-witted as the rest of us. You had a choice and you decided to help. So let's not look at how you see the future. If your help leads to solving our problem then we'll see what we can do. I can't say more.'

'They know me,' said Halin, 'they know what I have. You don't understand. This is new for me; before there was never any danger. I've been picked to do a job I should not be doing. I don't want to do it – for them, for you. They know what I have.'

'You mean a wife and child.'

'You know what they could do?' He looked at Fraser who

gave nothing away. 'If you have a problem why should I risk my family to help you solve it? Why?'

'Because, Mr Halin, our problem can't wait, we need to find the answer as quickly as we can. We don't want to put anybody in a position of danger and we don't accept that that is what we've done with you. Your choice of employer from the very beginning was an unwise one, wasn't it? The moment you signed on with them your life could never be as safe as it once was. Didn't Fisher's death tell you that?'

'They didn't kill him,' blurted out Halin.

'They told you that?'

'Yes. It was someone else, they said.'

'It's not like the Russians to confirm or deny.'

'Fisher was good,' said Halin, 'they had no reason. I thought about it and I realised it must be true.'

'You realised?' said Fraser.

'If they had planned to kill Fisher they would have planned to replace him, no? They replaced him with me. Don't you see there was no plan, and so no kill. Someone else killed Fisher.'

'Now, who could that have been?' asked Fraser, moving Halin on.

'I don't know.' He quickly got up. '*Excusez-moi* . . . I must go to the toilet.'

Fraser watched him stop at the bar counter then disappear through a small entrance to the back. There was a lot of activity at the bar, with cups and glasses lined along the counter-top. Lots of joking going on, lots of happy faces exchanging the soft sounds of the French language.

The toilet was a single cubicle with a flickering overhead light, a closet within a closet. Just in from the toilet door was a metal bucket with mop and cleaning fluids; the complete floor area had the glistening look of wetness. It took time for Halin to empty his intake of two beers and his relief did not encourage him to hurry. As he finished and covered himself, he pulled at the dangling chain that hung from the cistern high on the wall, then opened the cubicle door. It was the click that brought his eyes up, right up to the barrel of the gun. He stared at it, at first unsure what it was. Then with ice-cold clarity the object was identified. An English joke, he thought, but there was nothing English about the gun or the man with his grip on it. Halin stuck to the floor unable to say anything. The only sound was the cistern filling up.

'Turn,' said the man. The voice was quiet. Halin was pushed round. 'Sit,' he was ordered. Halin lowered himself to the seat and faced the wall. The chain dangled on his left as he sat astride, and when the last drop of water had fallen into the tank Halin shuddered, his breathing heavy and tight. 'Pull it,' said the man urgently. But before Halin could comprehend the man's final demand of him, the chain was pulled violently and the water ran, roaring down from the tank. The gun cracked then and the bullet tore open the back of Halin's head. Halin had asked for nothing, no pleas and no mercy. The laughter from the bar filtered through but there was no one there to hear it.

It was a few minutes later when Fraser rose; Halin, he thought, had slipped away or had an intestinal problem. He made his way through and stood by the bucket and mop. The cubicle door was closed. 'Halin,' he called. He pushed the door wide and peered into the semi-darkness. Halin's face was smashed against the cistern pipes that ran down to the bowl, his forehead and nose split. Fraser turned him a little, the nervous light catching his pale skin; it was as if every bone in his body had crumpled, softened and bent. He placed the Frenchman's head back in its position, but his body had sunk further and his face slowly slid down the pipe raising a cheek abnormally high, which in the unsteady light gave an even more grotesque picture. Fraser left.

The girl in tight jeans was busy serving, she had become hot, all the bodies in the small bar, drinking and laughing, had made her brow glisten. She had removed her pullover when Fraser passed, her arms were bare: slim arms, beatifully shaped. Fraser glanced.

She called after him, '*Aurevoir, Monsieur.*' He wanted to reply but nothing came. 'Goodbye,' she said haltingly, before he felt the air on his face. It was always the same, when you had a worry, something climbing all over you, everyone else appeared to be free. The streams of people Fraser found in the street were so happy looking, their voices, their faces. He found this mixture of Halin's death and Parisian laughter explosive and made to get away.

Early the next morning he flew out of Charles de Gaulle for London. The flight passengers were informed of conditions outside the craft; the sea below was approaching storm force, but for Tom Fraser conditions had deteriorated long before and they could plummet even further.

London, March 1983

'Pierre Halin was all we had, there was nothing else.' The voice was soft. 'Our position now is extremely difficult. Without this Halin we are brought to an abrupt halt. You do see that, don't you?' said Sinclair.

'Yes, I do,' replied Fraser.

'For Christ sake, how did it happen?' Sinclair was like that, far from anger in one sentence then crashing into it in the next.

'I don't know. I arranged to meet him. I let him wait for twenty minutes. I could see no sign of anyone who could have been following him. We went to a bar of my choosing, and we talked. After two beers he left the table and didn't come back. I heard nothing.'

'Then you found him – shot?'

'Yes.'

'Alright, what did he have on him?'

Fraser lifted Halin's slim-lined briefcase, whose contents were all Paristec data sheets. He then produced a wallet with PH inscribed on it. It was exactly what he would have expected of Halin, this kind of personal touch.

'Money?' asked Sinclair.

'It's all in the wallet,' said Fraser and passed it across.

Sinclair opened up the compartments then thumbed through the impressive pile of notes. 'No coins?'

'Not a centime,' said Fraser with the tone of a man whose honesty was being questioned.

'Didn't mean that. I suppose you've cast your eyes thoroughly over this.' He held between his fingers a notebook of such slimness that it fitted into one of the compartments without bulging.

'I've gone through it, yes.'

'Discover anything?'

'Not really. Mostly work stuff. But somewhere he's written a reminder.' He took the book from Sinclair and leafed through the pages. 'Here. It says: Rosalind 23.' He passed it back to Sinclair who repeated the name. 'Not quite French, is it?'

'Could be, Fraser.'

'Not this time. Fisher's wife is called Rosalind. She was born 23 February.'

'Alright,' said Sinclair, 'no big mystery there. Not really. Nothing terribly unexpected about that. It was natural she would find a boyfriend. No, Fraser?'

'I don't know. There seems to be a lot of connections here; Fisher and Halin and their Russian master, Levchenko. Now after her husband's death, Mrs Fisher still remains in the picture.'

'Halin was a colleague. A woman could look for comfort from that kind of friend. I'm sure it does happen.'

'Yes, I know,' said Fraser.

'Don't stop there, if you know something, well, get it out.' Sinclair stretched his legs and walked over to the window. Fraser sat and kept it in. The view of the outside was a terribly dull one from his position, as if someone had pulled a large sheet of off-white paper across the panes. But Sinclair stood there, up against it: he might have been watching children play in the street if it had been that kind of street.

'I was sitting in the train the other morning, hoping that the sky would clear, just once, and a touch of blue could be seen. When you get older, Fraser, things like that matter; despair and joy are so damnably close and only a few clouds can shift the balance. Anyway, as luck would have it, the awful dullness was to stay all through the day. I was in one of those open carriages where you dare not do anything and be sure no one's watching. No bad habits to pass the time. The ticket collector had snipped at our tickets: it was a surprise to see him, I had almost forgotten how they looked since they placed the machines on the platforms.' He rubbed at his nose while sniffing something away. 'Well, this day he had returned, small, old with thick-rimmed spectacles. It was difficult to determine what made his appearance so sadly laughable. Was it him making fun of his shapeless uniform or was it the other way around?' He turned and took a few steps forward. 'I watched him in his silly seriousness with each passenger, and if one had some difficulty in locating one's ticket, his face would frown more. It was then I realised something. As the collector made his way he stopped at four giggling youths who promptly produced their tickets. Then one, with all the decency in his face, informed the collector that there were two young rogues hiding in the toilet without a ticket. And the fool, such as the man was, hurried to the top of the carriage. The laughter roared and I almost joined in.' The story so far failed to rouse Fraser, who sat unmoved. 'Well, the collector reappeared after some minutes; his expression hadn't changed. He spoke with the youths and their faces became honest and innocent and suggested that he should try the toilets farther down. The man was easily put in chaos. He ran down and made his search, and the boys laughed. It was a normal day for them, to do what they could to brighten their lives, and to torment the collector was wonderful.' He paused. 'You see, they made up a story, Fraser. Is that what we have here? Are we the ticket collector? There's no real evidence that there's a leak from here. Nothing's been located to suggest a department, a section. All we have is Gull's body and now Halin. But is it enough? If the Russians thought they could create chaos within the agency, my God, they would do all kinds of things for that. Just to sow doubt, suspicion, then build on that.'

'They would kill Gull for no other reason but to make it look as if he was getting close?'

'If they thought it would work, they'd do it.'

'Too close to nothing. Just for appearances. Is that what is being believed?'

'No, I didn't say that. It was a thought on the train and nothing more at present.'

'I don't believe it,' said Fraser. 'Some might think they're capable, but I don't believe it.'

Sinclair stood by his desk, his fingers on some sheets. 'You don't. Will you tell me why?'

'Maybe it's because I've never been impressed with the Russian mind as others have. I've never seen their cleverness in this way and I don't think their intelligence people would plan out such a scheme which had so little certainty.'

'All they had to do,' explained Sinclair, 'was offer to stir our interest over Fisher's death; then the officer investigating would be eliminated – in this case, Gull. Our interest would deepen and . . . before you know it we're chasing our tail.'

'Why pick out Fisher?'

'Ah, good question. Well, he had to be English and where do you find an Englishman in Paris?'

'I don't know. Where?'

'Berlitz. Language schools. They wouldn't pick the first one, of course, they would check out a few, see if they fitted. It's all possible, Fraser.'

'Are we chasing our tails?'

'Not so they'd notice. Let's say we'd rather think the worse. We're playing it safe.' Sinclair lifted a hand and patted his hair as if a sudden gust of wind had somehow entered the room. 'And your man, Halin, is dead.'

For a moment Fraser went back to Paris, to the bar, to the toilet. If the light had been constant the sight would surely have sickened him – the gaping hole, the bloody mixture. But he had no real memory of that, only the awkward position Halin was forced into and left.

'When you buy a man a beer,' Sinclair said, 'and then he abruptly dies like that . . . well, feelings can turn amazingly positive.' He looked at Fraser for agreement. 'Halin was small-time, a man who grabbed where he could. The Russians are too controlled to forget a man's real worth. This Levchenko, for what we know of him, has the ability of slamming the door shut on people.'

Fraser leaned forward and gave Sinclair a look a half-back might to an opposing forward. 'I don't feel guilty if that's what you're asking. They had Halin tailed, that's now painfully clear, but hell knows where he was in that street. I'm sorry about Halin . . .' He leaned back. 'Professionally speaking.'

'Write it down,' said Sinclair, 'we've got to read it.'

'Things have come to a stop now,' said Fraser, 'I'd like to try and get them moving again.'

'How?'

'I'm not sure yet, but I'd like to return there. Keep my ears to the ground sort of thing.'

'I don't know what you mean. I can't approve anything, not after Gull. But go back, we don't want them thinking we've been chased away. Live a quiet tourist life for awhile. But any ideas . . . no one wants to know.'

33

Tom Fraser had a wish he had harboured for many years, many people do, have something they wish they had done, but it never happened. It was about doing the right thing, to ease the conscience. He knew from personal experience about unfulfilled wishes, he had heard of them and he had been there when the time had run out on them. He learnt something from those faces and it frightened him that he might follow. Tom Fraser's wish was born in Paris when Levchenko had run out of places to go and he was there in front of him. He remembered the Russian like yesterday, he could still smell his clothes and the hint of something on his face, when he pulled his ace card and walked away. It was the hardest thing and yet he regretted having the discipline to watch him go. The hardest thing, allowing even for Halin's cruel killing and Rosalind Fisher's run to be free from herself. These memories were now embedded in Fraser; they could wake him in the night, it was the torture he knew he had to bear, and because of that it reduced the importance of his own life and of those in it. On American soil, he thought of the life Levchenko must have, the dollars, the easy living, the success he must think he was and wondered how close he was to seeing him again. So more and more Fraser created in his head the

228

dream life he was certain the Russian was leading, finding some comfort in that and a whole lot of pain. Maybe pain was Fraser's comfort, but, if he could only know how Levchenko felt, how bare he was, if only he could know . . .

In Levchenko's home the telephone rang, the caller identified himself and spoke briefly but with interest in the man. Levchenko, alert of procedure and government calls, was taken by the warmth of the man's voice. So many years in California and yet so distant. The caller spoke of a little help that would be appreciated. Maybe a meeting the next day, it was suggested. Levchenko became unsure. A meeting? He didn't have any meetings anymore. He didn't know. Maybe he was busy. 'Do I know you? Have we met before?' There was a pause. 'What is it you want from me?' 'Need to talk. It's about our long lost general,' the caller said.

A long pause followed. 'That was a long time ago.' Levchenko was uncomfortable with a slippy hold on the phone and his eager questions that had almost escaped him. 'Tomorrow? Mr Cullen, you said.'

It was surprising how lives could be lived through the certainty of youth and the doubts of afterwards, and then the shaking of the soul when there was nowhere to go. Levchenko felt that way not all day but every morning; by noon he was better, yet he knew that would change, too. Cullen had never touched the flesh of Levchenko and did not have the same feelings Fraser did. Fraser had allowed Levchenko to sink him, he hated the Russian for exposing him to himself, where before he had thought so much of himself for too long a time. Was he not a man apart, a race apart with his family tartan which failed to give the kindness and generosity he thought was in his blood; he wanted to be loved without returning love, to be sought after without ever seeking. He wanted to be more than he could ever be, but more, he wanted to discover and be found, instead he was lost. Five years earlier when life was asking less and less of him, something somehow bit at his heart. People, he realised in a few moments of spitting anger, were not to be lived with, and in most cases sadness was all that was to be gained with each passing decade.

Fraser had a son who was everything and nothing to him. The boy was going to be many things, it was sure, and Fraser held to that belief while Helen, his wife, felt a growing discontent within the house which kept her quieter and her ambitions subdued. He brought this up with her once or twice and she told him that if he was surprised that she never quite understood what plans she should have for their son, then maybe that was because he didn't live in her world, the real one. Words used to mean something to her; communication, she thought she was good at, sharing thoughts and ideas, but not anymore. They were all self-centred, she said, he the husband, she the wife. In their house she felt defeated, but the sad thing was, it was either him or her. Fraser thought she hated him and asked her to say so. 'Hate, love, I have neither, and I'm sorry if you don't either. It wasn't supposed to be this way, we were supposed to be happy with happy hearts. What happened?' Fraser wanted to speak, tell her what he knew in a way that would surprise her with his insight and tenderness, but nothing came. Helen could only be sorry that her proud man had to pay such a price. But there had been sweeter moments when Tom looked young and so did she; maybe it was that, aging, looking old to each other which stirred her – every day he was telling her with his looks that she, too, was getting older, and that was the message she received every day of her life from her girlhood sweetheart. Their son was never felt as a presence, maybe in his early years, but afterwards he was sure he had stopped growing in their eyes and then in his own. He should have been more, they should have made him more and not the shadow he found himself to be. He could have spoken with his young ideas, his urging for things, he could have loved them more, he could have, and they him. But Fraser did not know what he had when the boy came into his life. The picture of the Fraser family was not what each one of the Frasers wanted, they wanted the usual thing like everyone else, loyalty and pride, but that's not what came about, somehow they couldn't gel and they drifted from each other.

Fraser with his few skills at home blossomed outside, he was a better human being, he cared or at least he showed he did, he was warmer and steady, more a man than his son ever thought. Yet he gave his boy the same attention he received as a son and the boy grew up and apart from both parents. It was upsetting to see for Tom and Helen, and when they exploded with each other she could not find her part in their sadness and he could not care in his. It had been years since they last saw their son: he thought he was on a ship going down, and he . . . jumped. He would telephone when no one was at home, so he could leave a message, a few words of, *I'm okay*. Helen warned Fraser that he might never see him again, with each passing year the journey home would be greater. She would sob at what she had said. 'People, who are they?' questioned Fraser, not with pain, only mystery. His own boyhood in Scotland never prepared him for the hell much of life had been, and every time he returned to that place where he knew himself as a boy, he could only think of one friend in particular, one kitchen smell and taste, a broth, a chunk of bread and a woman with her back to him. Simply he knew it would have been better if he had never outgrown those days.

He was in a car some years before with the old school friend, one time when years had started to cull very personally. He had travelled north and had noticed that the tightness around his chest was becoming less and less, his heart was in fine condition; the anxiety that had been hanging to him and could grip and grip around him was slowly receding. Back home he parked round a familiar corner, like the old school bike shed. Every time he came back it was the same, the same feeling, the same questions: Where was he? Where had he been? Where was he going?

He was met by his friend in a tiny square where the cobbled stones had been left and the buildings, which seemed to have been built for tiny people, stood as though welcoming Fraser home.

'Well, well,' said his friend on greeting him.

'Christ, man,' replied Fraser, 'you're ten years older and I saw you only yesterday.'

They could speak this way with each other, it was so much easier to them, to keep their masculinity up front. There was no embrace, only a touch of hand on the other's sleeve. There was much affection bottled up and that was the way of things. The men talked, a drink was had, both had time and a short journey to be taken.

'Isn't it strange?' his friend said.

'It seems so,' answered Fraser.

'Did you hear . . . ?'

'Yes, I heard. This is the time we're in, I suppose.'

'I suppose.' Pause. 'Let's take my car.' He emptied his glass, found his keys and stepped out.

They drove to the edge of town where the car stopped on the brow of a hill which Fraser knew well as a boy – bike climbing the brow, pushing hard on the pedals, the sharp left downhill and then a right. Oh it was fun, the chase, the speed, the pleasure. The car sat, its hazard lights flashing.

'Not a good place to stop,' Fraser remarked.

'It's been a while now,' his friend began, 'Mum and Dad were walking along here, they'd come from a cousin's house a little back there,' he waved his hand backwards, 'and they were taking their time.' He put both hands on the wheel. 'My mother had my dad's arm and they were fine, mum said.' He took a moment as two walkers approached and passed the car. 'Then suddenly Dad went limp, not dramatically, it was a kind of gentle limpness, if you can say that. Mum said she could feel his shoulder pressing on her and she called out to him at the stress she was being put under, but somehow she found the energy to keep him upright. My dad didn't fall,' he looked ahead pointing at where his dad had stopped walking, 'he was lowered to the ground. Someone saw them from a distance behind and said it was like the pair of them had their movements in slow motion.' The flashing indicator had become a thunderous sound inside the car as Fraser sat listening. 'Mum went down on her knees and Dad . . . She was trying to lower him gently.'

'I'm sorry,' said Fraser.

'Can you imagine your mum and dad like that? I wasn't there but I see them, even today.' He shuffled a little in his seat. 'I come here every day, I don't stop like this all the time, but I pass and I want to hit the horn, but I don't.' He looked across at Fraser. 'You doing alright?'

'Alright.'

Fraser had his own grief, but it was not beautiful at all, not to be spoken about and, if possible, to be remembered. He felt it odd that his old school friend, whom he didn't know anymore, had within a short time taken him to the spot where his father had died. Not understanding the actions of others had taken its toll on Fraser; why could he not understand? With scorn in his voice he could push people away, namely Helen and his son who had a name, but when did he last call it? He had sat in his friend's car being patient, then feeling envious that his friend would want to share with him, to bring him in to a most private moment. Helen was fine, their boy, too, he assured those who asked. Fine. Fine. Work? Went on as ever, he would reply.

34

Bayreuth, Northern Bavaria, March 1983

The snow had not returned, the sky was at last clear and there was now a stretch of blue as far as the eye could see. Bayreuth was a little south behind the hills, and the country road Alex and Jack were on had not seen a car all morning. The move was on, word had come through that Keech had been sighted, his appearance was well, and his escape, although unknown to him, was being prepared. Jack had informed Alex in an excited way: like a father proud of his child, the name of Willy Matthofer always lifted Jack, brightened him like nothing else. Alex had not seen this side of Jack, the parental side that was there in Bayreuth, but he had never spent so much time with him, been so physically close. Maybe it was because Kathleen and he never had a child, maybe they always wanted one but it just never happened. He could not understand how Jack had kept it secret; until now he had never spoken of the boy, and, yet, Willy Matthofer seemed to fill a large part of him. Alex could not be sure, people and their feelings and their needs were not a strong point with him, so poor was his comprehension on the subject he never bothered to make a little progress. He did not understand love, although he knew of it; there was Susan and Jilly and love, that was the reason for them,

234

but he was never sure. Instead of love filling Alex up, it left him wary that it could be caught and lost so quickly. He sometimes hated it for being so unreliable.

As the white barriers of the rail line crossing with their painted red stripes slowly came down, Jack brought the car to a halt. The unexpected stop unsettled him a bit and he sat tight at the wheel.

'I don't suppose they could have dug an underpass,' said Alex.

'I've seen worse examples of public spending,' replied Jack, 'but no, I don't suppose so.' He looked around at the flat fields. 'Lots of silence out there; one could easily get out of touch living like that.'

'Would that bother you?' asked Alex.

'Losing touch? I don't know. Sometimes I dream of just that, slipping away to the woods. But it's not me; my curiosity would pull me right back. I've got to find out what's going on.' He gave a little smile, 'I suppose you're the same?'

'I suppose so. We tend to build something up and make it important, and when we come face to face with it it's usually a let down, I think. Our curiosity demands drama and we're addicted to that: the drama on the road to fact.'

'What about Nick White then?'

'What about him?' Alex answered back.

Jack searched along as much of the track as he could. 'Where's the bloody train?' he said loudly. He looked back at Alex. 'I heard he wanted to get out, not to retire but to run.'

'Oh, for Christ sake, Jack, what is this?'

'Steady on, Alex. It's true. Nick White told his wife a crazy story: he said Control was going to pin him for the leak and he was ready to take her and run. Now for me, paranoia and Nick White are worlds apart.'

Nothing seemed to be happening outside. A slight breeze had picked up but the stillness was hardly disturbed.

'What are you saying? That Nick wasn't stricken as we all will be one day, and that he'd been leading a double life for years. Is that it? The whole thing is sickening.'

'Yes, it is.'

'Do you believe it? Would White open up to Marian, tell her such a story and then ask her to go with him. It doesn't make bloody sense.'

'No, I don't suppose it does, but sense has little to do with it.'

There was a pause. Jack could see that Alex had stopped listening: he had wound down his window and had stuck his head out. The crossing barriers stretched in front of them, firmly held in position for a train that had still to pass.

Alex rolled his window back up. 'Are you telling me it was White's love for his wife that did it?' he asked. 'After all those years of never having her he would go to her with that, knowing damn well it would only lead to her final rejection.'

'Would you not do the same for Susan?'

A tractor had climbed the slight rise on the other side of the crossing, its engine noise roaring into the car. Jack straightened himself in his seat, one hand on the gear stick. He had complete faith that the local people would not wait unnecessarily at a crossing, they would know exactly at what time the train passed. The whistle in the distance brought him to turn the key and start up. The barrier rose and by the time the tractor had rolled over the rails like a tank, Jack and Alex were some distance away.

'I don't think you're enjoying your stay in Germany,' said Jack. 'Are you?'

'I live here, don't I? I have thought of living somewhere else. Kathleen and I have discussed it. England would, of course, be a natural move, but we don't know.' His foot had eased up and the car now ran smooth. 'England alright for you?'

'If you mean politically,' replied Alex, 'the answer's no. If you mean financially, again the answer's no. England's a habit for many. We never talk about going elsewhere. A fresh start.' He looked at Jack with a dubious expression. 'Who talks like this? No one talks like this!' This made Jack laugh. 'We should be very close to the border,' said Alex. 'I hope all this is for something – no errors, no losses.'

'No one expects that. But who can tell.'

The car came upon a busy road; there were heavy articulated lorries on both sides with Czech, Polish, Hungarian and Greek number plates.

'Right, Alex, we'll be there shortly.'

One of the lorries, its large silver sides painted with its foreign name, had boldly come right over to pass the stream of traffic, and as it thundered by Alex said, 'I'm expected back in London.'

'Yes, I know. You've got people waiting.'

The line of traffic ahead of them had reduced their speed to almost a crawl.

'Did you know that *I would* do the same for Susan.'

Jack looked out ahead then nodded two or three times. 'You'd better not; look what happened to Nick White.'

Hansbach, East Germany, March 1983

'It was one night, there was a moon shining, I remember; I looked up and tried to zoom in on it, tried to pick out parts where I wished I could have been.' He stopped as the moon of that night became clear to him again. 'It was funny, no, strange, to see it like that, because in the States you see it the same way and the longer I looked at it the more I was back in the States. Maybe all countries should have their own particular angle of the moon, that way you might not know where you are but you sure as hell know you're not at home.' Keech lay lost in his memories. Hanna tucked into him, her shoulders uncovered and bare, their pillows discarded on the floor.

'That night I wished I was up there, so far away from the hell down here. But that night I knew I could never survive up there, you can't. To be there I'd have to be dead, and yet I prayed to be there, to be peacefully dead.'

Hanna listened – she was very good at listening – her eyes were so sincere that Keech emptied himself.

'It's not right that such fear should exist in people, but Holy Christ, it does. In Viet Nam you could feel your fear pricking at you like lots of little electrical shocks stabbing away in the jungle in the dark. To overcome it, you'd get stoned, that way you'd be drained but loose, everything was less threatening: the war, the killing, everything. If I'd been stoned I might not have seen the moon the way I did and . . . it brought out the meanest hate I've ever felt – hate for the moon, the earth, and everybody on it. I searched my mind for anything that was worthy of my hate – I can now look back and say I survived it.'

He turned his head and looked for Hanna's eyes. 'Go on,' she said.

'In Nam the killing was cruel; it was the way it must have been at the beginning of time. Maybe somewhere in your language you have a word, the right word that I can't find in mine.'

She thought. '*Grauenhaft*,' she offered.

'That sounds awful, what does it mean?' He smiled a little at her. 'Do you know it makes me feel good, better, that I'm not familiar with a word in my own language that could mean anything close to what I found out there. It gives my feelings no real identity and I thank God for that.'

'It was so terrible?' she asked in wonder.

'It wasn't just the night or the animal noises all around you, nor was it the slow death that I had seen so many have. It was more, and maybe the shining down that night brought it right to my eyes. Maybe good and evil were holding hands there where I was. Can you imagine all your protection gone, inside and out? I did then.'

'What happened?'

He had taken his hand away from her shoulder and placed it

behind his head. 'I met religious guys out there, GI's, officers, people who knew who they lay with or did before they stepped off the transports into their new world. I think they suffered most because they were not prepared for what Viet Nam revealed. The kind of guys who could travel to a distant planet with an all-American attitude. In Nam some turned against themselves, just blew themselves away.' He closed his eyes. 'I can see it still . . . the moonlight had caught it, I saw it but nobody else did. We were on our knees on the ground, we were scattered a bit, just too loose, and I saw it.'

'What?' asked Hanna. She had some difficulty following him, the way he jumped from thought to thought.

'Probably a bayonet, one of ours taken from some poor bastard who wasn't looking where he was going. I didn't call out, I just stayed put. I lifted a knee and tightened my hold on the gun. I thought that was it, we were going to be butchered and I was considering at that point turning the gun round and ending it quickly. But then a cloud passed and covered out the light; it must have been the only damn cloud in the sky because I had been searching the heavens earlier and there was nothing, just the moon and all the stars. Anyway, I lost it, the glint in the bush was gone, and my panic, because that's what it was, took my finger from the trigger and I got up. My movements, I realise now, were panic driven. I came away from the men, I couldn't speak, if I had tried only panic would have come out. I couldn't do that, still had some control I suppose. Jesus!' he looked away.

They both lay still for minutes, Keech's confession had taken away desire; bodies are not interested in minds, when it comes down to it bodies could get on very well without the wonderings of the mind. With Keech talking and Hanna listening, their bodies had turned cold.

'A young corporal started walking towards the bush where the Viet Cong was, I was sure he'd seen something and I knew he would call out and we'd be jumped and Christ, we wouldn't have a chance. I went after him, I pulled at his shoulder, he turned and pressed a finger to his lips. The young fuckin' idiot pressed a finger to his bloody mouth. My heart was thumping.' Keech's voice had become louder and nervous. 'He went on and on and there I decided, if you can really decide in panic, that I had to stop him. It must have been seconds, ten at the most, the moon was clear again and the soldier was somewhere at my feet. I'd killed him, pushed the knife and all my panic into him.' His heart was thumping again. 'I let him lie there, I'd hoped he'd died immediately but I couldn't be sure. I wiped the knife along the ground and left.' Keech's breathing had become disturbed, bringing heavy sighs from him. 'That night was quiet, one of our quietest patrols. We all returned to camp in the morning, our relief brought out our laughter. We were mighty pleased. The young corporal's disappearance was just that, no one could say what happened to him. I think they told his mother that he *was missing in action.*'

Hanna took her arm from around his belly and lay with her head flat on the bed. Her eyes were sleepy but her voice was not. 'Do you think you murdered him?'

'There was no Viet Cong in the bush, I don't know what it was that gave the effect I saw, but there was nobody.' A pause. 'Yes, I murdered him and I got away with it. *Missing in action,* that's what they told his mother. *I* killed him.'

'But you thought . . .'

'Nothing. I would have killed them all just to get away, far away. To the moon.'

Hanna had opened her eyes wide, the tremble in him brought out all of her attention. He got close to her and pulled away the sheet.

'Don't you see, Hanna, if I'm in the wrong place at the wrong time I'll do the wrong thing.' His hand slipped down her back, squeezed in between the bed and her body. 'I went back to the States, to my family, the house. I saw and heard everything different. The positive things of American life were gone. It was a lucky thing that I started to get moved about.' He took his hand away and lowered his voice, 'I was once in a whorehouse where this cute little thing taught me something awfully nice; let me show you.'

'Let's go to sleep,' she said.

He ran a finger from her breasts down. 'Let me show you.'

'Tomorrow,' she said.

'What did Andrei say, you're here to please me.'

'Why did you tell me about Viet Nam? What was it for?'

His finger stopped somewhere on her body. 'I thought, here I was, in so called enemy territory with a naked lady at my side. I thought I could let it go, this dark secret, just get it out in this foreign place with this foreign woman.' He beamed at her as if pleased with himself. She took his hand away and got out of bed.

'I thought I could tell you. Everybody has something only they know about themselves, and they'd be happy, if they could, to let it out, just to shout: I stole, I raped, I murdered. There should be something that one could go to, someone one could speak to without ever wondering about trust.'

'There are churches in America, you're supposed to be a Christian country.'

'We're supposed to be many things but we can't trust anybody.'

'Have you come here for trust? Do you hope to find it here?'

'Tell me?'

'There's nothing to tell. You're with people who don't trust you.' She wrapped her arms tightly around herself. 'They're going to find out, you know that.'

'Where does your mother live?' he asked.

'My mother?'

'She's alive?'

'I'm not allowed to answer.'

'Just tell me if she's alive. She is alive, isn't she?'

'Yes, she's alive.'

'You should be with her, helping her. Not here screwing around with everyone. Do you ever think about her?'

'Don't ask me.'

He began to mumble to himself, 'When am I getting out? Hanna, tell me.'

She walked slowly back to the bed, his voice had brought her shivering to his side. 'You're a strange man. I don't understand some things you say. I don't know if you're telling me real things or telling me dreams. They don't like dreams here, it's not what they want to hear. You have to give them something.'

'I have.'

'No, you haven't. Why do you think you're still here, in this house, in this room? You're causing concern, do you understand? It is not advisable to do that. If you want to live with them you have to make them happy.' She paused. 'This incident in Viet Nam . . . tell Andrei, give him the details, all the details.'

'Like hell I will. This is something that belongs to me, it's mine forever and no son of a bitch Russian's going to get it. For Christ's sake, Hanna, what the hell are you saying?'

'You will see Andrei in the morning, you must give him the details then.' A pause. 'It will be dangerous for you if you don't. Russian people are patient if they think it is in their interest to be.'

'Hanna.' He sat at the edge of the bed, his back to her. 'What is after Hanna? Your other name?' He began to laugh and laugh until it was a roar, shaking the bed. 'Hanna, you bitch. KGB. Right?'

She watched him keel over on the bed, his laughter almost choking him. She waited until his laughter released him. 'Did you not know . . .'

'KGB. You screw for the KGB, for your beloved Russia or are you really German?'

'It doesn't matter. I'm surprised you never thought before, that you never had an idea that I might be more than a whore

242

giving free sex. Why did it take you such a time, General. You are a general, yes?'

'Don't you know the difference between an ordinary screw and that of a general?'

Her hand came with such force from behind him striking the upper part of his face and pushing him from the bed. Cursing at him in German, she got out of bed and dressed.

He sat on the floor holding his face. 'Hanna, don't go. Help me.'

'General, you have a short time.'

'If you go now I'll have nothing in this God damn forsaken place. Hanna, are you here to break me, is that it . . . Stay.'

'General, we didn't meet at a party or through mutual friends. I was given to you, remember?'

'Stay tonight.'

'What for, General? I don't think you have anything to say.'

'I'll tell you everything if you will stay.'

'And Andrei?'

'Sure.'

35

Fraser was never going to meet Jilly, he was never going to see her and calm her young heart. He was the wrong person to be asked to fly over and tie up what seemed a loose thread from the past: he had too many threads of his own. He had quickly brought himself up to scratch with General Keech and Alex and family, and of course he wandered off to places that had not quite been filed away, off record ones.

The last few days with Helen were quiet, he seemed happy to be on the move again. She never expected him to come back home and back into his routine with his inner troubles bubbling, no, she would see him go and wait; but she was concerned, a concern which became a worry she tried to keep at bay and failed until it was everywhere inside her head. The Frasers had become noticed in the street; before his retirement things were quieter but since then their household had changed. Too old to start over and not old enough to die. The world was cruel to Helen and the enemy to Tom. She had laughed through a lunch time as she sipped a young bottle of romantic Italian red, she wanted an affair, she thought, a luscious profound one. Her body had not let her down so she had something to offer. Women were having encounters all the time. Yes, as she poured, she would do that. The visions of herself secretly removing her clothes, taking a shower, made her feel good. It would be fun and it would stop the pain in her eyes, remove the years she had become. Yes, if it were another day and her wounds were fresh.

What was the meaning of her son walking away? She had wanted to be close to him but it was difficult, even as a boy he seemed to be biding his time. So bit by bit he walked from the centre of the house to the door, it took years but to see him edge his way like that, her son, shook her to her stomach. She did not believe any knock on the door now would remove her feelings for him. The pain he brought her was okay for him, it was in the past, it happened, she had her life and he his. Helen found nothing sincere about him and didn't want her love tested further, she just wanted him to go and do well, and she would remember what was positive. She had learned a long time ago – whatever trouble comes along, be your own friend first – and that's what she did. Fraser thought that mothers and sons had a special bond so Helen must take some responsibility, there must have been something that could have prevented that, and he always looked at her for the answer.

'Some children,' she once said, 'cannot be explained, they can't. Our son isn't violent, he's harmed no one, he isn't reckless, he's just not kind and his feelings are limited, to us, anyway. He's his own person, he knows what he's doing and he can do it. How? Why? I don't know. Don't let him sink us, Tom, because he could do it if we let him. Tom. Tom!'

But now something had gripped Helen and she had an idea that Tom had a plan out there in America and she wanted those who sent him to know. Someone was going to call round and did, to see Mrs Fraser at home, amongst her things and alone. A man, maybe her own age, past that half century mark when a shout or scream can be heard somewhere inside one's head, stood at her door. There was someone with him, similar but different in a complementary way. They were quiet in their movements as they stepped in and Helen was not as she was when she had telephoned, she had put her worry away well. To arrive at her house her visitors had driven along what was a deserted street – no movement, no evidence that people actually lived there. Helen brought the men in and closed the door.

She spoke of Levchenko and how Tom hated him, how he blamed him for his failures, his sleepless nights and his angry days. She spoke about the way he had become since his retirement, about all the mistakes he felt he had made, how Levchenko got away with it all. Sometimes she did think he needed help. The men listened. Coffee was offered but they wanted to get to the point of things without delay. Before she could say more they reminded her that her husband was considered highly, and it would be a complete surprise if they were seriously being asked to re-think that.

'Oh, I know, I know,' Helen agreed, 'but that was working Tom, before retirement. He did live another life and he's tried to find more of that life since. You may not know it,' she explained, 'retirement either awakens a person or puts him to sleep.' She talked to the men as she would to students of long time ago, when still in the profession she had given up for her baby son. 'Tom couldn't sleep, not that I wanted him to, he's not that kind and, anyway, this man Levchenko was never going to let him.'

'What are you saying, Mrs Fraser?'

She came forward in her chair and opened her eyes wide in some surprise. 'I'm not sure.'

'Is this man Levchenko in danger?' The older man reached closer to her. 'Do you think that?'

Helen looked into space and saw Tom as a younger man, looking strong, all his strength lay in his eyes then, and she had hoped when their child was born that one day he would find his father's strength and become strong, too. But while she roamed in her mind at Tom's past with her, there was that day when their son's casual goodbye had meant an adieu. He never found his father's strength, only his own. Now on this day she sat alone, a son somewhere whose father had forgotten how to call his name. And alone in her still and impersonal world she worried about Tom, where he might be going and where she would follow.

'Danger, Mrs Fraser?' the man asked again.

Helen had wanted to say, *don't leave, don't go, I'm your mother,* while he packed his things upstairs but she was unsure of her standing as she leaned sadly on the wall at the bottom of the stairs. Tom was with himself, holding his feelings in. They both stood, she facing her son and he in denial of the boy's decision. They could not be stiffer, more awkward with their emotions. Their son could find no tears in them, no words asking him to stay. Two crippled people who had almost captured a third one. Their only child was going and maybe a part of them wanted him to go because they both believed they couldn't do anything about it.

'Mrs Fraser, why have you called us?' – Helen's thoughts closed down then – 'Mrs Fraser, we've never had any concern before and we don't think there is any need for it now.'

A storm had swept in from the Pacific Ocean, so far away from England, as two lines of small talk were spoken, and then unexpectedly the men found Helen's outstretched hand. The older man received it while the other stepped out through the doorway. They drove away and thought how lucky their lives were.

36

England, March 1983

The cliffs of Dover were almost sparkling as a chilly March sun shone down. The wind coming off the Channel gave the passengers who were stepping from the ferry bus an immediate indication of how the sea was – choppy and dark. The ferry terminal was filled with English housewives with permed hair and various colours of bell-bottom trousers that failed to reach the ankle – a fashion that had lasted more than ten years among the middle-aged and elderly of the country and it seemed more than probable that it would reach a score.

Jilly had been excused from school for the day. Mummy had some business to do, Jilly was told; Daddy was away and there was no one who could look out for her after school, not that day anyway. Jilly brightened considerably when she heard she was going to France, 'where they speak French and eat much better than we do.' Susan gave her a little of the language to work on the night before and Jilly took it to bed with her. Her eyes wandered around the room in search of the occasion she would be called upon to say, '*Parlez-vous anglais?*' She slipped into sleep repeating this over and over.

'Why do seagulls follow the boat, Mummy?'

'Because the passengers feed them, they throw food to them and watch the gulls dive for it.'

'That one there is not doing anything, it's just sitting watching us.'

'Are you cold?' asked Susan.

'No, I'm alright. I wish we lived at the sea, Mummy, with the seagulls and the boats.'

'You've taken to the sea very quickly, Jilly.'

'Oh it's better than the busy roads of cars and buses. It's empty here. Look,' she pointed out towards the horizon, 'there's nothing for miles and miles, just the waves.'

The gulls squawked as they dived for everything that was thrown and Jilly watched with delight. The wind had watered her eyes and her cheeks were rosé.

'Let's go in,' said Susan. 'The wind's biting through me.' She pushed her sunglasses high up over her forehead trying to control her hair, which was in a windswept tangle and kept falling in front of her eyes.

'Not yet, Mummy. It's great out here. Why haven't you taken me to the sea before, I mean on a boat like this?'

'We did,' replied Susan, 'when you were younger.'

'Did we go to France?'

'No, we were in Sweden, you, me and Daddy. It was a cruise in summer. You must have been four.'

Alex wanted away then, she remembered, away from London to somewhere new, he had said, and away from the bodies on the beaches in Spain. He had told her one night in an unusual way for him. He had brought home a gift that he said had caught his eye in a window in town; it was beautifully wrapped, but it was a bit strange that he should spring a surprise like that. Then he pulled out the tickets: a holiday cruise through the waters off the Swedish coast. She had complained a little that it would be freezing and she wouldn't be able to wear anything but winter woollens. She needed a little sun each year, she said. 'Why don't you open it,' he had asked, stopping her in mid-stream. Her gift had been left for a moment in all her surprise and it sat unopened beside her. She had untied the ribbon carefully while Alex watched and said that it would be a chance to meet an old friend he had not seen for a long time. The paper opened out and the box was revealed. Her eyes had widened as she removed the top. He had asked if she liked it and she nodded and said it was lovely. Why such a large box for a watch, she had wondered. Alex had left to pour himself a drink, explaining how the shop assistant couldn't understand why he wanted another box, a large one, she couldn't see. He had laughed.

'You have a friend in Sweden?' Susan had asked. 'I didn't know.'

'He's actually Danish. I met him years ago. He was studying here. We used to correspond but without seeing each other that eventually stopped.'

'Danish?'

'Yes, he's on an island . . . Bornholm, I think it's called. Off the south coast of Sweden.' He sipped. 'It would be a chance . . . You do like the watch?'

'I do.'

Alex never saw his friend, he was gone, somewhere out to sea, he was never found. Alex was stunned and Susan tried hard to help him, but she felt she had failed. It was a blustery day on the island and they were both lonely people; one unable to give, the other unable to take. His friend's sister, Birthe, and family were very kind and had asked them to stay a night or two. Alex's friend had been gone two years they said, it was over for them and they seemed uncomfortable talking about it. For Alex it was fresh, like yesterday, and no one was able to bridge this distance. When they left, Alex said a couple of times that maybe they'd come back again sometime. It was some months later when Susan found an envelope with a Stockholm postmark; Alex said it was just Christmas greetings from Birthe, but Susan never saw it.

But why should she think about that now, she wondered, there were other things on her mind, like the reason why she found herself in mid-Channel in her new role as messenger. Alex had phoned two nights before, his voice unusually quiet, a whisper almost. He said he wished he were back with her, and then spoke of how a difficulty had cropped up with his being away. He sounded soft and nice, and she wanted to be nice back so she asked him what it was, if she could do anything. Her offer slipped easily from her tongue, mainly because she didn't think she really could. 'You know I can't tell you anything like this,' he said, 'but I need you to go over to France as soon as possible.' 'France? What for?' she had asked, Jilly would be at school, there would be no time to journey that far. 'I thought it would be something else, something that I could help with here,' she said. Alex got angry. He swore at her, brought down Jilly's school saying that if she missed six months of the damn place she would more than likely have improved because of it. Then he paused, just let the silence reveal the distance from each other before Susan rushed out, 'If it's so important . . .' 'I could ask someone at the office,' he said, 'but I'd rather come to you, Susan. I want you to go over to France in a couple of days, but first, tomorrow, I want you to collect something at a West End hotel . . .'

Jilly was stuck to the rails watching the gulls and the salty spray come off the ship bow and splash on the deck. 'Oh look, did you see how it caught that?' she said excitedly. 'Maybe they're French seagulls, Mummy.'

'Seagulls don't belong to anyone,' said Susan, 'they fly where they want.'

'Are there seagulls in Sweden?'

'Yes, but I think they're smaller than these. Daddy likes gulls, he used to photograph them, try and get as close as he could and . . . . click. They must be in the house somewhere.'

She remembered how Alex had filled up his bag with film on that holiday. He would talk about what the evening light up there would be like, he had read so much about the sky in Scandanavia, the freak light that one could only find in such a northern place. After the visit to Bornholm he seemed to put the news behind him and tried to make the holiday work; he had gone through his film like a boy and brought Jilly out of herself. It became quite a happy holiday.

'When's Daddy coming home?' asked Jilly.

'Soon, I think. You're freezing me staying out here.'

'Oh Mummy, it's not really cold.'

Susan hung on a little longer. It was strange to find herself on a cross-Channel ferry, she didn't feel it as one. Boats, ships, always suggested a long voyage to her; an ocean away. A ferry to Calais was something she had not experienced before. Alex would have laughed at her thoughts, her great stone in her dreamy parachute, she would say to him, usually in the kitchen where her dreams tended to lift off. Alex always said he never had dreams but Susan didn't believe him.

'Come on, Jilly.'

The wind was not going to let up, it never did in March. The ferry rose and fell, some passengers had been unable to lose sight of the Dover coast before rushing to the nearest lavatory.

'I'm hungry,' Jilly complained. She had noticed some people eating chocolate bars.

'We'll soon be there,' said Susan.

'What are we going to France for?' asked Jilly.

'It's business,' Susan answered, putting on a schoolmistressy expression. 'It's a secret.' She smiled at her, and saw so much of Alex. For a moment she felt a little sad, alone, even though her daughter was sitting close to her. Alex was gone somewhere in Germany. At the moment she needed a warm climate, a strong sun and lots of laughter.

'Mummy, Daddy told me he had lots of secrets. He didn't tell me any and I'm his daughter.'

'If he didn't tell you it was because he couldn't. Anyway, his secrets mean nothing to you. It's just work.'

'Is your secret in your bag?' Jilly lifted it up onto her knees and made to open.

'Leave it, Jilly.' Susan stared at her, watching her disobedience. 'Jilly.' But Jilly pretended not to hear. Susan brought her hand down hard on Jilly's thigh and took the bag from her. 'That is one of your bad points, Jilly, you don't take me seriously as you do your father.'

The sting on Jilly's leg brought some tears but they were quiet and quickly wiped away. Susan had turned from her to where the other English women were sitting. Alex had been gone too long, she thought.

She and Jilly sat quietly until Jilly bobbed up. 'Mummy, is that France?'

Susan followed Jilly's outstretched arm. 'I suppose it must be.' As the coast of Calais drew closer Susan felt a thousand miles from England and a thousand miles from Alex. '*Bienvevue en France*, Jilly. Now you have to speak French.' She picked up her bag. 'Come on, get your jacket and we'll go out on the deck.'

The shops in the centre of Calais were a great disappointment to Jilly, who could see little difference between them and the ones at home. There was so much English about to guide the daily ferry loads of foreigners into the shops. Calais was not the best example of France on that blustery day or any other, but Jilly would go home and tell her friends that France was not a very nice place.

'Are we going to eat, Mummy?'

'Yes, we are.'

Susan stopped a young girl and asked the whereabouts of a street and then of a cafe. The street was a narrow cobbled lane, and the cafe was small and dark. Some early diners had arrived and Susan and Jilly settled at a corner table; the table had tablecloths, which impressed Jilly who felt she had to examine them and began touching the material with her fingers.

'They don't give you tablecloths in England, Mummy.' She was happy, she had found a difference between her England and now her France.

'Yes, they do.'

'No, they only give you mats and paper napkins.'

Susan thought. 'You're right, only mats.'

'And paper napkins,' added Jilly

They ordered and Jilly talked almost continuously through the meal about her observations of France. Susan was hardly listening; her little business trip had made her irritable to her daughter's chatter and she began to question what she was doing. 'I shouldn't have come. Why have I come?' She questioned aloud.

A man a little distance away had finished his meal; he laid his crumpled napkin beside his coffee and turned three-quarters round in his seat. He got up and walked over to them. Jilly had a large spoonful of ice-cream that vanished as she paused in mid-sentence – her table manners had dropped noticeably since her arrival, thought Susan.

'*Excusez-moi, est-ce que je parle avec Madame Dorian de Londres?*'

Susan looked at him, he was slightly bowed over the table and wore the expression of a person with something delightful to announce. '*Oui.*'

'*Ah, bon.*' He sat down opposite her and Jilly, who had finally decided to rest her voice, but still held her spoon tightly.

'*Nous avons un rendez-vous,*' he said.

'I'm sorry, my French is not what it should be.' There was the sound of an apology in Susan's voice.

He gave a nod of understanding. 'I will speak English.' He looked at Jilly whose eyes were stuck on him. 'I'm from Paris.'

'Yes.'

'This is your daughter?'

'Yes.'

He smiled at her.

'Are you a Frenchman?' asked Jilly.

'A little bit of one,' he replied.

Jilly returned to her ice-cream not sure what he meant.

'You know who I am?' the man asked.

'No, not really,' replied Susan.

'You have something I have to collect.'

'Yes.' Susan said that in a way that was not yes at all.

The man stared at her. Jilly finished her ice-cream and finally the sound of the spoon scraping the bottom of her dish ended.

'Would you like another?' asked the man.

Jilly turned her face to her mother and won approval. He called the waiter.

'How do I know I'm meeting the right person?' Susan asked.

The man raised his eyebrows. 'I'm here. Who else could I be?'

'In your kind of world you could be anyone.'

'This was a rushed appointment,' he said, 'your very presence here suggests that things are not what they should be, that much caution be taken. Our mutual third party brought us together.' He stopped while Jilly's ice-cream was served. 'I think we have been cautious.'

Susan placed her bag in front of her and untied the leather which laced through slits at the top, slackening it wide enough to allow her entry, then pulled out an envelope and handed it across.

'I hope I've done well,' she said.

'*Madame?*'

37

Young Greg Keech's name and police file had lain for a couple of days at the Sheriff's office in Percy, Idaho, after information had been received that he had broken probation and he should be detained on sight. There was some sympathy for young Greg at this news. Sheriff Bane felt for the Keech family for he knew about their struggles when and after the father had made the national headlines. There were reports from all the agencies from Washington DC to Idaho. The Keech family, it was made clear, after the initial outcry that the general was suffering at the hands of a cruel regime behind an iron curtain, were not an ordinary family, not one other Americans would recognise. Sure, the father was a general, but there were question marks at how he had achieved that. Betrayal, the television psychologists explained, was born with the character, it was not something anyone watching could catch. Sheriff Bane knew the family before their fall, when his son and Greg were friends, and the general, he remembered, was so pleased his son was calling at the home of a sheriff. A pleasant boy, thought Bane, who had a good future before the reports were written. It was sad that a family could be there one day and gone the next. Detain on sight, they ordered. Maybe he wouldn't go there, Idaho was no refuge for him. But there was a part of Bane that wanted Greg to come on home. Maybe home could help in a way it never had before.

But Greg had not yet reached the border, he was on an open road with Jilly and severe bad weather had made for changes in their plans and to bus schedules. They thought they could walk to a place called Mason, a town a couple of hours away at a brisk pace. With few features on both sides of the road they both felt without saying how empty, how useless and how lonely they both were. That empty stillness was to be broken by a crackle of thunder-burst about ten, maybe more, miles away; the approaching signs of a looming storm as the distant mountains harboured heavy laden rain clouds urged Greg and Jilly to a faster pace. The road was eerily quiet and the humidity in the air was affecting Jilly's breathing, which had become deeper forcing her to inhale through mouth and nostrils. With the last crackle and clash of clouds the hum of an old pick-up truck came hurrying along before them. As it passed, its horn was blasted while the driver was laughing in an insane kind of way. Tied to the truck with about fifteen feet of rope was an animal, a dog thought Greg, as it bounced past him. It was butcher red. 'Greg!' shouted Jilly. 'Come on.' He hurried. The pick-up had come to a halt and sat silently two hundreds yards behind them. 'What are they doing?' asked Jilly. 'Don't know. Just keep walkin'.'

The truck came back to life and turned. It passed them for the second time and stopped a little ahead. 'Walk past. Keep goin',' Greg urged Jilly. The driver and his passenger watched them pass and sniggered as they went. Greg wanted to walk on but somehow could not and turned to face the driver who sat staring with his mad eyes. 'Need a ride?' he asked. Greg shook his head and turned to the road ahead.

'Does the lady need a ride?'

Greg and Jilly walked on with the pick-up following at their pace.

While he walked Greg had a feeling he had always wanted to forget, a feeling of having no power when there might be a need for it, a feeling of having fear and nothing else.

'You guys need a ride? Sure you do. It's bein' hospitable, man,' said the driver, bringing much insane laughter from his passenger.

'We're walkin' into Mason. Thanks anyway.'

As he stepped on, the two men sprang out. 'Fuck you, boy. Get in the fuckin' truck. And you,' he jabbed a finger at Jilly, 'get in with my friend.' The expression on Greg's face aroused the driver, who tried to change it by opening much of Greg's left cheek with a metal instrument he had carried from the truck. The blow saw Greg fall heavily to the road, the pain delivering immediate unconsciousness while Jilly's distress brought her gasping for breath.

The thunder clouds of ten miles away had approached while Greg lay on the road, and the weight of the downpour had eased by the time he could feel his aching face. The truck had gone and Jilly, too. His face was open, he did not know by how much but it felt as wide as the road itself. It was almost dark as he made his way towards Mason. The storm had been torrential but brief, and he could see flashes of light in the distance, then flashes of Jilly's face. His clothes clung to him while he listened to far-off claps of thunder and his own soggy sounds with every step. The condition he found himself in triggered other sounds, human ones from a year earlier. Cries and shouts from those who might have made it if there had not been a policy to ensure that they didn't. The Penitentiary men lived their lives to their own rules, where success to them was failure to everyone else. It was fun, powerful fun, taking men where they didn't want to go, seeing the weak become weaker. God, it was something. The beer tasted better, sex, too, everything, self-delusion was perfect. Yes, it was fun taking a passive man to the edge, to cross a line he was not equipped to do, and violate another. Those men might have learnt from their mistakes if they had not been forced to cross that line.

A brilliant flash of lightening had lit up everything in front of Greg revealing a vehicle rear reflector down on a track off the road sitting amongst grass and bush. He shivered as the evening air penetrated his clothes while he searched ahead. There, its red colour black in the darkness, the pick-up truck stood. A lump was building in his throat and his hands had turned from cold to sticky. He hid himself. There was no sound to be heard from inside the truck, but he knew Jilly was there, had to be. Again he found himself somewhere he had no right to be, and it was a place where violence was all that was on offer. A cigarette was flicked out an open window of the pick-up and a voice was heard. Greg crouched more as if to squeeze his body, his mind and all that kept him aware of where he was, to pulp. 'For Christ's sake,' he could hear his father's voice, 'be that man you want to be. Life's a test, every day, I told you that. Don't fail me and yourself.' He owed Jilly so much, all her letters which had helped to keep him afloat.

Slipping down a slope to the track, he began to realize the likely outcome of his rescue of Jilly. There would be no conversation or negotiation, only violence would get Jilly back, there could be no surprise there. After that she would be safe and that was good enough. He found a piece of wood of arm's length and good thickness, and with it he climbed in a hush onto the back of the truck. The men's voices, low and secretive, could be heard, but nothing from Jilly. The rear window of the cabin was mud splattered, so Greg climbed unseen onto its roof. Below him he could hear only their generous remarks which brought his banging hard on the cabin top. As one door opened and the passenger raised his head, Greg swung forcefully at him with the wood. It was not quite full-blooded, but because of his fear that if he got it wrong it would do nothing for Jilly, it was enough to reduce the man to the ground deadly still. The driver, yelling and cursing when he heard the sound of the strike to his friend's head, would have killed Greg if he could have reached him. He became wild and threatening, his arms flaying, his insane smile gone, his mad eyes looking like he would devour Greg as he climbed onto the back of the truck, hands bare and lunging forward. Greg struck him across the shoulder and might have broken it there and then, because the man's arm was not used again.

'Pat!' the man yelled. 'If you've killed him, I'll kill ya!' And then his smile returned, with his dangling arm he could smile and say how sweet his girl had been. Accommodating was the word he liked. 'Pat! Where's Pat?' He looked into the darkness and then flew at Greg who fell onto the bonnet.

Jilly had remained where she had been for eternity, awake but closed in herself. It was the thumping sound of Greg's body on the vehicle that triggered her hysteria, whilst he was receiving continuing promises to damage him. Jilly's need for Greg to conquer probably gave him the added strength to resist, but it could only be temporary. As the man kicked hard, he plunged a small blade into a part of him. It was not over yet but it was all Greg had. As the thunder continued to growl lightly far away, the man's force was becoming less; his energy spent, he lowered himself to the ground resting against the truck.

There was blood, dark sticky stains in the dirt. Greg's cheek was wide open and his jaw ached more when he called for Jilly. The two men, one out cold and the other exhausted, were simply dark figures on the ground as Jilly was coaxed out of the cabin. Face to face with Greg she could not be touched, any movement toward her brought an extended arm from her. The driver mumbled some words of comfort to his friend while Jilly and Greg walked away, from him, the pick-up and the night.

Mason was their destination and it was dawn before they entered the beginnings of the town, two heart-torn people shuffling along together. With the bleak hour, the chilly air and the start of drizzly rain, it was not a good time to enter anywhere. Traffic lights had held up a cab which Greg approached with a tap on the window. His full face, beaten and with a look of desperation brought a gasp of *Jesus* from its driver.

'Could you . . .'

'Sure, get in.'

Jilly had nothing for Greg but her soft hand that would reach for his face without touching it. The driver had much to know and the sense not to ask. It was life for many, to keep out where curiosity and sympathy tried to pull in. The power of those feelings becomes less in time – a lifetime.

Mason County Hospital had a delivery, not one they had been expecting and not one they could not help. Greg and Jilly stepped into an empty corridor and as they slowly walked it, from the outside behind a floor-to-ceiling glass door the driver stood waiting, watching them make their way.

38

West Germany, March 1983

'Of course, an articulated truck with a concealed compartment was considered, but it was thought too chancy. I believe talks are still deadlocked, neither side will budge. Keech has to be returned and that is it, while the Russians want to deal. Look at this, Alex.' Jack lowered his eyes to the ordinance map which was held to the table by an ashtray and Jack's whisky glass. 'My boy, Willy, intends to bring Keech through this area.' He extended a finger and made circular movements over the area. 'Now, there are two watchtowers, here and here.' He marked them X with a pencil. 'There's one on top of a hillock here, and the other's here, on flat ground. They cover the northern part, here, and an eastern section here: two distant parts of the area. But there's another tower, back here, near to the turn-off point which brings you along this road.' He ran his finger along the stretch of road on the map. 'It used to be a road leading into this village, but its useful-ness ended with the erection of the fence and all the rest. Now, only farm vehicles use it. This tower here, as I said, is near to the turn-off and it's really only coincidental; the reason is because the land slopes fairly steep at this point, and from the tower they must have a magnificent panoramic view. Why we know all this

262

is because a few years ago this area was wooded, quite heavily, all you would see from the tower then were treetops. Well, they felled the trees and made a clearing. I don't suppose there's a tree of any size standing there now.'

'Then if this tower's a problem why don't we stay away from it, choose another spot?' said Alex.

'Because this road runs parallel to the fence, it's the main road that has access to all the towers in this region. Now Willy would be wise to get off this as quickly as possible and after entering it somewhere here, he can, within a couple of minutes, get off it again at this turn-off. If he did what you suggest he would come onto the road farther up or farther down and he would be on it for much longer, which would be damn risky. The other way is considered less so.'

'Okay, Jack, tell me. Back in Bayreuth you said we're here to help; now there's fencing all along here and all the things to discourage anyone from trying what you're saying your Willy boy is going to do. The towers along here are not to stop anyone, the automatic guns and mines will do that, the guards are only a presence so one never forgets what it's all about.'

Alex got up and complained of the cold. Although the radiators were burning, their rooms in the Gasthaus were draughty, the wind sneaked in through the wooden window frames lifting the curtains.

'There are so many ways a person can be smuggled out of the East,' said Jack, 'and all of them are risky. We've talked about it endlessly trying to uncover a safer way and we've discovered that there aren't any. To bring Keech through a border crossing is bloody mad. How long do you think it'll take them to discover that Keech has gone? And when they do, I don't think Keech would reach the border. They would just be bloody waiting.'

'Alright. But didn't you say your feelings were that the Russians were probably expecting a snatch, that they found little or no value in Keech? That's what you said, they'd be happy to see him go.'

'I still think that, but of course, I could be wrong. With your own life you can act any way you like, take your chances as you see fit, but I can't with Keech.' A pause. 'Alex, sit down, let me finish.'

Alex remained standing but encouraged Jack to go on.

'From the turn-off the road becomes mainly a farm one, there are some maintenance people who come periodically to inspect the fence etc, but it's unlikely they'll be anywhere near it when Willy arrives. The road's four kilometres long and there are seven farms leading off it, the nearest to the road is two hundred metres.'

'They'll be heard,' said Alex.

Jack nodded. 'Could be. This is where a bit of help comes in. You may have seen it as we came in, a farm with white house and white gate, well, the farmer's name is Fuchs, we know him. He's a prosperous man. He took to farming after the war, he and his brother; there weren't many options going in Germany at that time, their parents were dead, war victims, and their uncle sort of adopted them. Anyway, this uncle had land, quite a bit of it, here, where we are, and there, where the towers are and beyond, and as it happened there was also property on it, here and there. So, wisely as it turned out, Fuchs took ownership of this piece and the brother took the other. When the fence started going up, well, you can see their position, to have your brother locked in behind it or the poor fellow to abandon everything. A situation no one should have to face. Fuchs's brother stayed on, gave up ownership, of course, and became a sort of general manager instead, and it'll be his farm Willy will be nearest to as he comes along that road. Fuchs's brother knows about it; Willy will drive past for a kilometre and then get out.' He took up his glass, put the rim to his nose then lowered it, his eyes in the liquid. 'And then the fun starts.' He tilted his head back and let the whisky run.

'Willy and Keech are going to jump onto a waiting tractor, start it up and bulldoze their way out? It's too simple, Jack, in theory, maybe, but . . . They would have a better chance in a balloon.'

'The weather's against that,' said Jack seriously, 'but you're right about the tractor, you've just got it the wrong way round. We have the tractor and we're going in. You see, the fence, as everyone knows, isn't for keeping us out but for keeping them in, and the measures taken have been installed with that in mind. The guns do rotate when triggered and their spread of fire is . . .' He opened his arms wide. 'To cover this area takes many seconds – I'm not sure how many – and to obtain this degree of swivel an enormous heat is generated in the barrel, which, I'm told, causes malfunction in the gun – they simply jam. In other words, those automatic weapons don't do what they are supposed to do. There's a high percentage of jamming.'

Alex poured himself a drink, a little stunned at what he had heard. 'There's an electrical fence and mines. Christ, what the hell are we doing?'

'Listen Alex, the mines are there, sure, but they've been laid carefully. The East Germans have considered where an escapee would run for when he reached this point; at this point he'd have a couple of options: to enter an open area here, or to remain cautious and make it for here, the more sheltered area. When you get this far you might think you've made it and this would take you right in here . . . They understand the mind of a runaway. Of course, others would have us believe that every inch is covered, not only do the Russians spray the escapees with bullets, the mines then blow them apart as they thump to the ground. Overkill like this would be very expensive. No Alex, there's no worry there. The fence carries enough voltage to blacken the skin and this would have been a problem, but to have this power twenty-four hours a day would be immensely costly and that is why they don't. The power's switched off, for a time throughout the day. It's difficult to be sure even for someone in a position to know much more.' He paused.

'So it's a bit hit and miss,' said Alex.

'The power's switched off and on locally, it's all localised; that could be in our favour.'

Alex looked unimpressed.

'Alex, we're here to get Keech out and safely back to the States. If I thought this job could be done any easier I'd be delighted. We have to open the fence for Willy. That's why I asked for you; I didn't expect the two of us to have a cosy little time together, but I knew our differences would remain between ourselves, there would be no leak back to Control, and I was right.'

Alex sank into a sofa and sighed deeply. 'I've been trailed out here not knowing what I was getting into. I've tried to find out but you haven't been responsive. I haven't been getting answers from you. But you asked me here because of *trust*, you said, and yet . . .'

'You're suspicious of something? Is that it?' Jack looked alert as if he had just realised.

'Put it this way: I'm not mowing down any bloody fence into East Germany. If I had to do it I'd want to know everything.'

'Ask away,' said Jack. 'I'm not holding anything back. I want this to be a success, to get Keech out, but I'm not closing my eyes to anything that could later backfire on me. If you have something, ask away.'

Alex sniffed, a sign of a chill in a chilly room. He would have liked to have been somewhere else, another room with another person.

'I phoned Kathleen that night you went away.' He paused to give Jack a moment to think about it. 'I called.'

'Did you?'

'You never got the message.'

'What is it, Alex?'

'You said you were going back, remember, business overlapping, but you didn't see Kathleen, she didn't expect you.' He sniffed again. 'Let's start there.'

266

'It's difficult, Alex. And really it's none of your damn business, but fair enough, I understand your position. We can't go on until certain things are clear, I want that.'

Alex listened to Jack stepping backwards almost with his words, smoothing the ground before he was ready to reveal.

'But it's difficult, nothing serious for our business but . . . I've got a girlfriend, Alex, that's it. Kathleen doesn't know and it wouldn't do her any good if she did. Surprised?'

'No, I don't suppose I am. Who is she?'

'You want to know?' – Alex waited – 'She's Willy's mother, Mrs Matthofer.'

'So all this affection and concern for your boy is thanks to Mrs Matthofer?'

Alex's sarcasm disturbed Jack's calm, raised his temper well beyond where he wanted it to go. 'Stop calling him my bloody boy, will you. I care if he gets out of this. We're here for Keech but I won't sacrifice Willy for him if it should ever come to that. I want that clear.'

Jack had risen to a word, an expression, something that Alex had brought out and now Alex sat back waiting. Perhaps Jack was using this affair to bring out Willy, perhaps that was it. Willy was coming out with Keech and instead of leading, Willy Matthofer was following, instead of guiding Keech safely along, he was as blind as the American. The thoughts were racing through Alex as Jack steadied with another whisky. If only he could check out Willy Matthofer, check out Jack's story, call Sinclair. Christ, who the hell was Willy Matthofer?

'You left to see your girlfriend,' said Alex.

'Alright, alright. Put like that it doesn't sound good. But I didn't go because the flesh was weak, it wasn't that. Willy's mother . . .'

'Does she have a name?'

'Liesel. Her name's Liesel. She's wanted Willy back in the West, home, for so long. But either there was never an opportunity or he hadn't quite exhausted himself. Hadn't found rest within himself. Only he knows what he's done to them, what pain he's brought them. We don't know his measure. Well, Liesel heard of Keech, of course she did, it was everywhere here; we spoke about it and I told her what I thought. A deal would most likely be made between the big two and the incident would close. This was shortly after New Year, I hadn't been able to see her – it was a family time.'

Jack seemed to have forgotten his drink, he was calm again, comfortable looking as he spoke. The ripples Alex had created in him had been controlled; what might have ended in storm had brought the equivalent of blue sky. 'She asked if the Americans might try and get Keech out, she thought cowboy Reagan might just do that and maybe, she was wishing and hoping here, maybe they would want Willy to help. That's how it started.'

'So Willy is coming out with Keech?'

'If he wants to. If he has no option.'

'You mean, if a tower's been alerted and a light's gone on?'

'Something like that.' A pause. 'She wants him back, you can understand that, anyone could.'

'You're getting old, Jack, did you know? You'll have one eye on Keech and one on Willy. That's a hell of a way of doing this kind of work.'

'Look, Alex, I think Willy will come. I know it's got nothing to do with you, but we owe the Matthofers this, it's been a long time coming but now we have a chance to make up. It's right that we should help here, it's damn right.'

'Balls, Jack. We aren't here to right the mistakes of Control; if we were, there would be no time to piss, and that's what we're doing, pissing about in your private life. I don't know Frau Matterhof nor do I know her son and that's the way I want to keep it. As you said, we're here for Keech and nobody else; once he's over that's it for me, I won't be stalled for anything – for you, Willy, or some high moral cause.' He walked away from him, to the window and some noise in the street. 'When will they be ready?'

'I can't say.'

'You can't say? Is it in a day, a week?'

'I can't tell you. Orders, Alex.'

'What orders?' He walked towards him. 'Tell me.'

'When Nick White died it was 10.30 in the evening, his wife had just ten or so minutes before walked away from him. Well, it took us twelve hours to part with the news of her dearly beloved, that her Nick wasn't coming home anymore. She was interviewed of course, we wanted to know how Nick was the hours prior to his death. You know how it is: a senior man alone on a wet London night, we didn't know what was on his mind, if anything. But Marian gave us a picture, Marian would, nothing faithful about her.' He laid his sympathy down and Alex left it there. 'Didn't Sinclair give you any of this?'

'He only prodded me for responses.'

Jack laughed. 'Yes, he does that, doesn't he? Marian White had been away, an overnight stay, she said. It was checked and it was just as she said, the name and address of her friend, a younger man, in his forties. The name was Philip Knight. Now, that name may not ring a bell with you, not immediately, but Mr Knight is a freelance photographer and journalist on occasions and a damn bloody nuisance most of the time.' He smiled at Alex. 'How do I know all this when you don't? That's easy; Philip Knight caught my eye here, he lived in Cologne, working here and not exactly prospering at that. A couple of years or so back he seemed to be pulling himself away from his penny-pinching early days; he began travelling more, dressing better, he became much more visible. That was fine, we like to see an Englishman making it in foreign circles – that was until he started stepping out with officials from the press section at the Soviet Embassy. That kind of move got our close attention. It was treated very low key because that's what it was. How many Philip Knights are there at any given time? Quite a few I would imagine. Of course, this never really got around in London; a quiet eye was kept on him but inevitably it began to close more and more, that is, until Nick's death.' Jack stood up. 'You're right, it's perishing in here.'

'Do you think Nick knew?'

'He knew about his wife but he didn't, I believe, keep up to date with names and addresses. It was something she did and he turned an eye as best he could. Anyway, the discovery brought the usual tight measures, and one was that all information on present field activities must first pass through Control before taking appropriate action. All rule book stuff, I thought, but when I got through to Sinclair to clarify, he said that nothing which could endanger what we're doing here must be revealed, and I quote him here, "Not even to Alex". Don't take it to heart, they're just being themselves. I'm fully responsible for this one, that's what they want.'

'So, I've got to wait until a midnight hour, perhaps, when we go on the rescue?' said Alex.

'Yes, it will be dark.'

Alex gave a smile that didn't tell Jack anything; whether he had accepted the story or was keeping his rage in, keeping it for Control. 'If it's agreed that there's a leak, why are we not looking at Nick White? His last few hours suggest he was a man in turmoil, a man in some panic. He's all we have to go on, after all.'

'That's not quite true, Alex, I believe there's someone else. I don't know who, of course, but there's someone who hasn't caught on yet, someone who hasn't felt the hook in his mouth. If Nick White proves me wrong, then I don't think the leak's automatically plugged and that an error has been made with the other . . . No, I wouldn't think that at all. I think it would mean we should intensify our search, because if that happened it would indicate that there have been two leaks all along.' He drew air heavily through his nostrils and made to leave. 'Let's get something to eat.'

39

There was much driftwood scattered on the beach. The storm had blown in from the south and proceeded east for a good day before heading up north-west. It still had the energy of a storm in full cry and weather reporters admitted it could end up anywhere. Toby Cullen had ended up on the shore. He liked the sea and its movement; each wave rushing in was always welcome, somehow soothing. Levchenko was close but Cullen was advised not to be over eager, *on this one*. A remark he thought about when he heard it and now again on the beach. It was step by step. Was he the right person? But, of course, he knew he was the only person. He was there all those years ago with his ambition, and his Harvard papers told many that he was ideal and ready, years before he was. He had been to many places all on expenses, almost all in some kind of rush except for Germany, it was different in Germany. He had the language, he had the people and he had the army all in one place. It was his second time there but it felt like the first. Many things were like that. Germany at eighteen was not Germany at all. The second time was the real visit. That was a Germany he had not studied; the language was softer, a real surprise, people laughed, were emotional and he was welcome. The US army were in their barracks, in the streets, everywhere, a force within a force. Cullen had a German woman who was happy to be there whenever he called. She was tall, as much as he, and her legs were captivating: no matter what she wore, her legs were always to be seen. His relationship with her made him worse than he really was. Straight from a country that could only measure others by the threat they posed to them, he failed to see the value he had in Germany, he mis-interpreted words that he was so confident in knowing, he mis-read acts of affection and generosity to an extent that he began to believe that the woman was only attracted to his American status. He all but mentioned this to a colleague, another kind of colleague in another kind of department, who confirmed Cullen's suspicions that all people wanted to be American, that was why the world hated America. He decided it made sense.

Germany was only truly seen after he left. Cullen was a happy man stepping off the tarmac and boarding his flight home, but somewhere over the ocean he had a terrible feeling of loss.

General Keech, he had learned, was gone. A British guy he had only just met, someone he could have talked to more, had disappeared before him. And the woman he had had all the time he wanted with had, over a long period, been pushed away. Over the ocean, unsettled, he was not sure where his flight was taking him.

Toby Cullen was to meet with Levchenko and planned to give him some time. He knew his situation, his routine, it was all arranged. Levchenko knew the meeting place, a little place to which the rich could take the few steps from their villas and enjoy the small restaurant that extended onto the sand. Cullen waited to greet him as the friend America felt he was. The Russian had remained tall with time, always appeared deep in thought until a spark of a smile would change that impression immediately. As the two men met, a strong hand was offered and a strong one taken.

'Thanks for coming,' said Cullen. Levchenko nodded and said he was not going anywhere, not today and not tomorrow. 'A little lunch?' Cullen offered as they approached a window table.

'I like pasta. They have pasta here?'

Cullen looked around till someone came over for their order. It was suggested to Levchenko that the *pasta primavera* may be to his liking; the order was placed for both with a young woman who had still to be heard.

'You have something you think I can help with?' Levchenko asked.

'I hope so, but it can wait a little longer.'

'Yes, I can wait. It is a good day. After the storm is a good time.' Levchenko looked closely at his host for his agreement. Cullen nodded. 'Things are blown all over, then there's peace. It's a good peace.'

'You've been here . . .'

'Yes. It's been a long time. Too expensive for my pocket.'

'A long time in the States, too.'

'I know the years, Mr Cullen, the months and when I know the days, I will die.'

We all die, Cullen thought, and not all of us where we want.

'I know things about America I never did before,' said Levchenko, 'not immediately, it took some time. I always thought I knew the American heart, but there are many, many hearts in America. Did you know that, Mr Cullen?'

'But there's a general beat,' replied Cullen.

'Is there?' Levchenko leaned over a little closer. 'Do you know why that is so?' – Cullen did not try to answer. – 'Because the people out there do not know their beat – their own beat. But it's there, they have it.' He sat back with that smile looking comfortable and softer than in his Paris days. 'The body America does not hold as I believed it did,' he continued. 'There is a general heartbeat, a beat called America, you believe? I think that is not so. America is a myth, is it not? Your system is reckless and indulgent. I'm unhappy with America. I've lost to America'. Levchenko looked lost then a little sad. He did look, for that moment, like a man who had wandered far from his birthplace. 'The flat plains of my country may look bleak, Mr Cullen, but I have seen bleakness here, a world of pain is here.' Levchenko touched the cloth that covered the table as if examining it. Cullen was not sure where to look. 'Yes, I have dollar bills in my pocket, I breathe American air, I am alive.' He ironed out the cloth on his side of the table with his hand. 'We are brothers . . . maybe different fathers, maybe. But the American beat is phony and it will destroy you and your land.'

'That sounds mean.'

'Does it? I don't want to be.'

'Human life, are you not talking about that?'

'No, I don't think so. I am talking about your America, about your hypocrisy. I am sure the American heartbeat is a rhythmic sound to some, but it is a pounding hostile drum to others,' he said, before turning round to the sound of diner chatter – a busy restaurant with happy diners, at ease with each other.

Levchenko, on stepping onto American shores after his hurried flight from Paris, had tried to put to sleep all his past, all his deeds and all his losses. He tried to start over, untie his links to everyone he ever knew, stop being the man he ever was and embrace his new home, but America, oh America! 'Ah, life in your country'. He had a rage behind his eyes but he smiled it away. His day had not started well, too many clouds or too much sun, things remembered instead of forgotten, too many days to manage alone. 'I was thinking, Mr Cullen, after your call, about your America, and I don't know what but I was fascinated'.

'By what?' Cullen asked.

Levchenko put a hand on his chest and patted where his heart was. 'Imagine, Mr Cullen, that you are a man who's getting by and you think you know who you are for many years. Your beat is a general beat, as you say, then a day comes when your wife has a charity need, you know, women do. Clothes must go, yours, hers, everyone's, but just in case a dollar bill lies in a pocket your hands search each one; you expect nothing, yet maybe something, and then you find a ticket'. He smiled again. 'You know, a dream ticket, as you Americans would call it, something that will change your life, bought, who knows how long ago, when there was fun or desperation. Do you know,' asked Levchenko, 'how many people never make a claim? Oh, thousands.' He raised his arms to give some idea of the size. 'Can you imagine if this ticket, which has been in your pocket for years, when times were bad, happiness far, could have softened your whole life, maybe have saved a child when you could not, rescued a marriage that was dying, maybe even opened your eyes after a lifetime of them being closed. Imagine, Mr Cullen, this ticket could now kill you'. He inhaled deeply taking comfort from knowing that life and death were so easily lost and found. His eyes turned to the outside where a few sea birds were flying silently, around and around, while the white foam of the waves ran up the beach. 'Ah, there are many American hearts, one in everyone's pocket.'

The young woman returned and served. Cullen asked his guest if he would like wine. A glass of red was requested. The woman said that the wine came in bottles, which Cullen said was fine as long as the bottle was accompanied by two glasses.

Levchenko thought of happiness far, in days different from these, where he had places in his heart for all areas of his life. Then one day he had a meeting, one not dissimilar to the one today, in lovely Paris. Maybe it was because he led a lonely life that he gave time to another American man then, again and again. At the window with a forkful of pasta, he looked out and back on that road that was Paris, and those he could remember who were no longer anywhere. Tania was gone, but the truth was, Tania was never his life. Then she died. He gave a little resigned shrug and sipped from his glass.

Cullen had been speaking, some small talk about what he knew of California, which Levchenko didn't hear. There was a change in both men which remained until their plates were cleared.

'Have you been back to Paris?' Cullen asked.

'Mr Cullen, when I came to America, it was only for America. This is my world. No more Moscow, no more Paris. This is my world here, no other exists.'

'That's a pity,' Cullen remarked.

'I'm a marked man.' He laughed loudly. 'It is true.' He looked certain. 'Very marked.'

Cullen took the opportunity to mention Keech. Levchenko brightened.

'Ah, your general. An amazing man. Not a stupid one.' He paused. 'Oh come, Mr Cullen, you cannot think that. He should be thanked for waking up America.'

The table was cleared.

'I don't want coffee. I'm a little tired and when the body is like that coffee only beats it awake.'

'Feelings for Keech have changed for some,' said Cullen. 'At the time . . .'

'At the time,' Levchenko laughed, 'it was inconceivable to the American mind that they could harbour a General Keech. I remember.' Levchenko stopped for a moment. 'We could all be like the general.'

'Is that so.'

'We are all traitors, Mr Cullen. There are some good ones and some bad ones. There is the international one: the spy! And there is the other: the politician.' – Cullen sat unimpressed – 'Nationhood,' Levchenko went on, 'can be a lukewarm feeling because it is not always a grip on the heart. My homeland is a wonderful place inside my head, but in reality it is not like that. I hate nationalists and that's what your America wants. People for the nation and not simply part of the nation.'

'I don't know about that.'

'Mr Cullen, half the population have had meetings with aliens.

They've been abducted and they want to be again. Half, Mr Cullen, do not want to be here, they'd rather be out there.' He raised a hand to the heavens. 'We're all prisoners, Mr Cullen, in one way or another. What does it mean to be alive? What does it mean to be dead? It is something I have questioned a long time.' He thought of that. 'Prisoners in prison; maybe our world is just that in the heavens.'

'Is that a fact? Prisoners? You, me, General Keech . . .'

'I don't know what it is you want. Your general was a long time ago. I don't want to talk about it.' He took his eyes away from Cullen, away from the table.

'You've got nothing to worry about, it's just that something's come up.'

'I'm sorry, Mr Cullen . . . '

The buzz in the restaurant had become cheerily loud with every table taken. 'Some say,' Cullen added, 'Keech is not dead.' – Levchenko looked at him – 'Not dead, Mr Levchenko. Is that your feeling?'

'I don't have feelings about that.'

'No?'

'That is a world away from me. I am not a reliable source anymore. I'm suffering from a stroke of old age.'

'I need to know from you . . .'

'Mr Cullen, you surprise me. You are a senior man, what are you doing out here? To see me? No, Mr Cullen, if Keech is not dead your office will have known that for a very long time. Please, do not play games with me.' He moved in his chair and both agreed to leave. 'I don't have my lunch bought for me usually. I rarely eat out.'

'If Keech were alive,' Cullen started again, 'would he be alright? Would he, after all those years, be as you are here?'

'As I am here? I don't know. If Keech is alive he will be like me, I suppose: getting older and finding himself listening in the quiet of the night to his own sounds, listening to his life.'

'So you're saying he'd want to come home?'

'Mr Cullen, if Keech knows where home is he's a better man than I am. No, he will want and want, but in reality he could never know what it was he wanted.'

Cullen had led the way down to the hard sand. The beach was not large nor was it long, but many local dogs ran on it to their heart's content every day. Before the men went their separate ways they walked the stretch there and back.

At the same time on that grey windy day, a little distance from them a car parked outside a small hotel was approached by two suited men. The car driver was in the hotel lobby checking in. A hotel off the highway could be a bit hit or miss, but after a journey the traveller usually looks for the positive. Tom Fraser was making light talk with a heavy receptionist when the men entered and took him aside; a few words and a touch of his arm brought Fraser outside and back to his car. His luggage remained placed against the desk, suggesting his return. The woman could not remember much about what she had seen because she had not followed the men into the parking lot, instead she was answering a call. It must have been ten or more minutes when she remembered her new guest, his luggage still on the floor and his car still in the lot. With sharper eyesight she would have seen Fraser at the wheel – he sat unmoving and remained that way until ambulance personnel removed his body and drove it away.

* * *

Helen Fraser had been visited again and now they had gone. It was all unreal to her as she sat with them; she had taken a better seat, looked more certain in her manner and her voice remained strong. But Tom was dead, she was told more than once, and with his death, or just before it, he somehow passed along some of his strength to her. No one knew about that and no one knew much about Tom's sudden demise. The police over there had put it down to a mugging, the usual things were missing. There had been a struggle, they said; it was unfortunate that Fraser was clearly in the wrong place at the wrong time. The men who called on Helen were to tell her that they would of course do all that was necessary to make this tragedy a little lighter.

'Haven't you noticed,' asked Helen once, when time with Tom was more and words seemed to have a little more meaning, 'that we don't live on the things we used to. We used to have love and lust. We had hopes and plans. Now look, we have blemishes, we have tests and results. We used to have fun and laugh. Tom, are you listening? We used to have our son, Tom. TOM!' She wept and wept that day.

Tom had said he didn't know why or how, but every step when he believed he was right, he was wrong. He'd lost his son and he didn't know why. It wasn't fair to be punished without knowing why. They were both being punished, Helen remembered saying. If he were somewhere else, Tom continued, not there in that country, he could have a gun in the house, and did she know, he spoke sadly, he couldn't think of a better time to use it. He was a weaker man than he thought he was, but he had reasons, reasons. Helen remembered the break in his voice and, caught by surprise, felt something of the same in her own.

She had tears now for Tom, she wanted to see him. She had been offered a flight out but she didn't want to cross an ocean alone, so she asked for help to find her son. It was not known to her then that her husband had used his resources to find him some time before, but he had kept it from her because of what he had learned – the pain of not knowing he considered better than telling her where he was.

Should anyone need to see where their father died? Would it not be best he be remembered another way? Helen didn't want to be asked. She didn't want to know how difficult it would be for her and her son, who was presently in prison and had been for over two years. What she was asking for could not be done. But Helen persisted, and she was reminded that her son didn't want to be found, he had made that perfectly clear. It was too much for Helen, to be spoken to by a civil servant who knew nothing, nothing.

'His father's been murdered.' She all but screamed, 'He's his son.' She could have struck the man, again and again. 'My husband's gone, do you understand? Do you?'

Tom Fraser had gone when his son's face had become unclear to him. He had said to Helen that he could not find a strong picture of him in his mind. He was, he said, remembering less of everything. Helen tried to be positive by saying that the reason why their son had turned his back on them was something that only he knew, didn't he see, she'd say, it was his world, and when his eyes cleared and he could see as everyone else, his reasons would die a natural death. It was what she believed and Tom, Tom should believe that, too.

When the son was told of where his father lay, Fraser, if he could still have been part of life on earth, would have seen all those angry and bitter years fall away in him. He would have seen his son young, alone and filled with grief. If he could have seen. The young man was slim and pale without the same fight he had when his father thought he hated him and he thought so, too. When someone approached where he quietly sat to say that his mother needed him now, he nodded and thought maybe his need was greater. Whatever he had been fighting for was for nothing; years of building himself, using the cheapest of materials, had brought him down bit by bit. He had fucked up when he thought he was on the road to growing up, and now his father, cold and stiff, was about to do him a last good turn. He was stretching over an ocean and pulling his son to him.

*   *   *

'So that's the way you say it happened?' – Greg said it was – 'A pick-up truck, it hit you?' The officer wanted to be clear. Greg's face had by now been x-rayed, cleared of fractures and stitched. It was a mighty thump a doctor had said.

'Its door. It was the door,' corrected Jilly.

'Your name sounds familiar,' the officer noted when he read it on the hospital chart. 'Should we know you?'

Greg had difficulty saying much but assured the officer that he should not know him.

'Why are you here in Mason?'

Jilly answered that he was showing her America.

'From California you travel to Mason? Mason ain't America, it's simply Mason. And those men in the truck ain't necessarily American. There's a whole lot of different kinds around here, in the hills, in the mountains.'

Jilly and Greg looked gone. Greg was losing it as the painkillers were taking effect.

'They talk American? You know, speak American?' The officer was hoping they were not.

'Think so,' said Jilly wearily.

'You think so. Okay, I'll speak with the doctor on the way out, and I want the two of you to come and see me when they let you out of here.' – Jilly understood – 'Your boyfriend by the look of things will be staying over. And you, miss?'

'I don't know.'

'Come and see me later.'

The officer walked away with his notes and a friendly nod to Greg, who lay feeling battered, and Jilly, who had begun to shiver again, sat with her hand in his; no words passed between them as he slipped into sleep.

The nurse who appeared at the door waved Jilly to come away, to be with her for a moment. 'Your friend,' she said, 'he has insurance?' She looked at Jilly. 'He needs to stay overnight, at least. And he needs to pay. Can he pay?'

Jilly gave a smile of acknowledgement and lifted herself in an upbeat kind of way.

The nurse, who was more than that, smiled, 'Good.' She watched Jilly leave her and Greg behind and walk out of the hospital into the town of Mason.

40

Paris, March 1983

The door was wide open; two large men had each their grip on a bulky piece of furniture that could not, unfortunately, fit in to the narrow lift; they had to use the stairs. Inside the apartment a room had been completely cleared and another had been entered, everything was going. A window was open and the air and the traffic noise came in together. Fraser had noticed the big Renault in the street, its back doors wide open and some household pieces waiting on the pavement; the furniture was being manoeuvered in the back by a man with a cigarette sticking out of his mouth. He entered the building and made his way into the apartment; his knock on the door had brought no one and he had yet to call out. There were many boxes waiting to be taken and many pieces covered with blankets. The two large windows facing onto the street were naked and Mrs Fisher was looking out of one; she had not heard Fraser's steps on the uncovered floor as he approached.

'Mrs Fisher?' – she slowly turned to him – 'My name's Fraser.' He took a few steps forward and extended his arm to her. Her hand was more taken than given as she looked at him.

'You're leaving?' – she nodded – 'Going back to England?'

– she nodded again – 'It can be a sad time, packing up for good.'

'I haven't been here very long.'

'Why are you leaving?'

'What is it, Mr Fraser, what do you want?'

'It's Monsieur Halin – Monsieur Halin is dead.'

'Yes.' She closed her eyes, his news had not surprised her.

'Who told you?' he asked.

'A call on the phone. I don't know.'

'Mrs Fisher, your friend Halin was shot in the back of the head – I found him.'

She opened her eyes. 'Why did you find him, was he with you?'

He turned and walked over to a far wall. 'Halin had taken up from your husband's business, he replaced him although I don't suppose he had much choice. He was murdered because he wanted to help us, that's their way, if there are any doubts they simply eliminate them.'

'What do you want? I'm leaving. I'm going away.'

'I see that. Paris has been unlucky for you. I'm sorry. Yes, you're going away and I hope things will be better. I'd like to go, too, just clear out; much can be said for it. It's not running, it's learning to get yourself in a more favourable position in an equally favourable place. You don't need any help to get out of here, Mrs Fisher, you've got everything packed, I saw them loading in the street. What help could you need? A fresh start back in England I would imagine looks wonderful right now.' He moved away from the wall and came into the centre of the room. 'There's no good reason at this moment that I can think of why you shouldn't go ahead with your plans. Empty this place completely and go away.'

'I'm still waiting, Mr Fraser,' she said.

'Can we sit?' He pulled a protective cover from the sofa and they sat down. She took only the corner of her side with her back resting on the arm.

'I want to speak to a man, Mrs Fisher, the man who followed Halin the night I met with him. I met Halin three nights ago at 6.30 and I want to know where he was an hour earlier. Was he here? Did he leave from here?'

'I last saw him then, he left here about five.'

'Had you seen anyone else that day?'

'No. I went shopping in the morning and came back. I didn't go out again.'

'What about the afternoon, anyone?'

'I've been living quietly, Pierre was my only call. There was a little work of course, some of my husband's classes, I didn't want to lose them, so I kept them coming.'

'And the day before?'

'Just one class.' She looked down and away.

'Mrs Fisher, don't return home with all this weight, lighten yourself here.'

'Oh no, it wasn't really a class, he's far too good. But he keeps coming.'

'Who?'

'A Russian man, called Levchenko.'

Fraser was ready to jump in with questions but he waited until she had no more to say.

'The classes were hourly?'

'No, they weren't strict like that. If he had more time he stayed.'

'This class you had the day before . . . did it overrun?'

'Maybe it did, yes, maybe.'

'If his English was so good, why did he keep coming?'

'He wanted conversation. It was a conversation class. We'd talk, about England, about life in Paris.'

'Did he ever invite you out? A cafe? A restaurant?'

'Why are you asking? Why am I sitting here answering?' She leaned her body fully back on the sofa and covered her eyes with her hands. 'Yes, he did.'

Fraser got closer to her. 'He did. That's just fine. How often?'

'What?' There was a shout in her eyes and in her tight angry face, but it didn't quite come out in her question.

'How often did you go out?'

'I don't know, a few times.'

'Mrs Fisher, it's important. Two men, one your husband, the other your friend, have been murdered. Mrs Fisher, does this man Levchenko feel for you, is he in love with you?'

'No, no, he doesn't. We've been out together but . . .' Her words died away.

'It's very important that you make no mistake. If Levchenko has feelings for you, if you've taken his heart, then I would ask if he's taken yours?'

'Taken my heart, Mr Fraser. That's a nice way of putting it but I've lost nothing to Mr Levchenko and, as for him, you'd have to ask him.'

'You've lost more than you think to Levchenko, lost, Mrs Fisher. Why do you think we're talking so much about him? Because he belongs with the Russian Intelligence Service. Because he had your husband on a hook. Because he did the same with Halin. You've suffered, Mrs Fisher, you've suffered and lost. If Levchenko has lost his heart to you he, of course, has felt no pain. You must tell me.'

Mrs Fisher stood and quietly stared across at a bare wall. There were voices coming from another room where the removal men had moved into. Voices under strain as something heavy was challenged and taken. 'Nikolai? I don't believe you.' She kept far from him, her face towards the pattern on the wall.

'I'm not lying to you,' said Fraser.

'My husband's dead because of Levchenko?'

'Yes.'

'My God . . . My God!' she whispered. Suddenly she felt everything heavier, all her recent pain rushed back with an intensity that spilled out the only way it could. 'I've gone out with this man, slept with him, done everything.' She wiped away the wet from her cheeks. Her face was tragic, lost and empty and ready to howl the moment Fraser would decide to leave.

'We need your help, Mrs Fisher. When are you seeing him again?'

'I'm sorry, but I have to be alone.'

'He does know you're leaving?'

'Please.'

'There's no time, not now.'

'I'm sorry, I'm not . . . can't you see.' Her tears came back. 'I can't help, I, I, just can't.'

'Mrs Fisher . . .'

'NO!' Her howling could not wait. Her head fell forward onto the wall. Sobbing and sobbing.

Fraser listened to her and remembered Halin and what was his damage, the awful damage. Later he had tried to imagine how it was done to stand there and squeeze the trigger and open up someone's head like that. He had asked himself if he could have done the same, so coldly and brutally.

'I know there should be time for oneself, but for you, Mrs Fisher, there's nothing here for you, everything's gone. You'll be leaving Paris in distress, your life and belongings and also your memories of your life here won't be taken back to England the way they could have.' A pause. 'What I'm saying is that it's not time for you to leave. I know you want to run but I hope you won't.'

'What have you got in mind? What have I got that you want?'

'I want to talk to Levchenko and I want you to arrange it.'

She shook her head.

'If I don't get to him now the chance will slip away,' he said.

'I don't want to stay here another minute longer than I need to. My things are packed and they'll soon be on the boat back to England. I might never return to France, I don't know. But let me get away now, please. Let me just go, will you?' She left Fraser and walked into the bathroom. A mirror still hung above the wash basin and there she positioned herself.

Fraser followed. 'I don't know how or what is needed to make you stay that bit longer. You're right to want to leave as quickly as possible but you're also right to want some justice for your husband. That is right. If you go to England now there'll never be anything for him, he'll be gone and life will continue and the questions will have long stopped. It happens, people die when they shouldn't and they receive precious little, the French police have by now filed his case away, their investigations halted by lack of direction. But you are right, it's natural to want to close the door here, but Mrs Fisher . . .'

She had stared at herself all the time he spoke, all the while he tried to turn her and coax her to give him her help. 'Tell me, Mr Fraser, what would you do if I stayed and they killed me too?'

Fraser looked around the bathroom – it was almost square-shaped, with a large radiator below the window and an old boiler hanging at the left of the door, the tiles on the floor were blue, a dull deep blue set in a pattern. Then he walked out.

'Is it right I should take the risk?' she asked loudly.

'Goodbye, Mrs Fisher.'

She ran a few steps after him. 'I've got no choice, have I? I've got nothing, not even a choice.'

One of the removal men approached. 'Is there anything else?' he asked.

She looked after Fraser. 'When do you want him?'

'As soon as you can,' he said.

The furniture was unloaded from the van and brought back up the tight stairway. All the floor space that had been filled before was filled again, everything was put back, and it was strange: in her heart she had already left. Rosalind Fisher went over what Fraser had said, how she would phone Levchenko and tell him how depressed she had been, how she felt like leaving Paris; she would sound confused and he would come round and hold her. That's what Fraser said, that when he came she must ask to be taken to a restaurant, bright and lively and high above Paris. He told her which one and why, if he should ask, she wanted to go there, because, she was to say, she had been there once before and the feeling she got from looking down on the river, sparkling under the *quai* lights, filled her with something she had not forgotten. Levchenko, thought Fraser, might not understand her insistence to return, but a man in love would see it as his duty to help, there would be no suspicion, nothing that would dilute his love.

But Rosalind Fisher could not build herself back up for her coming revenge. The smart young Englishwoman whom Fraser had found by the window and who stood forcefully demanding why he had come, the young broken woman who began to comprehend only in parts before the whole of Fraser's story came over her was not able to think solely of Levchenko and what Fraser had planned for him. She could not free herself for the short time Fraser had asked for, to make a call and meet the Russian. It was no use, she thought, her defeat had set in deeper than she had realised and she walked about, looking at her elegant bits and pieces acquired since arriving in Paris. She felt how an old person must, when age and loneliness drive them out of their home to something new and temporary, where things remembered just pass by as if they had never been. She was going over, remembering in that way and something must have climbed high inside her, something that breaks down barriers and walls that we all live within, because she took herself back to the window where she had listened to the traffic and all the city noise and in a tearful finale she covered her eyes with her hands and let herself fall.

41

Before Tom Fraser's body could be released for its flight home, it had to await the necessary documentation. It is hard to begin the walk from the outside to that innermost room where the dead congregate. It is a strange walk, one of hope, hope that who is to be seen is not known to you, hope for a mistake, that your loved one is elsewhere, and one of fear that if death has called, there is now the opportunity to say goodbye. Death does not always allow a meeting, the holding of hands, a last look. So few rules in this world, it has been thought over and over, no rules for those precious times for everyone, no consideration whatsoever that if death could encourage love, kindness and patience, there should be a rule that all come to know the softer side of death.

Before Helen, who had banished all the darkness that was too many times her marriage, could take that walk, Jack Kirkland was on his way to meet with Cullen. Jack's face years on had not really changed, but Cullen had no image of the man he had briefly met one night in Germany. It was a moment Cullen didn't want to have, but there he stood waiting, as Jack's flight touched down.

'I don't know very much,' started Cullen, 'I mean, I don't really know why you've come all this way.'

Jack could see the Cullen he remembered, a little fuller, maybe. Less sure, certainly. 'I'm afraid our old job's been resurrected,' he said. 'Bloody big surprise to me. Your general and our . . . , how shall I call him, he wasn't a ranking but he was something.'

Cullen remembered the bar in a small West German town, where he watched Alex and Jack together. Both of them attracting attention. It was amazing to him then that, while he was there unnoticed, they were in full view.

'You won't want this story opened up again,' Jack went on, 'we don't.'

'So you've come here to keep the lid on things?'

'We want to take Jilly Dorian back – home.'

'How do you propose doing that?' Cullen asked.

'I'll talk to her.'

'She thinks her father's alive and she can't rest.'

'That's right, not a day since he vanished.'

'You were a family friend. Right?'

Jack noted and said, 'You've been reading up.'

'She could have called you uncle,' Cullen said accusingly.

'She never did,' replied Jack.

'I don't think our general's dead.'

'Mr Cullen, you mustn't say that. Your general's an old story and we can't let old stories change their endings. Your general's dead and our man's dead, no matter what anyone says.'

'Well,' explained Cullen, 'the politics in this country have changed since that time and if it gives us all an opportunity to look again, that's what we should do.'

Jack stood and placed a hand on the table. 'Just tell me where Jilly Dorian is.'

'I don't know where she is. We're not monitoring her every step, nor are we searching for her in any determined way. We think she might find some calm here and we don't want to disturb that.' There was a pause that made the bar seem silent.

'She should return to England as soon as possible, she's not . . .

the healthiest. She should be with her mother. Her father's been dead many years, you know that, you were bloody there. But she can't accept that. She's lost her youth because of her refusal to get on with her life, and now she's halfway through her twenties and it will go on until she's made to realise that no matter where she goes, her hopes of finding her father will be in vain.' Jack sounded deeply concerned and reasonable. 'She must be helped. She cannot lose more days of her life.' He took his hand away. 'Help me, Mr Cullen, to take her home.'

Cullen put some money on the table and told Jack that two minutes from the building was a hotel, sufficient for a short stay, and he was expected. 'I'll be in touch.'

'Mr Cullen . . .'

Cullen had smartly walked out.

*　　*　　*

Jilly had walked around Mason, a nice kind of town, with a feel to it that she found comfortable. It was strange to be so well as if she were part of the local community. She felt like stopping someone for anything, asking a direction or the time of day, and the words she had ready were – *parlez-vous français?* In America, feeling comfortable, she wanted to speak French like the child she was when she sailed with her mother to Calais. A day out of school, so unexpected, with no time to think and dream of it. To go to France where it was so cool to say anything in that language. Oh, she loved her mother then. There was the breeze, the gulls, oh, she was going away. *Parlez-vous français.* The squawking could be heard, the water swooshing and the white foam from the ship propellers. Mum. Mum.

Mason was some hundred miles from the sea and its leafy streets were unlike any kind of boulevard, but her mind was quiet, she was tranquil, the last twenty-four hours had not yet had their effect. She was blessed, she would have said, if there had been anyone nearby to ask her. Like the clouds above her head, doubt and then despair could hang over her that she had taken too many wrong turnings for too long. Dad was surely gone, she had heard the devil say. Why could she not hold onto the memories, why could she not? She would never really know how her mother had lived the years by herself as she did not know why she had walked around her little England when so many times there had been a longing to walk out on life. Many times she had heard the call. Now in Mason she saw women who looked like her mother, alone and with another, strong and elegant they appeared to her, like any would in any boulevard. If she had been a degree more uncertain in herself, she would have gone to one and embraced her. Home had a feeling of being close, in Mason things had come back to her, and it was good to feel all the muscles in her body just ease because only by their easing could she feel what she had been carrying. Home was all around in Mason, the garden and the swing of early school, around her dad's neck and holding her mum's hand. Around and around Mason until the clouds thickened and the heavens cried. Jilly found herself too alone and returned to Greg.

*   *   *

Deep in the Heart of Texas was playing, and it was a place where some people wanted to be, but Toby Cullen, who had distanced himself from Jack Kirkland, was far from that state as he travelled north with his eyes on the road and the picture of Jilly on his mind becoming more and more that of Margaret. *Deep in the Heart* was in his ears and in some way it reminded him of what America was: hot and cold, thoughtful and indifferent. His meeting with Levchenko had in some way helped him to remember people who used to be important in his life and although many could be found again it would not be the same. There was no use in returning to old ground. When his father died, Cullen felt he could say nothing. Without the old man, the door had closed on both of them. But while Texas was still on the air, he knew that was a lie. All the distance east of him, in a state where nature was in love with itself, his mother lived, less close to him today and that was not what she wanted. So many questions people ask themselves about loved ones that always end in why. Why. But a flight away Cullen could hear her at any time asking him to unburden himself, become an honest man, perhaps for the first time, and tell her where he was the day Margaret went away. Deep in the heart the weight of Margaret lay more; some nights, some days. For how many years had his mother and father carried their pain. The years it took Cullen to even say sorry alone in the darkest of closets where secrets are born and where they die. Cullen had for so long refused to raise his hand and whisper his guilt.

It took a Texas matter to shake him, a Texas matter to make him raise his hand. So far away and still in America, there was a story of how a young man was to die. It had happened again and again in all the years Cullen had been a citizen of his country. It was known and not known that evil begat evil but Cullen never had much passion for the good Lord, nor for the devil, it was a battle that never involved him. To live or die was a matter of the law and there could be no argument. He could turn his eyes away, worry entirely of himself, and whatever was going on elsewhere, went on. But somewhere in Texas a death was being prepared. A young man who was born vulnerable and remained that way all his life had been promised that all his loneliness and uncertainty were to come to an end. Life was precious but not, it seemed, his. An act of gross disrespect for human life had put this man on a journey, immature and blind to his road ahead, following the sky from light to dark, night to day, he now lay at journey's end. Respect was a one-way street for some people, and those demanding it took some pleasure in withholding it. Before reaching his last day, the young man had heard of people at the gates outside urging the state of Texas to think again; they called themselves friends of Leroy . . . but it was too late because there was a swollen number of those who saw and felt no shame. Cullen could remember the glee in their faces and how convinced they were that their state knew what was right and where the truth lay, but he knew that Texas was as far away from the truth as every other state in the Union, yet Texas was sure it had seen the light in such matters and death was it.

Cullen's mother had mentioned the young man on the phone one night as she sat on her bed, dressed for sleep. It was an unexpected call for both of them. She had gone about her preparations like every other night when she had an over-whelming urge to speak to her children. In the mirror on her dressing table she saw what she had become and all her emotions pulled at her. *Oh Margaret*, she would hear herself quietly call. *Toby*, she would call next. Her husband never had a name at that time of night, for night could be remembered as the time words kept subdued in the day were released and feelings of anger and loss became gigantic. Night was when they turned on each other. If only he could feel her loss as she did, if only his pain could be seen. She thought she needed that from him. After he died she found her lost Margaret more in her life and sometimes she could not cope. Sitting on the bed she had asked her son if he thought of his sister at all. Could he see her sometimes as she was dressed in a particular way that she wanted him to remember? But he never could. Life was poorer without her, did Toby know that? Toby knew he had become poorer and, as the years passed, it would be downhill all the way.

'They're going to kill a young man in Texas,' his mother said. 'The news was saying this and that, but they're going to kill him.' She sighed and asked, 'What happened to Margaret? I'm too old for all my tears.'

Cullen could say little.

'You can't kill people anymore,' his mother reminded him. 'What is Washington doing about the state of Texas?' she sighed again.

'Go to bed, Mom,' Cullen coaxed.

'I can't sleep, Toby. Margaret's in my head and for some reason so is that young man. Why is that? Why do I have my lovely daughter and a stranger together?'

The minutes passed and then the line between them closed; Cullen could see his mother in bed with her table lamp on, her head a little sunken in the pillow, and for a little while he thought of Margaret and himself, and where they had come from.

Cullen rested poorly. What could he do? His mother, three hours ahead in the middle of the night, and he with his hand on the phone urging himself to call. She was tormented every night, she had told him more than once, and he was sure he had said something but she never heard it. With the night over he ran into the new day and a new stretch of road.

'They don't give a fuck about the man they lost, but they do about this Dorian woman. They want us to find her for them.'

Cullen had pulled off the road to speak with his caller back east. 'I don't think we should do that,' he advised.

'You don't? Cullen, you've left one of theirs in a shitty place, and they seem to want some kind of trouble.'

'Jilly Dorian,' Cullen began to explain, 'is simply looking for her father. It's sad, but she believes he's still alive. She's got dreams of their reunion.' He stopped as the signal faded and then returned.

'It's a bag of worms,' the caller stated.

'We don't need to enter the scene yet.'

'And Keech?'

'Same story. Everyone knows that one.'

A lightning flash and a peel of cracking noise brought a ton of rain which blackened the sky. Cullen decided to sit put with a photo of Jilly with her details in front of him. She looked nice, no, more than that. Did she take that from her father? He couldn't say. A beer in a foreign place with him couldn't tell where her features came from. Two foreigners, one not knowing the other, and the other pretending the same. It was all a blur now. While traffic splashed heavily on the side of Cullen's car, he took time to consider all his successes, what he had built his reputation on. He seemed to be highly regarded for his approach to things then, the way he could be cold, how he could show it and how it never faltered. That was his success, keeping people on the far side of the room.

Parked off the road he studied Jilly's notes and her two photos, one fairly recent, the other, for some reason, a long time ago. He remained still while others on the road sped past. It was while on-coming traffic was dazzling him that a patrol car pulled up behind. The officer's knock on his window startled him before he was asked to step out of the car. Cullen protested claiming he had nothing to protect him from the rain.

'Don't say anything, sir. Please step out of the car.'

The rain fell in torrents as the officer in full weather gear frisked Cullen who had been asked to spread himself against the car.

'Is this your car, sir?'

'It's a rental,' Cullen said in a half shout.

'Identification?'

Cullen produced his wallet. The rain was running down his face.

'I'll have to check this. Please do not enter your vehicle.'

Cullen stood until all of him but the socks on his feet had felt the rain water. The patrolman started his engine and came up alongside requesting him, through an open window, to follow behind. Cullen made little protest and sat in. He felt like he glistened as every part of his clothing he touched was wet and runny; he sat while the screen wipers swooshed back and forth, swoosh, swoosh, and the patrol car waited.

42

Paris, March 1983

The ringing telephone was unexpected, Tom Fraser could not have known what was waiting for him. He hurried to his room and quickly opened the door and reached for it. Mrs Fisher was dead. Suicide. He placed the receiver and lay back on the bed. 'Mrs Fisher,' he whispered, and for some time all he saw was her, all he heard was her voice. She cried, he could still hear her, her crying and crying. He had always some doubts about a woman's pain, he didn't trust it sometimes, he had never found women very accurate – their words, their thoughts, their tears, they never seemed to penetrate him as they should have, different faces trying hard to be meaningful. Everything was too shadowy, not enough black, not enough white. He lay on the bed searching where the point had been that took her out and down into the street. Had he pushed her? In his attempt to get to Levchenko had he by-passed her reactions? He let it rest, and wondered if he now had lost the Russian; he couldn't leave Paris, just pick up his tourist bag and head home.

Then something came into his head: some trees, wet and dark, and a small crowd all with umbrellas standing close together. He held to this picture, firm, not one that could be lost in a second.

There was a stone wall nearby, he could see it stretch away towards the green rising fields in the distance. The rain didn't seem hard, a drizzle maybe. Some umbrellas had been folded and others followed. Everyone was quiet. It was clear to him – the wet grass, the hand on a shoulder, the silent sadness that this funeral gathering felt back home in Scotland. He could not recall who had died, and many of the mourners that day he had not seen since, he did not know if they were still alive, it was a long time ago he was sure. And then they walked away, umbrellas up, their cars waiting. Little stone walls round a field; was that where Mrs Fisher would be taken?

The bed creaked as he swung his legs over the side. Levchenko would not go near, it would be stupid. He picked up the phone, dialled and spoke. 'Where is she?' Pause. 'Mrs Fisher.' Pause. 'Her body?' Another pause. 'Right. I'm going there. I'll get back to you.' He pushed the receiver hard into its cradle. A window shutter had come loose and was flapping noisily in the wind. He opened the window and held it back, while studying the view over the rooftops – Paris had become grey as a rainy spell was approaching. Funerals in the rain, he wondered; would Levchenko be attracted, would he make an appearance?

'I want a service for her. Put it in the evening paper. Do anything but get it in.' – Lee looked – 'I can't let her go,' said Fraser. 'I know she's dead and should be left peacefully like anyone else, but that's not how it is. Death is a terrible thing, Lee, never get used to it simply because it's inevitable. I know there are people around who don't give a damn – in Paris, in London – people who should struggle to the last for you, but they won't, they'll let you go and they'll go home and somehow what happened earlier that day will never come back, never creep up on them. They can live with it, you see. Well . . . Mrs Fisher's dead, and before, there was Halin and Gull . . . Am I taking their demise too seriously, is that what you think, Lee?' – Lee looked down – 'I

want Levchenko to have an opportunity to pay his last respects.'
'Yes,' said Lee. 'She told me he loved her,' Fraser went on, 'and
maybe that will bring him, maybe this love will finally bring the
two of us together.' He thought of that. 'You'd better get going.'

He watched Lee walk away down the gravel path towards
his car. Through the misty windows of the hospital he saw Lee
slip his car through the gate. He stood listening to the hollow
sounds of footsteps close by and those out of sight in the corridors and on the stairs; he waited, there was nothing else to do.
A smell seeping into the corridor, thick and sickly coming from
nowhere, hit Fraser bringing up all his recent memories, and he
struggled to cover his mouth as he quickly made to the door.
There, the wet Paris air rushed into him. It was then the large
black Peugeot stopped outside the gate; he did not see it, his
sickness had taken his attention. Even when the car moved a
further fifty metres, he still did not notice. The rain had begun
to fall harder and Fraser stepped back inside taking his position
by the windows. It was the crunching steps of someone on the
path that wakened him from all his thoughts, all that had locked
him away for the time he stood there. He stepped away from the
door as the visitor hurried towards him. Inside from the door
was a small desk with a white-coated clerk giving out information and directions: Levchenko pushed through the door and
stopped at it. Fraser had no time to walk away and he could
have caught Levchenko's eye while he asked for something from
the desk. Fraser had his handkerchief out, crumpled in his hand;
there was an expression of sorrow on his face, a sadness that his
handkerchief emphasized. Levchenko spoke a soft French and
was given a direction that took him past Fraser and along the
corridor, following the sign to the mortuary.

There was loud laughter coming from two female hospital
staff who had entered the corridor. Their laughter bounced off
the walls before they returned through a door that echoed its
slam everywhere. Mrs Fisher was through another door and

Levchenko, thought Fraser, was paying his last respects, he was saying goodbye, inside, and very privately.

He walked over to the clerk and explained a sad situation, then took the lift to a floor above. The clerk had phoned ahead and a nurse waited to show Fraser into a compact room with a table laden with magazines. She then left him and closed the door. Fraser picked a magazine, one full of tragedy with pictures of human pain. They would have loved Halin, he thought, '*Poor French Boy Caught in the Middle.*' There would be a picture of the wound and the lavatory. What would they have done with Mrs Fisher, he wondered.

'*Monsieur?*'

There had been a tap on the door, Levchenko had turned the knob and his foot was in.

'*Oui,*' replied Fraser. 'Ah, you are the friend of the late Mrs Fisher?'

'Yes, I am.'

Fraser pushed his arm out and took Levchenko's hand. 'I'm doctor Martin. Please sit down.' They sat across from each other with the small table separating them. 'When Mrs Fisher . . . A neighbour telephoned me when she was discovered. I live nearby.' – Levchenko looked – 'I entered her apartment, I went in, I don't suppose I should have but . . . There were a few letters all sealed and all with a name on each. They were obviously addressed to friends. Some don't, some suicides don't leave anything, nothing. They've been cut off before their final act. Mrs Fisher had still something and if circumstances had been right, if someone had called round or something had just got in the way . . . We'll never know.'

'I see,' said Levchenko.

'Suicide is a terrible way in which a person should leave this world. I have great sympathy for those people. Mrs Fisher was my patient, she called me her English doctor.' He smiled. 'I'm half and half, actually, but to her I was more.' He paused. 'She was a lovely woman, and I've taken it upon myself to do this for her, to assure her letters reach their destinations.'

'The police would have done that,' said Levchenko.

'Yes, I know. But there was nothing else I could do for her. And rather than have official hands on them, beaurocratic ones, I thought . . .'

'Is there one for me?'

'I don't know yet. I thought one or two of her friends might go to her and I was in the area. The clerk told me you had called. You didn't leave a name with him.' He paused. 'If you could give me your name I'll be able to tell you if the remaining letter is for you.'

Levchenko nodded. 'It is a very sad affair; I had known her a short time. You were her doctor, did she suffer from anything?'

Fraser shook his head. 'She was a healthy woman, she gave me no indication that she was capable of this. But it happens, a certain despondency that can sink deep in a person. There's melancholy in all of us and in the right conditions a person can see their own destruction as the only step. It can be a clear-headed decision in a depressed sort of way, their values are turned upside down.'

Levchenko sat still and looked as if he understood the workings of the human mind.

'Now is the letter for you, *Monsieur?*'

'My name is Levchenko.'

'Ah, that is your surname, *Madame* has written a Christian one.'

Levchenko straightened himself, his suspicion mounting. Fraser buttoned up his coat.

'*Monsieur?*'

'Nikolai. My name is Nikolai.'

Fraser beamed. 'Good. The letter's for you. I have it in my car, just ouside. I'm so pleased I've found you. I thought I might not.'

'What would you have done?'

'Oh, I would have been obliged to hand it over to the police, but now there's no need.'

Fraser opened the door and Levchenko walked out. The lift was occupied; as they waited, Levchenko said nothing and Fraser complained a little that hospital lifts were either inefficient or that not enough of them were installed. At that the large steel doors of the staff lift opened and a bed trolley was pushed out by a male nurse. Fraser put his hand on Levchenko's arm and walked him in. The doors then closed and the two men descended. One floor down the lift stopped and the door opened. Fraser slammed his hand on the button panel on the cabin wall, the doors closed and the lift continued down. He then pushed a finger on the white stop button and everything shuddered to a stop, movement and noise. He raised an open hand in front of Levchenko and lifted a finger of the other.

'You can struggle with me and get this thing moving, but a smart man like you would know what that would mean. *Top KGB Officer Stranded in Hospital Lift* is not a good headline. There's a newspaper photographer waiting in the car park.'

'Who do you think you've got?' asked Levchenko as he backed away from him.

'There's no mistaken identity, I have no worry there. You're Nikolai Levchenko and that's all I need to know. You've just visited Mrs Fisher's body, her death brought your intimate relations to an unexpected halt. You knew her husband, Edward Fisher, who's also dead, murdered by persons unknown. You knew Frank Gull who was murdered most certainly by you. And then there's Halin. A man of little importance gets a big-time killing.'

Levchenko took a step forward and Fraser allowed it. He was lean compared to the Russian's bulk, his hands looked quick and sharp and eager for Levchenko.

'I'm going to call the police. You can't hold me here. You're mad.'

'Sit down. Things will be better if you do.' Fraser folded his arms and waited for Levchenko to ease himself to the floor. 'I suppose you wish right now you were back in Moscow or wherever else you come from in your country. And I suppose you're right to do so. It's natural for those afraid to wish they were somewhere else, Gull must have wished it. And if you're not afraid now, you will be because there's nothing here in Paris to protect you.'

'Have you got a gun?' asked Levchenko.

'Perhaps we both have,' replied Fraser. 'Halin was shot and before, Gull. Yes, perhaps you too have a gun, but I'm not interested, I don't care about your weapons, it's your information I want.'

Levchenko looked comfortable with his back against the wall and his legs folded up. Although Fraser worried, trapped in the lift like that, he kept it and showed only irritation, the way he might with a man from the French beaurocracy.

'My name is Levchenko, should I know yours?'

'Fraser. Same business as yours.'

'British?'

'You know damn well.'

Levchenko smiled. 'You're going to kill me because of those people you named? Oh, I don't think you will. Everyone threatens at the beginning; it's a sign of unsureness, they lose their aggressiveness after a while. You're not going to kill me, Mr Fraser, here in this ghastly illuminated elevator. But talk is fine, I'll listen.'

'As you killed Halin so coldly, don't underestimate human revenge. The KGB knows all about that, it never stops returning for that.' Fraser held his hands tightly, keeping some distance between them. 'One of our officers has recently died, you will know about that because he was working on your side. Well he left some things behind as one usually does at the end – you know, papers, letters, private things like that. We had to go through it all, check up on the dead, sort of thing. It was startling what we came across, good quality material I can say. It revealed so much to us: names and places . . . you know what I'm talking about . . .' There was less anger in his voice, less tension, as if what he was saying was a kind of relief to him, happy to tell. 'So much we learned from this man's death that we now seek no name: we have his name. Your lovely relationship has ended, but before it did you saw it threatened and that's why you killed Gull and Halin. Mrs Fisher was your mistress, which was fine until I told her who killed her husband. I regret that now because it took her out through the window. While I was looking for you I forgot to look at her; if I had, there might have been a telltale sign, something that would have told me. But it's late now and I've got you.' He slipped his hands into his coat pockets.

'Why kill me? You've got everything you want. Take the elevator down, you can hand me over to the police.'

'You won't be released if that's what you think. Oh yes, for Gull and Halin you'd probably be safely flown home – out of sight and mind – the press would try and stir something but you'd be gone. Yes, it would all die down. But there's Mrs Fisher . . . It's the French, you see.' A pause. 'Did you see her body?'

'No.'

'Nothing at all?' – Levchenko shook his head – 'I'll tell you why. It's being considered that Mrs Fisher was pushed. Oh they knew about her recent bereavement, but they're not thinking suicide, they're thinking something else.' – Levchenko stood up, his face caught in astonishment – 'There are some who want an investigation into her death. An investigation means digging into her private life, you know, diary, letters, phone numbers, people in her life, and that means you.' He looked into Levchenko's face, a face which had begun to loosen, where the shape of his middle years had taken hold. 'It would be a murder enquiry and you'd be exposed, that is if I weren't going to kill you, but I am. You're a cold-blooded man, I have to get heated up before my violence comes out. I believe in revenge, I believe in going after and striking back, all the way to mother Russia if the blood demands it. All of you who have come out of that country, with your sickness and your hate should never get any other treatment.'

'Mr Fraser, I'm getting weary of all this, there's nothing to trouble me,' he smiled, 'and you have nothing in your pocket. Now, shall we get out of here.' He stepped toward the button panel but was stopped by Fraser's fist sinking deep into his stomach. He took a step back and fell.

'You're filth,' said Fraser. He wanted to lash out and his control was in the balance. He crouched to him as some colour was slowly returning to Levchenko's face. 'I want a name, nothing more. I'm not interested in what the French courts would do to you. I want a name. The leak in London, you run him, don't you?' Fraser stood. 'Don't you?' – Levchenko gave an indication that he did, a movement of the eyes, something in the face – 'This senior officer left a name and we need it verified. Who are you running there?'

'You don't understand, you can't expect me to answer. You're being ridiculous, no one anywhere would give you that kind of information.'

'You will, Levchenko, by God you will.'

'Violence, is that your method. You hope to cause me physical pain, break my arm or leg. Either way you will get no success. Russian people have had pain, they know what it's like but they've never submitted to it. We're of the same kind, it's just that we in my country are more threatened than you are, we have to be right in all our actions.'

There was a light flashing on the button panel but neither saw it.

'We have friends in the West that we must protect,' said Levchenko. 'We don't betray loyal friends. Were you not brought up to trust in friendship?'

Fraser ignored the question. 'You have a friend in London,'

he said, some of his recent anger hotting up again, 'and for years you have been running him, squeezing him, blackmail maybe. With your kind of friendship no one's allowed to end it but your lot, you possess the ultimate ending. If I deviate from the truth here, my truth, you'll correct me, won't you. Now, this friend has got a wife . . .'

'Most have, Mr Fraser,' broke in Levchenko.

'Yes, most have. But this particular wife is suspicious, she doesn't exactly know what it is but her husband is causing concern. So, she tries to follow him – to the office in the morning, who he has lunch with, that sort of thing. And then one day he drops in to a city hotel and leaves a small package at the desk. This lady's suspicion heightens. Naturally, no?'

Levchenko listened, trying to keep his surprise inside, behind his own defensive wall.

'She decides to approach the desk,' continued Fraser, 'and discovers that the package is addressed to a Mr Brown who's expected to collect it the following day. The lady leaves and returns the next day. She waits and waits, behind a magazine, a newspaper; it's uncomfortable for her, alone like that in a hotel lobby that caters for the busy and the lonely. Then Mr Brown calls and collects. What's discovered at this point is that Mr Brown is, in actual fact, Mr White, the senior officer who died. Now isn't that interesting. And what's more, while White was collecting at one hotel, you had Halin collect an equally small package at another – just before he was picked up.'

Levchenko sat silent trying to work out what was known and what was not. It was clear there was a gap in Fraser's knowledge, and Levchenko had to decide how wide it was. 'You're telling me stories. You'll tell me anything to get what you want out of me. I don't believe you; why should I?'

'Because it matters to you that you survive, one way or another. I can't accept that your own loyalty, dedication, call it what you like, goes beyond your personal survival. Maybe in another place, different circumstances, where a person's emotions have lost touch with reality . . . a battlefield, maybe, but not here. There's nobody watching or with you here, Levchenko. There are places like that; Halin was caught in one and now you're in one.'

A bell began ringing from the button panel, a muffled ring that caused Fraser an anxious moment. Levchenko did not move. Fraser removed a key that hung inside a small perspex case below the row of buttons and quickly opened the small door below it. Inside was a telephone hanging on a hook. He answered and explained he was stuck and had pressed all the buttons but there had been no response. He said there was another gentleman with him who was feeling unwell and would appreciate if they could get to them before too long.

'They are having difficulty locating the fault,' said Fraser. 'They'll be looking for a while yet and that suits me fine, I have time to prise from you what you want to keep, your secret friendship, your secret life.'

'I can't take it much longer.' Levchenko inhaled deeply. 'I can't.' – Fraser looked – 'Claustrophobia. You understand.'

'You suffer from claustrophobia?'

'Ever since I was a boy.' He took his jacket off while he inhaled more and more deeply.

'Don't lie to me,' said Fraser. 'Give me the man you're running and you'll be out of here, in the fresh air and free.'

Levchenko put a hand to his chest. 'Mr Fraser, I realise you're working alone, you're on your own time here with me. London doesn't know. Your people don't know what you're doing. Is that not so?' A pause to inhale. 'Is that not so? You have a guilty conscience, you have Mrs Fisher on your mind. Is that not it?' His breathing had eased and his vulnerability had disappeared, and like a man with his confidence returned, Levchenko was coming back at Fraser, jabbing his finger towards him as he spoke, as if to pin him to the spot. 'Can you see her fall, fall. You went there when she never wanted you, and you spoke to her; you told her anything.' He stopped and loosened more at his tie. 'And you left her shaken and in such distress that she killed herself.' He lifted up his jacket. 'You need to be careful, Mr Fraser, you can't go alone, there are rules, you know that. It's dangerous what you're doing.' He walked past him. 'I'm getting out of here.'

Fraser pushed him hard against the thin metal walls and held him. 'You're not going anywhere. Nowhere!' He pulled Levchenko by the shoulders close in to him and raised his knee, squeezing all the Russian's power away. Levchenko fell to his knees, his body bent and his hands soothing. 'You don't understand,' said Fraser, 'we've got a man who's been passing things over a long period of time, passing them on to you. But now we know, we've discovered what he's been doing and we're excited. Yes, through the pain of discovery there's excitement. You can understand that, can't you?'

The lift began to move. Levchenko put on a wide grin, it was what he had hoped for, that the mechanics of the damn contraption would get it moving and then both men would be brought down. But it was not to be, not yet. The lift shuddered and stopped again. Some pain returned to Levchenko's groin.

'Our time's running out,' said Fraser, 'and when they open the doors they'll find you here on the floor, dead. Your identity will become known and so will mine: two foreign intelligence agents. The French will listen to your embassy's protest and the British will claim it was natural causes and that will be more or less that. Now, I want to hear the name of this man from you and I won't ask again.' He took off his jacket and let it fall on the floor, then removed his trousers belt. Levchenko watched all his movements. 'You see,' Fraser went on, 'with this around your neck your claustrophobia will be triggered; this confined space and the decrease of air into your body will set it off, and through your panic will come restrictions on certain parts: your muscles and your nervous system. Do you think you can survive that?'

– Levchenko did not say – 'I doubt it, and if I'm right then – you'll be dead.'

'I can't tell you the name because the Americans already know.' Defeat had come all over Levchenko, had set into him like the gloom any defeat is. 'I'm working for them.'

'What?'

'I contacted them four months ago; I told them I wanted out. Of course they had to be convinced and I've been working for them since, supplying what they ask for. I must not endanger my chances of starting a new life in the United States.'

'Christ Almighty!' Fraser was lost for some moments. 'The Americans?'

'I can't prove it to you, not here.' A pause to ponder his proof. 'If you kill me they won't be happy. And the . . .'

'Shut up.' Fraser paced before him. 'I don't believe this because there's no doubt that you were involved in the killings of Gull and Halin; now why would you do that if you were already under an American wing?'

'This man of yours is valuable and his identity was only known to a select few; he had to be protected, it was in every-one's interests. But your man Gull was getting closer and he had to be stopped. I told this to the Americans, I asked if there might be a way of getting him out of Paris, but they couldn't find one, but I did ask.'

'So you had to act?'

'I had to behave as I would have had to normally; to do other-wise would have aroused suspicion. The Americans understood that.'

'Halin was the same.'

The lift shuddered again and began to move.

'I was so ready to kill you, I had never been so ready. You're a lucky man, tell your children that. Tell them the Americans saved your life.'

Levchenko put on his jacket. 'It's moving,' he whispered. He dropped his head into his hands then began rubbing his brow and nose with a handkerchief.

'Recently I saw a little girl,' he said, 'she was eating an ice-cream the way children do, with a sort of concentration . . . There were moments I thought you were going to kill me.' He paused. 'And this little girl came into my mind. My own children are much older; I don't even know if they eat ice-cream anymore.' The lift continued down.

'Now you can ask them.'

The lift had arrived and before its doors opened Fraser asked, 'The girl with the ice-cream, did she have a name?'

Levchenko was taken at that moment, the light from the facing windows had suddenly blinded him. 'A name?' he smiled. 'Don't all little girls have a name?'

A young nurse with very white arms asked how he felt. He was fine, fine, he replied. Fraser watched him go, all the way along the corridor. When at the last few steps he turned his head, he was a little stooped, a little older looking from that distance, then he turned away again and disappeared through a door.

43

'It's the fuck in my vocabulary that's kept me strong.' A rare moment had passed between Greg and his mother when the days were bleak and ready to turn bleaker still. His mother had lost hope in herself and hope of holding things together while Greg kept pulling hard to be free. Those years after her husband had hit all the headlines, when no one called anymore and no one smiled, something inside her was damaged, so she stopped seeing Greg, she recognised who he was to her but the importance of it had faded. When love like that dies it affects the spirit, and day by day Greg tried to place little importance on his loss until he could not live with it anymore and drove himself away. For a time – his mother's presence gone, the look in her eyes, her physical shape – all he could see were rainbows in everything he looked at and every-thing he touched. It was a magic time and his affection for himself returned. When he met Carla, he believed the moment could not have been better. He was more complete than he ever had been; she was everything. There was an immediate bond, a happiness between them, but it was not always enough to remove what personal baggage they carried. Words could be easy some days; many things on her mind, she would say, but thoughts would run from her and feelings, which she would shrug her shoulders at, remained in her eyes. At other times, when she knew of no one watching, all her loveliness could be seen.

Greg sat on the bed dreaming as he waited for Jilly and thought about Carla. 'You're not very tall for an Idaho boy,' she had said to him in a poor little place that played music when you paid for it. It served mainly beer and the broken people who lived around it took some relief there day and night. Those people had something they never wanted, so they isolated themselves, in a forced way, to hide it. Greg had his name which he could hate then love then hate again; Carla could smile for awhile and remove the hate from the forefront to the back of his mind. She was happy fun. She spoke of no ache or sorrow and neither did Greg. For a time Greg was just Greg, no Keech, no junior – just Greg, alive and happy.

'You'll need to wait in the waiting room,' a nurse said, waking him from his daydreams.

Behind a windowed door in the hospital in Mason he found himself closer to Carla than he had known, he could still feel her hand whenever he wanted to. There were moments he wanted not to think of her smile, not to remember too well what she had told him, not to dream of the land from which she came. But there were times like now, when all those things were forgotten and it became so easy yet achingly hard to remember her. 'If your father loved Berlin,' she had said, 'then you must go there, you must.' Greg had told her a story about the city of Berlin, a city his father had often spoken of before it was one. Carla listened eagerly, so Greg told her more. He felt it therapeutic telling her things his father had supposedly said, it was an old story, one he was convinced was true. 'To be in a place like that, who knows, Greg, who knows.' It was a soldier's city, Checkpoint Charlie and all that, God, it was America, Greg's father used to say when the house was still a home, still liveable and secure. Greg would watch him when his passion was rising and tried being hot like that, but his flame was never burning in that way; not then as a boy or today as a man.

Greg sat humming a song that was being sung on a nearby radio. When he was happy he used to sing, it was a way by which he could measure his life and how it was going. But too many songs were already half forgotten, the music was there, but the words were gone, so he would hum more. Dad could sing. He could sing. What did he sing? His humming had become louder while he waited until he saw Jilly's figure coming along the corridor.

'There's a car waiting for us. We're being taken to the Sheriff's office,' Jilly announced.

'Our journey's ended,' replied Greg, 'and maybe that's best. Where were we goin'? Anywhere?'

Jilly examined his cheek where the wound was covered and now could see the full extent of the swelling. 'For years,' she spoke softly, 'I've abandoned my life because I couldn't begin to pretend that my father was dead. I've let go all my roots. I've changed in ways that, if my father were to walk along here now, I can't be sure he would know me.'

'Maybe he'd cry,' Greg did not mean to say that. Her eyes swelled up and she whispered with an open mouth, 'I know.'

Greg put his hands on her shoulders and pulled her into him. 'Let's go.'

*   *   *

'We don't know the procedure too well in this matter. We don't know what we should rightly say to this woman.' – Cullen sat drying out while a suited man spoke – 'Her husband's here, stone cold. It wasn't an unfortunate killing, being in the wrong place and so on, it was deliberate.'

'He'd just arrived and you're saying he was hit on?'

'We don't know too much. His name was Tom Fraser and the

Brits here are claiming he was nothing more than a retired civil servant. No one knows why he was here.'

'The woman?' enquired Cullen.

'She's quiet. She's with her son, through there.' He pointed at the door at his rear.

'You pull me off the road for this?'

'We asked for help after they were brought here. They got off the plane and we were told to expect them. We don't know what's goin' on.'

Cullen slipped his jacket on and made for the door.

Helen Fraser looked as she felt, tired and troubled beside her son who had become a stranger to them, and now only to her.

'My name's Toby Cullen.' He stretched his hand out to them both.

'I want to see my husband. I want to know what happened to him,' said Helen.

'An act of violence. I'm sorry.'

'My husband's dead?'

'Yes.'

'He came to America.' She sat with some mystery on her face. 'He came to America . . . He's dead.'

Cullen looked at mother and son, her body slumped against her wishes of upright and strong, the son with nowhere to look except the floor.

'Why is he dead?'

'He was shot. I don't know why. Things aren't clear.'

'He was an unhappy man, and I believe he thought coming here would change that.'

'Unhappy?' asked Cullen.

'With his life, his past. Always the past.' Helen looked at her son and wanted to stretch out to him to reduce the distance.

'Can I get you something? Coffee?'

'Some cigarettes,' the son asked. 'Marlboro. If you can.'

Cullen briefly left the room. On his return and before he had closed the door, Helen spoke hurriedly: 'I can't go home. If I go home you'll forget all this, our tragedy. It doesn't take long to forget someone else's loss, Mr Cullen.'

'I'm sorry. I don't know much. I've been asked to speak to you. I'm waiting for details.'

'My father was in the Intelligence Service,' said the son inhaling and exhaling quickly from his cigarette. 'He thought he kept England safe.' He had lifted his head to speak showing his full face, his pale cheeks and emotional eyes. 'I shouldn't be here.'

Helen tried to say something to him but spoke to Cullen instead. 'Father and son.' She thought that would be enough to explain. 'We used to have more,' she went on, sitting tightly in her chair.

Cullen did not know what she meant.

'She means,' intervened the son, 'they had more when I was in their lives.'

'And you're not?'

'Not for five years.'

Helen heard her son sounding pleased to say that. 'I've lost my son,' she said, 'I don't know why he can't tell me.'

Cullen listened, attracted to the Fraser story.

'In some ways I got used to him not being around, we both did, even when we had no idea where he was, we could, and I speak for his father, always find a tender part in our days to say a little prayer for him.' She felt exhausted, almost weepy. 'You may not know tears, Mr Cullen, but they don't really cleanse in any way, they're just reminders of the pain you no longer think you feel. My husband knew this. He believed his son eased his own hurt, whatever it was, by hurting us. And the more we screamed at each other and chipped away at our love over the years, the more we began to believe our son was feeling easier inside himself. There was some relief in thinking that. But Mr Cullen . . .' Helen's voice disappeared. The room had become smoky and each of the three sat quietly. 'It was terrible when I heard that Tom was gone. The first question is: gone where?

Isn't it? They shouldn't say gone and they shouldn't say dead.' As she spoke she turned her head more to her boy. 'I don't know words anymore. Do they have any meaning at all?'

'Dead means dead, Mum. Dad's dead and he's in a mortuary here waiting for our visit.'

'I know. I know. My husband, Mr Cullen, thought he could save people, but he couldn't, people have to save themselves. Tom thought what he couldn't save he lost. They were dead because of him.' Helen spoke with tenderness, all the feelings that had been locked away in her were coming out more and more with each sentence.

The son who had made up his mind about his mum and dad had given them up quicker than any cigarette – they were losers. He thought they were nothing and this nothing was there for good so he stopped looking and never tried. On his chair, a few feet from his mother, he played with the cigarette pack from hand to hand, weak in body with the look of defeat on his face.

'My son,' Helen said, wishing to tell someone where she had come from and how she got where she was, 'he's got himself into prison. He's got a record now. He doesn't have anything. No future. And he doesn't have a dad.' She sighed and held her eyes on him. 'I love my son, I really do, but I can't help him. I'd like him to stay here, Mr Cullen. He's got nothing to go back to but to complete his sentence. He doesn't have to do that. If he could have a new beginning . . .'

Cullen didn't know what he had walked into.

'My mother's right, I need to get out of England. It's a small country and it's difficult to recover from your mistakes.' He looked back to the floor. 'It's difficult. I'm not free to be as generous as I should be. I'm not free to be myself.' He raised his head. 'I'm not the person that . . .'

'Have you seen my husband?' Helen interrupted. 'Have you seen the bullet that killed him? Was it an American bullet from an American gun?'

'And lying cold on an American table,' the son added.

'It's true, England's too small for young people. England took our son from us where sons are encouraged to go. There can't be any healing process there. Help my son, Mr Cullen. It would be a chance.'

'You'd like him to be an ocean away?'

'But he'd be closer. I know he would.'

'I hear what you say, Mrs Fraser.'

When Cullen last saw mother and son, they appeared to have found something they had not arrived with, something positive. Through the rain of the day and into evening, Cullen called home, back to his mother's room where she would be at that particular nightly hour on the east coast. Through the rain and in the semi-dark of his hotel room he sat with his back to the door, and in the stillness he found comfort in his voice as he called her *Mom*, like a boy.

44

London, March 1983

The rain had been lashing at the window long before Jilly climbed into bed. It was dark and wintry like a day could be in any month. When the storms seemed to have exhausted themselves and blown away, something sinister in mid-Atlantic would materialise and blow right back again.

Jilly was in bed, playing a game with her mother, a little fun before sleep. It was a word game: searching for words that rhymed; Jilly would start off with a word and Susan would match it, the game speeded as the words came pouring out. There was a lot of excitement and laughter. Jilly was getting older, growing up quickly, more in her speech than in her look. Asking and questioning things that her mother did not know or was not ready to reply to. Since Alex had left, Jilly seemed to ask and question more, and Susan wished he would hurry up and come home. Alex with all his secrets could handle her curiosity better and she regretted that, regretted that there could not be a balance, where he could be at times as unable as she. But Alex was able and Jilly knew it. The words were not coming so easily now and Susan was suggesting sleep for Jilly when the telephone rang. She gave Jilly a quick kiss, switched off her light and ran down the stairs.

'Hello. Yes.' Her voice revealed someone unexpected. 'Please do. Goodbye.' She rested the phone and walked into the kitchen. She brought out two cups and saucers from a cupboard, then her quality coffee, which she rarely used for herself, and her coffee pot. It was not long after the doorbell rang.

'I hope it's not too late?' said Sinclair.

'No, no. Please come in.' She took his coat, which was splashed heavily at the shoulders, and they walked through to the sitting room. 'I haven't seen you for a long time,' she said, and only then she began to wonder why he had called.

He noticed and said, 'Nobody has died if that's what you mean.'

'Would you like coffee?'

'Maybe later. Sit down. Let's have a chat.'

They both sat, Susan still wondering what could have possibly brought him over in the rain.

'How's the little girl?'

'You mean Jilly? She's fine. She wants to know when her daddy's coming home.'

He nodded. 'Susan, you know our business, secret and delicate, so I want you to bear that in mind while I'm here.' He looked at her. 'I want to know about you and Alex – your marriage, your life . . .'

'What? You want to know . . .' She looked perplexed. 'I don't understand.'

'This is difficult but there are some things I've got to ask. I can't tell you why but I hope you will be helpful.'

'You sound serious.'

'I don't mean to, it's part of the business I can't brush off.'

'Everything's fine,' she said, 'a happy threesome I can say.'

'Jack Kirkland asked specifically for Alex to work with him. Did you know that?'

'Yes. Alex did say Jack wanted him. They're good friends.'

'So Alex was happy?'

'Well, I don't know. I think he had some work here. It took him away.'

'He said that?'

'I think so.'

'Has he been in touch? Telephoned?'

'He phones, of course. He lets us know that he's fine.'

Sinclair had something to say but was not ready to say it, so he kept skirting around with questions that moved them along. He turned his head to a photograph of Jilly not far from him, on the wall, and studied it for a second.

'Jilly?' he asked. 'Lovely. Alex is lucky.'

'So am I,' Susan said, 'we both are.'

'Of course. Maybe that's why he didn't want to go with Jack; he didn't want to leave her behind.'

Susan smiled. 'Your family are much older, aren't they?'

'Ah yes, gone to bedsits. The family's still together in the sense that we talk to each other, usually on the telephone but I don't know if it's as valuable as it should be or as I'd like it to be. You and Alex and Jilly are still valuable. Allies. Kisses and hugs. Affection like that tends to stop later.'

'How sad,' Susan said sadly.

'It is a bit,' he replied and then moved off the subject. 'There's a problem,' he said, 'in Germany. Someone there is leading a double life.'

Susan kept her eyes on his. His head was resting on the sofa and he spoke in a matter of fact sort of way.

'A double life?' she asked.

'Do you understand, Susan, there's your husband over there and there's Jack.'

'Alex? I can't believe we should be talking about either.'

'I'm here tonight, Susan, in the rain; if you had no interest in this I simply wouldn't be here, but I'm afraid you do. Whether it be with Alex or Jack we haven't arrived at that point yet.'

'How do you know? How?' She stood and looked at him. 'Alex

is your friend, isn't he? Why have you come to tell me this? You know it isn't true.' She walked over to a part of the room that was chillier and turned to face him. 'You won't be allowed to tell me any details, will you?'

'Not really.' Sinclair sat forward and spoke softly, asking her to return and sit again. Now the uncomfortable bit had passed, she returned and sat, her body tight and shaken – a natural response, he thought as he began to probe into Alex.

'I can't believe Alex . . .' she stopped. 'There's no reason. There's no money. I haven't seen any money or any extravagance. What could it be for?'

'I don't know. I know Alex, spoken with him, became friends, but he's a rather closed person, difficult to get inside. We can't be sure.'

'And Jack?'

'Jack's different.'

'And he's in Germany. He's been there for years. You're talking about two men who work apart, far apart. Whatever you know, surely the distance would separate them. Surely.'

The more she thought of it the more she realised that if the double life was rooted in London then it had to be Alex. If in Germany, then Jack. 'You know,' her mouth opened in surprise and shock. 'Why are you here if you know?'

'Susan, it isn't as simple as that. Nothing is.'

She found his hand resting on hers and she wished it was Alex's. She would have taken it then, and he would have found all that was waiting.

'We aren't sure, not yet. But we will be very soon,' said Sinclair. 'I know it must be terrible for you, out of the blue like this, but I'm thinking of Jilly. Until this is all over I have to ask you to be careful, careful with Jilly.'

'Jilly?'

'Would Alex go anywhere without her, I mean for good? Do you think he could do that?'

Susan thought of them, one sleeping above her, the other spending another night in Germany. Sometimes she could feel some jealousy when Alex and Jilly were together, the way she always beamed at him, the way she hugged him and the way she took his scolding her. Susan knew that she tried privately, to herself, to think of their relationship as wrong. Alex was not a conventional father, he did not play in the conventional way with her, he did not feel burdened to make her happy with giggles and screams, or to promise gifts; he just talked and she talked, the way any two people would and Jilly was very happy. She could not be like Alex, her conversation and tone were much more conventional. She thought of Sinclair's question and she realised if Alex could, then Jilly could not.

'Jilly could be approached,' said Sinclair. 'How did he sound on the phone?'

'Fine. He didn't say much, he never does on the phone.' She gave an anxious smile.

'On the phone the last time . . . did he say he loved you? Did he tell you that?'

'Alex doesn't speak like that.'

'Did he say anything that was a bit unusual, you know, unlike him? A word, anything?'

She thought about the call and the others but he hadn't said what Sinclair was looking for.

'Susan, there must have been something.'

'Why? Why must there be?'

A pause.

'It's natural, I think, that a man away from home feels the wish to be back. Did he speak with Jilly?'

'No.'

Sinclair frowned. 'He didn't. Susan, if we're getting closer to Alex . . .'

'Or Jack,' she interrupted. 'It *is* still Alex and Jack?'

'Yes, it is.'

Their voices had woken Jilly who was now out of bed and sitting half-way down the stairs. The sitting room door was open enough for the light to shine through, enough for Jilly to have slipped her young body through, and enough for Sinclair, whose voice could sound rough, tho' there was little rough about him, to be heard clearly, so Jilly stayed on the stairs and listened.

'Let me tell you this, Susan. Not too many years ago, when you were single and childless, there was this chap who, after forming a friendship with this other, a foreigner – let's call him Olav – lost touch with him. Nothing mysterious about that, we have all done it, lost an old friend who's buried somewhere back in time. Well, this chap, we can call him Jim, begins to plan out his life, gets married, takes out a mortgage and sort of settles down. To those who knew him it would have been a surprise seeing Jim choose such conventionality, but they never did see him; like Olav, they too were somewhere back in the past, out of sight.'

As he went on with his story the rain kept hitting the upstairs window with a violence that frightened Jilly, sitting in the dark listening.

He pulled a cushion from behind him and sat back. 'Then Jim got a call: now it's not sure if it was a telephone call or if a letter came for him, but it was one or the other. It was Olav, he was going to be in the city and he thought, of course, of Jim. After a long absence they were to spend some time together. Olav was booked in to a city hotel and that's where Jim would meet him and together they would talk about their memories – the university, their old ideals and the girls.'

He brought his tongue round his lips and asked for a drink. Susan rose and poured two vodkas.

'I'm probably keeping you out of bed, Susan, but I'm sure you would rather hear this.'

'Yes I would. Any sleep I had you've chased away.'

'I understand,' he said with some apology. He sipped at the vodka the way someone sips at a new drink, but it was unlikely it was the first time, more likely he hated it. 'Jim didn't tell anyone that Olav had contacted him, which was a little strange. The news must have delighted him and yet he didn't say to anyone.' He paused. 'Jim went along to the hotel at the agreed time – it was early in the afternoon – and approached the desk, got the room number and took the stairs to Olav's room. But when he arrived and the door opened there was no sign of Olav. There was a very attractive girl but no Olav. She invited him in explaining that Olav had been detained and would arrive shortly. So Jim sat and waited, his human weakness for affection completely controlling his doubts and suspicions.'

Sinclair finished the rest of his drink politely refusing another since, he explained, he was driving.

'This has got something to do with Alex and Jack?' asked Susan.

'Well, let's say this is a road we must go on to get back to Alex and Jack.' He still held his glass and was looking at it as if it might be a fine piece of crystal, which it was not. 'It was there something happened to Jim. We know he was not very long alone with the girl because she left and two men arrived. There was no sign of Olav, he never appeared, it was just a way of getting Jim there. And once there he was worked on; not beaten, more threatened, the only kind of promises certain people can keep – that of malice.'

'Threatened?' Susan could not understand; what could have threatened him?

'Let me go on,' asked Sinclair. 'Jim wanted to know where Olav was. After building himself up for their meeting his concern for him was as strong as it would have been for his closest friend. They told him he was living in Stockholm, that he was well and hoped to see him soon.'

'But how was he threatened?' she asked with disbelief. 'What was it? What?'

'Susan.' He paused as if searching for the right words and

the best way to explain.' You see, Jim's politics were difficult to define, he could be this or that and he knew it, and this for labelling sake tended to put him under the liberal label, which he certainly was not. It could not be clear where he rested, if he ever did, politically speaking. And so, as I'm telling you this story about him, he was told a story by them.'

'What? You've come here tonight to tell me exactly WHAT?' Her emotions were in the balance: angry at being taken along his well prepared road, and fearful of what the end would reveal.

'Allow me to continue, Susan; a few more minutes . . . Try if you can, to imagine yourself with, say, a problem, that of identity, not being able to say who you were or where you should be, and for comfort's sake you decided on one, maybe you were offered one, one far away from where you were, one that was new and full of hope. It changed you there and then; ended your self-questioning and even brought you some happiness. Of course, there would be a cost, there's always some kind of payment. But it could be made and that was important. There would be no pain there. For the benefit of identity all your other actions would be justified and therefore painless. Supposing that's what happened to Jim. After years of not knowing where he stood, what he wanted and where it was, this fog somehow cleared in that hotel room.'

There was a creak on the stairs and Susan got up and went out. Jilly had gone, scurried back to her room and under the covers.

'How could that happen?' she asked, her body stiff, her voice under strain as she returned to Sinclair. 'How could a man switch like that? Tell me?'

'I don't know, but it looks like that's what happened. From that day on Jim was no longer with us: he'd taken a new master.'

Susan looked grieved, unable to release her tears. She sat hunched in her chair as the squawking of gulls the day she took Jilly to Calais, the day Alex had asked her to deliver to someone there, entered her thoughts. She had never felt happy about that, although Alex's voice was full of urgency, it was too urgent and it was asking too much of her, which he had never ever done.

'What will happen?' she asked.

'It depends on what we want and what he wants. I don't think he knows that he's been uncovered; so he'll come back, we'll bring him back.'

'I don't understand all this; if you knew Alex was doing something criminal why was he allowed to go to Germany? Why? Why?' Her tears had risen and began to spill out; her threesome she had mentioned was breaking up and there could be nothing left. They needed each other too much. She shook in her chair as she saw everything crumble.

'We wanted Alex away from England, we wanted to see what he would do and we wanted to see what his KGB controller would do. Of course, things never go as they should and certain things we should have known were kept from us. But Susan, I'm afraid Alex won't be treated lightly, he'll go to prison.' He looked at her while she tried to gain some of her control. 'But he's not here yet and if he catches on, he might prefer another alternative. Do you understand my meaning?' As she shook her head hesitantly, he explained. 'He might not come back. He probably knows if you would follow him and he might not expect it.'

'What are you saying?'

'He might want Jilly with him. It wouldn't be unusual. A loved one such as a child can become as precious as their wayward ideals. It can remind them of who they are. Not all want to forget that.'

Sinclair paused and Susan clung to her handkerchief that had wiped her eyes dry and red. She was numb; her lips felt swollen and her hands had lost their grace and felt fat and clumsy as she squeezed on the already crumpled handkerchief. She sat unable to think, not of the past or the future. Alex might well be dead now: a car accident, something abrupt and final. She could feel no need to see him, he was already lost, Sinclair had more or less said so, and what was lost was gone.

'Take Jilly away, a few days from school won't do her any harm.' He sat forward and placed his hand on hers. 'Susan, I had to tell you. I didn't want Jilly to be up, I didn't want that.'

'If there's a court-case the papers will get hold of it, won't they?' She seemed surprised. 'It'll be splashed everywhere. Isn't that what you want to avoid, all the publicity?'

'We can't let Alex retire quietly, if that's what you mean. The damage is too great. Some people would want their pound of flesh.'

'I see. The security business can take a back seat, is that it?' She pulled her hands away. 'Alex is going to be nailed no matter the cost.'

Sinclair took himself out of his chair; he had delivered the unpleasant news and he did not expect any gratitude. Alex had been deceiving everyone and Susan was hurt, more than at any time in her life; her romantic notions that had taken her into marriage, that had brought Jilly into the world, that had given her a sense of achievement had now also brought, so unexpectedly, disaster. She did not know what or whom to cling to; Alex had broken her life, Sinclair had come along on a wet night to let the pieces fall as gently as he could. The pieces of betrayal and sorrow. Her anger inside wanted to shout, *go, just go*, to Alex, to Sinclair, she could not feel anything else. But she was not there yet, not completely ready to let go; now she was turning on the bad news messenger. Sinclair understood and could sympathise. He made for his coat, buttoned it up and turned to Susan who had not moved.

'Take Jilly, remember, and tell me where you are.'

She did not reply. The front door closed hard shaking the letter-box: Sinclair was gone. Susan was ill, drained and limp. She turned off the light and slowly climbed the stairs; at the top Jilly called to her.

'When's Daddy coming home, Mummy?'

'I don't know. Go to sleep.'

'If Daddy doesn't come home I'll die.'

Susan put her head inside the doorway. 'Don't say that, Jilly.'

'But I will. I want Daddy to come home.'

'Daddy is coming home. Who said he wasn't? Go to sleep.'

She took herself away and closed the door of her room before letting her weight fall heavily on the bed.

45

'There's someone to see you,' said the fat man who was
the Sheriff's deputy, 'says he knows ya.'

Greg and Jilly had found themselves with little
choice but to make the stop as the deputy had asked. All Greg's
possessions had been taken from the hospital and lay waiting on
the desk before him.

'Our Sheriff ain't here,' the Deputy added, 'just me.'

'How long will we have to wait?' Jilly asked.

'As long as it takes, miss. He's comin' a distance.'

'From where?' Greg enquired.

'From out of state. Idaho. A place called Percy.'

Jilly sat on a bench against the wall and Greg sat beside her.
'Somebody know you?' she asked. 'Yeah, suppose so,' he said
with a sigh. 'It's Sheriff Bane, ain't it?' he called to the Deputy.

'That's the man. He your friend? Need some help?'

'Need a coffee,' replied Greg.

'There's a place over the street. Coffee's good. Food, too.' The
Deputy spoke as if remembering some recent food he had.

'Can we go?' asked Jilly with a lift in her voice.

'Sure. But you'll come back, won't you?'

Greg leaned toward his wallet on the desk.

'Ah, you gotta wait till your man from Percy gets here. Can't

330

have that right now. But the lady can buy you coffee, if that's alright by her.'

The deputy took a call, and Greg and Jilly took to the door. The sun was shining on half the street as they sat in Bett's coffee house. Jilly looked a bit dishevelled and Greg painfully bruised.

The coffee came more as a friend than anything else before Greg asked Jilly when she was going to stop.

She looked at him and beyond. 'Stop,' she said, 'to stop you need brakes – I don't have any brakes.'

'You must. We could stop together.'

Jilly considered what it would mean to stop. 'Can you imagine . . . Can you imagine a long stretch of road, long, you don't know how long, and you're just driving, mile after mile. Can you imagine?' She looked as if she was. 'Then after hours when you're still on the road, you need to pee,' she gave a smile, 'a silly thing like that. So you look for a place and slow, slow right down to stop.' She brought the coffee to her lips and buried her eyes into it, as Greg waited amused. 'Can't you see, there you are on that long road, you've switched off the engine and you can never restart it, never. Try as you will nothing gets you going again, not forward and not backward, you're stranded on an empty road forever. I don't want that and that's where I'd be if I stopped.'

'I don't see it that way. Look at this place, never heard of it before, maybe never pass this way again, all these people who have lives here, have stopped.'

Jilly knew that. 'But they've got reasons to stop, this is their place, where they want to be. There are families here. Family, relatives, Greg. I'm looking for my father. I'm looking, looking.'

'Jilly, your dad, my dad . . .'

'Greg, suppose as you sit here you turned your eyes to the street and there,' she pointed out, 'where the sunlight's striking that corner, you saw your dad. All those years later, here he was, in Mason.' She sat back more at ease and asked if he was hungry.

'I can't imagine that. My dad!' said Greg. 'I don't believe that'll ever happen.'

Greg's expression made him look less than what he was. It made Jilly angry and she told him he looked like a bum, his defeat on his face. 'Christ, Greg. GREG!' Her shout brought everyone's attention.

Greg looked down surveying all the items on the table, lifting and putting down every object until customer talk and kitchen noise picked up again. He had the face of a young man who seemed stuck in his teens, who wanted nothing from life and did not believe anything was on offer. 'I don't know why I'm livin' this agony. I don't,' he said with his teeth almost clenched. 'Across the street, you say. I don't know. I might just ask for another cup of coffee, because, you see, I say I want him to be alive, but I really want him dead. Dead, Jilly. He's best that way. How could he be alive? How could he explain? How could I tell him where I've been?'

Greg's hand movements had caught the eye of a waitress who now stood waiting.

'Hungry?' asked Jilly.

The waitress noted the order and left.

'I don't want what I can't get. I don't want to feel that if I could find my father I'd have found my feet. My dad's gone, Jilly. Dead or alive, he's gone.'

Jilly sat getting angrier and ready to walk out when Greg said, 'That's my dad. That's me. I can't go on like you. You've got a light in your tunnel, I wish to God I had.'

The food came and they ate in silence. Jilly felt the need for someone's arm around her, really around her. It had been so long. England seemed far and she was thinking more and more of her mother than at any other time. Who was holding her, she wondered. When she last saw her she was beautiful. They had spoken when Jilly was angry, an angry meeting with angry words and the fault lay, Jilly wanted to believe, with beauty.

Her mother's beauty had somehow distanced Jilly from her. It was a mixed-up, confused train of thought that had taken hold and pushed their closeness away. Like blondes without brains, her mother had been given a downside, a price to pay, and that was dishonesty. Somehow, before Jilly could fully see, her mum and her beauty had pushed her dad away, and away from his daughter. It seemed to be an answer to her until it grew to become The answer. So lovely, beautiful Jilly fled from beauty for long years thinking that would be what her dad would have wanted. But Jilly was wrong about beauty. In the silence between them in the coffee house, she could see the man who had called at her home to talk about Dad and how he had gone missing. Jilly could remember how much she loved her mother before her life became a darker place; she could remember just how much. She could look back to those years when she had rage and some kind of freedom was the bite she took out of life. But it was not real because freedom was beauty and not something that entangled people. In truth she didn't know what she had, with her bearings misplaced, inside and out, in the company of young men fleetingly known, who were driven by other things to crash time again and again on their cool, cool road to nowhere.

'Dad never called my mother Sue,' Jilly said like that, 'never.'

'Susan's nicer,' Greg replied.

'I've got this picture of my mother and father,' her thoughts were running. 'It's in colour but they look like people from an elegant black and white time.'

'Can I see it?'

'Oh no, it's in my head. All my pictures are there.' Jilly sat, happier than at any other time. 'They say that memories of when you were a child come back to you as you get older, but I have mine now. I can sit anywhere in the world and think for a minute, and then without realising I'll have a smile as wide as your canyons.' She thought on. 'It's always been Dad in my pictures. Mum was there, too, but Dad was in every frame. Maybe Mum will be in every frame, too, for the later years.' She looked up. 'Here's the Deputy coming. I like him; I think he's kind.' She watched him approach.

'Maybe he's got news for us. Maybe the game's up.'

'Maybe he's coming to spill the beans.'

'Spill the what?'

'Never mind. All's going to be revealed,' Jilly sighed.

The Deputy approached and smiled. 'Would you folks like to come over?' He invited them nicely.

As the three walked to the door the waitress ran to them with the bill. The Deputy said to put it on the Sheriff's tab as all those folks' money was tied up in jail. He laughed, and the waitress, too.

A room was made available for Sheriff Bane who had now arrived in town. He did not come in uniform and did not have an official car, he had travelled down with no usual business on his mind. There had been plenty of time for him to consider what he was going to say to young Keech, the general's son who had taken on the world and lost every round. Young Greg would have changed, of course, he would have physically grown, he might not even recognise him well. It was a journey to find out. When Bane walked in, there was Greg, dusty hair and battered looking, but still, if things could be put back in place, he would still see the boy who used to mess about his house with his son.

'How you doin'?' He walked to him and took his hand. 'God, Greg, I'm happy to see you.'

Greg was a bit overwhelmed. 'Good to see you, too.'

'Don't worry,' said Bane, 'I know your story. You've had a hell of a hard time.' Both men looked at each other while Jilly stood back at the door. 'You're tall, gee, as tall as me. Less bone,' he said with some affection. 'And,' he paused, 'you're not far from home.'

Bane looked over Greg's shoulder at Jilly at the door. 'Miss, come on in.' He took her hand as Greg introduced her. Bane spread his arms and invited them to sit. 'What brings you over here?' he asked Jilly.

'My friendship with Greg,' she said quickly.

Greg knew that Sheriff Bane must know everything or there abouts, so he asked him what he did not know.

'Good question. I don't know how you both are. I don't know that.' Out of uniform and out of the clothes he used to wear when he would sit on his verandah drinking cool beer while Greg played with his son Jeff, Bane hadn't changed too much, in fact it was a good feeling for Greg to see something of his past so warmly. 'It's been years since we talked, remember, you, me and Jeff? You're a man of what now?'

'The same as Jeff, we're just months apart.'

'Oh, Jeff says hi! I was calling him and, gee, he was excited when I told him.' Bane smiled. 'He was happy about that. Here,' he went into a pocket, 'I have his number. Maybe . . . Sometime . . .'

Jilly watched the friendliness in Bane and hoped it was sincere.

Bane enquired where they were heading. Temperatures were dropping, he added.

'We're tryin' to get some reason into our lives,' explained Greg, 'just makin' our way.'

'I'm sorry things turned out the way they did,' Bane began, 'all that stuff.'

Jilly looked at Greg for something.

'You left so quickly. Your family. No one knew where you'd gone.'

'We'd no choice. Mom was told it was for our safety.'

'How's your mom? Your sisters?'

'I don't rightly know.'

'It's your dad you think about.' Bane knew. 'I liked your dad.' – Greg tried to remember if that was true – 'I might have been a military man, too, if I hadn't taken this direction.'

Jilly was there feeling invisible. The room had become different to her, maybe it was the two men there urging themselves toward each other but she felt a whole lot of caution holding them back. She did not feel comfortable when she sensed tenderness and affection, she just realised her need for the same had yet to be met.

'Who knows where any of us might have gone and done if . . .' Bane came forward in his chair. 'If . . . You've jumped parole and here you are sittin' talkin' with me.'

'I'm goin' back to jail?'

'You don't wanna go back. Nobody wants that.'

'My father's still a big problem?'

Bane stood. 'It would seem so. Big decision, big problem. I think he took years to make it. Some decisions shouldn't pass without an explanation, a reason, something that others can understand.' He walked around the desk before leaning against it with both hands on top. 'I'm an officer of the law, a cop, to the people out there in the streets, but I'm many things, Greg, and so was your father. We didn't speak a whole lot but I got to know him quite well. If you cut out the bullshit between people, you can make progress. He always spoke well of you, always. But he wasn't a family man, whatever that might mean. What's a family man in our country today? Food on the table, clothes on their backs? Your father wasn't a family man. Some men can't live with women, they can't.' Bane now sat on the desk with one leg off the floor. Jilly was silent and almost forgotten.

'Why?' asked Greg.

'It's not a bad thing,' explained Bane, 'it's a view-of-life thing. Things were goin' on and your father told me he couldn't hold what he had together. He sounded disappointed when he said it, but anyone would, I guess.' He could see that Greg wanted to hear more. 'Hey, let me get you guys somethin'.' He pressed on the intercom and asked for coffee and coke. 'He did like women,' Bane continued, 'he just didn't like his wife.'

'My mother.'

'He thought that she devalued the important things in life, his life. This had an effect. He said that much to me.'

Greg didn't know any of that.

'How could you know, you were a boy and unhappiness was somethin' else to you. If important things are made small, we're made small. Many men feel like that sometimes, but with your father, he blamed himself and his country.'

'I don't understand, what's the country got to do with it?'

'Everything.'

A rap on the door brought the deputy with drinks. 'These young people stayin' some nights?'

Bane laughed at the worry he found on Jilly's face. 'I don't think so,' he said, 'but . . .' he looked at her with eyebrows raised. 'In Mason, maybe.'

She did not disagree. The Deputy closed the door.

'America had become a big problem for your father,' Bane went on. 'I have had time to look at your dad and what he did, it may not be obvious to us or to you as a boy back then, but he had to make that decision, it had nothing to do with him being a bad man, nothing.'

He spread his hand over his face and could see himself with Keech one evening when the crickets had never been so loud. A police siren could be heard even louder, although it had to be at least a mile away; Keech remarked then how he hated the police sound, the chase that they loved to perform. He asked Bane what he thought about it, what he thought of this urgent side of law and order, and, without pausing, he said with a passion, 'I hate it. Hate it more and more. I don't know your kind of people.' He took some beer and wondered, 'Cops. What are they?' Bane replied that they weren't too unlike the military. Men, he thought, were men wherever they were. But the Sheriff was wrong, men weren't the same. Where had he got that idea from? 'Christ,' Keech raised his voice, 'you're a cop, you see other cops every day, and you're saying you're among the elite of men?'

This confused Keech as to what emotion he should have, and Bane noticed the uncertainty about him, how shaky he seemed to stand. He wanted to say to him that it was not always that cut and dry, good and evil lived side by side and had always done so. On the verandah Keech stood that night, through the hours after Bane had said goodnight, when the crickets refused to hush and those officers on the back shift could no longer hear the ridiculous squealing of their own urgency.

'Let's say,' Bane put to Greg, 'that you'd become a father. You've had months to prepare yourself, you even thought you knew the sex of your child, but you lived in a time when there was no way of knowing that beforehand. A boy or girl, it was part of you and you'd been caught up with the very idea that you were introducing a new person to the world. And all the things wrong in the country, you would somehow see that they'd pass your baby by. You didn't know it then, but this was the beginning of your war with all things American.'

Greg and Jilly were hushed. She had sat her bag on her lap and was embracing it. Bane continued.

'Your baby entered the world but before too long you thought that this small piece of you was born all wrong. You didn't think this at first as you lifted it in your arms, walked it a little, along the corridor, to and fro like that. But there was a moment that you couldn't shake off, as you walked. At the other end of the corridor another parent walked toward you, a teenage girl with her baby held tightly to her breast. A maternal picture, you could say. But somehow she looked out of place to you, far out of place. She was reducing your magical moment with your new baby and making it a trash experience. This girl wore no beauty and no dignity you could see. Here you were in a maternity hospital where new life enters and this solitary girl with long black hair seemed miles from what you were experiencing with your new baby. This girl represented the ugly side of America to you. In that corridor no new life could say that they had arrived into beautiful America. And

338

you began to fear that that baby would grow up to disgust you in the quick years to come, but worse than that, so might your own. Nobody, you thought, could see it as you did and that was the start of your hope disappearing. Cultural America was dead and you would be, too, if you didn't act. Maybe you were right about what you saw, but it was a corner, a big corner of your life in your America; there were other Americas you would never discover.' Bane had removed his jacket and hung it over a chair as he gave Greg the best picture he could of his father. 'When your father was all over the papers, I took some time to know what I could about him. This is my experience. There'll be other people who'll have a different view. Your father somehow felt that this country was for small people, there were the mountains and the canyons but the people were small and weak, and now it had infiltrated his home. By the time you and Jeff were getting to know each other, I think your father had made his decision. It would've been pounding in his head, I'd say. But out there in Germany it might . . . at Christmas time, there might have been something, with all the Christmas emotion, something that took him that long walk.' Bane searched for a little more he could say to Greg and failed. 'I don't know.'

'Is he dead?' was all Greg could ask.

'If he's not, where is he? You and Miss Jilly have produced a minor miracle in your own way. Since your run, everyone's kept the lid on this. That's why we're talkin', if your name wasn't Keech, well . . . You get the picture. The last thing anyone wants is your father's story back in the papers. They don't want that.'

Jilly thought Greg's father was alive and someone in America knew where he was, but Bane did not respond.

'Jeff thinks you should come home and so do I.'

'I've got no home. No door key. Nothin'.'

'He's doing well. So could you.'

'It's an offer, Greg,' warned Jilly, 'to take you off their conscience. It'll be the cheapest college. I know.'

'They want to send Jilly back,' Greg worried. 'She doesn't want to go. Her problem's my problem.'

'Greg,' Bane revealed some irritation in his tone, 'this is the world we're in. Security. Embarrassment. Don't do that. Don't think about it. You've got no power. If anyone thought you had, what do you think they'd do? Jilly's not the problem, you're the problem and that won't change.' Some silence crept into the room. 'It's been a long time. You've got your life and you've got your wounds. Don't open that wound.'

Jilly jumped up from her chair. 'Don't listen, Greg, they'll say anything to make you bury your father alive.'

'Let's take a rest,' suggested Bane. 'The Deputy knows of a place where you can look at things away from this office.'

Greg took steps to the door and walked them back. He looked at his wallet on the desk and Bane picked it up and pressed it into his hand. Greg and Jilly left Sheriff Bane with the Deputy and stood outside in the fading light. Bane's story, where the hospital corridor seemed as long as the street they were about to cross, had struck Greg – the girl with her baby was standing before him and there in the silence of this picture his hands were full.

In Mason in the middle of the night Greg was still, there was not a shadow of an intruder felt to worry him. Still in the night he heard Bane again, talking to him like that in the jail. Sometimes he couldn't believe he had been to jail, if anyone had told him when he was a boy that he was going to jail he would have run to his daddy. It had been all a mess. He had heard from guys inside that jail was everything. Some had become deep thinkers and some thought that five, twenty years didn't matter: everybody, everywhere, they were all doing time, it was just that a lot of folks were not awake to it. He could have been sucked into those thinkers, another couple of years and he could have gone over to the other side, like his old man. When he thought about it . . . In the middle of the night he lay still holding Jilly's hand. Not a word had passed between them, not an intimate stroke of love. It was a room not for sleeping or for pleasure but for being still.

Mason had made an impression on Jilly, a place her mum should see, dad too. She urged her thoughts along and for a time she was everywhere she had ever been. She felt the rhythm of her body and instinctively she squeezed Greg's hand: in the stillness she had a little burst of hope. He said, 'Hi,' and squeezed back.

'Hi,' she replied. 'What you thinkin'?'

'Everythin' and nothin'.'

Neither had turned their heads to each other, both just gazed at the pocket of light reflected on the ceiling.

'Do you trust the Sheriff?'

'I used to. Don't know now.'

'Everyone's going out on a limb for you.'

'Looks like that. Yeah!'

'What a world,' Jilly sighed.

Both rolled over and put their arms around each other, as much for protection as for desire. 'Greg,' she whispered.

It was some hours before the town of Mason rose and the weight of another day was felt.

46

West Germany, late March 1983

It was early evening and the spring sun, which had been clear in the sky all day, was now setting. There was no movement anywhere. Not in the fields or on the country roads that could be followed a long distance before disappearing into the trees. There were two guard towers nearby, both wooden, with two guards whose surveillance seemed gone with the light. The darkness was creeping over the area and it took a few minutes more before the lights were turned on in the farms of this small corner of East Germany and in the streets and houses of the nearby West German village.

Alex was alone in the Gasthaus, downstairs in the bar trying to gather some news from a local newspaper. Brushing up a language he had allowed to slip away so many years ago was frustrating, and with every difficulty he met he would turn the page. But with a litre of beer in front of him he tried to make some sense of the foreign news page, and it was a four-inch double column piece from Leipzig that took all his attention. He went down it slowly then stopped and read over a sentence. *"Gestern haben die Ostdeutschen jegliche Hoffnung, dass Keech in die USA züruckkehren könnte, verworfen indem sie angaben, dass jedermann, der*

Schutz suche, nicht abgewiesen würde." He went on, but he could
not be sure what he had read. Was Keech a man ready to run?
He lifted the heavy beer and allowed the liquid to run past his
lips, then returned to the paper. He had to be absolutely sure that
this was not a new development, something fresh on the Keech
affair. He looked at the faces in the bar and wondered if any
of them knew some English, but he could not go round asking,
'*Sprechen Sie Englisch?*' It was a country place and it was unlikely.
He drank some more and began to worry. He could feel things
were not right. If Keech could not, or worse, was never intended
to be taken back . . . rescued, then . . . then it was a lie – Jack had
lied.

His thoughts were gnawing at him when someone asked for
the paper. It was when the young man with dark hair repeated
his request that Alex caught on and handed the paper over. In
a distinct German accent the man thanked him in English. Alex
watched him take a seat in an empty corner; he lifted his beer
and let a moment pass before he made his approach.

'Do you speak English?'

The man raised his head and gave a mixture of yeah and *ja*.
Alex smiled.

'I picked it up in America,' said the man.

'Did you.'

'But it's not perfect.' He smiled.

'It sounds very good; very American,' said Alex.

'Are you on holiday?'

'For a few days. Look, there's something in the paper that I'm
having difficulty with and I wonder if you could translate it for
me?'

'Sure.' The man seemed happy to help. 'Which page?'

Alex picked up the paper and opened out each page. 'Here.'
He placed it back on the table. 'This bit down here.' He put a
finger on it and kept it there while he turned the paper round.

The man folded his arms on the table and read it over to himself.

'Right,' he said, 'I'll try to be accurate. "The East German authorities today have made contact with the United States about the
mysterious case of the US Army General, Gregory Keech. It has
now been three months since Keech left his barracks in north-
east Bavaria on the first of January and disappeared in the East.
The Americans have claimed since that Keech was abducted by
the Soviets in hope that it could bring about an exchange deal –
a senior KGB agent was recently found guilty and sentenced in
the United States. The Russians have put Keech on television to
speak for himself hoping to remove any doubts that the general
had defected. Yesterday the authorities dampened any hope of
Keech's return to the US saying that *anyone seeking refuge will not
be refused*. General Keech has made it clear that he has no wish
to return to his home country. He is said to be anxious that his
life could be in danger and fears that the American government
might make a… a snatch . . ." Snatch?' The man looked at Alex.
'Is that the right word?'

'Snatch.' Alex nodded, 'Yes, yes. Go on.'

"A snatch for him. The American general has been well
received here and has been staying outside Zwickau; this is
expected to come to an end soon when he moves further east
to Moscow where he wishes to begin his new life and where he
would feel safer." He stopped. 'I hope I have been clear,' he said.

'Yes, it was fine,' replied Alex, 'thanks. So damn frustrating
not being able to understand. Can I get you a beer?'

'No, it's alright.'

'I insist,' said Alex. 'Be right back.'

He left to order and the man went through the paper.

'Here.' Alex returned with two massive beers. 'Where I come
from we have pints and we think they're big, but this . . .'

The man laughed and Alex sat down. 'You were in America?'
– the man nodded – 'From what I've heard you Germans like the
country better than the English do.'

'It's a beautiful place. I had a wonderful time.'

'I think people should see it when they're young,' said Alex, 'see it with fresh eyes. I think that's what America needs. It doesn't need old visitors who are set in their attitudes. I've got a feeling America isn't that easy to like if you're late in getting there.'

'You haven't been?' asked the man.

Alex shook his head as he took a mouthful; the beer seemed to have taken its effect, as if the alcohol had raced into his bloodstream and clouded him. Jack's lies had brought no panic, no biting urge to run. 'No, I haven't,' he replied, 'and I've got, I regret to say, fairly fixed ideas about the place. It's difficult to change that.'

'But think of all the people who went there, people who ran there, all different ages.'

'But they were getting away from horror, and no matter where you go, after horror any place looks good.'

The man did not want to show his disagreement and masked it in his beer.

'Do you know this story about the American general?' asked Alex.

'Ah, this Keech.' He pointed to the paper. 'Yes, there was a lot about it at first but it died away as everything does. I think he is a CIA plant fronting as a defector.'

'Do you?'

'If he were a real defector he wouldn't have gone over like that; he would have made contact, they would have expected him.' He laughed. 'No, he just ran across.' He laughed again.

'If you're right he's as good as dead,' said Alex.

'No, they won't kill him, it wouldn't look good. They have accepted him. Anyway, it might put off other defectors by killing him and they don't get that many.' He laughed a little more and Alex put on a wide grin.

'Your English is very good,' remarked Alex again, 'a holiday in the States has done a lot for that.'

'Oh, you're getting the best just now, after a while it all falls apart. But it's okay with beer.'

'Another?'

'No, no, thank you. I have to go after this one.' He held the glass mug in an odd way, Alex noticed: it seemed uncomfortable to him. 'German beer is better than English?' the man asked.

'No, not really, but everybody thinks theirs is the best. It's a nationalistic thing – like football. Maybe here it's different, a divided country and that. Yes, maybe it's different.' He watched the man take another mouthful and swallow, then he would do it again, all the time keeping the glass in position at his mouth.

'What do you do around here?' asked Alex. 'Farm?'

'I'm a teacher.'

'English?'

'Yes, and French. I'm not from here, further south. My school was here, so I am here. And you?'

'I'm little more than a clerk in a disorganised office.'

'An army office?'

'Army?'

'Yes, the American,' he pointed to the paper, 'is in the army, I thought . . .'

'You thought I was professionally interested. No, no, just a story I have been following; I'd like to hear the end of it.'

'Well, I hope you do.' The man finished his drink and said he had some classwork to mark. He stood and shook Alex's hand and said he hoped to have another beer with him before he left. Alex returned to the paper.

On the other side of the village was a hotel, large for the area and expensive. It was white with a timber roof overlapping at the sides, with timber shutters and frames on the windows and timber decoration cemented into the wall. It was like a mountain hotel, everything in its architecture was taken from there. Alex walked in through the hallway to the desk where a man, grey and distinguished-looking was filling in the details of a form into the hotel book. His writing occupied him while Alex waited.

'I would like a telephone directory,' asked Alex.

The man kept his head down as he pointed in the direction of the public phone box.

'I'd like the directory of Frankfurt?' said Alex.

The man raised his head. 'Frankfurt?'

'Yes, do you have it?'

The man looked through the shelves under the desk, his search bringing colour to his face. 'Here you are.' The thick book was allowed to fall with a thump on the counter.

Alex made to walk away with it.

'You will have to look at it here,' said the man ,'it belongs to the office, it is not really for public use, you understand.'

Alex walked back, placed it on the desktop and leafed through the pages. He found his page and from the top followed his finger down. In a city the size of Frankfurt he had expected a full list of Matthofers, instead there were only two out of a population of almost a million. He was surprised. Matthofer Carl-Otto was the first and Matthofer L. the second.

He dialled L. Matthofer. 'Hello . . . Frau Matthofer?'

'Matthofer. *Ja.*'

Alex presumed she could speak English, it was more than likely, Frankfurt being a bilingual city. 'Frau Liesel Matthofer?'

'*Ja,*' the voice was hesitant.

'I wonder if you could help me.' There was a pause. 'Do you speak English?'

'*Ja,* a little.'

'Good. I would like to speak with Willy. Is Willy at home?'

There were some seconds of silence.

'Who is calling?'

'I'm a friend of Jack's.'

'Who?'

'Jack. Jack Kirkland. Is Willy there?'

'My husband is not. I'm afraid there has been a mistake . . . Who is calling?'

'Mistake?'

'Yes, my husband died many years ago.'

'Dead! . . . Your son then, it must be your son I want.'

'There has been some confusion,' her voice changed, she was frightened.

'I do have the correct number, don't I? Jack . . . you know?'

'No, you have the wrong number.' She placed the phone.

'Lies. Lies,' Alex whispered into the humming phone. The realisation brought his fear almost to overspill. He took a small address book from his pocket and hurried through its pages. Holding it open with his finger he pushed at the box door. 'Excuse me, can you give me another line.' Then pulled the door shut again and dialled quickly. After the ringing there was a click and silence which seemed to calm him.

'It's London,' he said, 'I've been discovered.' There was a long empty silence that seemed like an eternity. 'You know where I am.' Alex could feel his inner self shake. 'Can you get me away?'

'I don't know,' said the voice at the other end.

'For God's sake, London's finished and I need help.'

'Can you get yourself here?'

Alex could feel an uncaring in the silence that followed, and it spread over him like water over a sinking man. 'Impossible, I need help.'

'We won't let you go, London, someone will come.'

'I'm waiting,' said Alex. The line then cut off.

The receiver had become slippy and loose in his hands: the calls had brought his fear out in his palms, turning them cold and damp. Alex began to dial again but the tone was different, he couldn't get through. He pushed at the door and asked for another line.

As the first ring began he was there, in the hall at the foot of the stairs where the mirror hung above the telephone, where all your expressions could be found with the in-coming news.

'Hello.'

'Susan.'

'Alex.'

'Susan . . . Have you had a visit from anyone from the office?'

'Yes . . . Sinclair came round. Alex.' Her voice began trembling. 'Alex, we're alone here, me and Jilly. I'm frightened to be alone. Oh Alex.' Her distress came all the way to him.

'Susan, I can't explain on the phone, I can't say anything. It was a belief, it was for that. Susan, listen to me. They will call me misguided, wilful, treacherous, but I'm none of these things; just tell Jilly that. I'm none of these things.'

'Are you coming back? . . . For Jilly? For me?'

'Are you there anymore?'

'Alex, please, think of us, of your daughter. If you go you'll never see her, how can you?'

Jilly came rushing into his mind: her laughter, her tears, one immediately after the other. He had thrown her away, that was it, put her at risk then at the end thrown her away. The love that he could never understand, could never trust, was squeezing at him as Jilly was everywhere in him. 'Is Jilly there?'

'Yes.'

'Jilly . . .'

'Daddy, when are you coming home?'

'Listen, Jilly, I can't come home just now. I don't know when I can. Remember I used to to tell you about all the secrets I have?'

'Yes, I remember.'

'Well I gave them away because I thought I should, and some people at home are not very happy with me . . . Jilly, I can't come back . . .'

'Daddy, come back. Daddy!' she shouted and began to cry. 'Daddy says he's not coming home.'

Alex listened as Susan tried to calm Jilly but her voice had also broken, 'Alex, Alex, can you hear her?'

He said nothing as he brought the receiver slowly away from his ear and let their sounds of anguish become barely audible before silencing it. They were gone, left to themselves. He never thought he would lose them, not now, after all those years of playing the spy game. It had become so much part of his routine that the threat hardly existed. Someone would come, that was what Paris said, he would be rescued.

There was a knock on the booth door. 'Alex, are you coming out?' Jack was standing with a drink in his hand. 'Saw your shape through the window. I never would have guessed I could recognise you from the back.' – Alex stepped out – 'Phoning Susan?'

'Yes, I'm anxious to get home, Jack. I want to get back.'

'Everything's alright I hope?' – Alex nodded – 'Willy's coming over tomorrow.'

'The two of them?'

'That's right, Willy and the American.'

'Tell me, Jack, just to satisfy my curiosity, how did you receive this information?'

'I'd hoped you wouldn't ask me that but I know how certain things have to be known. Let's walk through here.'

'Excuse . . .' the man at the desk called out, 'your telephone calls, sir.' Alex dug his hand in his pocket as the man tallied up the bill. 'Twenty marks eighty.' Alex fumbled a little as he searched his coins, then placed them on the counter and turned away. '*Dankeschön*,' said the man.

'You and Susan must have lost none of your youth if you can talk for twenty DM,' said Jack.

'You were telling me.'

'Oh yes. We have a newspaper correspondent in Leipzig who helps us when the need's there, you know, someone who's got something else to do. Well, Willy puts his message through this way. The paperman sends in a story with an additional item, which is Willy's message; when it reaches London this bottom piece is given to us. It's all in code, of course, and it's not for emergencies. Alex, you used to be active, you must have known.'

'What does Willy do in an emergency?'

'There's not much he can do, he still needs time. If he's running, he's on his own.'

'Tomorrow?' asked Alex.

'You'll be home the day after,' said Jack.

Jack placed his glass on a nearby table and left.

It was the clearest night of Alex's stay in Germany, there were thousands of little dots of light all inviting the same question. Alex and Jack walked back to the Gasthaus; nothing had changed, everything was as before.

'I must say I don't like this,' said Jack – Alex turned to him – 'doing what we have to do.'

'It's the people we work for,' Alex answered, 'they make us what we are.'

'They wouldn't accept that,' Jack disagreed, 'I don't think anyone would.'

'I don't care. If you happen to live in a country that is wrong, work with people who are basically wrong, you either close your eyes to it or try somehow to correct it. Now ask yourself, is it wrong?'

'It depends, I suppose, on how you go about correcting it. If you're putting bombs in the streets or going for influential individuals, that would be wrong.'

'Yes, that would be. There can be nothing but wrong, all directions lead that way.'

'Is that what you think?'

'I've never seen the sky so clear,' Alex remarked. 'Look up there.' He had stopped while he took in the view. 'It's so amazing it hurts.'

'I used to be interested in astronomy. At school,' said Jack, 'our science teacher talked with such familiarity on the subject that we half-expected a postcard over the summer break from the Crab Nebula to the boys of Lab 5C . . . I let the subject go, it wasn't real, I thought. There's got to be some comprehension of what's going on, as people we need that. I asked this science freak, as he was affectionately known, what one could expect from such a career and he told me that in practical terms . . . nothing. Everything was theory one day and ash the next. That's what he said.'

'An honest man,' said Alex. 'Let me ask you a question: if I sent you a card from the Crab Nebula would you hate me or would you be happy I got there?'

'The Crab Nebula is a hell of a distance away, I wouldn't want a friend to go that far.'

'I've no choice. I know I won't have Susan and Jilly but I wouldn't have them anywhere.'

'Come back.' Jack stopped. 'Come back, Alex.' Jack's hand held to Alex's arm. 'They're not stupid enough to lose control of this. It'll be quiet, of that I'm certain. They'll punish you, you know they will, but you can take that. Come back, there's no life for you anywhere else.'

They reached the Gasthaus as the night air gripped them. Jack wanted a private chat, Alex wanted the bar.

'Can you get anything to eat here?' asked Jack looking around the tables for someone enjoying a meal.

'What have you been told to do?' Alex questioned.

'You mean, have I got orders to shoot should you run? Well, not quite. They want you back, sure, but through persuasion and common sense. You know how they are.'

'What am I here for? I shouldn't have been allowed out of England.'

'You've got to thank Keech for that. When he switched sides things began to move. So an elaborate story was hatched for your benefit; I was brought into this because of our friendship, it was felt any paranoia you might suffer from would be better controlled by my presence. Friendship is supposed to be reassuring.' A pause. 'I didn't want this, Alex, but they convinced me that you'd be less likely to run if you were with me.'

'What did they expect to get from sending me out here?'

'They wanted your contact, they wanted him out in the open, they wanted your absence to create an error of judgement, a slip-up.'

'And?'

'Who knows, they didn't tell me that.'

'And Willy?' asked Alex.

'Yes, you know about Willy.'

'Keech, too.'

'Keech?' questioned Jack.

'He's going to Moscow. It's in the paper.' – Jack sat silent – 'All a story.'

'I don't know what you read, but Keech is coming out . . .'

'Tomorrow, you said.'

'No, tonight.'

'Oh come on. Here you've got the boy Control want, no more stories.'

'Keech is coming out with Willy tonight – yes, Willy. I don't know who the hell Willy is; I was asked to give him some background, but there *is* a Willy, a real live one.'

'Well I won't be here to meet him,' said Alex. 'You make your preparations, get your boy out, go home to Kathleen or Frau Matthofer or whatever other story you're living but I won't be here.'

Alex's raised voice had turned a few heads; two foreigners arguing in a bar, it was not something that happened everyday, not there, in a place so far off the beaten track. It might have been amusing in an English pub but there was nothing on the faces of the locals to suggest that they were amused.

'Where do you think you're going?' asked Jack. 'Do you think there's a new home waiting for you, for services rendered?'

Alex's hand sprang out and grabbed Jack's tie and pulled it toward him with such force that brought out a heavy grunt that everyone heard.

'You've become one of these self-satisfying senior clerks who sits at a desk crafted by a man of talent, something you've lived your life wholly without.' The tie was stretched fully bringing Jack's chin jutting over the table; the knot had disappeared.

'For God's sake, Alex, we're not here to fight. Let me go.'

Alex wanted to strike him, just to bring his hand across his face, but he thought, after the first swipe, he might never stop. He released his hold just as someone came over to have a word. Jack assured him that there would be no further disturbance and this was accepted.

'I understand what it must be like,' said Jack as he worked away slackening his tie. 'On edge. But I want to help.'

'It's very clear that I've got two options: one is to be a good boy and go back with you, the other's to abandon everything and live the best I can. At the beginning when I felt the danger I thought I could never run, not from Jilly . . . nor Susan. But that was a long time ago and I've never considered it since . . . not until now.'

'You had a very high-up contact, you were a special case. They treated you differently. We know that. Who was he?' Jack stared at him. 'Come on, as I've said, we know.'

'You'll say that anyway.'

'You phoned this contact tonight, didn't you? You told him you were in a mess and you wanted assistance, right? Christ, you phoned Nikolai Levchenko. It was Levchenko, wasn't it? And now you're waiting, but Alex, there's nothing, nobody's coming. Your situation is worse than you thought.'

Alex listened patiently. The sounds of German laughter that erupted from different areas of the bar each time seemed to lessen his worries.

'Alex, you've been had, Levchenko defected to the Americans some months ago and before they lift him out of Paris, he's got to prove his worth. Levchenko, probably the only one you had communication with, the one who would protect you before his own mother, has left you alone.'

354

'Another story, Jack? Another lie?'

'Levchenko, to get himself safely to the States, told it all. We got it a bit late and by the time we did we'd already put our own wheels in motion.'

'Levchenko has defected?' Alex laughed. 'Oh Jack, why do we bother, it's all so tragic.'

'Why did you do it, Alex? I can't believe the ideology bit, I'm sorry but I feel there must have been something else. What was it?'

'What does it matter, why do you have a need to know? What will it do for you?'

'At this moment you don't have many friends, don't isolate yourself anymore than you are.'

'You're right, you're right.' He paused. 'Before Susan and I married I never thought I would. Couldn't see anything in that direction at all. I'm talking about the sixties. You'll remember. You and Kathleen got married about that time, didn't you?' He sat back from the table, putting a little more distance between himself and Jack. 'That period opened up a lot of people's eyes and I suppose it did mine. It was difficult . . . . a difficult time.' He looked at the other tables and the foreign faces while Jack sat in front quietly. 'It was a time I began to shed old ideas and old beliefs. Instead of always being cold, I was now heating up.' He sighed heavily. 'What are you expecting, Jack, my confession? Do you think I need to bare my soul, to bring it all out? That's what you want, isn't it?'

'No. Confessions are for priests and I'm not one. No, I don't want that. Just a why. Something I can understand. Is that too much?'

'You're false, Jack, there's not an ounce of sincerity in you. By bringing me over here you had to convey a side of you that doesn't exist. It was all planned out before; you were to lure me with your talk and lies. Now tell me why you would do that? Why you would accept this part, this dark, low side of human nature?

You can understand that, can't you? Why are there people like you?'

'Do you think by attacking me you can justify your own ways? You're a traitor, and in my book there's nothing lower than that.'

'What book? A book of ethics? There is no book. Whatever you possess it can't be that.'

'You're still a traitor. Think about that.'

'Traitor . . . What does it mean?' He thumped the table hard with his fist. 'WHAT?'

'Lower your voice,' said Jack.

'You see, I know you and the rest of you back there think that a dissatisfied customer should just leave and not return, just bugger off elsewhere. But that's not it, I'm no customer. No, I believe in changing that attitude; getting rid of all of you and putting new people entirely in the shop, because I can't live with you anymore, with any part of you. Traitor? I don't believe it's treacherous, I don't believe that at all . . . Let's get out of here.'

'Wait, Alex. What about Susan . . . and Jilly, what happens to them? When this gets out, they'll be hounded by the gutter press – we can't protect them from that. While you're picking up a new life in Moscow, they'll be suffering. You'll have left them stranded, can't you see that? Mother and daughter alone like that . . .'

Alex thought about them in silence, their faces in his head pressing at him.

'Tell me,' asked Jack, 'why did you marry Susan, an Englishwoman? That's the surprise out of all this. Why?' There were a few moments when they just stared at each other, then Jack leaned slightly forward. ''Was it a career suggestion from your handler?'

It was too much; Alex's hands pulled Jack's head down with a mighty thud on the table top. 'Why do you think you can say that to me?' He kept his hands pressing Jack's face against the wood. 'Why?' Around them the tables had quietened and every head had turned before Alex released him and got up.

Jack massaged his face, where a red splash had appeared from brow to nose-tip. 'Tonight I need your help,' he said. 'After, there'll be no more trying from me, you can go, I won't stop you. But you're wrong, your courage has deserted you and I wish I wasn't here to see that.'

Alex looked down at him, at his profile which made him appear very different. 'You'd better tell me what is supposed to happen.'

47

Jack Kirkland found Cullen on a highway, after obtaining his number and calling him as he sped along. 'Pressing business,' said Cullen to explain his sudden departure.

'I've got a job to do, too,' snapped Jack. 'Are you going to assist me, Mr Cullen?'

'I don't know what I can do.'

'Yes, you bloody do,' Jack snapped again. 'I'm here to take Miss Dorian home. She can't be allowed to wander the great American wilderness alone.'

'I don't know if she is alone.'

'We've been promised . . .'

'I've made no promises,' Cullen cut in, while he changed his direction and headed north-west to a small landing strip.

'What's your interest in this woman?' Jack inquired. 'You've never met her, have you?'

'No, I haven't.'

'Why then?'

Cullen had Jilly's photograph and Margaret's picture clear in his mind as Jack questioned.

'Why?' Jack asked again.

'You had a colleague back in Germany, didn't you?'

'Alex. He was also my friend.'

'Was he?' retorted Cullen. 'I was there, too. Remember?'

'That was a difficult time. I lost a friend, and his daughter has suffered. She needs help.'

'You've had years to help.' As he drove on, Cullen asked, 'Aren't you here to silence her? Take her home and do what you Brits do so well. You'll bury her and hope the whole fucking affair'll be buried with her.' His speed had increased as he thought of what lay ahead of Jilly.

'She's got a mother who's alone. They haven't been together for years, Cullen.' Jack had lost his composure, his voice raised as the telephone signal repeatedly broke up. 'She's got a mother,' he said finally.

The telephone connection ended and it was some miles before Cullen's speed slowed. She had a father, too, he said under his breath. The car was quieter and the scenery clearer. She had a father.

'We've all got something, someone; never feel you are being asked to forget.' Cullen could still feel the hand on his shoulder, the words in his ears. It had been a bad day. And now, if asked if his journey to lighten himself had begun, what would he say? On a day, on a road, Margaret had become his companion. The days were always forward, always pushing ahead beyond the grip of the past. On a day like today, on a road somewhere Cullen struggled with past and present. *Margaret's gone*, he heard himself say. There the sound of lapping water receded from his mind as he recalled before the journey straightened out ahead, while sitting tightly at the wheel, mile after mile.

Cullen had been called on to take a short flight to a place he had not heard of, a small community within a mountain range. There was a man there called Bill Lawrence of whom no one at Cullen's home base knew much. It was suggested to him that if young Keech could keep his head down, take some mountain air for a while, his breach from parole could be set aside. It was an offer not to be turned down. The man Lawrence could straighten him out, he knew the Keech story, father and son, but before anything he needed a personal visit. Cullen was to call. But before there was still a drive to take.

The roads of America are strange and wonderful; the country's history has passed along all and each one and there has been pain and there has been laughter going back to when the American native had the land. Now the road that lay before Cullen, empty and still, with only a breeze sweeping through the air, carried memories of all those he was thinking of. It was a strange drive for him, with Margaret, then Jilly in the landscape. Somewhere out there and he rushing to them.

The rush of his life brought him anxiety and his anxiety had brought him on to many roads and today to a clearing that was an airport. He fastened himself into the silver turbo-prop that had been kept grounded by a late passenger. With its engines at a roar and all on board, the plane left the tarmac in record speed. And now with its mad dash behind it, its eight passengers and crew seemed to crawl through space. Within minutes the terrain below had changed from rusty colour to green and before a range of mountains was crossed Cullen sat uncomfortably, wondering where he might be going to.

There was a road in Germany he had travelled on, it was snow covered at the time when a new year had just begun, and it took him to Camp Braddock, a US camp set in thick forest. The army had lost one of their own, so Cullen had been called to see the camp general about the loss and how best it could be understood. He was told the army lost men in different ways, that war took men without too much fuss: some disappeared in a combat zone, some died in front of fellow soldiers and had to be left, some came home, or thought they did, but many of those who were still present among them had also gone. Life was about loss, young Cullen was told. We think we try hard to avoid loss, but that's a lie, we only encourage it. Loss gives us all the sharpness we need to stay alive. Fly over Nam in something that cannot manoeuvre, like an old dog in the sky, fly like that and you can feel all your movements inside that keep you awake. Cullen now knew what an old dog in the sky was. The general had remarked then how Keech was not a brave man because he had returned. It was his personal opinion. Maybe an angry one, he admitted, maybe he couldn't help. Army men saw themselves as something else on the planet; they had thousands of years of history and the general at Camp Braddock did not see Cullen as an equal, did not believe that he in hand-to-hand combat could have survived. And maybe it was just the time in his life because neither did he.

Months later when he was back in the States, Cullen spoke with his father about how, weapon in hand, a man could struggle with an enemy. His father told him that such fighting, face to face like that, could only be performed when the human being in the man was jettisoned. In a situation like that what was left standing with weapon twitching to kill was a biological unit. For however long it might take, the man had, if only temporarily, left the scene. Hand-to-hand combat was not between men as they were known to be, it was much less than that. There could be no hero in such a struggle, no admiration that good had triumphed over evil. Hand-to-hand combat was all evil.

Cullen had stopped talking with his father a long time before, around college time, maybe, when he was growing hard and then when he decided that the Security Services was where he wanted to be. While he wanted a softer son, his father got a discreet but hard one. What in God's name did he want from that kind of life? He would ask his wife. But Cullen's mother was just happy that her son was doing what he wanted. 'America faces a world threat, people want to injure us, to take away what we have,' she explained, 'our son is protecting his country.'

'That's bullshit. Our son has been sucked into a mindset that Americans have a right to kick their way around the world. We still have Viet Nam clear in our heads and that's killing some people in Washington. They can't accept it. I don't think Toby can either. My son should know, because I tried to tell him years ago that there is a time to win and a time to lose. America needs to give its young men compassion and a sense of real history. But today fear is in the American mind. We have enemies, sure, we made them. And boy, how good were we? Then we take them on, knowing damn well we can destroy them, just end their existence. How's that for being the good guy? The American way is not for everyone but living is, on this good earth where there are natural enemies threatening millions of people every day. Why can't I have a son in those zones where he's giving comfort instead of being a hard American with violence hidden in his pocket? He's my son, too, but I can't talk to him, not anymore. My son's gone and I fear his father is, too.'

A crew member broke into Cullen's thoughts offering drinks in plastic cups and warning that the weather could become a bit choppy, but they would all be down, soft or hard, in twenty minutes.

Bill Lawrence had been told to expect a visitor who would be coming in on the daily flight to Dew Falls where he had made his home for a number of years. The reason for his visitor was little more than a courtesy call from those who still remembered him, even though he had not received such a call for a long time. Lawrence had stepped out of mainstream life, like many others in Dew Falls, and while mainstream was out it was never far away. The people who had chosen to live in that mountain retreat knew each other only up to a point. Lawrence was thought to be a medical man who had made an error too far, and the profession had let him go. Ideas of crime and passion had surfaced, too.

With the slightest of bumps the aircraft was down, and shortly after Cullen was waiting in the tiny lounge area of the equally tiny airport for someone to identify himself to him as Bill Lawrence. He sat alone while the craft was preparing a quick turnaround, which due to a change in the weather was going to be quicker than other days. A long twenty minutes in an isolated building was enough before Cullen took himself away, out to a wind that had picked up with a biting chill and brought him a shiver from head to foot. The only car in the parking was a pick-up Buick waiting for him to place his eyes on it before its headlights flashed twice. The driver then got out and walked briskly to him.

'You the man I'm waitin' for?'

'If your name is Lawrence.'

Lawrence put his hand out and Cullen took it.

'Nice part of the world from what I saw of it up there,' Cullen remarked.

'Sure is. It's getting colder every day now and this place becomes smaller in winter.'

'No tourists, then?'

'We've had developers here promising everything, but the people don't want to hear. They kept their money and we kept our beauty.'

'The price you pay,' Cullen smiled.

'Yeah, that's right. The price you pay.' Lawrence looked at the holdall Cullen had brought with him. 'Got anythin' for me?'

'No. Should I?'

'I don't know. Provisions, maybe?'

'I'm sorry.'

'I understood . . .' Lawrence turned to him. 'Nothin'.' He turned back. 'Let's get out of here, Mr Cullen.'

As the men sat in the car and the key was turned to start the engine, Lawrence suggested, 'As you've brought nothin', you can tell me over a few beers what you've come all this way for.'

Lawrence had appeared to Cullen as a man with one foot in the woods and one in his own backyard, a Washington type, one of those finger-up-the-ass suits he had met all too bloody often, every time he looked in the mirror. Was that it, a man like himself, older but stronger, yes he was stronger. As Lawrence drove them away he would point at this and that on the route with some affection.

'It's a small place, Mr Cullen, too small to fight with anyone. You're not a small town guy, are you?' – Cullen was not – 'I honk my horn sometimes to see if I get a honk back.' He smiled. 'It can be a real welcome sound up here. Things like that are important.'

'I know what you mean.' Cullen understood.

'Do you? Hey, that's somethin'.'

The car bounced along some uneven road, and nothing more was said until they came to a halt on the edge of a forest of pine.

'Have you brought me good news,' asked Lawrence standing by the truck. 'They say no news is good news.' He studied his stranger. 'No, you've brought me news, but first a beer.' He patted a pocket of his jacket in search of something. 'This is home. Beside the trees.'

Home wasn't very big but it was built well and its appearance was at one with the forest. There was the sound of a dog on the other side of the door, excited at the men's voices.

'I found this place as soon as I got here, it needed a whole heck of things you wouldn't believe.' He looked at it remembering the work. 'I got it for a song, which was just as well – a song was all I had.'

Lawrence opened the door and the dog leapt out, an average size dog with a brilliant brown coat that shone like silk. Master and dog showed a friendship that Cullen could only smile at. When the greeting quietened, Lawrence said that although it was not a bitch he had called it Hanna. Before Cullen could ask why, Lawrence added that to call it Hanna was like having a photograph of a person he once knew. He looked again at the dog, and said that every time he called out its name he remembered the person – every time. Lawrence appeared to Cullen as a nice man who had maybe become nicer with his wooden house and loving dog. Both men were at ease with each other as they sat in the dark but warm room about to drink some beer.

'Who are you, Mr Cullen?' The question was asked after much talk of America's wild side, where the animals still called the tune, as Lawrence liked to put it. 'You've come all this way and you've come alone. Is that the way of it? You're on your own?'

Hanna sat with its clear eyes fixed on Cullen, not to threaten, but it seemed to ask the same question as its master.

'Isn't everybody?' Cullen responded.

'I'm afraid you're right there,' Lawrence agreed as he placed his hand on Hanna's body.

It was then that Cullen caught Lawrence's look to the dog, his head down and turned away, an angle of his profile that he must have seen before which struck him. Hanna looked sure while Lawrence looked less so.

'You have a dog?' – Cullen shook his head – 'I had years of not considering things like dogs. Lost years, that's what they were. I'm mystified, you've come all this way without a question, which would suggest you're a tired man. I'd understand that. There have been things that I've done in that way.' He stretched out in his chair in a tired way, then sat up. 'I'm Bill Lawrence, Mr Cullen, and have been for a good many years, but now you've forgotten that name, it just fell away right back there, and you see me now as the famous General Keech. Don't do that.' Lawrence lifted a bottle from nearby and said, 'Have a little whisky with me.' He handed his guest a glass. 'Not too many people have been here, sitting where you sit and holding a glass for me to fill.' The dog made no sound but its presence felt strong in the room. 'When I was told you were comin', I was also told that my son needs me. That's what I was told. Is that true?'

'Yes, I think it is.'

'Why?' I haven't been needed for . . . . Why?'

'He's been searching for you, some might say all his life.'

'All his life,' Lawrence repeated.

'He's lived for a long time thinking you were dead, then maybe not, then you were dead again. I suppose I'm here to tell you that it would be better if we could avoid any recycling of old stories.'

'To remain anonymous.'

'No media headlines.'

'Do you know, Mr Cullen, out here it's very quiet during this time and I've seen myself walkin' in those very woods. They're alive, you know, with all different kinds of animal, but also on the forest floor I've come across those that couldn't stay alive long enough for another spring. I've been there, where the trees are tall and little light can penetrate, and I've seen dead, all kinds of dead. And when you find that, Mr Cullen, you want to look into their dead little faces and remember that they won't be completely anonymous, someone's come along and can tell another that they were there, they saw.'

Cullen had followed him into the forest as he spoke.

'Anonymous,' Lawrence repeated. 'Sometimes I think I'm dead. And to be left in this kind of peace I've had to adhere to everything from those who have power over me.'

'Can't you be Bill Lawrence and make a new life?'

'No, I can't. No flying out of here when I want. No driving more than half an hour in any direction. No money to send to my son, if I wanted to. I've been encouraged to forget my past, my personal past. Do you understand?' He sounded desperate with his last sentence.

Cullen sat silent while Lawrence and Hanna looked at the world sadly.

'Do you know how your son is?' asked Cullen breaking the silence. 'I mean, know?'

'No, I don't.'

He got up and switched on a lamp that stood like an observer a few steps from them. 'Out there things don't change much. I used to like that, something reliable there. But I've changed,' he said with glass in hand. 'God, I've changed. I'm another person.

I just wish young Greg could see me. How's he doin'? I'm sure he's well. He's done well.' He smiled at a memory. 'I saw a man in that young boy's face years ago, a great young man.'

'Maybe he could come up here,' Cullen brought the idea out. 'Some father son bonding?'

'I don't think so. He doesn't want to see me. It's not on. Better to stay away than be haunted by his old man.'

'I don't know, General.'

'Oh, no general around here. Around here I don't know what they think of me. They're kind people but they must wonder who the hell I am. An old battered Vet, that's what I am. Seen the cruel world and now I wait.' He seemed to take much comfort from stroking Hanna, and Hanna was always there.

The weather had changed as forecast and there was a strong gust blowing around the house.

'Here boy,' Lawrence called to Hanna who had been caught up with some rattling noise outside. 'I love this dog because he's vulnerable and he knows it. He doesn't holler when he's afraid, he just stands still and you see the quietness in him and then a quiver going through his body.' He looked down at the dog looking up and nothing more was said.

Out there in the cabin with Lawrence and the woods close by, Cullen found a patience within himself that he did not know was there; the general before him, out of sight for years since Germany, had slowed him down. Unknown to many, Lawrence had been living in the shadows, a world away from where he had been, and Cullen had his questions that were to lie somewhere on his mind.

'I'll need a room in town.'

'You could be here a while if the weather closes in,' Lawrence said looking out of the window.

Cullen stood. 'Can you give me a ride back?'

'Sure I can. Is that our talkin' over?'

'I didn't know who you were.'

'I was a surprise?'

'You could say that. You're supposed to solve our problem.'

'Can't do that.' Lawrence opened the door and Hanna ran out. 'Look,' – the sound of the wind in the trees brought a yelp from Hanna somewhere – 'things have got to be tied down, you could give me a hand.'

As the coming storm approached, the two men moved together tying and securing all that Lawrence thought he had.

48

West German-East German Border, late March 1983

Toby Cullen stood with his collar up over his ears. It was three in the morning and the road was dead. He walked a few yards then turned and walked them back again. It was cold. The Americans had agreed to receive Keech in Bayreuth but orders had been changed or so it would seem. Cullen had appeared alone, before Alex and Jack drove up. The car stopped and the lights picked him out.

'Who the hell is he?' said Jack pushing his face forward to the screen.

'Jack, I don't want any games.'

'There's no game.'

Alex studied the figure that stared back at them. 'I know him,' he said, 'I spoke with him earlier. He said he was a teacher.'

'German?'

'So he said.'

Jack wound down the window and called him over, 'Have you got a problem with your car?'

Cullen lowered his head and peered in. 'No.'

'Okay, what do you want?' Alex had opened his door and got out and stood with his arm leaning on the car roof.

'I'm waiting for an American citizen to come over.'

'You have orders to do that?' asked Jack.

'Yes, I have.'

'Christ, this is what sickens me,' said Jack in a shout. 'The Americans were out of this, they were to stay out. Oh, I understand it wasn't popular but that was the way it was to be. And I would appreciate if you saw our point and left. Wait in the village or something.'

'I can't do that. My orders are to stay with you men, wait for General Keech and only then, leave the area.'

'You lied to me earlier,' said Alex.

'You were a stranger,' Cullen replied.

'Maybe, maybe. We can't stand here all night, Jack.'

'Alright, get in your car and follow us.' Cullen nodded and started up.

'If they can't be in at the beginning, they have to be in at the end,' Jack said. 'But I don't like this, out of the blue like that. I'm afraid the secret service has long lost its secrets.' He realised what he had said. 'Didn't mean that.'

He slowed the car and brought it as much off the road as he could. Cullen did the same.

'Right, Mr . . .'

'Cullen.'

'Mr Cullen. There'll be no American assistance in this operation, do you understand?'

'Yes, I do. I'll wait until the American's foot has touched West German soil.'

'You'll do more. You'll wait until we deliver him to Bayreuth. Do you understand that?'

'What he means,' came in Alex, ' is that if you get in the way, become a bloody nuisance, you might not get to Bayreuth.' Alex walked over to the American's car and opened the door. ' Mr Cullen it's better if you stay nice and quiet in here.'

Cullen obeyed, no protest, nothing.

'A mannered fellow,' remarked Jack. 'We could have a little wait, there's always a wait at a time like this.'

'I've got some doubts.'

'Don't. Everything is ready. The tractor's been specially fitted to bring that fence down. The tower lights, if things go accordingly, won't have the full power to reach this distance. And although the sky's clear, thankfully there's no moon, so they'll be shooting at noise, sounds in the dark. I'm not too worried.'

'What do you want from me?' asked Alex.

'Well, I won't ask you to sit up in the tractor, I'll do that. Just be about.'

Temperatures were icy and the chill was biting on the open road.

'Will you keep in touch with Susan?' asked Alex. 'I know you'll be here in Bonn, but, I mean, a letter now and then. There's no reason to fade away because of me.'

'It's you who's fading away, Alex. If we're successful tonight then come with me to Bayreuth and then home. It'll look good, at a time when you could have run, you stayed. It'll look good.'

Alex listened and turned to see the American's face at the window. 'Has he really come to see Keech safely step over the dividing line?'

'Why not? I wouldn't be surprised if a TV network newsman popped out of the boot. The American people have got to know,' Jack laughed, more to conceal his nervousness than for anything else.

'I hope you're right,' said Alex.

They both looked over the fields and Jack pointed to a dark shape that was trees. 'Fuch's farmhouse is six hundred yards down there and if there wasn't a gap in the trees we wouldn't be able to see it. But there is and with these,' he patted a pair of night binoculars that were hanging round his neck, 'you can see two windows at the side of the house. When Keech passes the top light will go on for five seconds and off for ten. This will be repeated once. Should the bottom light go on, it'll mean that the time of waiting is over and they haven't appeared. Looking on the bright side, we should expect them anytime now.'

'When the tractor starts up, what kind of response will there be?'

'The first thing the guards will do is to find out what the hell the noise is, and as the tractor proceeds through bringing down the fence, one will frantically phone the local barracks, which is five kilometres from here, and the other will switch on his light and start shooting. There are a couple of things in our favour: one is that we'll be opening their eyes at the deepest point of their sleep – sure they aren't supposed to be sleeping but that's what they'll be doing – and two, the searchlight is powered from a generator and we hope it's not working too well.' He smiled. 'So other than that, I expect the tearing down of the fence to take no longer than a couple of minutes. But to get to that point, to get the vehicle from where it is will take about three.'

Alex looked back at Jack.

The cars sat silently on the road. Jack and Alex had no more to say as they waited. A wind had risen and was blowing through the wire and under the cars, disturbing all that had been still on the land and in the sky. It was some time later Jack said, 'They're coming.' He stirred in his seat then opened the door. 'The top light's gone on. Wait.' They both looked through the darkness. 'Yes, they're here.'

The American called from his car, 'A second, please.'

Jack hurried to the car. 'What is it?'

'Don't let your colleague up on the tractor. It's all I can say in the situation.'

For a moment Jack stared into Cullen's face then hurried back to Alex.

'Alex, could you bring the tractor along, I should stay here and keep my eyes open for them.'

Alex started the engine and was turning the machine onto the road while Jack peered through the fence and saw a figure running up the slight rise in the field. He waved Alex on as the tractor roared in the darkness. 'Come on. Come on.'

Alex had reached the point where he had to turn and go over a couple of metal ramps that had been placed to bridge the ditch. 'Keep going, Alex, you're doing fine,' encouraged Jack. He went on and on and then the guns began firing.

Jack fell to the ground then the firing stopped, choking at first. The guns had jammed, just as he was told they might. Seconds later there was further firing but Alex had cut through, ripping a hole from west to east.

'Alex. Alex.' Jack called no more. He knew where Alex was going before the tractor engine stalled. The sudden hush brought Jack to call again Alex in nothing more than a whisper.

The engine spurted to life and Alex tried to manoeuvre onto a new course as the gun-fire changed from mindless blasting to single rifle shots with more accuracy, and the power in the fence, which had been absent throughout, returned. The high voltage that then ran through the tractor illuminated it. Then the power died away bringing the stillness back to the country road. Jack stood some steps closer to examine the scorched area but he couldn't really see it, there was just the smell of burning. Alex was gone.

'Alex. Alex,' he whispered.

Cullen got out of the car and stood at Jack's shoulder. 'You knew he would run, didn't you?'

Jack looked away from Cullen to the spot where he last saw Alex. 'I knew,' he said softly.

'Less than forty-eight hours ago a US Army general was thought to have been shot trying to escape, there are no more details. The paranoia over there was too great, they thought he was a trick of yours, they never quite understood what. I'm here to see your operation conclude.'

'Whatever you thought of your general, we, unfortunately, had no such doubts of our man.'

'But where is he?'

'He's either burnt to a cinder on the earth . . . or . . .'

'Why did you let him go?' He paused. 'You knew.'

'How? How could I have known?

'But you said . . .'

'He was a rotten apple. That's what they do. He probably got away.'

'I won't be reporting that.'

'Go to hell.' Jack heard himself call Alex. He ran it through his mind. He wanted to believe he did call and call. He could still be there. Was he there? If there had been a moon he could have seen the curling wire, the break, but the darkness was too deep and had hidden everything.

With the recent noise the wind seemed blown away, but now it was picking up again, blowing back.

'Mr Kirkland, our reports should be as one; we lost our men and that's what we should say. We really tried to stop him.'

'How?'

'We took away his messenger; Levchenko was a big catch for us. With his messenger gone it should have been enough.'

Cullen got into his car as a figure stood in the shadows. 'Can you take Willy back?'

Jack didn't reply. Cullen took that as positive and drove off.

Jack slowly walked to the car and sat in. The man who had sneaked across the border only minutes before waited quietly in the passenger seat; Jack studied him for a moment.

'Willy?'

'*Ja.*' He looked like a soldier – his short hair, his jacket and trousers, in a sort of military colour all the way down to his high black boots.

Jack brought the car to life and drove very slowly. A story Alex once told him about Jilly came into his head; it was all Jilly,

Jilly, he remembered. He stopped in the little street outside the Gasthaus and sat in the silence.

'Okay, Willy, there's a room for you inside, the key's in the door.'

'*Danke.*' Willy slipped out and round the front of the car.

Jack sat and let the night pass before he phoned Sinclair.

49

Over a mountain range from Dew Falls, in Mason, Greg and Jilly had been asked not to leave town, not yet. Sheriff Bane had heard that a senior officer was on his way. Greg and Jilly could settle in awhile and maybe this could be over in a day or two.

The town of Mason was green on the inside and sandy on the outside. It was a place with some history, with old relics of the past preserved as much as possible. It looked like a town Jilly had trouble remembering. From a western, she first thought. Greg did not help her, he just listened as she unwound herself.

'Tombstone?' Jilly guessed and Greg laughed. 'It's got an east coast look, although I've never been to the east coast.'

'It's full of sand,' Greg said dismissively. 'You see there?' He pointed to a sign to the old cemetery. 'Let's take a walk.'

It was less than a mile when they walked trough the gate of the white-walled cemetery, less than a mile from the town, and Jilly found more dust than sand underfoot.

'There'll be a wind comin' down from the mountains, lifting all this,' Greg made lifting movements with his hands, 'it'll be everywhere.'

'It's not exactly Arizona,' remarked Jilly.

'This is how Vegas started out. It's got a cemetery, too. It's one big cemetery there, I've heard.'

'Sand or mud, I don't suppose it matters,' Jilly said as she looked at old gravestones. Life was a cycle, Susan had taught her, awake for the morning and asleep for the evening. Susan had thought of the beauty of it and Jilly of the mystery.

'Some were probably shot and then their families brought them here,' Greg explained, 'a hundred years and more, look, 1858, about hundred and fifty years. Must have been wild.'

'Who would shoot them?'

'Anyone with a gun. Wild, I said.'

'If I were shot . . .' Jilly stopped her sentence short.

'Yeah.' Greg waited. 'Yeah. If you were shot. What?' – Jilly stood silent – 'Do you want to be brought here? Sand and mud and all that?'

'I've got to see my mother again . . . before I get shot.' Jilly looked as if being shot was not far away.

Greg gazed over the cemetery wall and into the distance. 'I don't know what waits for us. Something good, I hope.'

Hope was all they wanted, hope and love. Jilly came close to him. All her wild talk as she pushed her mother away, came back to her as she now saw all of her: her features, her hair, her hands and the pleading in her eyes. 'I've given my mother a terrible time,' she confessed to Greg and herself as she leaned on his shoulder. 'I'm glad I came here. To America. To Mason.'

The sand beneath her feet had been passed along by many over the years, and now it was her time to pass along and leave the bones of Margarita Ducan, whose tombstone had witnessed her confession, to rest again in peace. Jilly was going to see a new way ahead. She felt stronger with Greg by her side; alone, she would not know with any confidence where she would end. It was a bit frightening, but he was there and there was the walk back to the green fields that was Mason.

*   *   *

The weather had closed in at Dew Falls, and Keech was not keen to drive anywhere. Cullen could stay over where he was, there was food and comfort, of a kind, said Keech, who asked to be called Bill.

Standing in the yard with trees less than fifty yards away, he said: 'Do you wanna know somethin', every day I'm here in the yard, and sometimes I look up and see the trees, I don't know if I'm here, I don't know where I've been. Don't know what it is, but it makes me think that here and there are the same.'

Cullen noticed that Keech might be better served telling his story all over again, where a sympathetic ear might learn his true value. 'I want you to come with me,' he said.

'Can't do that.'

'Why can't you?'

'Because this is Dew Falls and in Dew Falls winter comes when winter wants, next month or tomorrow.'

'I want you to come and meet your son.'

Keech stood and wrapped his arms around himself as the wind blew with more chill. 'My son? It's strange to hear that, Cullen.' He turned to him. 'Let me get one of my jackets, what you've brought will freeze your hide.'

'Tomorrow we could fly out of here,' Cullen encouraged.

'My son doesn't want to see me. For God's sake. Do you know how many years it's been?' He stopped to think about that. 'Cullen, I'm not his father, never really was. I just . . . was there a bit and then I went away. I can't return.'

'You're shit scared.' – Keech sighed heavily – 'There's fear everywhere, General. Some would say it runs the world.' Cullen walked over to Hanna who was only a few feet away. He crouched and stroked him. 'It's in your Germany, your Nam and your America. It's the same for everyone. Hanna here has got it. I've got it and young Greg, your son, has got it.'

'You don't know a bloody thing,' Keech barked.

'Tell me what I don't know, General. Tell me about your life

378

in the army, when you made that courageous walk out of one world and into another. Tell me about the consequences of that. Tell me, General, and maybe I can understand.'

Keech opened the door and disappeared. He let Cullen be alone with Hanna before returning with a jacket for him. 'We've got a walk to take.' He called Hanna who ran with him eagerly.

The single track they took led to a small lake about a mile away, and as darkness would soon fall Keech brought a long black torch whose beam could reach half-way across. As the men walked there were some shrills from high and some rustling of animal movements. It was a calming atmosphere and yet, in a moment, it could change to a startling one.

'On the day I took that walk,' Keech said, 'I was another man. To prepare, this was no five-minute decision, it had to come from another Gregory Keech. The old one had no guts, no spirit, nothing; he couldn't have done it. When I was on my way, groomed and polished, I was the best Gregory Keech the world had known.'

'And now?' asked Cullen.

'The greatest moment of my life. Not leaving, turning my back on my country. Not shaking hands with our enemy. But the walk, Cullen, the walk released me from my life. It was my test that I had to pass. Oh, when I remember, like I do now, it pleases me. For all my restrictions here, that move way back then was an honest one. Everyone should have a moment that keeps them afloat in life. I got mine.'

Cullen walked along with him on a track that was wide in parts and narrow in others, towards a lake where the fish, Keech told him, were five minutes away with a simple rod and line.

'Hope your boots are strong, Cullen, 'cause you'll be pretty surprised at what you've picked up when you get back,' Keech warned.

The darkness gradually fell as they arrived at the lake lapping at their feet.

'I love listening to that sound of water. Don't you?' Keech asked.

Cullen peered out over the water as thunder was heard and all the lake before them was peppered hard with rain. The two men sat on a bench made by nature with a view to the mountains on the other side, but visibility was being reduced by the minute.

'Should we be sheltering like this, under a tree?' asked a concerned Cullen.

'There are thousands of trees here, why would the one we're under be struck?' – Cullen made no reply – 'Is God out for you, Cullen?' In the dark watery surroundings with the faintest of light he was prompted to add, 'God, I wish the hell I knew who God was. As you get older the things you've done, back when you were dumb, when time was rushing through your mind, those things appear again.' He turned his head to Cullen, but in the dark he needed the torch. 'You still there?'

'I'm here.'

'Here, in the backwaters, you can see things you can't anywhere else. People out here are either strong or crazy. It's the things you remember, the sounds and smells of yesterday can be calling on you before you get your ass out of bed.'

'You've got things on your mind and on your hands. That it?'

The look Keech gave Cullen would surely have frightened him at any other time, but in the darkness he never saw the general's face. The sky seemed to erupt then and all the electrical power in it lit up the lake, followed by a mighty roar that seemed to rock everything.

'Jesus, the heavens are pissed off with someone,' Keech shouted. 'We'll give it a little while more, see if it lets up, then head back.'

The rain kept falling but the sky never lit up the same again.

'It's a haunting place,' Cullen remarked feeling the stillness.

'It sure is.' Keech knew. 'You haunted, Cullen?'

'I don't confess my soul, if that's what you mean.'

'You don't. Well hell, I don't know. All America's got soul, but how many do you think know of it?'

'I know if I had a boy whose life had lost direction because of me, I'd want to do something about it.'

'He never made it, did he?' Keech sank a little as the rain swept in.

'In his way I think he did,' replied Cullen, 'he could have let you go, just kicked you out of his life, but no, General, you're there, more than you could ever realise. He's been to hell every bit as real and terrifying as your Viet Nam memories and your courageous walk along that lonely road in Germany.'

Keech sat in silence. 'I wish I could see the stars, but this damn weather . . .' He paused. 'I'd have shown Greg the sky, the stars. I'm sure I would. I can't remember. I can't remember his face.'

There was a splash about twenty yards away and Keech jumped up and shone his torch in the direction. 'Hanna!' His voice a nervous shout. Hanna's body colour and the water made it hard to locate him. 'Cullen, he's in the water. Can you see him?' The sound of splashing was strong at first but was quickly becoming less. 'I can't find him,' shouted Keech, who would have jumped in if he had only half a sight of him.

Cullen heard the fear in Keech's voice; he began to feel his own and, in an unexplainable moment, waded into the water.

'Cullen! Cullen, come back! It's dangerous water,' Keech yelled.

The water had quickly risen to his chest and his own sounds of him making his way, arms raised for balance, deafened any sound from Hanna. Wading through a mountain lake for a dog had yet to surprise him, when he stumbled underfoot submerging himself fully. It was only a few seconds, but when he surfaced he was in some terror; his cry of anguish as he pushed his head from the water was in fear that he might return to the bank alone. In the pitch black of the lake Cullen called out, softly at first and then in a bawl, 'MARGARET! MARGARET!' His splashing was excited and continuous till there was no more. Keech waited, his beam finding little as he peered into the distance where he guessed Cullen was. But not far from him Cullen and Hanna had found each other, and, if there had been light, the welcome each gave would have been a joy to behold.

Back on the bank and shivering like the last of autumn leaves on any tree, man and dog made their return quietly. Hanna was carried part of the way till his legs were ready. Keech had wanted to embrace Cullen when he stepped ashore, but allowed him those moments when only by being alone with yourself could you see where you had been. For in the water Cullen saved three and came out a true hero.

The next day, after the wettest of nights, Cullen made some time for Hanna. All the vegetation around the house glistened and the timber on it had become dark, almost black.

Keech had information that the daily flight was cancelled and had come to find Cullen roaming around. 'You wouldn't want to take to the air with all that turbulence, would you?' Keech added after delivering the news. 'Another day's nothin'. Let me show you somethin'.' He made to open a shed door which was padlocked. 'Inside here I've got a treasure,' he said fumbling with keys, 'let me show you.' He unlocked and opened. Both men stood looking in. 'You see.' There, facing them was a motorcycle.

'When I got to fifty, I kind of lost all my hopes,' explained Keech, 'you know, Cullen, never lose your hopes.' He walked to the bike and placed a hand on it as he would have on Hanna. 'Look at it,' he urged Cullen, 'not only is it a beautiful red painted beast with arms of chrome and you must see how it positions itself on the road, it's not only that, it's a mirror of who I wanted to be and it tells me that I can still be. Can you imagine something so beautiful telling you every day you visit that you are that better man you thought you were.' He paused. 'I have, up here, Hanna and machine. That's how I survive.'

'Anything I've had of beauty, I've let it go,' Cullen let it be known. 'Beauty and me don't seem to get on.'

'That's a pity,' Keech replied as he rested his eyes on his bike.

'Come back with me, your boy needs you.'

The bike stood between them, beautiful. Strong and beautiful. 'It's so hard,' Keech said in a painful way, 'so hard.'

They walked back into the house and the day passed peacefully. A quick check next morning found the skies clear and the flight on. Cullen got his things together and they drove slowly off with Hanna in the back.

'Before I leave I want you to think of taking a flight.'

Keech shook his head. 'I wouldn't put a foot on that thing they use to get people over the mountains.'

'Then drive.'

'The truck wouldn't take the climbs.' He turned and smiled.

Half a mile farther on he said, 'Of course, there's that thing of beauty in the shed.'

Cullen almost laughed. 'There is indeed, and that's a fact.'

At some altitude, Cullen laughed loudly at the beauty he had come across in Dew Falls, and he realised that some things never die. He could still feel Hanna's body in his arms and wished it had been Margaret. The drone of the aircraft was soothing to him as he let all his body ease back in the seat. General Keech would not be forgotten easily, whole new vistas had appeared to him, like the sprinkling of lights on the hills across the lake when he thought he would drown before he saved. He smiled at his ordeal, and how he had met it well. It was just his secret, his and the general's, that, at a moment when all emotions came to the surface, he called the only person he had begun to love more and was not now of the world.

Two days later Keech took his bike, which had kept him young over his years as Bill Lawrence, and roared out of his territory.

* * *

At dusk the light in Mason could strike the buildings with orange and faint yellow colours. Jilly was at the edge of town, waiting perhaps for a bus to arrive and someone she knew to step off. Her hair was swept from her eyes and she looked as a child would, anxious and unsure. She wore something that allowed her arms to be seen, and while she looked into the distance the beat of her heart quickened. It had been a full day away from Greg, a day to be alone. Greg did not object. 'We'll just roam our own way,' he said. And while she saw him go, he did not see her. Sheriff Bane had asked them not to think of leaving town, he did not want anyone arrested. That was sure to spoil his visit.

Jilly had walked away for the day leaving nothing much stirring in Mason until the news reached Greg that his father was a day or so drive away. He received the news when he was alone, in town where people were meeting each other like any normal day in their lives. He was standing in the street watching the world of Mason go by when Sheriff Bane put a hand on his shoulder and told him that his father had been found, visited, and now he was coming to meet him.

'It's shockin' news, I guess,' Bane said with a smile. 'You might feel like runnin', right now. You might see a disaster comin' round the corner, but I don't think so.' Bane's hand never left Greg nor did his tone change.

Greg was lost, the blood seemed to drain away from his face and take the strength from his body. 'He's alive?'

'It seems so.'

'God! Are you sure?'

'Expect him soon.' Bane saw Greg's response to what he thought would be good news and was surprised at how he received it. 'Greg. Greg.'

Greg had lowered himself to the gutter where he vomited up all his fears. He looked positively ill when he stood upright again. 'I'm sorry,' he apologised for the open display but he felt sorrier that his father had become real. It was strange and made him feel aggressive. If the Sheriff had not been with him then he might have lashed out at anyone passing. An act of violence might have helped understand his feelings. He had travelled with Jilly because he thought he should and because she was too lonely to be alone. His own search was half-hearted, he did not have the same belief as Jilly, she had become amazing to him, she was fantastic, all her years and sacrifice. She had done so much for him that he felt sorry at the news. How could he tell her?

'Be happy,' encouraged Bane, 'remember what I told you about your father.'

'What do I say?'

'I don't know. Whatever it is will come. I don't even know where he's comin' from.' The men walked along the street. 'Be sure, he'll be as nervous as you.'

Greg blew out his cheeks as his stomach tweaked at him. 'It's a bad idea. A terrible idea.'

'Let's get away from here,' said Bane.

Greg was already away, re-visiting everywhere he could see or hear his father.

'Let's go, Greg,' repeated Bane.

As they walked, somewhere in the mountains the general was heading their way.

Jilly saw Greg approaching. He looked good to her as she made to meet him half-way. But with every step the clearer the message on his face. She knew, she just knew, and there on the edge of Mason something died in her.

'Just watching the sunset,' she said, and turned to it. Greg stood at her side. 'Margarita's over there.' She looked over at where Margarita was. 'All the sunsets she's seen.' There was a stillness between them.

'My father's on his way.'

She nodded. 'I'm happy for you.'

'I know.'

'But I don't know how to show it. I'm sorry.'

'I'm sorry, too,' said Greg.

'Sssh,' she whispered as her eyes glazed over, putting her fingers over her lips.

They stood quietly for awhile, Greg thinking what to say and Jilly what to do.

'Can't we go out there?' She pointed to the stretch of road to the mountains. 'Before your dad gets here.'

'I'll ask the Sheriff, it's his car,' Greg said with a doubtful expression, 'I'll try.'

'I'll wait here.'

In the time Greg was gone Jilly stood being bathed in the sunlight. All the roads she had been on came flooding into her mind, some so long and faraway and others like the sand that had got into her shoes, every step felt, every sound heard. Her American journey was over, and she could hear her mother reminding her that all good things must come to an end. When she asked why, she was told because they must. There was never an explanation that could be acceptable for her, not for the good things and not for the bad ones. She was becoming sad on her own like this; she'd phone, she promised herself, before the day was out, she'd call and hear her mother's voice. She would say sorry a hundred times, then dream a little of putting her arms around her. There was a surge of excitement rushing through her as she imagined their words together. She was somewhat at ease when she said aloud, 'Dad won't be there.' There was that last call from Germany, she remembered, when Dad had frightened her. To say goodbye like that when the night was cold and dark and she had just stepped into her pyjamas, with Mum shaking as she sat by the phone.

Whatever happened there between mother and daughter, a look at each other, perhaps, a moment when both had let the other down had taken Jilly through primary school, teenage years and into her mid-twenties. Her losses piling up. But now there was going to be a call.

Greg had given her some time before picking her up and heading into the mountains. The Sheriff had handed him the keys with a look of, *don't do anything crazy.* There seemed to be no hurry for speed or for words as the miles passed. Greg had his window down and his arm out, like on a summer's day.

'I'm nervous,' he said.

'Yes,' Jilly replied.

'Bloody scared, to be exact.'

'I'm nervous for you. Really scared.'

Greg laughed. 'You are?' He laughed again. 'God, my heart's thumpin'. Feel it.' He took Jilly's hand and held it to his chest.

'Boom, boom, boom,' Jilly shouted.

'He could be here today. I don't know,' Greg sighed to himself. 'Never really thought I'd meet my old man again.'

'Let's go faster,' Jilly urged in an excited way.

'Faster?'

'Faster on this lovely road.'

'I'm sorry,' Greg said holding her hand, 'I'm sorry you're still out there with all your hopes.'

Jilly sat looking out, her ears picking up the sound of the road and not much else.

'I don't know how this will turn out, me and my dad. I'm excited but it could be for five minutes. I wish, I wish . . .'

'Don't.' Jilly wanted to be quiet and said little more. How would she be watching Greg with his dad? How would she be observing them together?

'I'm glad you're here, Jilly. If it wasn't for you I'd never have got to Mason. It's because of you, Jilly. Because of you.'

As the car sped past the sand coloured terrain, Jilly, feeling all her strength suddenly fade, put her hands on the door and pushed herself out. The wind noise sucked into the car drowned out her final moments on the ground as she tumbled over and over. With her body painfully beating the asphalt, memories of her young life flashed by. A long ago bedtime and a long ago

I-love-you-Jilly from Dad: his smile and her impish reply *I-love-me-too* made her heart leap with all her laughter for Dad slumped heavily onto her pillow wounded, then dead. Her long ago happiness when she had him close. The slow motion of her fall brought his face again, distant and worried, looking out at her from a car rear window while she stood on the pavement looking back. Her skin had broken on her face as it met the road and below her body ached in defeat and in her silence. Then Mum with her sailing to Calais. The sea and the gulls and the *parlez-vous français*. The last happy moment was quick and the feeling of Mum's hand in hers on the windswept ferry deck was gone.

Greg's braking was so hard that the car lunged violently to its left while he fought to bring it back again. The screeching sounds from the tyres could be heard echoing deep into the mountains. Jilly lay still, half on the road and half on the dirt. Greg's moans were heard before he reached her. Her eyes were wide like a baby's when he spoke to her. Little words full of nice things before the trauma in Greg's body raced his heart and before the trauma in Jilly's brought hers to a slow stop. He held her hands, fingers, touched her cheek until her eyes closed. There on the road he stood, Jilly at his feet, and as he began to tremble and the cold set in on him, he wrapped his arms around himself and squeezed, his body folding under his own power.

The engine noise of a beautiful bike could be heard in the distance, while Greg squeezed more and more.

THE AUTHOR WISHES TO THANK:

Valentina who, in her Genovesi and Acquesi days,
helped enormously to get the project off the ground.
She was a true supportive presence in those sunny early times.

Nadia Vercelli for her long-time friendship, spirit and enthusiasm.

Paola Barbetti in Torino, Marisa and Abramo Barosso
in Genova for their views on reading the final draft.

Yannick Martinez in France whose long-standing
support was much appreciated.

Tony Kiening in Germany who generously
introduced me to Bavaria.

Cristian Fassi and German Revilla of Revilla Networks
Italia who kindly offered their office space and time to drive
the project along. With great spirit and expertise
they helped bring the title to the Web.

A *grande grazie* to all the Acquesi, Alessandrini and Novesi
friends who gave their support and their *in bocca al lupo*.

The Comune di Sezzadio for the photo opportunity.

K

www.kappamakbooks.com